Storm Testament V

Storm Testament V

LEE NELSON

Council Press

ISBN: 1-55517-356-1

Published and Distributed by:
925 North Main, Springville, UT 84663 • 801/489-4084
CFI
Publishing and Distribution Since 1986
Cedar Fort, Incorporated
CFI Distribution • CFI Books • Council Press • Bonneville Books

Lithographed in the United States of America

Chapter 1

Hundreds of Mormon women had left their homes and their children to flee from the officers of the law; many had been behind prison bars for refusing to answer the questions put to them in court; more were concealed, like outlaws, in the houses of friends. Husbands and wives, separated by the necessities of flight, had died apart, miserably.
—FRANK J. CANNON,
"Under the Prophet in Utah"
C.M. Clark Publishing Co., 1911

I usually don't have much stomach for shooting a horse, but when Ike pulled his Henry rifle from its scabbard, I was in no mood to stop him. Circumstances demanded the horse be stopped.

We had been chasing the sorrel gelding through the foothills of the Sheeprock Mountains most of the day, and though we had come close to getting a rope on the gelding several times, it looked now like the animal was on the verge of getting away forever, our saddle horses simply too jaded to continue the pursuit.

Patrick O'Riley, the oldest son of Sarah, my second wife, had ridden the horse into the west desert from Salt Lake City about a week earlier to escape United States deputy marshals who had a warrant for his arrest.

Patrick was just an infant when I married his mother, several months after her first husband, Pat O'Riley, had been killed under the wheels of a runaway wagon. I adopted

Patrick, Jr., who became the big brother to my own children who came later.

When Patrick had married his second wife a year ago, we had figured the authorities would leave him alone because he was a medical doctor. We were wrong. Even though Patrick had taken every precaution to keep the plural marriage secret—even keeping the new wife, Lydia Sessions, in a house more than a mile from the home of his first wife, Beth—the deputies were still able to uncover the plural relationship.

Under the Edmunds Law polygamy was punishable by five years imprisonment and a $500 fine, a punishment that could be repeated for each time the man had been with a plural wife. If polygamy couldn't be proven, the punishment for cohabitation, or adultery, was six months in jail and a $300 fine, which could be repeated for each time the man had been with the other woman. Hundreds of Mormon men had gone to prison, some sent as far away as the federal prison in Detroit, Michigan, a prison rapidly becoming known in Utah Territory as Mormon Siberia.

Beth, Patrick's first wife, hadn't borne any children in nearly 20 years of marriage. Lydia, who was nearly 15 years younger than Patrick and Beth, was healthy and headstrong. Everyone in the family hoped she would bear the offspring Patrick and Beth had longed for for so many years.

The year since the marriage to Lydia had been a troubled one. Lydia was jealous of Beth's position of influence as first wife, and Beth was depressed, having failed to bear children. Added to these problems was the necessity of keeping the relationship secret from the law. It was an unhappy time for all concerned.

As soon as I received word from Beth that Patrick had fled into the desert with deputies on his trail, I loaded up a pack horse with supplies and set out to find him. Pat had never been much of an outdoorsman. He wasn't a man who could live off the land. I guessed he would try to hide out in one of the hunting camps he had become familiar with as a young man. If so, I hoped to find him and give him supplies. With winter coming, he would need them.

Near Camp Floyd I ran into my old friend, Ike, the escaped slave who had come to the mountains with me nearly fifty years earlier. He and some of his Indian friends were headed east to hunt elk. Ike insisted on joining me, telling his companions to continue without him.

Several days later we spotted Patrick's gelding running with wild horses. We had no trouble recognizing the animal because it was carrying a new saddle, the same one I had given Patrick as a wedding present a year earlier. There was no bridle on the animal, and there was no way of telling how long the gelding had been running wild.

The horse was a little taller and fleshier than its mustang companions. Still, it was not a well-bred horse. Its neck was too short, its head too big, and it was not well-muscled through the hindquarters. Though Patrick earned a good living as a doctor, he never spent more than was absolutely necessary on horses.

Patrick's horse seemed every bit as wild and slippery as its mustang companions—perhaps more so. We wore out our horses in our unsuccessful attempts to get a rope on it.

The first time we got close to the gelding, a sick feeling settled in my stomach as I noticed something long and pink in the right stirrup. I'm sure Ike saw it too, but neither of us said anything. We were only more determined to catch the horse, knowing it carried clues as to what had happened to Patrick. Besides, if we let the animal get away and it was unable to get rid of its saddle, the skin on its back would rot and the gelding would die a miserable death.

The horse was at the edge of the foothills, heading straight for the open salt desert to the northeast, when Ike finally leapt from his horse and rested the barrel of his Henry rifle across a smooth boulder. Though using a white man's saddle on his big buckskin mare, Ike was dressed like an Indian, wearing leggings, loincloth and moccasins. He was bare above the waist, his huge muscles rippling in the afternoon sun. Though his curly hair was partly gray, he still had a young man's body thanks to a hard, active life with the west desert Indians.

Ike dropped the running horse with his first bullet, a clean shot to the neck. By the time we reached the animal, it was dead, the blood from the single hole spreading in a blur across the gelding's sweat-soaked skin.

The shock of seeing a once beautiful animal dead and bloody on the ground was forgotten the moment we saw what was in the stirrup—a man's lower leg and foot, or what was left of it. The foot itself was still covered by a low-topped shoe—the same kind worn by Patrick—and was wedged tightly in the stirrup opening. A partially flesh-covered bone with a clean break at one end extended several inches beyond the stirrup.

The sight of the mangled foot and leg wasn't nearly as disturbing as the thoughts that came to our minds as to how the accident might have happened. How could we know for sure if it was Patrick's leg? How was he unseated? How did the leg break? How long had he remained alive and conscious while being dragged about? Minutes, perhaps hours? Could he still be alive somewhere?

While Ike removed the remains from the stirrup, I opened the saddle bags. I was still too numb to feel pain at the apparent death of my adopted son.

Inside the bags I found a box of bullets, some wooden matches, a candle, a plentiful supply of dried meat, a bottle of pills, and an iron pan. Beneath the pan was a brown envelope. Carefully, somewhat hesitantly, I removed it from the saddle bag. There was no writing on the envelope.

Opening it, I found a sheet of neatly folded white paper, a letter from Beth.

Dearest Patrick,

You must go immediately. Skunks saw you leaving Lydia's place this evening. Now they have seen you with both of us. I'm sure that even while you read this, they are preparing documents for your arrest. Don't worry about us. We'll be fine. It will be as if you were on a mission.

Please be careful. Let us know how you are as soon as it is safe. I'll see that the people on your appointment calendar

are contacted and referred to other doctors.
If only these troubled times would pass.

Your loving wife,
Beth

Standing up, I crumpled the paper in my fist. The last words of the letter, "If only these troubled times would pass," rang in my ears. Those words had been penned too late for Patrick.

Since passage of the Edmunds Act in '82, hundreds of Mormon men had been arrested for polygamy or unlawful cohabitation and sent to prison. Many more had been forced to abandon their families to avoid arrest by federal deputies called "skunks."

"Doan seem right a man should die dat way," Ike said. "Not for keepin' two squaws."

"Amen," I said, turning away, beginning to feel the pain, fighting back the tears, wondering how I would tell Sarah what had happened to her only child.

"What should we do wid dis foot?" Ike asked.

"Wrap it up," I said between clenched teeth. "We'll take it home."

"Now?"

"No. First we've got to look for Patrick's body by trying to backtrack the horse."

Chapter 2

I, for one, shall not be a party to the enactment or enforcement of unconstitutional, tyrannical, and oppressive legislation for the purpose of crushing the Mormons or any other sect for the gratification of New England or any other section. . . . The clamor is not against the Mormon for having more than one woman, but for calling more than one his wife.

—U.S. SENATOR JOSEPH EMERSON BROWN,
Georgia
In Senate debate on Edmunds Act, 1882

"Give a man a new gun and put 'im on a tall horse. Add to dat a good woman, or two, to go home to. What moah could a man want?"

Ike was talking, partly to me, partly to himself, as we backtracked along the meandering trail left by the band of wild horses. Occasionally, we'd spot the unmistakable mark of an iron-shod hoof, evidence that Patrick's gelding had been traveling with the wild horses at that particular place.

"What moah could a man want?" Ike repeated. "Guns, horses and women. 'Cept maybe a little firewater now and den." He paused. "Dat's all an Injun wants. But whites is different. A white man, he got to have land and money and git everyone else to agree wid him on politics and religion. Doan understand it. Can't figure why de soldiers, de judges, de preachers, de female crusaders, de politicians—everybody seem bent on stompin' on de Mormons for takin' plural wives. Can't see where no one outside Utah will be any richer, poorer, smarter or happier because some Mormons have more dan one wife. Can't see why it should matter to nobody, 'cept de Mormons dat's doing it. Ain't like a body's holdin' a gun to de heads of dose Mormon ladies who wants to be plural wives."

"I suppose it's a religious thing," I said halfheartedly. "They think we're sinning and going to hell."

I was thinking about Patrick and the mixed feelings I had about looking for his body. On the one hand I wanted to find the remains and take them home for proper burial. On the other, I dreaded what I might see upon finding a loved one who had been dragged to death beneath a horse and left to lie in the sun for several days. I shuddered beneath the burden of taking such a body home to the woman who had mothered it. But if I didn't find the body, how would I ever know for sure what had happened to Patrick?

Ike stopped talking, sensing my desire to avoid a discussion of the polygamy question. We rode in silence for what seemed a long time.

After a while my thoughts turned to revenge. Who was responsible for Patrick's death? The Congress of the United States, which passed the Edmunds Law and was getting ready to pass a more severe Edmunds-Tucker Act? The U.S. Marshal and deputies who relentlessly hounded Mormons suspected of polygamy, or the judges who consistently found Mormons guilty of polygamy or cohabitation, even when the evidence was practically nonexistent?

It wasn't right that the death of a good man like Patrick go unnoticed. Someone should pay. But who?

At the top of a gentle sagebrush pass, Ike reined up and pointed to the right side of a marshy spring in the valley ahead.

The smoke from a lone campfire snaked lazily into the blue sky. Beside the fire a man, his hair long and black, sat cross-legged and still as stone, staring out across the marsh. Behind him in the sagebrush stood a gray mule.

"Know only one Injun who rides a big gray mule," said

Ike. "Flat Nose George." He urged his horse forward.

Ike said the old Indian was a shaman, or medicine man, of the Ute tribe, and that the old man's home was hundreds of miles to the east, near the Green and Colorado rivers. He also said it was bad luck to pass a medicine man without giving an offering. Besides, the Indian might know something about Patrick.

Flat Nose George was alone, sitting on a worn Army blanket and wearing elkskin leggings and a blue Army coat without any buttons, not even on the sleeves. He was a big Indian, apparently at one time strong and athletic. Now, in his old age, his muscles had lost much of their firmness but had not yet turned to flab. There were crater-like scars on his face, perhaps the result of smallpox many years ago. His black, loose hair was streaked with gray. But in spite of his many years, his back was straight, his jaw firm and his eyes steady. Like a statue he gazed over the marsh grass, ignoring our approach.

It wasn't until we dropped a bag of apples and dried beef in front of Flat Nose George that he acknowledged our arrival—not with a smile or handshake, but with a grunt and a nod of recognition when he looked at Ike.

He didn't look at me until Ike explained to him, in Ute, that we were looking for my son, and that we thought he had been dragged to death beneath a horse. Though the old man's face was still expressionless, I couldn't help but notice tears welling up in the corners of his black eyes as they looked into mine.

"Come," he said in English. "I have found your son."

We followed Flat Nose George for a mile or more through the tall marsh grass. He picked his path carefully, avoiding the soft areas where a man could sink from sight. We left the horses behind with his gray mule.

We worked our way past the main freshwater springs that fed the marsh to a more barren area, and finally to a large alkaline or salt spring where no vegetation was growing in the white-gray mud.

We walked through the muck to the very edge of the spring, which was about 15 feet across and at least 20 feet deep.

The water was not as clear as a mountain spring, but it wasn't murky, either.

"Your son," Flat Nose George said and pointed into the water.

Looking down into the spring I saw Patrick, standing upright in the heavy salt water, his head about six feet below the surface. The body was held down by a big rock tied to the remaining foot. What was left of his shirt and pants was shredded, and numerous cuts and bruises were visible on his gray-white skin. One of his arms was broken. Attached to the wrist of that same arm was a frayed piece of hemp rope. An eye was missing. From the condition of Patrick's body I figured he must have died long before he had broken free of the horse.

There were other upright bodies in the spring—four near Patrick and more further down. Indians, I guessed, covered with white salt crust. They looked like stone carvings.

"Indian burial spring," Flat Nose George said, anticipating my question. "Legends say those buried here come alive again after a hundred winters."

"Want me to get him out so's you can take him home?" Ike asked.

"Don't know," I said. "Looks pretty content right where he is. Soon he'll have a crust of salt like the others. Suppose it'd be all right to leave him here?"

Flat Nose George nodded.

"Could I offer a prayer?" I asked.

Flat Nose George just shrugged his shoulders.

The Indian and Ike bowed their heads while I offered a short prayer dedicating the spring as a final resting place for my son Patrick and his Indian companions. Feeling the emotion and hurt well up in my chest, I was tempted to include in the prayer a curse on those responsible for Patrick's death, but I didn't do it. At the conclusion of the prayer we walked back to Flat Nose George's camp.

The next morning we headed home bearing the horrible tale of an unjust death, evidence the persecution of Mormons for polygamy had gone too far.

When the salt spring was four or five hours behind us, the

thought occurred to me that perhaps I should have buried the foot—the one we had taken from the stirrup—with the body, down in the salt spring. The foot was still in the saddle bag.

Pulling my horse to a halt, I turned to Ike.

"Think we should have tied a rock to Patrick's foot and tossed it in the spring beside him?"

"Doan know," Ike said. "I been wondering 'bout dat rope 'roun his wrist."

"What about it?" I asked, remembering the frayed rope that had been tied to Patrick's broken arm.

"Why'd a man have a rope 'roun his wrist, 'less somebody else put dat rope dere?"

Suddenly I realized my earlier notions of how Patrick had died were probably wrong. All along I had assumed he had been alone in the desert, trying to hide from the authorities. But a lone man wouldn't have a rope around his wrist. I wondered why it had taken so long for me to realize the significance of the rope. Perhaps Patrick had fallen from the horse because his hands were tied behind his back or over his head. Perhaps he had been jerked from the horse by someone holding the other end of the rope.

There were still a lot of unanswered questions, but this new understanding of the rope changed one basic circumstance of Patrick's death. He had not been alone, and therefore his death was possibly not an accident. Perhaps his death was more than an accident; perhaps Patrick had been the victim of a cruel murder.

I felt the adrenaline surging into my veins. That sick, helpless feeling that had haunted me since finding the foot suddenly gave way to anger and hate towards the individual who had tied that rope to Patrick's wrist. The man responsible was probably a U.S. marshal or deputy marshal.

The frustration at blaming Patrick's death on generalities—a law, a social problem, two value systems in conflict—evaporated. Somewhere in the Utah Territory was the man who had tied that rope around Patrick's wrist. Maybe I could find the man and make him pay.

"Wanna ride back and bury de foot wid de rest?" asked Ike.

"No, I'm taking it home."
"Gonna bury it?"
"No," I said, without offering an explanation.
"What you gonna to do wid it?" Ike asked.
"Got a feeling there's a man I'll want to show it to."
"Who?"
"The man who tied the rope around Patrick's wrist," I said. "Then I'll kill him."

Chapter 3

The Mormon Church . . . offends the moral sense of mankind by sanctioning polygamy. . . .
—U.S. PRESIDENT JAMES A. GARFIELD,
January, 1880

Nellie Russell slowly raised the fountain pen to her lips, her clear hazel eyes intently scanning the three sheets of white paper on the pine writing table in front of her. Her hand quivered slightly as she put the final touches on the story that would have the Mormons screaming. There would be official protests, petitions, and a likely confrontation with Grace Woolley, the fiery young Mormon who was rallying plural wives to defend their polygamist husbands. The story would guarantee a sellout. Perhaps a reprint would be necessary.

Nellie was in the front office of Salt Lake City's newest publication, *The Anti-Polygamy Standard,* founded by the non-Mormon women of Salt Lake City to open the eyes of their ignorant Mormon sisters to the evils of polygamy.

In her early 20's, Nellie was a woman most people, especially men, would call beautiful. Her red hair was not long, but thick and full, bouncing in full curls on her shoulders. Her complexion was white and smooth, except for a slight hint of freckles on her cheeks. Her body was lean, but full in the places that would attract a man's attention. She moved gracefully, even in her many petticoats.

Nellie had arrived in the valley of the Great Salt Lake

from Glasgow, Scotland, just weeks earlier. Her experience on a Glasgow newspaper, the fact that she was a Mormon woman courted as a plural wife, and her determination to fight polygamy were all factors helping her land the job as assistant editor and staff writer.

The pay wasn't much, only a few dollars a week, but she didn't care. After what had happened to her, she would have worked for free to help in the fight against polygamy.

Nellie had been converted to Mormonism three years earlier in her native Scotland by a very sincere and persuasive missionary named David Butler. They had begun writing each other, and upon his departure for home from London, David had sent Nellie a note proposing marriage, asking her to come to Utah as soon as possible to become his wife. He had finished law school before his mission, and he wanted Nellie to be at his side as he became one of the territory's top attorneys. Nellie accepted his proposal and began making preparations to go to America.

Everything was so romantic for Nellie—pulling up roots, saying farewell to loved ones, and traveling halfway around the world to meet her lawyer fiancé in the heart of the American frontier. But those feelings ended abruptly the moment Nellie arrived in Salt Lake. David did not come to the train station alone. Beside him was a wife named Alice, pregnant and clinging. Nellie was speechless.

At first she tried to be understanding, or at least appear so, when David tried to explain why he had not told her about Alice. He said something about being unable to contact Nellie because she had already left Scotland. But when he suggested they go ahead with the marriage anyway, with Nellie becoming his second wife, that was too much for her. She hit him with her umbrella, screaming that she never wanted to see him again.

Nellie had known about polygamy, but somewhere in her courtship with David she had concluded he would never do it. But he did. The whole thing seemed so wrong, so unfair. She had traveled halfway around the world to marry the young man she loved so much, the missionary who had brought her the true gospel. Now he wanted her to become his second wife, to be subject to his pregnant first wife, Alice. Deep inside, voices were shouting no, no, no. Nellie couldn't do it. She didn't want to do it. She wouldn't do it.

David and Alice left, and Nellie found herself alone in a city of polygamists, with barely enough money for a single night's lodging. What should she do? Where should she go? She felt so lost, so alone.

She sat on the wooden bench in the train station trying to decide what to do. It occurred to her that in her current situation perhaps she shouldn't have been so quick to drive David from her. Perhaps her desperation demanded that she marry him.

Then she figured that maybe she was lucky the way things had worked out. If David had married her first, how would she have felt a few years down the road—when perhaps she was pregnant and feeling fat and ugly—if he had brought home a new young wife? What a horrible thought. No, things had worked out for the best. Nellie wiped the last tear from her eyes and looked around.

A minute later she was scanning the ads on the back page of the *Deseret Evening News.* Perhaps she could find an opening for a live-in maid or cook—anything to hold her over until she figured out what to do with the rest of her life.

That's when she saw the advertisement for Angie Newman's House of Refuge, a haven for "destitute" plural wives. As Nellie later learned, Angie Newman had received a $30,000 grant from the United States government to establish a home of refuge for women trying to escape the shackles of plural marriage.

Nellie had not been a plural wife, but she had come close and therefore thought she might find a warm welcome at Angie Newman's home. She did. In fact, the welcome was much warmer than expected, perhaps because she was the first "destitute" woman to show up at the refuge in many weeks.

Nellie was welcomed into the home by Angie Newman herself, a middle-aged woman with stern features. Angie was so skinny she didn't look much like a woman. Her black hair was in a bun pulled tight enough to remove any hint of wrinkles from her face and make her dark, oversized eyes look like they were about to pop from her head. But she was a friendly, religious woman, eager to offer Christian service to those in need, especially plural wives.

It didn't matter to Angie Newman that Nellie wasn't a plural wife. That she had come close was reason enough to roll out the red carpet. Nellie received a warm bath, a private room and a hot meal. She was told she could stay as long as she wished, within reason.

It was Angie Newman who, upon finding out about Nellie's newspaper experience, had introduced her to the publishers of *The Anti-Polygamy Standard.* Three days after arriving in Salt Lake City, Nellie had a job. But not any ordinary job. She had an opportunity to get even, to help crush the institution of polygamy that had played such a dirty trick on her.

Nellie removed the pen from her lips, unconsciously dipping it in the inkwell in anticipation of making another correction or two before turning the story over for typesetting. She loved the first sentence, especially when she thought about the uproar it would cause among the Mormons. She read it again: "There is new evidence that Charles J. Guiteau, who assassinated United States President James A. Garfield in 1880, was acting on orders from Salt Lake City."

This was Nellie's first story for *The Anti-Polygamy Standard,* and without doubt it was a very controversial one. She had received her information from several leading non-Mormons in Salt Lake, including Harry Chew, an editor at the *Salt Lake Tribune.* When she asked why this information hadn't appeared in print earlier, she was told that many publishers feared reprisals from Mormon Danites. Well, the publishers of *The Anti-Polygamy Standard* didn't fear Danites. Neither did Nellie. She continued her last check of the story:

"Mormons in Colorado, Texas, and New Mexico were greatly elated over the success of Guiteau, or Utah, as they called him. New evidence taken from secret Mormon records indicates that the assassin was a Josephite, baptized a Mormon in 1874. Shortly after the assassination of the President, Mormon leaders presented Guiteau with five new wives, who now live in Ivingston, Utah.

"When the Mormons saw that the late President in his inaugural address stated that he meant to put his foot on polygamy, the leaders at Salt Lake were heard to say, 'Yes, if we do not put our foot on you first.'

"Mormon leaders, of course, deny having given Guiteau five wives after the assassination. They also claim there are no secret records showing that Guiteau was a Mormon. . . ."

Satisfied the story was as good as it was going to get, Nellie pushed her chair away from the table and walked over to the editor's desk, where she deposited the story in the basket designated for typesetting.

She looked up at the clock. It was 12:30. Everyone else in the office had already left for lunch. She hurried out the door, not wanting to be late for her luncheon engagement with *Tribune* editor Harry Chew.

Chapter 4

The Salt Lake Tribune, strongly anti-Mormon . . . was without doubt the greatest single enemy of the church. The Trib was a most potent force in blocking statehood for Utah and in bringing the church to the brink of destruction over the issue of polygamy.
—SAMUEL W. TAYLOR
"The Kingdom or Nothing"
Macmillan, 1976

"Nellie, you made a big mistake not becoming Butler's plural wife," Harry Chew said as he and Nellie seated themselves at a small table in the City Creek Tavern on Whiskey Street.

The comment caught Nellie by surprise. If anyone was possessed by contempt and disgust for polygamists and their church, it was Harry Chew.

"What do you mean?" she asked.

Harry, looking across the crowded room at a blackboard listing the luncheon selections, seemed not to hear her. He was a thin, wiry man, his sandy hair receding prematurely. In silhouette his face was like that of a ferret or rat, the nose nearly forming a straight line with his sloping forehead. Harry's gray eyes were unfriendly and darting—eyes that seemed to keep track of everyone in the room. His hands were white, thin and soft, not accustomed to hard work. Whenever his hands rested on a hard surface, his forefingers tapped nervously.

"What do you want to eat?" Harry asked, as if he had forgotten his earlier statement. But Nellie wouldn't let it drop.

"What do you mean about me making a big mistake in not marrying David?" she asked.

"Oh," Harry said, as if suddenly remembering his earlier comment. "Had you tied the knot, then come over to our side, we could have gotten a polygamy conviction on him and sent him to prison. Three years, for sure. Maybe we could have gotten him shipped to Detroit."

Now Nellie understood. And she had to admit the idea had a certain appeal. Still, she was glad she had not married David. As angry as she was at him for marrying that other woman, she couldn't have married him just to send him to prison, even if he had deserved it for being a polygamist.

"Now he's defending every cohab coming down the pipe," Harry continued, "whether they can pay or not. Judge Zane says David Butler is giving him fits in the courtroom. How about the beef platter?"

Nellie nodded that that would be fine. Harry waved down a white-aproned waiter and ordered two beef platters and mugs of beer. Nellie became aware that some of the men at nearby tables were staring at her.

"Got it," Harry said, slapping his open hand on the table. There was enthusiasm in his voice. "I'll find me a cute little gal like you. Somebody who wants to help fight polygamy. Just let her circulate around, getting engaged to as many of the old goats as possible."

"What in the world for?" Nellie asked.

"Soon as she marries one, she then runs down to Zane's court and files charges. Not even David Butler could keep that man out of prison. She'd annul such marriages, of course."

"You couldn't get me to do that," Nellie said.

"Why not?"

"It's trickery and deceit. Lawyers call it entrapment."

"The cohabs use all kinds of trickery and deceit to hide their secret marriages. To catch them we've got to employ the same methods."

"Not me," Nellie said, not wanting to sound self-righteous, but still opposed to using dishonesty.

"Come on," Harry said, slamming his palm on the table for the second time. "These people are trampling the laws of the Bible, the laws of the land. They are marrying off innocent young girls to dirty old goats in the name of sacred religion."

Harry's voice was getting louder. Nellie was aware that men at neighboring tables were listening to his intense monologue.

"John the Revelator," continued Harry, referring to Mormon Church president John Taylor, "is nothing but an old gobbler fattening sleek on the tithes of the poor. Anything that will push that ruffian and his fellow bandits out of power is justified in my book."

The waiter in the white apron suddenly appeared at the edge of the table, setting down two thick white plates piled high with sliced boiled beef, potato salad, and long slices of dill pickle. The beer had arrived a minute earlier.

The arrival of the food ended Harry's tirade against the Mormons. He was hungry, and without another word, stuffed a huge piece of steaming meat into his mouth.

As Nellie began to eat, she noticed some of the men still watching her. It annoyed her. For the first time she noticed that she was the only woman in the place, which made her angry.

"Harry, why did you bring me here?" she asked. "I'm the only woman."

"Does that bother you?"

"Yes."

"Do you want to leave?"

"That won't be necessary," she said. "It just seems rude on your part, bringing me to a place where you knew I would be the only woman."

"Brought you here on purpose," Harry said after gulping down a mouthful of partially chewed meat. "Wanted to test you."

"I don't understand," said Nellie, picking at her potato salad.

"Got to be tough to take on the Mormons. They won't give up their polygamy without a fight. Some will die for it. Some will kill for it. Will Nellie Russell turn and run when things get hot and mean?" His gray eyes were locked on hers. She didn't look away.

"Did I pass your test?" she asked.

After a long moment, Harry looked down at his plate, using his knife to cut off another big chunk of meat.

"You didn't get all flustered like some women would. I suppose that's good."

Nellie remembered how when she had first met Harry, several weeks earlier, she had liked him, even admired him. A young man who had worked his way up to editor in a major publication like the *Salt Lake Tribune* was a man to be admired, especially when he had offered to help Nellie develop her own writing talents. He was the one who had told her where to get her information for the article on the Mormon tie-in with the Garfield assassination.

"How's the article coming?" Harry asked, changing the subject.

"Finished. Type is being set."

"Ready for another?" he asked.

"I think so," she said, feeling a sudden elation at getting a second story assignment when her first one wasn't even printed yet. Maybe Harry wasn't so terrible after all—not if he was going to help her become a writer.

"I want you to write a story calling for the vote to be taken away from Utah women," he said coolly.

"You can't be serious," Nellie said, beginning to laugh. She remembered that Utah had been the first territory to give women the vote in 1870. Now some states were giving the vote to women too.

"It's almost the 20th century," she said. "Everyone is giving the vote to women. You want me to call for a step back into the Middle Ages?"

"No," he said, looking annoyed at her reaction. "I'm just asking you to help cut the Mormon vote in half so we can get rid of this barbarous polygamy. Congress is considering including the disenfranchisement for women as part of the new Edmunds-Tucker Act. An article from a Utah woman calling for removal of the female vote would help persuade some congressmen. That's all I'm asking you to do. When polygamy's gone, Utah women will get their vote back."

Nellie didn't say anything for a long time. Harry was persuasive. She certainly wanted to be included in the fight against polygamy. But how could she write an article calling for the vote to be taken away from women?

"I'll have to think about it," she said.

"Look at it this way," Harry said, surprising her with a smile. "When that article on the assassination hits the streets, everybody in Salt Lake will be asking, 'Who is Nellie Russell?' And when the article to take away the female vote appears, everyone will know who Nellie Russell is. She will be right there alongside Harriet Beecher Stowe, Mrs. Rutherford B. Hayes—even Angie Newman—as one of the heroines in the fight to end Mormon barbarism. When this is all over you'll be able to run for public office and win."

"What makes you think I want to run for public office?"

"If that's not your fancy, how about a job with the *New York Times*?"

"Now, that I could take," Nellie said. "I'll give it a try."

"Great," Harry said as he forked the last of the potato salad into his mouth. He pulled a watch from his vest, frowned, then pushed his chair from the table.

"Want to be in on a little secret?" he grinned, suddenly leaning forward.

Nellie nodded.

"The little Mormon town of Tooele is electing a new mayor today."

"That's a secret?" she asked.

"The People's Party candidate is a stake president, and he's going to lose. That's the secret."

"I don't understand."

"I keep forgetting you're new to Utah. Today will be the first time a stake president loses an election in a Utah town. The Liberal Party candidate will win."

"Isn't Tooele about 90 percent Mormon?"

"That's right."

"Then how is the stake president going to lose?"

"We've got an entire trainload of voters heading out to Tooele this afternoon," he whispered. "They'll arrive just before the polls close. We'll have it won before the Mormons know what happened."

"But that's not right," Nellie protested.

Harry pulled his chair back to the table and leaned closer to Nellie.

"Polygamy is not right," he hissed. "The Mormon Church is a blight on the land. A bloodsucker draining off the wealth, trodding on the poor, and destroying human beings. It must be stopped, regardless of cost or method. There are no rules in crushing it. Whatever works is right."

"You really believe that, don't you?" Nellie asked, overwhelmed by Harry's intensity.

"Nellie," he said, his voice suddenly much quieter so only she could hear, "if a collection were being taken to hire an assassin to kill old John the Revelator, I would donate my entire paycheck, even mortgage my house. We are going to win this thing."

"What do you mean when you say 'we'?" she asked.

"The Ring, the Utah Ring. Surely you've heard of the Ring."

"No," Nellie said.

"My boss at the *Trib,* Oscar Sawyer; deputy marshal Sam Gilson; district attorney George Peters; former governors Eli Murray and Caleb West; Judge Charles Zane; Supreme Court Justice Tom Anderson; me and some others. We're in it together, working to curb the filthy tide of Mormonism."

"You're after more than polygamy, then?" she asked.

"Heavens, yes," he said. "Polygamy is just one branch. The whole tree must come down. The economic and political power of the church must be destroyed forever."

Harry pushed his chair away from the table for the second time.

"Got to get down to the train station," he said. "Going out to Tooele to cast my vote. Want to come?"

Nellie shook her head. "No, too much to do at the *Stan-*

dard this afternoon. Go ahead. I'll walk back by myself."

Harry left some money on the table for the lunch, then headed out the door. Nellie remained seated for a few minutes longer, not finishing her partially eaten meal. She thought about Harry Chew and wondered how so much anger and hate could be bottled up inside one man. She felt afraid, but wasn't sure why. She thought about all those influential men in what Harry had called the Ring. She wondered if the others were as determined as Harry to put an end to Mormonism.

Nellie pushed her chair away from the table and walked out onto the wooden porch. It was a sunny fall afternoon, but as she walked down the steps, she pulled her shawl close about her shoulders. She had an uneasy, cold feeling, like before a storm, so she didn't notice the warm sun in a cloudless Utah sky.

Chapter 5

The people of the rest of the country are our enemies. . . . God is greater than the United States. And when the government conflicts with heaven, we will be ranged under the banner of heaven and against the government. . . . We want to be friendly with the United States . . . but not one jot or tittle of our rights will we give up to purchase (such friendship). I defy the United States. I will obey God.
—JOHN TAYLOR
January 6, 1880

Nellie didn't get much done the day *The Anti-Polygamy Standard* ran her assassination story. It wasn't that there were an unusual number of distractions. There weren't—at least, not early in the day.

It was just knowing that her story was out there making waves. Knowing that hundreds, perhaps thousands, of people were reading and talking about her story made her feel excited, so much so that she found it difficult to concentrate on anything else—especially the new story Harry had asked her to write on why the vote should be taken away from Utah women.

It was early afternoon when Nellie received her first visitor. She had half-expected one of the leaders of the Mormon Church to be the first to challenge her story, but she was wrong. The first to come was Grace Woolley, the young activist who was stirring up Mormon women to express public support for their polygamist men.

Nellie's first reaction was one of total surprise. Grace Woolley was not what Nellie had expected her to be—a matronly, forceful, dogmatic woman with a cause. Instead, Grace Woolley was one of the most beautiful women Nellie had ever seen. Young too, not more than two or three years older than Nellie, at most.

As Grace walked across the wooden floor toward her, Nellie noticed the neatly brushed light brown hair, satin complexion, clear blue eyes, neatly tailored dress and trim, womanly figure. There being no wedding ring, Nellie couldn't help but wonder if this striking woman was someone's plural wife.

Nellie wondered if she dared ask. Why else would a beautiful woman be so active in defending the barbaric institution of polygamy? Nellie decided to hold the question, at least until she and the woman had become better acquainted.

"Thank you," Grace said when Nellie motioned to a chair across the table from her.

"I'm Grace Woolley," the young woman said upon seating herself.

"I know all about you," Nellie said, wanting to find out more about this woman before discussing the story.

"You do?" Grace said, sincere surprise in her voice.

"Yes—you are the one who obtained 5,224 women's signatures on a petition to the United States Supreme Court to repeal the Idaho test oath prohibiting Mormons from voting."

"It was 5,234," Grace corrected.

"And, wasn't it you who testified before the United States Congress on the injustices of the Edmunds Law?"

"Yes."

"Didn't you have a petition on that one too, signed by over 3,000 women?" Nellie asked.

"It was 3,319."

"Isn't it discouraging, going to all that work and not having the petitions do any good?"

"I wouldn't say that," Grace said. "Can't have all you do-gooders thinking you are being too humanitarian."

"Please explain."

"You know what I mean—all the talk about saving Mormon women from polygamy and all those dirty old men. Before my petitions it never occurred to many of your friends back East that perhaps Mormon women, on the whole, want polygamy too. My petitions prove that. The women want it. You are not rescuing Mormon women. You are only taking away their God-given freedom of religion."

"Do you really believe that?"

"Of course. How else do you explain all those empty beds in Angie Newman's house of refuge for plural wives?"

"Ignorance, perhaps."

"It's simpler than that. Mormon women don't *want* to leave their husbands. That's why you and Angie have the whole house to yourselves, except for an occasional prostitute."

Nellie remembered Angie's frustration at not being able to attract unhappy plural wives to her house of refuge. During the evenings they had spent many hours discussing the problem. Angie firmly believed Mormon men had some kind of devilish, even hypnotic, power over their women. It was Angie's mission in life to figure out a way to break that power.

"Are you a plural wife?" asked Nellie, trying to catch Grace off guard, thinking the element of surprise might bring a truthful answer.

"If I were I wouldn't tell you," Grace said, smiling.

"Why not?" Nellie asked, realizing this pretty woman was too quick to be so easily tricked.

"Because you would tell the authorities. There would be a deputy trailing me within the hour. The first man I stopped to talk to would be arrested. You would testify in court that I told you I was a plural wife, and the man I stopped to talk to would be sent off to prison, even if he wasn't my husband, just as long as he was Mormon."

"There's more justice in the system than that," Nellie said, concluding Grace was prone to gross exaggeration.

"Have you ever sat through a polygamy or cohabitation hearing in Judge Zane's court?" Grace asked.

"No."

"Don't pass any judgment until you have. He's getting a conviction almost everyday, and most of them on evidence a lot slimmer than what you would have if I told you I were a plural wife."

"I don't believe that."

"You don't have to take my word. Just spend a day in Judge Zane's court."

"Maybe I will," Nellie said. "Zane's court might be an excellent place to find some sensational stories on the abuses of polygamy for the *Standard*."

"Speaking of stories," Grace said, changing the subject. "I have brought you a rebuttal on your recent story attempting to link Mormon leaders to the Garfield assassination."

Grace reached into her purse and handed Nellie a single piece of white paper.

"I assume the *Standard* is not afraid to print an opposing point of view," Grace challenged, as Nellie began to read.

Nellie, totally engrossed in what she was reading, did not answer. The words seemed to jump from the page and grab her by the throat. She felt a flush rising in her cheeks, despite her efforts to suppress it.

Upon finishing the rebuttal, she reread the middle section:

. . . There is no evidence, including anything said by the assassin himself during his trial, that he ever joined the Mormon Church. The claim in the article that Church leaders rewarded Guiteau with five wives now living in Ivingston, Utah, is absurd because there is no such community in the Utah Territory.

The article referred to Guiteau as a Josephite with five wives. That would be something to see because the Josephites are an offshoot of the Church, strongly opposed to polygamy. . . .

"Ivingston, Utah, does not exist?" Nellie asked in a timid voice, forcing herself to look Grace in the eye.

"That's right," Grace said.

"Josephites really don't believe in polygamy?"

"Don't take my word for it. Ask them yourself," Grace said.

Nellie's mind was spinning. Her embarrassment was fast turning to anger—not at the beautiful woman in front of her, but at Harry Chew. Why had he and his friends given her obviously false information? Why had they let the story get into print? Why had Harry sent the story over the telegraph to other newspapers? Harry would have to do some explaining. Was it possible he would have a reasonable explanation? Nellie didn't see how—not if the facts in the rebuttal were correct.

"Will you print it?" Grace asked.

"I'm not the editor," Nellie said, "but I'll see he gets it. If the facts are correct, I think it will end up in print. Thank you for coming in."

Grace stood up and turned towards the door. Nellie watched her walk to the door, wondering again how such an attractive woman could be a defender of something as ugly as plural marriage.

She thought about Harry, too, and the rebuttal to her story. She had the same sick feeling she had had the day Harry had asked her to write the story calling for the vote to be taken away from Utah women. She picked up Grace's rebuttal and read it a third time, feeling all the more embarrassed and angry.

Chapter 6

The political power of the Mormon sect is increasing. It now controls one of our wealthiest and most populous territories, and is extending steadily into other territories. Wherever it goes it establishes polygamy and sectarian political power. . . .

To the reestablishment of the interests and principles which polygamy and Mormonism have imperiled . . . I recommend that the right to vote, hold office, and sit as jurors . . . be confined to those who neither practice nor uphold polygamy.

—U.S. PRESIDENT RUTHERFORD B. HAYES,
1880, in his annual message to Congress

"Damn you, Harry Chew!" Nellie shouted as she marched unannounced into the *Tribune* editor's office. Harry didn't stand up; he just slouched lower in his chair, raised his eyebrows in mock surprise, and let a sly grin break across his thin lips.

"Why did you let that story go to press?" she demanded. "You knew it was full of inaccuracies. I've been humiliated and you could have stopped it."

"Welcome to the world of journalism."

"What in heaven's name is that supposed to mean?"

"Look," he said, waving for her to be seated. She remained standing. "Around here we let every new reporter do that. Best way in the world to teach a new writer to be careful about facts."

"But the story is inaccurate, misleading, and false. The sources you sent me to lied to me!" Nellie cried.

"Should have doublechecked the facts," Harry shrugged.

"But why didn't you tell me before the story went to press?"

"Because you might come to depend on me to check your facts for you. Need to do it yourself. Editors can't catch things like that anyway."

"That's stupid and dishonest."

"Look at it this way," he said calmly. "Next time I send you out to do a story, do you think you'll be more careful about what ends up in print?"

"You bet I will."

"See, it worked. I taught you an important lesson."

Harry removed a large rumpled handkerchief from his pocket and blew his nose. After putting the rag away, he looked up again at Nellie, who was still standing.

"Now that I've learned my lesson," Nellie said, "you won't be sending the story out over the telegraph to the Eastern papers."

"Already gone out, this morning."

"You can't be serious!" Nellie cried. "But you knew it was full of errors."

"Calm down," Harry said. "Those Eastern papers don't care if a few facts are wrong."

"A few! The guy wasn't even a Mormon, let alone a Josephite."

"If your story is printed in enough papers, it will stir up a lot of public sentiment in favor of the Edmunds-Tucker Act," Harry said, standing up and walking around his desk until he was facing Nellie.

"Just think, Nellie," he said, an intensity in his voice Nellie hadn't noticed before. "Your story is another nail in the coffin of the Mormon Church. A little crooked and rusty, perhaps, but another nail just the same."

"I'm not out to destroy the Church," Nellie said, "just to stop polygamy."

"Don't think you can cut out the heart without killing the

whole thing. All of it has got to go."

Harry turned and walked back to his chair, looking down at his feet.

"Say," he said, "how would you like to have dinner with me tonight?"

"Aren't you married?" Nellie asked, realizing the subject had never come up in their conversations.

Harry shook his head.

"I didn't know that," Nellie said. "You must be in your thirties." She hoped her comment would cause him to say more about himself. She wanted to know more about this man who had not only tricked her into writing a libelous story, but who had sent the story out over the telegraph to the Eastern papers.

"Was engaged," he said, a wry smile breaking across his thin face.

"Tell me about it."

"Not much to tell," he shrugged. "She decided to marry someone else."

"Why?" Nellie asked, determined to keep probing as long as Harry was willing to give answers.

"The other fellow had more money."

"And?"

"More prestige in the community."

"More prestige than a *Trib* editor?"

"He was a Mormon stake president."

"And?"

"What do you mean 'and'?" Harry hissed, obviously annoyed with her persistent questioning.

"Was he a polygamist? Did your fiancée become one of his plural wives?"

"Yes," Harry said, a faraway look in his eyes. He didn't seem angry anymore.

"Did you love her?"

"Of course. I asked her to marry me," Harry said, becoming annoyed again at Nellie's questions.

"How long ago?"

"Seven and a half years."

"And you haven't found anyone else?"

"Why are you suddenly so interested in the romantic adventures of Harry Chew?" he asked.

"You haven't found anyone else?" Nellie repeated, not wanting to be sidetracked.

"Yes!" Harry stormed, his hands placed defiantly on his hips. "Two years ago. Lydia Sessions was her name. Very beautiful."

"Lost her to polygamy too, I suppose," Nellie quipped, hoping to inject some humor into a situation that seemed to be getting too serious.

"You didn't say if you would have dinner with me tonight," Harry said, ignoring her question. There was still an unhappy scowl on his face.

"What happened to the second one?" she persisted.

"You already said it. Lost her to polygamy too. An Irish doctor. O'Riley was his name."

Nellie realized her attempt at humor had only opened the wounds more. There had been no humor in the truth. But how could she have known? It wasn't her fault.

"So you're asking me to dinner, thinking I'm safe, having already rejected the opportunity to enter polygamy," she said.

Harry smiled.

"That may be true," he said. "What about the dinner?"

"No," she said firmly.

"Why not?"

"I suppose I could say I have other plans, but I don't," she replied honestly.

"Then why?"

"Because I'm still mad over the story, so mad I could scream. I still can't believe you did that to me. It'll be a long time before I'll go to dinner with you."

"I can understand how you feel," he said quietly, looking down at his thin white hands resting palm down on his thighs.

Suddenly he looked up at her, his eyes smoldering.

"But you'd better get over it quickly. Forces are gathering to rip the throat out of the Mormon movement. If you want to be part of it, you can't remain all strung out over what you perceive to be a personal affront over that silly little story."

Without another word Nellie turned and marched out the door, still angry at what Harry had done, but marveling once more at the intensity of this man's hate for the Mormons and his willingness—even eagerness—to do anything to undercut the Church. She was frightened at the thought of getting closer to a man so unprincipled in getting what he wanted. Still, she felt determined to remain in the fight against polygamy. She needed to work with Harry, but she would have to be careful.

Harry's only response to Nellie's sudden retreat was to slouch lower in his chair, fuming at a religious system that allowed polygamy.

Chapter 7

Polygamists must go to jail or betake themselves to Turkey.
Brooklyn Eagle, 1882

Even though we had left Patrick's body in the salt spring in the west desert, we still held funeral services for him at the new church in American Fork. We buried his foot—the one Ike and I had found in the stirrup—on a hill above the house. A small stone tablet marked the grave.

Sometimes when an old person dies, a funeral can be a happy occasion. There is relief at knowing the person is finally free from the pain and suffering of old age and a deteriorating body.

This was not the case with Patrick. In his prime—not yet 40 years old—he had died a miserable and painful death. He had been a physician with a busy life, doing much good. It was not his time.

Patrick's first wife, Beth, had not borne him any children, and there had not been enough time for his new plural wife, Lydia, to bear him any, either. There were no sons to carry his good name to future generations.

This was the very subject I was contemplating as I sat with family members in the front row of the church as Bishop Miller delivered Patrick's eulogy. I found it hard to concentrate on what the bishop was saying because the words he had spoken to me earlier in private were gnawing away at me.

"Dan," he had said, "perhaps the worst part of this whole thing is Pat not having any posterity."

I nodded my agreement.

"The Lord has provided a way around it," he said simply.

"What do you mean?" I asked.

He opened his Bible and read a scripture about a man who had died, only to have his wife go to a brother to raise posterity for the dead man.

"What are you suggesting?" I asked, stopping him before he finished reading.

"I would think it entirely appropriate," he continued with confidence, his voice low, like he was telling me secret, sacred things, "if a close relative of Pat's were to step in and raise seed for Pat through his new wife, Lydia."

"Wouldn't that be adultery?" I asked, taken back but with enough curiosity to want more information.

"No. Lydia would become a lawful—in the eyes of the Church—plural wife to the new husband. Only the resulting children would carry Pat's name, like in the Bible."

"I have never heard of anything like that before," I said.

"One of the beautiful doctrines of the new and everlasting covenant of marriage," he said.

"Is it being done anywhere else, in other families?" I asked. "I mean, Lydia wouldn't be the first, would she?"

"Things like this must be kept very secret. All the trouble with the law, you know. That's why you don't hear about it. Yes, it is being done elsewhere."

"Who do you have in mind to team up with Lydia?" I asked. "Couldn't be me. I'm almost 65. And my youngest son Ben is only 18 and scared of girls."

"I was thinking of Sam," he said. "He's nearly 40, strong in the church and doing well in his business. It would be good for him to take a second wife."

"I'm not sure how good it would be for Kathryn," I said, thinking of the beautiful Kathryn, pregnant with their first child after nearly 16 years of marriage and a number of miscarriages.

"Just remember, such a union would be an act of

unselfish love for a stepbrother who otherwise would be denied the blessings of eternal posterity," said the bishop.

"When do you plan on presenting this idea to Sam, Kathryn and Lydia?" I asked.

"That's your job as family patriarch," he smiled.

Those words continued to gnaw away at me through the funeral services. The more I thought about it, the more I figured Bishop Miller was right. If it was right in the Bible, why wouldn't it be right in modern times? But how could I present something so bizarre to those involved? I wasn't so much worried about Sam. We could talk about things. He might not like the idea, but we would be able to discuss it.

I wasn't sure about Kathryn. She had been a good mate to Sam, but she was a jealous wife—not the kind to welcome another woman into their relationship. She was strong in the church, but not that strong. Being six months pregnant wouldn't help matters, either.

Then there was Lydia. I wasn't sure about Lydia at all. I looked down the bench at her.

She was the perfect mourner, dressed in an expensive black lace dress with full petticoats. Her hair was perfectly combed, a little black hat pinned exactly on the top of her head with long, ivory-knobbed straight pins. Her complexion was clear and smooth, and her dark eyes were looking down at just the right angle. She was a beautiful mourner—too beautiful.

In contrast, Beth, Patrick's first wife, looked awful. Not only was her dress mildly wrinkled, it was specked with white lint. Her hair had been brushed in a hurry. Her cheeks were white as death, and her eyes red with silent weeping. Her jaw was limp with exhaustion and pain.

Just looking at her caused a tightness in my throat and chest, knowing she was hurting so much and there was nothing I could do about it. I couldn't help but wonder how Bishop Miller's suggestion would set with Beth. I wouldn't say anything to her, not until she was over this. I had already told Beth she could live with us if she wanted to, and she had said she would let me know later.

I had often wondered why Lydia had married Patrick, and why she had broken off her engagement with *Trib* editor Harry Chew. Why had she decided to become Patrick's plural wife? She was not the pious type. She might have married Patrick for love, but not for religion. Perhaps for money, but not for social status. There was none for plural wives.

Maybe I would learn more about Lydia when I presented Bishop Miller's plan to her. But I still had no idea how I would go about it.

Without warning, the ramblings in my head were interrupted by shouting outside the church. I could hear the thundering and churning of hooves, then a horse skidding to a halt at the church door.

"Skunks!" shouted a young man who had just dismounted from a sweating horse and was charging up the steps. "Vandercook and three deputies. Be here any second."

U.S. Deputy Marshal Oscar Vandercook was responsible for bringing more polygamists and cohabs into Judge Charles Zane's court for trial and sentencing than anyone else, so everyone knew what to do. Besides, skunks had been trying to catch cohabs in church meetings for several years now. With the women and children moving aside, the men tumbled behind Bishop Miller down a secret chute behind the last row of choir seats. Even those who didn't practice polygamy slid down the chute to a secret tunnel leading to the general store next door. Non-polygamists had gone to prison too, on no more evidence than being in a church with a group of unescorted women. Nearly everyone brought before Judge Zane on polygamy or cohabitation charges was found guilty. All the men followed the bishop down the chute.

The oldest male remaining with the women and children was my youngest son Ben, just turned eighteen. A socially backward boy and a stutterer, he had dropped out of school early, spending almost every waking hour with his animals—horses, mules, and a little gray-brown dog named Dix, which was sleeping on the porch during the services.

Ben was a thin, thoughtful boy, wiry and brown from his outdoor labors. His hair was bleached and unmanageable from sun and wind, his eyes blue and clear. He was eager to please, but cautious and shy in his dealings with people. He was still a boy.

Oscar Vandercook, in contrast, was confident, pushy, loud, and intimidating. Over six feet tall and weighing close to 250 pounds, Vandercook was a man used to getting his way. He was unshaven and smelled of sweat and manure. His face was round as a bulldog's, with nearly as many wrinkles. His mink eyes were small and black, too close together.

Vandercook was an unmuzzled fighting mastiff on the loose, incensed at the wrongfulness of polygamy. There were hundreds of arrests to his credit. Most of the men had gone to jail, and if Vandercook got his way, hundreds more would follow.

Heavily armed like his three followers, Vandercook stomped into the church, leaving the door open behind him. "Got to be a secret passage," he barked to his followers when he noticed the men were gone. "Probably up front somewhere." Vandercook and his men thundered down the center aisle to the front of the church, women and children scampering out of the way.

Except one.

Feet apart, fists clenched, Ben Storm blocked the front of the aisle.

"Th-this is a f-funeral," the boy stuttered. "You d-don't belong here."

"Out of my way," Vandercook hissed.

"N-no!" Ben shouted, his voice breaking.

Without warning, Vandercook's fist shot forward and down like the hoof of a pawing horse, striking the boy square in the chest. Ben flew backward and, losing his footing, landed on his rear. His back crashed against the base of the podium, his head striking the hard wood.

"What's yer name, boy?" Vandercook demanded as his partners scurried around the pulpit looking for the secret passage.

Ben didn't respond but just looked up into the cruel, black eyes.

"Got to know who's interfering with the law," Vandercook said. "Now tell me yer name or I'll break yer neck." He stepped closer to the boy, who pushed a few inches closer to the podium.

"B-Ben Storm," the boy volunteered in a quiet voice, all the time looking down at the floor.

Vandercook slapped his hip, beginning to laugh.

"No wonder the little grunt tried to stop us," he said to the other officers. "He's Dan Storm's son."

Then, turning to the boy, he said, "Yer old man is a sex pervert. Not satisfied with one woman in his bed. Got to have two."

Vandercook reached out with his right arm, pointing a dirty finger at the boy.

"I aim to see yer old man in prison or six feet under ground, or my name ain't Vandercook."

Beginning to sob, the boy suddenly jumped to his feet, doubling his fists like he was about to attack the big deputy.

The deputy began to laugh. Then just as suddenly as he began, he stopped. The room was quiet.

Vandercook removed one of his big horse pistols from its holster.

"No!" one of the women cried.

Instead of firing the pistol, Vandercook tossed it towards the boy, watching as it clattered to a rest between the boy's feet.

"Want to fight, huh?" Vandercook jeered. "Pick up the gun and shoot me. Go ahead."

Ben looked down at the pistol, then up at the big deputy. The big right hand was a few inches above the second pistol, ready to draw.

"Coward grunt, son of a pervert, pick up the gun," Vandercook ordered.

The boy continued staring at the gun.

"Don't do it!" Caroline cried, beginning to rush forward. Someone grabbed her and held her back. Caroline was dressed in black too, her long hair partly gray now, her thin body still strong, her blue eyes clear and alert.

When the boy didn't go for the gun, Vandercook bent over and picked it up by the barrel, offering it to the boy. Ben didn't move. He was still looking down at the gun.

Without warning, Vandercook's hand shot forward, the palm striking the boy on the side of the head and sending him to the floor a second time.

This time someone came to the boy's rescue. Dix, the little gray-brown dog, had come to the open door to see what all the noise was about. Seeing his master knocked to the floor by the big stranger, the dog dashed forward and sank his sharp teeth into the back of the deputy's leg, just above the boot top.

Vandercook didn't yell. He didn't even try to jerk his leg away. He calmly lowered the barrel of his pistol and pulled the trigger. The explosion made the windows rattle and temporarily deafened everyone in the church. By the time the little cloud of smoke began to disperse, the hole in the dog's neck had already filled with blood.

Ben scooted across the floor, beginning to cry, taking the limp, lifeless dog in his arms.

"Coward grunt," the big deputy said as he turned to help his friends who were still looking for the secret passage.

Chapter 8

Mormon insolence increases. In the face of a national effort to crush polygamy, the proud (Mormon) hierarchy sent out 300 additional proselyting hellhounds to make perverts. Let the law just framed for dealing with them be fairly tried, then if it fail, let the territory be placed under military law, until rebellion against the United States is terminated.
Syracuse Standard, 1882

Vandercook and his men didn't find the secret passage, but even if they had it wouldn't have done them any good. By the time they could have followed the tunnel to its end, the Mormon men would have been dispersed to the four winds.

It was unsettling news for me to learn that Vandercook was on my trail. U.S. deputy marshals had been to my home once in recent months, but I had conveniently been up in the hills thanks to American Fork's lookout system, which gave all polygamists advance warning whenever skunks entered the valley. When the warnings came, we polygamists disappeared. I had never known for sure whether the skunks were after me until Vandercook had said so in the church.

It all seemed so unjust. I had married Carolyn and Sarah back in 1848, fourteen years before polygamy became illegal. I had obeyed the law in that I hadn't married any more wives since 1862. How could they expect me to abandon the wives of my youth, the women who had given me their best years and had borne my children? Rather than turn them out, I would die. Never would I obey such an unjust law.

But what good would I be to my families in prison? Hundreds of Mormons had gone to prison and perhaps I would too. Even if the authorities didn't catch me, I didn't figure I would be much good to my families if there was a concerted effort to catch me, forcing me to go into hiding as Patrick had tried to do. I wanted no part of such living.

The only alternative seemed to be to leave the United States. The most talked about places among polygamists were Canada and Mexico. Most appealing to me were the sprawling grasslands and abundant water of western Canada. A few days after the raid on the church, a group of us decided to make a trip to Canada to investigate the possibilities of settlement.

It seemed strange to have to leave the land of the free to find freedom. But the United States was filled with the stench of bigotry, hate, religious intolerance—the very things early Americans thought they had left behind in the old countries of Europe.

Utah Territory wasn't the only place the persecutions against Mormons raged. Idaho had taken away the certificates of all Mormon school teachers. Idaho Mormons could not vote because of a new test oath at the polls requiring every voter to swear he or she did not belong to a church that taught celestial or plural marriage. In Utah, only polygamists were not allowed to vote.

I could not vote in the land I helped settle, and if the Ring got its way, not even monogamous Mormons would be voting in Utah.

In an effort to offset the increasing practice on the part of the Ring to haul large numbers of gentile voters to the various polling locations, the Mormon Church instituted a program to get its newly arrived foreign converts naturalized as U.S. citizens as quickly as possible so they could vote. The Ring protested, resulting in a ruling in federal court that foreigners who came to the United States to be with the Mormons were not qualified for U.S. citizenship. The decision was upheld by the Utah Supreme Court.

I felt uneasy about leaving the land I had worked so hard

to settle, but I felt little reluctance about leaving a country that would not let Mormon converts become citizens and people like me vote.

Still, I felt reluctant to leave a good fight in process. Mormon leaders had dug in their heels and said no to the orders to give up polygamy. All hell could rise up against them and they would not abandon a commandment of God. A year earlier, President Taylor had sent a letter to stake presidents calling all members of stake presidencies, bishoprics, and high councils to take plural wives or be released.

The storm clouds over Utah were getting increasingly black. Both sides were becoming more determined in their efforts to win. Patrick was one of the first casualties, and there was no doubt in my mind but what there would be many more.

While I felt an urgent need to get my families away while I still could to a safer place like Canada, I didn't want to abandon my church when it needed me to defend the faith.

My neighbors, like me, felt torn and confused. They wanted to do the right thing, but were not sure what that might be. We viewed the trip to Canada as insurance, a trip to check out a safe place to go just in case life became unbearable in Utah, as it appeared it would.

I decided to make a secret trip to Salt Lake one night soon before I left for Canada. I had to talk to Sam, Kathryn and Lydia about what the bishop had said. The more I thought about the unusual proposition, the more uneasy I felt. The times were not right for Sam or anyone else to enter plural marriage. If caught, he would go to prison. But what if there was a divine responsibility, as the bishop suggested, for Sam to sire posterity for Patrick?

I decided to relay what the bishop had said to Sam, Kathryn and Lydia. What they did about it would be up to them.

Chapter 9

And I say again, wo unto that nation or house or people who seek to hinder my people from obeying the Patriarchal Law of Abraham which leadeth to a Celestial glory . . . for whosoever doeth those things shall be damned.

—Revelation dictated by WILFORD WOODRUFF, January, 1880.

Accepted by John Taylor and the Twelve Apostles as the word of the Lord the following April

It was a crisp fall afternoon, and a steady west wind was pushing puffy white clouds across a blue Utah sky. But the beauty of the afternoon went unnoticed by Kathryn, who was marching east along tree-lined West Temple Street, several blocks east of Salt Lake City's busy center.

Kathryn was wearing a black wool coat, her pregnant belly preventing it from being buttoned in the front. She was walking faster than she should for a woman in her condition, and was trying to go even faster, but her gait was unsteady because her feet were too far apart.

Behind her was a frustrated Sam, trying to catch up, but every time he did, she turned off in a new direction, widening the gap between her and her husband. He was holding his hands in front of him helplessly. She had tear-stained cheeks.

"Leave me alone!" Kathryn cried, turning away as Sam made another attempt to move beside her.

"We've got to talk," he said.

"What's there to talk about?"

"The way you're behaving," he said, gently taking hold of her arm. "Please."

She stopped and turned towards him, wiping her nose with her free sleeve. Her eyes were red from crying.

"I just didn't think you'd do it," Kathryn said in a voice not totally under control.

"But we discussed it ahead of time. You said it was all right for me to marry Lydia."

"But I didn't think you'd do it."

"Then why did you give your permission?"

"I don't know," Kathryn said, her voice suddenly firm. "Must have been out of my mind. Bishop Miller made it sound so right with you not being able to hold important church callings without a plural wife. He said I'd be holding you back from exaltation in the Celestial Kingdom if I didn't go along with it."

"Then why are you crying?" Sam asked innocently.

"Because I'm fat and pregnant," she cried, pushing him away and jerking her arm free from his grip. "And because she's young and beautiful."

"Kathryn, listen to me," he said, reaching forward and taking both of her reluctant hands in his. "You've never looked more beautiful to me than you do now. To see you pregnant—nothing has ever been more beautiful to me than you are now."

"I bet you say that to all your wives," she mocked, visibly softened by Sam's remarks. Both of them began to laugh.

"No, only to you," he said.

"But you don't even know her," she said, her voice serious again. "And neither do I."

"Maybe there should have been some courtship," Sam said sheepishly as he looked down at his feet. "But how would you have responded to that, me coming home and announcing I was going out with Lydia?"

"That would have been better than the way it is now," Kathryn cried, "you not even coming home because you're spending the night with her."

"I haven't done that yet and you know it," Sam said.

"But you're thinking about it, aren't you? Don't tell me you don't want to."

"What do you want me to do?" he asked, throwing up his hands in desperation.

"I don't know," she said, beginning to cry again. "I just thought things were so good between us that this would never happen."

Sam tried to take her in his arms, but Kathryn wouldn't let him.

"I'll go to Bishop Miller and get the thing annulled," he said.

"Then I'd feel guilty, like I was hurting you, holding you back," Kathryn said, crying louder.

"Then what should I do? What can I do?"

"I don't know what to say," she sobbed.

"I'm going to Brigham City tomorrow to deliver some horses," he said, clearing his throat. "Be gone two days. Let's think it out. Give it a lot of prayer. We'll talk again when I return. I'll get an annulment, if you want me to."

"Don't you ever wonder why Lydia married you?" Kathryn asked, not seeming to hear his words. "She is so beautiful, and there are so many younger, wealthier men around."

"No," Sam said simply. "Never thought about it."

"I don't suppose you would," she smiled, looking with fondness at him for the first time.

"When I get back, maybe things will be clearer. Now come home with me."

"You sure you wouldn't rather go to Lydia's tonight?"

"Not tonight," Sam said, taking her by the arm. This time she didn't pull away.

Chapter 10

The excesses employed in enforcing the Edmunds-Tucker Act will yet be read with surprise and wonder.
—JOHN TAYLOR

Ben pushed the shovel deep into the soft black earth and underneath the dead vines at just the right angle to avoid cutting the big red potatoes he was digging. He liked the smell of raw potatoes and fresh, moist earth and the feel of his muscles straining in his arms and back. He was keenly aware of the strength that had been surging into his body over the last year or so, the broadening of his shoulders and the hardening of his thighs and arms. He could haul hay all day, shoe four horses without stopping to rest, and dig more yards of ditch in a day than any grown man he knew.

And he could ride. Ben had no fear of green colts who wanted to buck, and on a well-broke horse he could do things bareback at a full gallop that most men couldn't do mounted on saddles. Ben loved his horses and the things he could do with them.

But he couldn't figure out why speech was so difficult when physical things were so easy. He could run full speed over rocky ground without stumbling, but he couldn't spit out a simple sentence without stuttering.

Ben wondered about the incident with Vandercook at Patrick's funeral. He was ashamed at his own cowardice. The deputy had disrupted the funeral and killed his dog, Dix. Still, Ben had been unable to stand up to the man.

Why? There was no doubt in Ben's mind that side by side he could outwork, outride, outrun—probably even outfight—the big deputy, so why had Ben backed down? Why had he been paralyzed with fear, so sick to his stomach that he thought he would throw up? Even when Vandercook had shot Dix, Ben had been unable to do anything but crawl across the floor and cradle the dying dog in his arms. Ben hated himself for the way he had behaved. He was so ashamed.

His shame kept him awake at night. He thought about little else. The only escape was work—hard, physical work—the kind that made a man sweat and his muscles quiver.

Ben dug faster, overturning potatoes like he was getting paid a dollar for each one. The sweat was running down his bare back and chest, glistening in the morning sunshine. He could feel blisters beginning to rise on his palms, but he didn't care. He didn't stop. He wished he had a hundred acres of potatoes to dig, not just the small patch in Kathryn's back yard.

Knowing this was a busy time of year for Sam and that Kathryn was slowed down by her pregnancy, Ben had gone to Salt Lake to help her get her garden harvested and gather in a good supply of wood and coal for the winter.

Normally, his father would have handled such a chore, but Dan was off to southern Alberta, checking out the possibilities of moving there, away from the intense persecutions over polygamy. Many Mormon men were off on scouting trips to both Canada and Mexico. Some families had already left. There was even a lot of talk about the Church moving its headquarters to Mexico.

"Ready for a break?" Kathryn called from the back porch.

Ben straightened up, one hand on the shovel handle, and looked towards the porch. His vision was blurred by the sweat in his eyes. Someday when he married, he hoped he would find someone as beautiful, nice, and friendly as his sister-in-law, Kathryn.

He slipped into the blue long-sleeved shirt that had been hanging over a raspberry bush and started towards the back porch. For the first time that morning, his nose caught the scent of fresh cinnamon rolls. He was suddenly very hungry.

As he reached the back steps, Kathryn appeared in the doorway, a pitcher of cold milk in one hand, a basket of steaming rolls in the other. Together they sat down on the top step, Ben biting into the first roll while Kathryn poured two glasses of milk.

"The doctor said I should drink lots of milk," she offered.

Ben didn't say anything because his mouth was full.

"Sam should have been back yesterday," she said. "What do you think's held him up?"

"M-maybe some of th-the horses got away and r-ran into th-the desert. It'd take a c-couple of days to catch th-them," he stuttered, after a big swallow.

"That sounds reasonable," Kathryn said.

Ben was about to ask if she had checked with Lydia, in the event Sam had gone there first, but decided against it. He didn't know how Kathryn felt about his brother's new wife, and he didn't dare ask. He couldn't understand how any man with a wife like Kathryn would want another.

It had been different in the home where he had grown up. His father, Dan, had married Caroline and Aunt Sarah on the same day, and it had seemed a natural situation. Sam marrying Lydia seemed different somehow, but Ben wasn't sure why.

"I th-think I hear s-someone knocking at th-the front door," Ben said.

"I don't hear anything, but I'll check," Kathryn said, standing up and disappearing into the house. Ben reached for another roll.

He didn't finish it.

"Ben, come here," Kathryn called, louder than necessary. The alarm in her voice was unmistakable, even through the closed doors.

Ben jumped to his feet and charged through the door.

"Git yer things. Yer coming with me," demanded a

gruff, familiar voice from the front room. Ben stopped. It was Oscar Vandercook, the big deputy.

Looking about for a gun or knife but seeing neither, Ben hurried unarmed into the front room.

"He says they've arrested Sam on polygamy charges!" Kathryn cried. "He's in jail."

"And that's where yer going too, polyg squaw," Vandercook bellowed. "Git yer things, or I'll take you the way you are."

"What are the charges?" Kathryn demanded, not moving.

"Got a paper says I'm to take you in for protective custody, so you can testify against that pervert husband of yers," he explained.

"But I'm his wife. Wives can't testify against husbands," she insisted.

"Except for polygamy and cohabitation violations under the Edmunds-Tucker Law. Come on, lady, let's go."

"No," Kathryn said.

Vandercook grabbed her arm. She pulled back. He didn't let go. Ben stepped forward.

"Going to try something, grunt?" Vandercook asked, his mean black eyes aimed at Ben's. "I'd just love to break her arm and yer neck."

"You're hurting my arm," Kathryn said, beginning to bend as the deputy twisted her wrist.

Ben felt his fists clench. A sick feeling welled up inside him. His legs were frozen. He opened his mouth to say something, but no words would come out. He was helpless, sick with fear, and hating himself for his inability to act. He knew he was strong enough to whip this man in a fair fight, but he could do nothing but stand and shake like a wet pup. He felt so ashamed. Tears began welling up in his eyes. Vandercook was backing towards the door, dragging Kathryn with him. Ben didn't move.

"Tell David Butler," Kathryn yelled, as she was dragged out the door. "He'll know what to do."

When they were out of sight, Ben was finally able to move. He rushed to the gun cabinet in the corner of the room and jerked out his brother's Winchester rifle. Pulling open the drawer below the cabinet, he grabbed three cartridges and quickly inserted them in the magazine. He levered a cartridge into the chamber. The rifle was ready to fire.

Using the barrel, Ben pushed back the curtain covering the nearest window. At the edge of the yard, he could see Vandercook pulling the protesting Kathryn into a carriage.

Ben unhooked the latch and pushed up the window. Then dropping to one knee, he pushed the rifle barrel through the window, taking aim at the deputy's head.

Ben knew how to use the rifle. He had grown up with firearms and killed his share of deer, elk and predators. He was a good shot, so hitting Vandercook in the head at thirty or forty yards would not be difficult.

But Kathryn was beside the deputy, and Ben couldn't chance hitting her. Still, it was an easy shot. But the man was a deputy, an officer of the law.

Ben remembered Patrick's funeral. He remembered the insults. He could still see Vandercook lowering his big horse pistol and blowing a hole in Dix's neck.

If anyone deserved a bullet in the head, it was Vandercook, but Ben couldn't pull the trigger. His sweaty palms were slippery on the cold steel. His hands were steady, but no matter how he wanted to, he couldn't pull the trigger.

As the carriage drove out of sight, Ben, sobbing quietly, gradually lowered the rifle.

Chapter 11

Let the carpetbagger . . . lift up his head once more and turn his face toward the setting sun. Utah beckons him to a new field of pillage and fresh pastures of pilfering. Let him pack his grip sack and start. The Mormons have no friends, and no one will come forward to protect their rights. . . . I would not place a dog under the domination of a set of carpetbaggers . . . unless I meant to have him robbed of his bone. A more grinding tyranny, or more absolute despotism, was never established over any people.

—SENATOR HOUSE of Tennessee, 1882, in response to the Edmunds Act, which would put Utah under the power of an appointed commission.

"Doesn't look good," David Butler said as he paced back and forth inside Sam's cell.

David was a young, intense lawyer. His curly brown hair didn't seem to want to go where he combed it, if he bothered to take the time to try. His black suit was a little too small for his lean, muscular body, and several days beyond a good pressing. Though he spent little time in the sun, there was no pallor to his healthy skin. His eyes were blue and alert, his enthusiasm for his trade electric. David often talked so fast it required extra effort on the part of the listener to catch every word. He paced the jail cell like a caged lion, eager—even hungry—to take on the judge, jury, and prosecuting attorney.

In contrast, Sam sat on the wood frame bunk angry, worried and frustrated at the unfairness of his arrest. He wanted to roll up his sleeves and do something, but because of the uncertainty of the situation, he was not able to.

"They've got to let her go," Sam said. "She's about to have a baby."

"Judge Zane says no. He says in these polygamy cases too many wives, even the pregnant ones, disappear during the trial. Says he can't take a chance on Kathryn disappearing."

"I thought wives weren't supposed to testify against their husbands."

"Not so in polygamy cases. Too tough to get convictions without involving the women."

"How about getting me out on bail? If I were free, maybe I could do something," Sam said urgently.

"Zane doesn't let polygamists out on bail."

"You're not serious," Sam said. "It's not like I killed someone."

"No bail for polygamists. Actually, it's left to the discretion of the court. In Judge Zane's court there's no bail."

"The law's heartless, and so is Judge Zane!" Sam hissed, his jaw set.

"Not entirely heartless," David objected, a twisted smile spreading across his lips. "Zane said he would make things easier for Kathryn by moving up the trial date. She can go home as soon as it's over."

"When's the trial?" Sam asked.

"Tomorrow."

"But that leaves us only one day to prepare."

David nodded. "That's why we need to sit down and get to work. Right now."

David sat on the edge of the wooden cot beside Sam and retrieved a file of papers from his satchel.

"The first thing I need to know," David said, removing a pencil from behind his ear and looking at his notes instead of at Sam, "is did you really marry Lydia?"

"Yes," Sam said. "Bishop Miller sealed us a week ago Friday."

"Question number two," David said, suddenly looking

up into Sam's face. "Are you willing to lie under oath?"

"What do you mean?" Sam asked, not answering the question.

"When asked if Lydia is your wife, will you say she is not?"

Sam paused and looked down at the floor.

"Lying doesn't come easy. Can't we win fair and square, by telling the truth?"

"If you want to know the truth, chances are we can't win either way. I do think the chances are better if you lie, but there's a catch."

"What's that?"

"Kathryn and Lydia have to lie too. They'll both be on the witness stand. They'll both have to say you didn't marry Lydia. Will they do that?"

"Kathryn probably would," Sam said. "But Lydia, I don't know. To be honest, I hardly know the woman."

"But you married her," David said, grinning to himself like he had just struck upon a private joke Sam would not appreciate.

"There's a way to rationalize the lying," David continued. "You see, legally you really aren't married to Lydia. The government doesn't recognize our church marriages, so in the eyes of the law you aren't married to her. So when the court asks you if you are married to Lydia, you can say no with a clear conscience. Besides, celestial marriage is a sacred thing, not to be mocked and made fun of by gentiles. If Joseph and Brigham tried to maintain secrecy concerning their sacred sealings, I suppose you would be justified in doing the same."

"If I lie can we win?" Sam asked.

"Getting over the polygamy charge is just the first step," David said. "If you say you didn't marry Lydia and they can't prove it, then they will come after you for the lesser charge of cohabitation."

"Will that be easier to beat?" Sam asked.

"Not exactly, but the sentence is usually less. For a polygamy conviction you get up to five years and a $500 fine. For cohabitation the law says you can get up to six months in jail and a $300 fine. But there's a catch."

"There always is," Sam said, looking very grim.

"The penalty can be repeated for every time you cohabitate with a woman. If you've spent four nights with her since the wedding you could possibly get a $1200 fine and two years in jail."

"Where would I go to jail?"

"More and more people are being sent to Sugarhouse, but there's always the chance you'd go to the federal prison at Detroit. That's bad duty, two thousand miles away."

"At least we won't have to lie about the cohabitation part," Sam said, not wanting to even think about going to the Detroit prison, shifting the focus of their conversation back to the trial.

"What do you mean?" David asked, looking up quickly.

"Didn't cohabitate with the woman, not once," Sam said, simply.

"You mean you never consummated the marriage to Lydia?"

"Nope. Kathryn wasn't too happy with the whole thing, even though she went along with it. Then I was off to Brigham City with the horses. Ended up here before I saw Lydia again. In fact, Kathryn and I were talking about undoing the whole thing."

"You're not lying to me?" David asked, carefully watching Sam's face for any sign of deception.

"I swear I'm telling the truth," Sam said.

David slapped his thigh and stood up.

"Think we just might win this one," he said cheerfully. "They'll probably back off the polygamy charge fairly easily, thinking they've got you on cohabitation, then when we prove you didn't cohabitate, they won't have anywhere else to turn. Yes, sir, I think we have a good chance of winning this one."

"You really think so?" Sam asked, standing up too.

"Yes, but there's still a lot to do. I need to know where you spent every night since the wedding, and the names of witnesses who can back you up. Write everything down for me."

David handed Sam a piece of blank paper and a pencil. "While you're doing that I need to talk to Kathryn and Lydia, making sure they understand how to answer the marriage questions, that you are not legally married to Lydia. If they handle that right I think we have a chance. Oh yes, and Grace will want to stage a protest for Judge Zane. Got to find Grace."

"Guard!" he called through the bars. "I'm ready to go now." Sam sat back down on the bunk and began writing down the information requested by the young lawyer.

Chapter 12

For a quarter of a century Asiatic polygamy has grown, strengthened, and fortified itself in the heart of our domain. This American cancer has grown and spread till it has filled all Utah with its poison. . . . There should be enacted laws whose supreme object should be the utter and complete extirpation of this un-American institution which defies our national law, denounces our national judiciary, mocks our national authority, and reviles all who dare lift their finger against it.

—SMILER COLFAX, Speaker of the House
United States Congress, 1882

It was a gray, windy morning as Nellie approached the federal courthouse. Still, two blocks away she could hear chanting female voices. She hurried her pace eagerly.

As soon as she could see the federal building, it was obvious to Nellie that there were two separate groups of women hindering entrance to the building. All the women were dressed about the same, in long, full dresses and shawls. Only the lettering on their placards and banners distinguished them.

The group on the left, led by an enthusiastic Grace Woolley, carried signs with the messages "Mormon Men Love Wives, Not Harlots" and "Judge Zane Would Send Abraham, Isaac and Jacob to Prison."

The group on the right, led by Angie Newman, held up banners with opposite messages like "End Mormon Barbarianism Now'' and ''Polygamy is Slavery.''

Nellie knew both female leaders and would have liked to have stopped and talked to both of them, but she didn't. She just hurried up the steps and into the courtroom. She didn't want to miss anything, sure that if she kept careful notes she would come up with at least one, and perhaps several, good stories.

Judge Charles S. Zane had already called the court to order. He was an erect, proper man, in his late forties or early fifties. With slightly graying hair and a very sober demeanor, he looked like a preacher at an altar, about to handle the business of God.

Zane had already invited the prosecuting and defense attorneys to make their opening remarks. By the time Nellie took her seat, David Butler, dressed in the same wrinkled suit he had worn the previous day, had marched to the front of the bench.

After a brief but courteous greeting to Judge Zane, Butler walked over to the jury, which consisted of both men and women. Facing them, both hands on the wooden rail separating the jury benches from the courtoom floor, Butler began to speak.

''Most of you probably remember as you were sworn in that I asked if you believed in the Bible, the Old and New Testaments,'' he said in a calm, matter-of-fact voice, as if he were talking to a son about the morning chores. ''Is that right?''

Most of the jurors nodded their acknowledgement.

''Then I can assume you also believe in the resurrection, as described in the New Testament.'' Some of them nodded again.

''Then you also believe that families will be united in the resurrection—that husbands, wives, sons, daughters, brothers and sisters will meet again in joyous reunion.''

Butler waited for the jurors to nod their agreement, finally singling out one squat man on the end who did not.

''Sir, do you believe families will be reunited in the resurrection?'' he asked. After an uncomfortable pause, the squat juror nodded that he did.

"Will parents and children in the resurrection have the same filial feelings towards each other that they have here?"

"Perhaps more intense," offered one of the women.

"I think you are right," Butler said, turning thoughtfully away from the railing, as if in deep thought.

Then turning back to the jury, Butler spoke more quickly and with more intensity.

"We see in this life that among Christians, ministers of all faiths and classes of men, a man marries a wife and has children by her. And if she dies, he marries again and has more children by the second wife. If this one dies, the man will marry a third time, perhaps even a fourth and a fifth time, each new wife bearing the man children. This is considered right and proper by the entire Christian world as long as the man never has more than one living wife at a time. Am I correct in this assumption?"

Most of the jurors nodded their agreement.

"Now, in the resurrection," Butler resumed, every word clear and precise, "this man and all his wives and children will be raised from the dead and reunited. We all believe that."

He paused, waiting for his words to sink in, making sure everyone had a chance to think about what he was saying.

"But which one of the women will be his wife in the resurrection? The first? The youngest? The oldest? The one with the most children? What about the others?" His voice was getting louder. "Will God throw them out? Will God prohibit those other wives from being with the only husband they ever knew? Will some of the children be driven from their true father?

"No. God does not allow evil in His heaven. It is only right and logical that the women join their legal and lawfully wedded husband. All of them. You must agree with me. There is no other answer.

"Do you agree with me that God would permit such a family relationship in His heaven?"

This time no one on the jury nodded their agreement. They knew where Butler was leading them, and they weren't about to be drawn any further into his trap.

"Though none of you are nodding your agreement, I think you know in your hearts that I am right," Butler said. "What else could a just and loving God do but let that man be reunited with all his wives and children?

"Some of you have probably already guessed my next question, so I'll go ahead and ask it. If the Lord would allow a man to have more than one wife in heaven, where no evil exists," he said, his voice soft, but suddenly getting very loud, "then why wouldn't He allow a man to have more than one wife on this earth?"

There was a spontaneous outbreak of talking among the jurors, as well as among the spectators. It seemed, all at once, that everyone had something to say about Butler's argument, both for and against.

Judge Zane banged his gavel on the bench three or four times. Finally everyone was silent.

"I don't expect to convert all of you into polygamy today," Butler said, and there was a loud eruption of laughter. Again the judge hammered the room to silence.

"Objection!" shouted William Dickson, the prosecuting attorney, who up until now had been silent. "Your honor, this is a court of law, not a Sunday school. We didn't come here to be preached at."

"I agree with the prosecution, your honor," Butler said, his voice clearer and louder than his opponent's. "But every juror entering this courtroom today saw signs and banners referring to so-called Mormon barbarianism. I am merely attempting to show that during the course of this trial we are not dealing with barbarianism, but a practice with foundations in Christianity and Christian beliefs. That's all."

"Then continue," the judge said in a gruff voice, adding as an afterthought, "objection overruled."

Butler then gave a brief history of the man on trial, concluding with, "The man you are judging is a horse trainer, and a trader in carriages and wagons. He has a reputation for being honest and forthright in all his dealings. There has never been a legal judgment against him. He has no criminal record whatsoever."

He turned and pointed at Sam, washed and clean-shaven

in his Sunday best. Sam was a healthy man in his mid-thirties, normally a cheerful, friendly man, but today he looked very sober.

"He is a family man," Butler continued. "His wife Kathryn is expecting their first child in just a few months. He should be tending business and taking care of his wife, not defending himself in this courtroom. His wife should be home resting, getting ready for her first child, not sitting in this courtroom, compelled against her will to testify against the man she has taken sacred vows to cherish, honor, and obey."

Butler turned back to the jury, walking up to the railing and placing both hands on it, elbows straight.

"I will prove beyond any reasonable doubt this day that the defendant Sam Storm has but one wife, and that he has not cohabited with anyone except his legal and lawful wife, Kathryn Storm.

"Though none of you jurors belong to the LDS Church—the Edmunds Law prohibiting this man from being judged by his peers—I hope each of you has the Christian decency to be just and fair in the decision you will make today. The future of this young family is in your hands. I hope you handle that responsibility in a manner pleasing before God."

Slowly, head bowed as though he were carrying a heavy burden, David Butler returned to his chair at the table where Sam was seated. The room was quiet as he sat down.

No one in the room had listened to Butler's remarks more intently than Nellie. While still angry at her former fiancé for not telling her about his first wife, she was impressed and pleased with his performance before the court. He was an excellent attorney, a powerful persuader. She couldn't help but think that if she were his wife she would see that he was better dressed when he went to court.

Nellie's thoughts were quickly turned back to the business at hand as U.S. attorney William Dickson strode to the bench, offering a crisp greeting to the judge, then turning to the jury. His black suit was as neat and tidy as any on the new mannequins in the front window of the ZCMI store.

Dickson was older than Butler, more experienced, more confident, more polished, and not at all intimidated by Butler's opening remarks.

"Since my opponent began his remarks with talk of the scriptures and the resurrection, I would like to begin in a similar manner," he began, his voice easy and confident.

" 'Wherefore, my brethren, hear me, and hearken to the word of the Lord,' " he began, reading from a piece of paper inside an open folder. " 'For there shall not any man among you have save it be one wife; and concubines he shall have none; for I, the Lord God, delight in the chastity of women. And whoredoms are an abomination before me; thus saith the Lord of Hosts.'

"Have any of you Christian jurors ever heard or read this passage before?" Dickson continued, closing his folder and looking directly at the jurors. "Where is it found?"

"Sounds familiar," one man said, but no one could say exactly where it was found.

"Well, don't feel bad if you don't know," Dickson smiled. "This passage isn't from the King James Bible, but comes from a different sort of bible, a Mormon bible. They call it the Book of Mormon. The reference is Jacob, chapter two, verses 27 and 28.

"The hypocrites," he yelled, "are going against their own sacred scripture!"

"Today," Dickson continued, his voice again quiet and confident, "there is not just a man on trial, but a system—a barbaric system—like you might find in Turkey and Arabia, but not in any of the civilized Christian nations. Polygamy has emerged in Mormondom like an uncontrolled cancer. Though their own scriptures oppose it, it continues to grow and spread, corrupting otherwise good men, enslaving young women. It is a worse evil than Negro slavery, which this country just rid itself of.

"And just as slavery was cleansed from our national conscience at great cost, so must polygamy be.

"You, the jury, must make a decision today. Whether to encourage the spread of this cancerous evil, or to help eradicate it. I hope you have the courage to do what is right."

When Dickson was finished and had returned to his chair, Judge Zane addressed the jury.

"I'm sure you were taken in by the eloquence of the opening remarks on both sides, as I was. But I want to remind you that polygamy is not on trial here today, but a man by the name of Sam Storm. The Congress of this country has passed laws against polygamy and cohabitation. Whether or not those laws are right or wrong is a subject to be discussed in the halls of Congress, not in this courtroom. The business for us is to determine if Mr. Storm has violated those laws, and if he has, to punish him accordingly. That is all."

Zane turned to address both attorneys. "Counselors, I hope you will limit your future arguments to the subject at hand—the guilt or innocence of Mr. Storm in reference to the charges against him. Is that clear?" Both attorneys nodded that it was.

Sam was the first witness, and David Butler didn't waste any time getting to the heart of the matter.

"Mr. Storm, did you marry Lydia Sessions on October 16th of this year as has been charged?"

"No, I did not," Sam said, looking at the floor.

"Ladies and gentlemen of the jury," Butler said, "please note that I have personally gone through the marriage records at both the county and city offices and there is no record of Sam Storm ever marrying Lydia Sessions. Unless the prosecution can produce such a record, the jury must assume that no such marriage has taken place." Then he turned back to Sam.

"Have you cohabited or been alone with Lydia Sessions in a private place at any time between October 16th and the present?"

"No, I have not."

"Would you kindly tell the court where you spent each night from the 16th to the present?"

"I will," Sam said, and proceeded to narrate in detail his actions from the 16th to the time of his arrest. When he was finished, Butler sat down and Dickson approached the witness stand to crossexamine the witness.

"Do you believe that Joseph Smith was a true prophet

and a righteous man?''

''I do,'' Sam said.

''Do you try to follow his example in your own personal life? Do you try to pattern your life after his?''

''I try.''

Dickson turned away from Sam and walked over to the jury, opening his folder.

''I would like to read to the jury a comment by Joseph Smith published in the July, 1838 issue of *The Elders' Journal,* an official publication of the Mormon Church.'' He held up a copy of the *Elders' Journal* for all to see.

''The article I will read from is a self-interview in which Joseph Smith answers some of the questions most frequently asked of him.'' Dickson began reading.

'' 'Question 7: Do the Mormons believe in having more wives than one? Answer: No, not at the same time. But they believe that if their companion dies, they have a right to marry again.'

''Ladies and gentlemen of the jury,'' he continued, handing the *Elders' Journal* to the clerk, ''it is common knowledge that Joseph Smith not only taught, but practiced, polygamy. The statement I just read to you out of this journal is an obvious deception, a lie.''

He pointed at Sam, still in the witness chair. ''The defendant has already told the jury that he tries to follow the example set by Joseph Smith. If Smith lied about his polygamous beliefs and relationships, as I have just shown you, wouldn't the defendant do the same? Of course he would.''

Then, turning to the judge, he said, ''I have no further questions for this witness.''

Nothing much happened as numerous witneses were brought to the stand to verify Sam's whereabouts on various nights between the 16th and his arrest date.

When Kathryn was asked to come to the stand she did so, reluctantly, getting up very slowly from her chair and walking even more slowly toward the bench.

''Do you swear to tell the whole truth and nothing but the truth, so help you God?'' asked the clerk.

Kathryn looked at the clerk, then up at the judge.

"No," she said in a shrill but firm voice.

The courtroom was suddenly noisy, as dozens of people commented on the totally unexpected response from Kathryn. The judge once again hammered the room to silence.

"Would you care to explain that answer?" the judge asked Kathryn.

"Yes," Kathryn said, turning to face the judge. There was emotion in her voice, like she might cry, but no uncertainty in what she said.

"Two days ago I was forcibly taken from my home by a United States marshal. I have been locked up in a room against my will for the past two days, and brought here today to be used as a witness to help send to jail the man I love, my husband." Her voice was getting stronger, more sure.

"We live in a country where women are not required to testify against their husbands. If the Edmunds Law says wives must testify against husbands, then it is a bad law and must be changed. I refuse to help this court send my husband, a good man, to jail."

"Mrs. Storm," the judge said, trying to remain calm. "The law says you must answer the questions."

"And if I don't, are you going to order me shot or beheaded?" challenged Kathryn, her voice angry now.

"No, not that," Zane said, still calm, "but I can send you to jail."

"Me and my unborn child?" Kathryn responded.

"Yes, and I will do it, if you don't answer the questions."

"Then send me to jail," Kathryn said, marching back to her chair.

"For contempt of this court, I hereby sentence the witness to one week in the county jail," the judge bellowed, ending his comment with a fierce blow of his gavel.

Nellie marveled at Kathryn's courage, standing up to a federal judge like that. She wanted to talk to this Kathryn, maybe interview her for a story.

Nellie looked over at Sam, who was looking at his wife. Nellie thought she could see tears run from the corners of his eyes down his cheeks. He seemed like such a good man. Nellie was angry with herself for feeling so much empathy for polygamists.

The last witness was Lydia, who had never looked more beautiful, wearing a new, neatly pressed light blue cotton dress with white trim. Her long black hair was brushed loose, which gave it a partly wind-blown, natural look. The flush of her cheeks, her long black eyelashes, her full breasts, made her an item of extreme interest to everyone in the room. Lydia did not hesitate to take the oath.

Butler was the first to question her.

"Is O'Riley your maiden name?"

"No," Lydia replied. "It's the name of my late husband, Dr. Patrick O'Riley. My maiden name is Sessions."

"How did your husband die?"

"He was dragged to death by a horse about a hundred miles west of here. His foot was caught in the stirrup," she said coolly.

"What was he doing in the west desert?"

"He was a polygamist trying to escape U.S. marshals," she said, still calm. "I was his second wife."

Some spontaneous chatter erupted. The judge called for silence. Butler continued with the next question.

"Were you married to the defendant as a plural wife on October 16th?"

Lydia paused, looking first at Butler, then at Sam, then at Kathryn.

"Yes," she said.

"I think you misunderstood the question," Butler said, a stunned, helpless look on his face.

"I don't think so," Lydia said. "I was sealed to Sam Storm as a plural wife by a Bishop Miller on October 16th."

Butler turned to Judge Zane. "Can we have a recess?"

"I don't see any need for that," the judge responded "Do you have any more questions for the witness?"

"Yes," Butler said, trying to gather his thoughts. Lydia had agreed to deny the marriage. Why had she changed her mind?

"The defendant, Mr. Storm, has told this court that he

has not been with you privately since October 16th, that there has been no cohabitation between the two of you. Is that true?'' Butler's voice had lost its confidence. After the previous answer, he had no idea how Lydia would respond.

''Are you asking if my plural marriage to Sam Storm was consummated?'' she asked boldly.

''Yes,'' Butler said.

''Do I have to answer this?'' Lydia asked, turning to the judge.

''I apologize for the embarrassing nature of the question,'' the judge said, ''but I think it is imperative that you answer.''

''The answer is yes,'' she said.

''That's a lie!'' Sam shouted and came out of his chair but was grabbed by two guards as he tried to approach Lydia. The judge ordered silence as Sam was forcibly returned to his chair, the guards remaining there, one on each side.

''Mr. Butler, please don't look so shocked,'' said Lydia. ''If I had been sealed to you as a plural wife, would you not consummate the marriage?''

Spontaneous hooting and laughter filled the room, and no amount of hammering on the part of Judge Zane could bring silence, at least not for several minutes.

Some of the jurors were laughing too. Sam was glaring at Lydia, who seemed to be enjoying the fuss she had created. David Butler was shaking his head in discouragement. Kathryn was crying.

Chapter 13

What would be necessary to bring about the result nearest the hearts of the opponents of Mormonism? . . . Simply to renounce, abrogate, or apostatize from the new and everlasting covenant of marriage in its fullness. Were the Saints to do that as an entirety, God would reject the church as a body. The authority of the priesthood would be withdrawn, with its gifts and powers.

Deseret News editorial by JOHN NICHOLSON, editor
April 23, 1885

"I still don't know why Lydia turned on us," David Butler said. "It just doesn't make sense."

"Maybe she had her feelings hurt when Sam didn't consummate the marriage. Maybe she was striking back at Sam," Grace Woolley responded. She was with David in his carriage heading north from Salt Lake City along Beck Street, almost to the hot springs. It was early evening, and they were on their way to a secret meeting with George Q. Cannon, counselor in the First Presidency of the Mormon Church.

The First Presidency, including President Taylor, and the apostles had been in hiding to avoid arrest by U.S. marshals for over a year now. Through Angus Cannon, president of the Salt Lake Stake, David had asked for a hearing with the First Presidency. He was concerned that he and other Mormon laywers were having little success defending Mormons accused of polygamy and cohabitation in Judge

Zane's court. He also wanted to make sure the church was doing everything it could in Washington, D.C. to get the law changed so a Mormon could at least have a chance at a fair trial. The two things most urgently in need of change were the disallowing of Mormons on juries, and the requiring of women to testify against their husbands.

Grace had requested an audience with the First Presidency for different reasons. She wanted to discuss the possibility of sending a delegation of plural wives to Washington to show all who would listen that Mormon plural wives were not slaves, but educated, articulate women who had acted intelligently and rationally in deciding to enter plural marriages. Some people were reluctant in helping Grace set up the trip because the idea had not been endorsed by the First Presidency. She was going to Centerville to seek that endorsement.

"Had Lydia not turned on you, do you think you might have won?" Grace asked.

"To be totally honest, I don't think it mattered what happened in the courtroom," David said. "I think these non-Mormon juries would send Jesus himself to prison if he were brought before them on charges of polygamy or cohabitation. Unless there are some major changes in the law, a lot of Mormons are going to jail in the next few years."

"Do you think there's a chance the Church will back down and give up polygamy?" Grace asked.

"I don't think so. It's not an administrative thing. It's doctrine. I think we'll go to Mexico or Canada before giving it up. Storm's father and a lot of other people are up in Canada right now, checking on land values and places for possible settlement."

David and Grace rode in silence for a few minutes, both contemplating the possibilities and ramifications of the entire church attempting a move to Canada or Mexico. When the Mormons had been driven from Nauvoo, Illinois, in 1846, their numbers had been about 12,000. Now there were 160,000 Mormons, which would be a migration of huge proportions. Grace was the first to break the silence.

"Do you think Sam will have to serve the entire five-year sentence?"

"If the mood stays like it is, I'm afraid he will," David said. "But hopefully attitudes will soften so he can come home early."

"There ought to be a law against sending a man so far from his family. Detroit is almost 2,000 miles away," she said.

"We live in hard times, Grace," David said thoughtfully. "With things changing so fast, it's hard to make long-term plans. Takes a lot of blind faith just to keep going."

"I hope our meetings with President Cannon are productive," she said. "It's so hard to get anything past the First Presidency with them in constant hiding and on the move all the time. Do you know if anyone else will be there?"

"Angus Cannon said he'd be there. Said he had some names to clear for celestial marriage."

"You're joking," Grace said, surprise in her voice. "Who'd want to enter plural marriage now with all that's going on? That's stupid. Everybody involved in polygamy is either in hiding or jail. It's crazy."

"It's still the doctrine of the church, and I suppose people are still falling in love," explained David, amused at her strong reaction to his comment.

"Do you know who any of them are?" she asked.

"Grace, I didn't know you played the great Utah guessing game."

"Who doesn't?" Grace said. "Who's on the list?"

"I know one of the names."

"Is it someone I know?"

"Yes."

"Who?"

"A young woman who's very well known in the Salt Lake Valley."

"What's her name?"

"I don't think I should tell you."

"If you don't I'll push you out of the carriage," she said, grabbing him playfully by the right arm and beginning to push him away from her. With one of the horse's reins in each hand, David didn't try to jerk his arm away.

"Are you sure you want to know?"

"Stop teasing and just tell me," she urged.

"You."

"You're lying," she laughed, once more beginning to push him toward the edge of the seat.

"No. Honest, it's the truth."

Grace let go of David's arm and faced forward. There was no longer any humor in the situation. "You're not playing games with me?" she asked soberly.

"No, I'm not."

Both rode in silence for a few moments.

"But I haven't been seeing anyone," she said. "I've been so busy with the movement and the rallies, my romantic life has been nothing. I can't imagine who might be asking . . . not Bishop Thatcher?"

"Bishop Thatcher?"

"He sometimes calls me into his office to see how things are going, asking if there's anything he can do to help with the cause. Sometimes he's asked me if I'm getting any closer to getting married, but that's all."

"Not Bishop Thatcher."

"Then who?"

"Me."

"You're serious," she said, looking straight ahead, both hands in her lap.

"I hadn't planned on saying anything until I obtained a tentative go-ahead from the First Presidency. If the answer was no, my intention was to drop the whole thing and never say anything to you."

"And if they say yes?"

"Then I'll start courting you, to see if things might work out."

"What about your wife Alice? Does she know about all this?"

"It was her idea. At least to begin with. When things didn't work out with Nellie, it was Alice who suggested if I ever wanted to try again, it ought to be with someone like you. She said she thought it would be fun having you as a sister-wife. Married Mormons talk about those kinds of things, you know."

"I can't believe this!" Grace exclaimed. "It was Alice's idea, and she said she thought it would be fun?"

"That's what she said," David replied sheepishly.

"You know it can never happen, you and I getting married," she said, her voice once again soft and serious.

"Why not?"

"Because neither one of us could continue doing what we're doing if we were into plural marriage."

"Why not?"

"We'd be too vulnerable to discovery and arrest. How good would you be in the courtroom, knowing you might be the next one to go to jail? Half the women in Utah want to help me, but don't dare, knowing they'll make their own plural marriages more vulnerable. You and I are effective defenders of the system because we have nothing to hide. If we married, we would lose much of our effectiveness."

"Don't you ever feel like a hypocrite?" David asked, cutting in on Grace's monologue.

"A hypocrite?"

"Yes, defending something you don't practice yourself. How can you be a true defender of plural marriage if you don't practice it? When you go to Washington, how much credibility will your words have if you aren't a polygamist?"

"Do you love me?" she asked, catching him by surprise with the sudden change of direction.

"Yes," he said, looking over at her. She didn't look away.

"Well, I don't feel the same way about you," she said, her voice breaking like she was about to cry.

"Should I have him take your name off the list?"

Grace looked ahead, not answering his question.

"It seems so strange, so awkward," she finally began, "talking about marriage when I've never even been kissed by a man."

"I find that hard to believe," David said, beginning to laugh.

"And why is that?" she asked, indignation in her voice.

"What's so funny?"

"I'm sorry for laughing. It's just that it's hard to believe a woman as attractive as you hasn't had a lot of boyfriends."

"I've had my share," she said defensively. "Just not the kissing kind." Both of them began to laugh.

"Would you like to know what it's like?" he asked, putting both reins in his left hand while placing his right arm on the seat back behind Grace.

"Would you tell Alice?" she asked, putting David on the defensive. He hesitated before answering.

"I wouldn't tell anybody," he finally responded.

"Even if she asked? You wouldn't lie to your wife, would you?"

"No, I wouldn't. If she asked, I would tell her the truth."

"Then I'm not in the mood," Grace said, pushing herself to the far right side of the seat. David removed his arm from the seat back and took the right rein back in his right hand.

"You didn't answer when I asked if you wanted me to have your name removed from the list," he said.

"I'm sure he'll deny the request for the reasons I already mentioned," she said confidently, "but if you wish to leave our names on the list that is your choice."

"You mean . . ." he began enthusiastically.

"I don't mean anything," she said firmly. "I'm not in love with you. But if you wish to court me, assuming you get the go-ahead, I might let you—on one condition."

"What's that?" he asked, unable to hide the eagerness in his voice.

"That you go down to ZCMI and get a new suit."

"I'll do it tomorrow."

Chapter 14

We may say, however, if any man or woman expects to enter into the celestial kingdom of our God without being tested to the very uttermost, they have not understood the gospel. If there is a weak spot in our nature, or if there is a fiber that can be made to quiver or to shrink, we may rest assured that it will be tested.
—JOHN TAYLOR, 1885

Ben pulled the sorrel gelding to a halt by the small muddy stream. He didn't know what the stream was called, or even the names of the mountains around him, but he wasn't lost. He was in the west desert where the wild horses ran, and he could easily find his way home. But that wasn't important. He didn't plan on returning home. Ever.

He swung out of the saddle and dropped to one knee, carefully eyeing the brown-stemmed plants growing in the sand near the water's edge. The leaves were long and green, like willow leaves, but different.

Carefully Ben pulled one of the dead plants from the sand and snapped it in two. While the top of the stem made a clean break, the bottom was held together with tough, stringy bark.

It was dog bane, all right. He remembered as a small boy his father, Dan Storm, showing him the plant, cautioning him never to burn it in a campfire and never to tie a horse near it when there was nothing else to eat.

"If you breathe the smoke," his father had said, "first

you'll feel kind of crazy in a good kind of way, then you'll die. You'll be crazy as a drunken Indian before it kills you."

His father had then shown him how to make a tough twine from the stringy bark by holding one end of a long strand between thumb and forefinger and rolling the other end along the thigh with the palm of the other hand until the bark twisted.

Ever since that time, Ben had avoided dog bane. He had never needed the deadly plant, at least not until now. He picked a handful of the brown stems and stuffed them in his saddle bag while his horse drank deeply from the muddy water. Then he filled his canteen, figuring he'd let the murkiness settle to the bottom before he took a drink.

The horse finished drinking. Raising his nose a few inches above the running water, he slobbered half a mouthful back into the stream. Ben stroked his palm along the animal's sweaty neck and shoulder.

"I'll m-miss you, Sonny," he said. "T-tomorrow you'll be r-running with the wild horses because t-tonight I'm going to s-smoke myself dead on d-dog bane." The horse swallowed more water, then began reaching for the grass along the edge of the stream.

"I w-wish I'd been b-born a horse," Ben said. "W-wouldn't have to worry about s-stuttering, or . . . " Tears began welling up in his eyes.

"Or b-being a coward. That's what I am, Sonny. The deputy shot old Dix and all I could do was c-cry. I c-couldn't f-fight him when he dragged K-Kathryn out of the house. I couldn't even p-pull the t-trigger when I had him in my s-sights. I'm so ashamed."

"If you c-could talk, old boy," he continued, taking the horse by the reins and leading it behind him along the little stream, "I'd want you to t-tell me why I'm such a c-coward when my f-father and brother are s-so brave."

Ben walked a long time without saying more, eventually leaving the stream and working his way along the side of a sagebrush hill. Following closely behind, plenty of slack in the reins, the sorrel horse occasionally cropped a bite of grass.

"If that d-deputy came along now and t-tried to steal you," Ben said after a while, "I'd s-start shaking and c-crying and just h-hand him the reins. I can outwork almost any m-man around, but I ain't n-no man at all.

"Pat's been k-killed. Sam's going to p-prison. Kathryn's in jail. Dad's off to C-Canada. Everybody needs a man's help, and all they g-got is Ben the c-coward. After tonight I won't be in the way anymore."

As the sun dropped below the snow-capped western mountains, Ben made camp beside a lone cedar tree on top of a sagebrush hill. After unsaddling the horse, he staked it out to graze, a long rawhide rope tied to one of its front feet. He didn't roll out his bed, nor did he do any cooking. He wasn't hungry, and he knew blankets would serve no useful purpose once he was dead.

Slowly he gathered a large pile of dead sagebrush, enough to maintain a fire most of the night. He started the fire.

When it was burning brightly, Ben retrieved the dog bane from his saddle bag, along with several pieces of paper. He had watched men roll cigarettes at the livestock sales, and figured he could roll the dog bane into cigarettes, as the men had done with tobacco.

Taking his time, Ben peeled the bark from all the dog bane stems. When he finished he had enough bark for a dozen men to smoke. It was dark now, the stars sparkling in a cloudless October sky.

Slowly and deliberately, Ben flattened the largest piece of paper across his right thigh, rubbing his open palm across it several times to make it as smooth as possible. After spreading a generous portion of dog bane across the middle of the paper, he carefully raised it to his mouth, licking one side. He rolled the paper around the shredded bark, the wet side finally sticking against the dry side to form a large, crude cigarette.

Ben held it out in the firelight, eyeing it carefully and critically—almost like it might not work if it weren't made just right. Then he reached down towards the fire, slowly extending one end of the cigarette towards a red ember.

Just as the cigarette was about to touch and begin smoldering, Ben quickly pulled back his hand, carefully setting the cigarette down on the ground. He stood up, walking over to the grazing horse.

"S-sorry, old boy. Almost f-forgot. C-can't believe I'd be s-so s-stupid as t-to l-leave you t-tied up to starve to d-death."

Ben stroked the horse's smooth neck and back with both hands, finally wrapping his arms around the warm neck and squeezing hard. He fought back the tears. He hung on for a long time before dropping to his knees and removing the tether from the horse's ankle.

"Sonny, you d-don't want to see a c-coward die. Git!" He slapped the horse on the rump and it trotted away into the darkness. Ben returned to the fire, dropped to the ground, and picked up his cigarette.

It was several hours before Ben finally pushed the end of the cigarette into the coals and raised it to his lips. He paused, wondering how the smoke would make him feel, how long it would take to kill him.

Concentrating on his hand with all his might, he finally forced it to move closer to his mouth, eventually pushing the end of the cigarette between his partially opened lips. The hard part was over. Now all he had to do was inhale. But that was even harder. He closed his eyes and clenched his teeth until his jaw began to quiver. Suddenly, he inhaled deeply. He had done it!

But there was no burning in his throat and lungs. He opened his eyes. He sniffed. The cigarette had gone out before he had inhaled.

When the stars began to disappear before the silver dawn, Ben was still sitting by the fire, looking down at an assortment of odd-shaped, partially singed cigarettes. His bedroll was still tied to the back of his saddle. The food was still in the saddle bags. The sagebrush he had gathered was gone, and the fire was nothing but a smoldering pile of orange-gray embers. Ben hadn't been able to handle death any more than he had Oscar Vandercook.

Hearing something in the sagebrush behind him, Ben

jumped to his feet, spinning around. A smile spread across his weary lips. Sonny had returned.

He walked to the horse, reached out, and scratched its ears.

"S-smart old horse," he said. "You know t-too that cowards can't k-kill themselves. Thanks for coming back."

Chapter 15

Mormonism is gathering momentum. A few batteries on the hill east of Salt Lake might once have put a quietus on this great outrage, but not now. God only knows by what national exhaustion the curse is to be extirpated. But go it must.
—REVEREND DEWITT TALMAGE, 1883

After a meager breakfast of dried apples and the last of his beef jerky, Ben saddled up his horse and began riding up the sagebrush ridge toward the higher mountain peaks.

"Even c-cowards got to eat, Sonny," he said to the horse. "Let's f-find us a deer."

He hadn't gone far when he suddenly dismounted.

"Looks like a barefoot Indian m-might have passed this way," he said to the horse while kneeling to inspect the unmistakable toe marks in the soft soil. The tracks were fresh. No debris had blown into them yet, and the steep sides of the toe marks were not caved in. The tracks were no more than a few hours old, at most.

Then Ben noticed the heel mark—that it was far too close to the toes. He laughed at himself for not recognizing the source of the tracks sooner. He was not following a man, but a bear. Perhaps it had come down the mountain during the night to check out his camp.

Without getting back on his horse, Ben began following the tracks up the mountain. He didn't particularly want to catch up with the bear or kill it. He just wanted to know where it was going. He thought back on his encounters with the deputy, his cowardly behavior, and wondered why he didn't fear the bear. But he was just looking at tracks. If he were confronting the bear face to face, that would be the true test of courage.

It was a gray, overcast morning, a cold west wind bringing in a new storm, perhaps the first snow of the season. The weather suited Ben's mood.

Hours later, in the steep high country in a patch of mountain mahogany trees, Ben spotted a small buck browsing quietly two canyons away. Tying his horse out of sight in a draw, Ben began his stalk, his Winchester in hand.

It was an easy stalk. The young buck was not as wary as an older one might have been. The deer was located directly north of Ben, so the brisk west wind carried his man scent off to the east. The noisy wind allowed Ben to step where he pleased without fear of the unfamiliar sound of his footsteps reaching the deer, even when he stepped on dry leaves and brush. Still, he was careful, keeping out of sight and being as quiet as possible.

Finally, about 120 yards away, Ben crawled to the top of a sandy ridge, using a fallen cedar tree as cover. Upon reaching the tree, he pushed the barrel of his rifle forward through the branches, resting it on the fallen trunk.

The deer was still browsing on the mahogany leaves, totally unaware of its stalker. As Ben lined the animal up in his sights, he couldn't help but think that the deer wouldn't have to die if he had been successful in killing himself. Who deserved to live most, this deer that bothered no one, or Ben the coward? How many more deer, cattle, rabbits and other animals would die in the future to provide nourishment for him? Was it worth the price, spilling the blood of so many beautiful animals to sustain the life of a coward?

Ben decided it wasn't worth it. He must die or change, but he didn't know how. How did one stop being a coward? Changes like that didn't just happen by accident. Perhaps such changes weren't even possible. Why did life have to be so hard, so uncertain, so confusing? Why couldn't life be simple like hunting?

"That's it!" thought Ben, almost crying out in the excitement of a great personal discovery, but stopping himself in time, not wanting to frighten the deer. By living off the land by himself and avoiding people, he could have the simple life of a hunter. Maybe once a year he could go back to civilization to get supplies and visit his family. The rest of the time he would be by himself, with his animals, in the wild, remote places, avoiding both white people and Indians. That's what he would do.

Ben squeezed the trigger. The deer leapt forward, then collapsed. Ben had aimed for the heart and had not missed.

After making sure the deer was dead, Ben—a man in a hurry, a man with a purpose—trotted back to his horse. The people back home could keep their messed up world. He would make his own world, in the wilds, in the mountains, with his horse and the wild animals, and maybe a new dog.

There was a lot to do with winter coming. He needed shelter, firewood, and plenty of meat. He would live like the bear that had made the tracks—a lone wanderer, doing pretty much as he pleased, avoiding people, responsible to no one.

Ben leapt into the saddle and rode back to the deer. Tying a rope to the horns, he began dragging it down the mountain. He didn't anticipate going far. He was just looking for a flat place where he could make a good camp. The sky was black and snowflakes were beginning to swirl in the churning west wind.

Chapter 16

Now sisters, list to what I say;
With trials this world is rife.

You can't expect to miss them all—
Help husband get a wife!

Now this advice I freely give,
If exalted you would be,

Remember that your husband must
Be blessed with more than thee.
—Mormon Pioneer Song

"Good thing we saw your fire," Deputy U.S. Marshal Charles Owen said as he guided his tall black horse into Ben's camp. He opened his heavy wool coat to show Ben the big silver star pinned to his chest.

"Wet as we are with all the snow," he said, "don't know if I'd a been able to start a fire on my own. Mind if I come in and warm up my prisoner?"

Ben nodded. It was almost dark, and though the snow had pretty much died down to a few flurries, the west wind had turned bitter cold.

Ben had heard of Charles Owen. Everyone in Utah knew of Charles Owen, who had come to Utah as a government engineer, then changed his occupation to something much more exciting—chasing cohabs. After less than a year he was catching more polygamists than anyone else, except perhaps Oscar Vandercook. Most of the polygamy and cohabitation convictions coming from Judge Zane's court were because of arrests made by Owen and Vandercook. Throughout Utah, Owen was rapidly becoming known as the deputy who always got his man, or woman—as was the case on this snowy evening.

Owen was leading a black and white pinto carrying a young woman wrapped in a wet shawl. Her red, bare hands were tied to the saddlehorn with a thick piece of hemp.

The woman was 17 or 18 at most—little more than a child. Her otherwise long yellow hair was wet and dark against her head. Her eyes were sunken, her lips blue with cold. There was a wet cat look about her, and her white teeth were chattering uncontrollably. Ben moved forward to untie her hands.

"You a Mormon?" Owen asked.

Ben paused, looking toward the deputy, wondering what to say, feeling paralyzed by his old enemy, fear. He waited too long.

"If you interfere with the official business of the United States I'll kill you."

Owen was a thin, muscular man with week-old whiskers and a long face. Under his pointed chin, an oversized Adam's apple moved up and down like he was trying to swallow a pine cone. He swung out of the saddle and stomped the stiffness out of his long legs.

"You w-won't g-get any trouble from me," Ben stuttered, reaching up to untie the girl's hands and trying not to take his eyes from Owen, who walked over to the lean-to and picked up Ben's rifle.

"I'll give this back to you in the morning," Owen said, checking out Ben's lean-to, which was on the downwind side of a huge boulder. A fire was burning just in front of the opening. Balanced on three rocks at the fire's edge, Ben's gold mining pan was steaming, half full of venison chunks simmering in their own juices.

"Government will pay you for the food and the use of your lean-to," Owen said gruffly. "We'll be heading for Salt

Lake in the morning."

Ben helped the young woman down from the horse, not an easy task as her legs tangled and her wet petticoats clung to them. As Ben helped her to the lean-to, Owen led the horses over to the fallen tree where Sonny was tied and began to unsaddle them.

"You'll h-have to g-get out of those w-wet c-clothes," Ben said to the girl as he dropped to his knees to show her the inside of the lean-to. "The b-blanket's dry. W-wrap up in it. I'll d-dry your c-clothes over the f-fire."

"My name is Stella Smoot," she whispered as she crawled inside. "Tell the Woolleys at Grantsville what has happened to me." Ben nodded that he would, then turned to the fire, his back to Stella as she changed out of the wet clothing.

"That meat smells mighty good," Owen said as he returned to the fire. "Could eat the whole panful myself."

"L-let m-me give the g-girl some," Ben said, stirring the simmering contents of the pan with a peeled stick. "I've already eaten. Y-you c-can have the r-rest."

"Taking her back to testify against her husband, Angus Smoot," Owen offered as Ben began to spill a generous portion of the pan's contents onto a clean piece of pine bark. "Going to send the old goat to prison. She's his third wife."

Ben reached inside the lean-to and handed the primitive plate of meat to the girl. "Eat," he said. "This'll h-help w-warm you up."

"Just can't figure out how the old goats get young things like this to marry 'em," Owen said, turning away and dropping to one knee to search for something in his saddlebag.

Quickly Ben reached into his shirt pocket and pulled out one of his homemade dog bane cigarettes. His hands were shaking, almost uncontrollably, but somehow he managed to rip the paper away, spilling the shredded bark into the simmering pan. Quickly, he stirred the dog bane into the stew, frantically trying to control his shaking hand and pounding heart. He knew the dog bane smoke was deadly, and he hoped the unburned bark would be too.

Owen turned back to the fire, fork in hand, sitting cross-legged like an Indian. Ben, using a glove to protect his hand, placed the simmering pan on the ground, right in front of Owen.

"You have some first," Owen said in a gruff voice.

"A-already ate," Ben said, not moving, looking into the fire.

"Eat some anyway," Owen ordered.

Ben didn't move. Owen had been turned away when he dumped the bark into the pan. He couldn't have seen Ben do it.

Taking the pan in his bare hands, Owen stood up and stepped to the front of the lean-to. "Stella," he said, "you take the pan and give me the piece of bark. Be less messy for you."

Ben knocked the pan out of Owen's hands, spilling the contents on the ground. The next thing Ben knew, Owen's pistol was pointing at his head.

"Looked like you were stirring awful fast," Owen said. "Too fast. Mormons have tried to poison me before. What was it? Arsenic?"

Ben didn't respond. He continued looking forward into the fire, feeling foolish, stupid, and cowardly—not unfamiliar feelings. Suddenly Owen's big black boot shot forward, striking Ben in the shoulder and sending him sprawling to the ground.

A minute later Ben found himself face down beside the fire, hands and feet tied behind his back.

Owen picked up a piece of the spilled meat and knelt beside Ben's face.

"Eat," he ordered.

Ben clenched his teeth as Owen tried to force the meat into his mouth. Owen drew a long, shiny knife out of its sheath.

"Open up, or I'll pry your mouth open," he hissed. Ben opened his mouth and accepted the piece of meat.

"Chew," Owen ordered. Ben began to chew, his face sideways against the ground. He figured the dog bane hadn't had time to poison the meat, only the juice, so he made a conscious effort to let as much of the juice as possible drain out the bottom side of his mouth onto the ground. Owen didn't leave him alone until all the meat in Ben's mouth had been chewed and swallowed.

Opening his bedroll, Owen prepared himself a bed across the fire from Ben. After wolfing down the unfinished portion of meat on Stella's wooden platter, Owen hung her wet petticoats out to dry over some tree limbs, threw some new wood on the fire, then settled down in his bed.

"Stella, can you hear me?" Owen called, yawning at the same time like he could hardly keep from going to sleep.

"Yes," returned a timid voice from the lean-to.

"I know what you're thinking," he said. Stella didn't respond.

"When I'm fast asleep you would like to crawl out here and untie your young hero." Again there was no reply from Stella.

"Before you try it," Owen continued, "I'll tell you what I'll do if I catch you putting one finger outside that lean-to." He paused, waiting for the words to sink in.

"I'll tie you up on the ground, just like your young friend here. But with one big difference." He paused for a moment.

"I'll tie you up naked as a jaybird, hands and feet behind your back, your belly on the rocky ground, snowflakes falling on your back, and everybody looking at you all night. Before you try anything, Stella, I want you to think long and hard about what I will do to you."

"I will," Stella said.

"You w-wouldn't really d-do that t-to her?" Ben asked, after a brief pause. His question was sincere.

Owen just laughed.

Ben turned away, convinced Owen was a man who carried out his threats. Ben's shoulder ached where Owen had kicked him, and his wrists and ankles were getting raw from the friction of the rough hemp rope. But he could feel nothing unusual in his stomach. The dog bane had not hurt him, at least not yet.

At first light, Owen was crouched by the fire, sharpening his long knife on a smooth rock. The big black and the pinto were already saddled.

"How long you figure it'll take to get yourself untied after we're gone?" Owen asked.

Ben didn't answer. For the past two hours he had been planning how he would scoot over to the corner of the big rock as soon as Owen and Stella were out of sight. By rubbing hard, he figured the edge of the rock could sever the rope in about 15 minutes, certainly not more than thirty. It was as if Owen had been reading his mind.

"Turned your sorrel loose, but he just stuck around. You wouldn't follow us, would you?" Owen asked.

Ben was more worried than he had been the night before. Owen was too smart, too sly. Ben felt sick to his stomach, but not from the dog bane. He was sure Owen was going to do something terrible, something unexpected.

A minute later, Stella crawled from the lean-to, dressed in her petticoats and shawl. Though soiled and wrinkled, her clothing was dry. Her blue eyes were still sunken, with gray circles, but the blue was gone from her lips. Ben thought she was beautiful, even without her hair brushed.

Without a word she marched over to a big rock and began retching. Owen walked back to his horses to make final preparations for the day's journey.

"You c-can't t-take her out l-like this," Ben said.

"Why not?" Owen asked.

"C-can't you s-see she's s-sick?"

"She's not sick."

"Th-then wh-why's she th-throwing up?"

"She's pregnant. Damn Mormons. Keep their women pregnant all the time."

Stella finished her retching and walked over to Ben, kneeling down.

"What's your name?" she asked.

"Ben S-Storm."

"He won't kill you," she whispered.

"H-how do you kn-know?"

"Against the law," she said, a wry smile on her face, raising her eyebrows warmly.

"H-how did you get c-clear out h-here with h-him?" Ben asked.

"I was at the Woolleys, in Grantsville, to have this baby. When we heard Owen was coming down the road to make a raid, I got on the pinto and rode out into the desert, thinking I'd just ride around for a while and return after he was gone. Somehow he got on my trail. It was a long chase. He was really mad when he finally caught me."

"Did he hurt you?" Ben asked.

"I think I'm all right," she said, avoiding a direct answer to his question. "But I'm bleeding. I don't think I lost the baby."

"I'll follow you, and when the time is right. . . . "

"No, don't," Stella said. "He's too mean, too cunning. Just let him take me to Salt Lake."

"Come on, girl, let's hit the trail," Owen growled.

"Can you get loose?" she whispered.

"Y-yes," Ben said. "G-good luck."

"You're very brave," she said, bending over and kissing him on the cheek.

Ben almost laughed. This woman wasn't very perceptive.

Before getting on his horse Owen tossed a silver dollar into the dirt beside Ben. "That ought to cover the food and lodging. If you get untied, you can pick up your rifle at the sheriff's office in Salt Lake."

A minute later Charles Owen and Stella Smoot trotted out of sight into a brisk wind that had changed direction during the night. Now it was coming from the east, bringing with it the promise of more snow. Stella's pinto followed the big black, the girl's hands once again tied to the saddlehorn.

Chapter 17

And if thou shouldst be cast into the pit, or into the hands of murderers, and the sentence of death passed upon thee; if thou be cast into the deep; if the billowing surge conspire against thee; if fierce winds become thine enemy; if the heavens gather blackness, and all the elements combine to hedge up the way; and above all, if the very jaws of hell shall gape open the mouth wide after thee, know thou, my son, that all these things shall give thee experience, and shall be for thy good.
—Revelation through Joseph Smith
March 1839 (D & C 122:7)

As soon as the horses were out of sight and hearing, Ben worked his way over to the jagged edge of the big rock. On his side, his back to the rock, he began rubbing the rope against the stone edge, all the time watching to the east for the possible return of Charles Owen.

Owen was smart and certainly knew Ben would be working to free his hands and feet. Ben feared the deputy would return to prevent that. Surely the deputy planned to do something; otherwise, he wouldn't have left Sonny behind. From close to the ground, Ben could see the top of his horse's back as Sonny stomped restlessly about, apparently wanting to follow the other horses.

It was all too simple. Something must be wrong, something Ben didn't know about. Perhaps Owen was in hiding a few hundred yards off, rifle ready, just waiting for

Ben to follow. Ben wondered about Stella's request that he not follow her, that he not interfere with Owen taking her to Salt Lake. Perhaps that would be the safest thing to do, for Stella as well as Ben.

Rubbing through the rope took longer than Ben had anticipated. It was a good half hour before the last threads of the rope snapped apart, allowing Ben to bring his upper arm forward. A minute later his feet were free. He stood up, stretched, worked out the cramps, and rubbed the sore places.

He looked over at Sonny. Suddenly Ben stopped rubbing and ran to the horse, yelling "No! No! No!" He knew why Owen had left the horse behind, and why the deputy hadn't been concerned about Ben following.

Ben remembered Owen taking a lot of time that morning sharpening his knife. Now he knew why.

During the few moments when Stella had been talking to Ben, Owen had reached under Sonny with the long knife and sliced open the horse's belly, letting the entrails fall to the ground.

Secured tightly to the fallen tree, the poor animal had been unable to do anything but stomp about. Ben's first reaction was to wonder why God hadn't made horses so they could cry out in pain like other animals and humans.

None of the vital organs had come down, only the intestines. Ben had to lift one of Sonny's hind feet to untangle the mess. Then he dropped to his knees, brushing away as much of the dirt, pine needles, and manure as possible before trying to push the tangled mess back inside the horse. In some places the intestines looked torn where they had been stepped on. The sweet, warm smell was sickening.

It would have been easier had the horse not been standing, but Ben didn't dare put Sonny down for fear it would be too hard getting him up again.

Ben knew it would be better to wash off the intestines and sew up the torn places before pushing them back inside, but he had no way of doing that. And he knew that time was critical—the longer the insides were in the open air, the worse it would be for Sonny.

Frantically Ben pushed everything back inside, but

without someone to sew the opening closed while Ben held things up, his efforts were futile. When he pulled one hand away to try to pull the skin across the gaping hole, the intestines spilled out a second time.

Ben decided his only hope for success, though a slim one, was to take the horse down on its side. He tied up one of the hind legs by throwing a rope over Sonny's back, then pushed the horse over as gently as possible.

With Sonny down, it was easy to push the entrails back into place, but they were dirtier and more lacerated now than they had been before.

Using a sharp stick to puncture holes in the edge of the hide along both sides of the opening, Ben began tying the opening shut with strips of cloth torn from his shirt. Every three or four inches, he tied holes on opposite sides of the opening together with narrow strips of fabric.

When Ben was finished, he tried to push Sonny onto his belly to get him to stand, but the horse was too weak. After repeated efforts to roll the horse, Ben finally resigned himself to the fact that Sonny was dying and was not going to get up.

Ben crawled forward and, taking the horse's head in his lap, gently stroked the smooth, firm neck.

"S-sorry, old b-boy," he sobbed. "My fault. Nobody'll ever g-get the d-drop on me again. I s-swear it."

Soft snowflakes began to drift down, disappearing as they touched the ground. But Ben didn't care about the snow. He didn't feel the cold, only the wrenching pain in his chest and throat. A good friend was dying and it was his fault. He didn't care about anything except his horse.

Now and then Sonny would pick up his head, as if to look back at his injury, only to let his head fall back into Ben's lap. Each new effort to lift his head was weaker than the time before. After awhile Sonny stopped trying.

That's when Ben heard some twigs break behind him, westward up the hill. His first thought was that Owen had returned to finish him off.

It wasn't Owen, but a brown grizzly, possibly the same one that had made the tracks Ben had been following up the mountain a day earlier. The east wind had carried the smell of fresh horse entrails up the mountain, and the bear had come to investigate.

Ben stood up to face the bear. It did not retreat, but stopped, one front paw off the ground. The bear paused, nose forward, ears back, lips curled and exposing long white teeth.

Ben looked about for a weapon but saw none. The bear stood on its hind legs, its ears remaining flat against its head. A deep, threatening growl emerged from the animal's throat.

Ben stepped back, tripping over Sonny's front leg and falling backwards. The bear dropped to all fours and started forward. It was only 15 to 20 feet away. Sonny was struggling to lift his head, but couldn't.

Ben jumped to his feet, but not to run away. He leapt across the horse and directly into the path of the bear.

"No!" he screamed, shaking clenched fists over his head.

The bear reared back, standing once again on its hind legs, snarling and swatting with its front paws. Ben did not back down.

"You'll have to kill me first," he growled and stepped towards the bear. Ben didn't notice that he hadn't stuttered.

The bear roared. Ben moved a step closer. The bear held his ground. Ben looked again for a club or a rock—any kind of weapon that could be used against the bear.

Still facing the beast, Ben inched toward the fallen tree where Sonny had been tied. The bear moved with him, remaining on its hind legs. While it refused to be driven away, it was reluctant to attack this man-creature.

Slowly, still watching the bear, Ben bent over and grabbed a rear hock of the deer he had shot the previous day. Taking a firm hold on the hind quarter with both hands, he pushed it towards the bear.

The bear reached out and hooked the meat with its right paw, pulling it to its nose. Ben's original intent was to beat the bear with the deer leg. Instead, he let the bear take it from him. Slowly, the grizzly began to back away, dragging the deer leg, growling a warning for Ben to stay away. When the bruin was fifty or sixty feet away, it turned and rambled out of sight into the cedars.

Ben returned to Sonny, once again placing the horse's head in his lap. Within an hour Sonny was dead. As Ben stood up, he felt no malice toward the bear. It was only a hungry animal following its natural instincts to find something to eat. He knew it would return to feed on the horse once the deer meat was gone. Now that Sonny was dead, there was no need to protect him.

It wasn't until Ben thought about Owen that he realized something had changed, something deep inside. Ben no longer feared the deputy who had killed his horse.

Without hurrying, Ben stowed his saddle and gear inside the lean-to. Slipping into his coat and hat, he filled his pockets with the deer meat he had begun to dry. After taking a deep drink from his canteen, he headed west, following the trail of Charles Owen and Stella Smoot.

Chapter 18

. . . *The pit which has been digged shall be filled with those who digged it.*
—*JOHN TAYLOR, 1887*

Ben knew that under normal circumstances a man on foot could not catch a man on horseback. But his circumstances were not normal. Owen had a pregnant woman with him and would have to stop and rest, at least at night. Besides, Owen's horses were heading into an east wind. They would resist and need pushing. That would slow Owen down too, especially if he had no reason to push, not knowing he was being followed.

Ben knew he could catch Owen. With a warm coat and a pocketful of meat, Ben could walk all day and all night too, if necessary. He was no longer afraid of the deputy or anything else. He had had too much fear already in his young life, and there was no room for any more. It didn't matter that the horses could walk faster. When night came, Ben would continue walking. He would follow Owen until he finally caught up with the man who had so cruelly brutalized an innocent and helpless animal. Ben wasn't sure what he would do to Owen. He only knew he no longer feared him, and that just and fair payment was going to be made for what had been done to Sonny.

The rest of the day Ben walked into a persistent east wind that brought with it occasional snow flurries. When night came, he didn't slow down. Even with a mostly cloudy sky, a new moon cast enough light across the new snow to make tracking easy. Occasionally Ben would stop for a few minutes to rest his feet while washing down a few mouthfuls of raw deer meat with spring water or melted snow.

Having hardly slept the night before while his hands and feet were tied, Ben was amazed at the pace he was keeping. He felt like he could go forever. Somehow, when he had cast off his fear in the face of the attacking bear, it was as if Ben had, at the same time, unshackled a vast reservoir of energy. He had no idea how long it would last. He only knew that as darkness fell he felt stronger than ever.

The night wasn't half gone when Ben found the camp. The snort of a horse first alerted him he was getting close and then he caught the smell of Owen's fire. He was glad Owen didn't have a dog. That would have made his stalk more risky. Still, Ben was careful. Owen was a smart man who certainly knew a few tricks Ben had never heard of. Ben wasn't about to chance Owen getting the drop on him a second time.

The camp was in a flat between two gentle hills, in a small clearing surrounded by tall sagebrush and spotted with cedar. The tall black horse and the pinto were tied to a lone cedar at the edge of the clearing.

In the center of the clearing, on opposite sides of the smoldering fire, lay Owen and Stella, wrapped tightly in wool blankets, a saddle pillow at the head of each rolled blanket. Ben didn't move until he was sure he had seen movement in the blankets. He wanted to be sure the bundles were not decoys and that Owen was not off in the brush or under a tree somewhere.

As Ben waited and watched in the frosty night air, he thought about the two horses tied nearby and how Owen might react to waking up in the morning and finding them with their entrails tangled around their hind feet. It made Ben sick to his stomach to even think about doing such a thing. Besides, if there was a belly that needed cutting open, it was the belly belonging to the man in the bedroll.

Ben slipped out of his boots and began sneaking forward in stocking feet. Should Owen wake up, he didn't want to be caught with his boots off, but he needed to move quietly. His goal was the rifle still in Owen's saddle. Ben couldn't see the pistol, so he concluded Owen had it on him. Ben couldn't see his own rifle.

Ben could feel the adrenaline surging through his veins. He felt the excitement of battle—but he felt no fear. The thought that Owen might awaken, draw his pistol and shoot did not frighten him. Ben felt removed somehow—as if he were playing a game.

Ben tiptoed up to Owen's saddle and slipped out the rifle. It was almost too easy. Neither Owen nor Stella moved.

Before retreating back to the cover of the sagebrush, Ben looked about, wondering if there were something else he might do while in the camp.

Owen's big snow-dampened boots were standing upright at the edge of the smoldering coals. Reaching out with the barrel of the rifle, Ben tipped one of the high-topped boots into the coals, where it began to smoke. Stepping forward and bending over, Ben picked up the other boot and set it right in the middle of the smoking embers. Win or lose, kill or be killed, no matter the outcome, Owen was going to have a tough trip back to Salt Lake, especially if the snow and cold persisted. Gliding like a cat, Ben returned to the cover of the sagebrush, slipped back into his boots, and waited for the dawn.

Stella was the first to awaken, sitting up in her blankets, rubbing her eyes, looking about. She reached under the blanket to slip her shoes on. Ben waved at her, to get her attention, but her side was to him and she didn't notice the movement. Ben didn't make any noise, not wanting to expose his presence to Owen until he knew where the pistol was.

Stella suddenly looked over at the smoldering fire, noticing for the first time the charred remains of Owen's boots. Quickly she looked over at Owen's sleeping hulk, then back at the fire.

"You kicked your boots into the fire," she said timidly.

Owen bolted out of his blanket, automatically reaching

for the boots. His hand was almost in the coals before he realized he was too late. The charred remains of his boots were not worth retrieving.

"Damn you!" he hissed, standing up and looking down at Stella.

"I didn't do it," she said innocently.

"Hell if you didn't," he growled.

"No, honest, I didn't. . . ."

"You won't think it's very funny when your shoes are burning," he said, stepping towards her.

"You wouldn't," she said, rolling out of her blanket, away from Owen.

Ben cocked back the hammer on the rifle, at the same time raising it to his shoulder. Owen and Stella were still not aware of his presence.

Stella scrambled to her feet, beginning to flee, but even in his bare feet Owen caught her in two strides. With Stella so close to Owen, Ben didn't want to risk a shot. He waited.

Owen wrestled Stella to the ground, jerking off her shoes. She began to cry. Ben looked back at Owen's bedroll and spotted the pistol in a holster attached to a cartridge belt.

With a shoe in each hand, Owen stood up and began marching back to the fire. Ben knew it was time to make his move.

He wanted to kill Owen for what the deputy had done to Sonny, but when it was time to pull the trigger, Ben had second thoughts. It wasn't that he couldn't do it. He knew he could. He wasn't shaking. He didn't have that familiar sick feeling situations like this had always caused before. His hand was cool and calm. Pulling the trigger on Owen was something Ben could do if he chose to, but he didn't want to. Some of the anger, some of his hate, had subsided. But not too much.

Ben lowered the sights a little and pulled the trigger. Owen's feet flew out from under him and the deputy hit the ground hard on his shoulder. Stella screamed, thinking that in his anger Owen was shooting at her.

As Owen yelled in pain, grabbing for his shattered heel, Ben walked up to the deputy's bedroll and picked up the gun belt with the pistol.

"You're going to pay for this!" Owen screamed. "I'm a deputy marshal."

"And a disgrace to your badge," Ben said, amazed at the calmness in his voice.

"You'll pay!" Owen screamed, not looking at Ben, but at the bloody mess that was once the back of his foot.

"Shut up," Ben said, "or I'll shoot your knee off."

"You wouldn't dare . . . ."

Ben didn't say anything. He just levered another cartridge into the chamber and raised the rifle to his shoulder.

"No. Don't," Owen pleaded.

"Toss me the shoes," Ben ordered, without lowering the rifle. "Easy, now."

Picking up both of Stella's shoes, Owen tossed them over to Ben. Stella was standing, looking back and forth between Ben and Owen.

"Can you saddle a horse?" Ben asked her.

"Yes," she said as if she were afraid Ben might shoot her too.

"Saddle both horses," Ben said. "I'm taking you home." Stella hurried over to the horses.

"Owen, I pushed the entrails back in Sonny and sewed him up," Ben said, "but he died anyway. Took about three hours. Swore I'd kill you."

"Then get on with it," Owen said, finally getting control of himself.

Ben didn't know why he was bothering to talk to Owen. He didn't know why he no longer wanted to kill the man. He didn't know why tears were streaming down his cheeks when he felt no fear whatsoever.

"I'll take good care of your black. Won't cut his belly open or yours either," Ben said.

"You'll hang for stealing my horse."

"Only if you can catch me," Ben grinned.

"I will, if it's the last thing I ever do."

"Hurry up," Ben said, looking over at Stella.

A few minutes later both horses were saddled and ready to ride. Stella had found Ben's rifle and tied it to her saddle.

''Let's go,'' Ben said, when he and Stella were mounted.

''But what about him? We can't just leave him here. No boots, no horse, and that foot the way it is.''

Ben didn't bother to answer her question. ''Let's go,'' he said.

''But how will he get back to Salt Lake?'' she asked.

''Yeah,'' Owen growled. ''How'll I get back to Salt Lake?''

''Crawl,'' Ben said, as he dug his heels into the ribs of the tall black horse.

Chapter 19

A republican form of government has no existence in Utah. The Saints will never obey the laws until the political power of the Mormon Church is destroyed.
—The Utah Commission in its annual report to
the Secretary of the Interior,
September 29, 1887

It was late afternoon when Ben spotted the smoke. Quickly he turned the big black up a rocky draw, Stella following.

They had not covered many miles during the day, having had to stop frequently for Stella to rest. There had been little conversation between them. For reasons Ben couldn't understand, she was upset by the way he had treated Owen, especially shooting him in the foot and burning his boots. While the conflict was intense between the skunks and cohabs, both sides had refrained from shooting each other, with one or two exceptions. "If we start shooting them, they'll start shooting us," Stella told Ben. She didn't think Owen deserved to be shot, even after Sam told her about Sonny.

At first, Ben thought that she was right and he had been too harsh, but during the long periods of silence as they rode through the sagebrush, he thought about Patrick's death and how Sam had been sent off to prison, and he began to wonder if he had been too kind to Owen. Perhaps a bullet in the belly would have been more appropriate. Everyone was pussyfooting around the U.S. marshals and their deputies. It was time someone stood up to them and said, "No! You can't do this to the Mormons, and if you persist in arresting good men and sending them to prison, we are going to fight back."

Ben didn't understand the laws or the political struggle. He didn't understand why the Mormons didn't fight back. He only knew that what was happening was unjust, and it was time for someone to strike back.

Upon seeing the smoke, Ben knew it was too early for anyone to know what he had done to Owen. Still, there were people who might recognize the black horse or Stella. It was best to keep out of sight, at least until he knew who had made the campfire.

Leaving Stella with the horses, Ben hiked carefully ahead, seeking a vantage point where he could see who had made the fire. From a high ridge he saw three men sitting around a fire, cooking their supper. Three horses were tied in the nearby sagebrush. Bedrolls were on the ground near the fire, evidence the men planned to spend the night.

The men were too far away for Ben to recognize any of their faces. He decided to try to get close enough to catch some of their conversation. If they were Mormons heading in the direction of Grantsville, it might be possible to send Stella with them while he returned to his lean-to to fetch his belongings. He wasn't sure where he would go after that, only that it would be far away. After what he had done to Owen, he knew the law would be looking for him, and he didn't intend to be easy prey for the marshals and deputies.

If the men at the fire were non-Mormons, he would want to get as far from them as possible, even if it meant making Stella travel through the night.

It was almost dark when Ben, only sixty to seventy feet from the campfire, finally stood up inside the protective branches of a cedar to get a good look at the strangers. He didn't recognize two of the men, but the third started Ben's heart pounding. It was Oscar Vandercook, the deputy who had shot his dog, the same man who had arrested Kathryn. Though he could not see badges, Ben figured the other two men were also deputies.

He couldn't hear everything they said, but from the way they were discussing a wrinkled map spread out on the ground, along with the occasional mention of Owen, Ben concluded they were looking for him and possibly for Stella, too.

Ben dropped to the ground and began sneaking back the way he had come, keeping constant watch in the direction of the fire, welcoming the protective cover of the increasing darkness.

His first inclination was to get Stella and put as many miles as possible between himself and Vandercook. But the more he thought about it, the less he liked the idea of merely fleeing. There had been too much of that already. Though there were three of them and only one of him, Ben figured he had the advantage because they didn't know he was there. He remembered how easy it had been to get the drop on Owen.

As Ben slid down the steep bank into the draw where Stella was waiting, he laughed quietly to himself. He was no longer afraid of Vandercook. The deputy had made him tremble just a few weeks earlier, but not anymore. In fact, Ben felt exhilarated at the possibility of making trouble for Vandercook. He didn't want to sneak away into the night. He wanted to stay and fight, regardless of anything Stella might say.

"Three deputies—Owen's friends," Ben said when he reached Stella. "At first light I'm going to take their horses so they can't follow us."

"Wouldn't it be safer to just put a lot of miles between us and them?" she asked.

"Could be," Ben said, "but I aim to take their horses."

Without further discussion he began gathering brush to make a bed for Stella.

"Can't have a fire," he said. "We'll leave the horses saddled. Don't take your shoes off, either. You've got to be ready to go as soon as you hear me coming. If I'm riding one of their horses, I want you to lead the black. If you hear some shooting and I'm not here in five or ten minutes, head out for

Grantsville without me. If you don't hear any shooting and I'm not back a half hour or so after daylight, head out for Grantsville. Don't let the horses get separated. They'll start whinnying to each other.''

Ben filled his mouth with partially dried deer meat, untied the blanket from the back of his saddle, removed his rifle from its scabbard, and hurried back up the hill. Stella wrapped her blanket around her and curled up in the bed Ben had helped make, forcing herself to chew on a piece of the half-raw deer meat.

It was still dark, the stars just beginning to fade, when Ben tiptoed into Vandercook's camp. As on the previous morning, Ben was in stocking feet. This time, however, he was carrying Owen's pistol. One of the men was tossing restlessly in his blankets, providing Ben with ample opportunity to sneak forward, the rustling of the blankets muffling any sound he might make.

Ben's original plan had been to untie the three horses and gallop away with them as soon as it began to get light. But the sight of six boots in a neat row beside the glowing coals was more than he could resist. The fire had been a big one, and Ben was sure there was sufficient heat left in the coals to do significant damage to the boots if he could get them in the fire without any of the three men taking notice.

No one moved when Ben put the first boot in the fire. There was no problem with the second, third and fourth, either. That's when one of the first boots, which had been wet, began to hiss—even whistle. All of the boots were smoking and stinking.

''What the hell,'' mumbled a voice from beneath a blanket. Ben cocked back the hammer, pointing the pistol where he figured the man's face was hidden.

Suddenly the blanket was pulled down, exposing the startled face of one of the strangers. Holding the pistol steady, Ben held a forefinger to his lips, signaling the man to silence. The man didn't move or make a sound as Ben proceeded to put the remaining two boots in the fire, all the while pointing the cocked pistol into the man's face.

With all the boots in the coals, Ben remained still. The pistol was steady as a tree as he waited for the boots to burn. He didn't want the man pulling them out of the fire before the damage was done.

The man's eyes were darting back and forth between his snoring companions, the smoking boots, and the cold steel of Ben's pistol. There was desperation in his eyes. He wanted to do something about the smoking boots, but he didn't dare challenge the cocked pistol.

"Vandercook?" whispered Ben, nodding to the two sleeping forms.

The frightened deputy nodded towards the sleeping form just beyond his head, apparently Vandercook. Ben took a step back, then two. Suddenly he pointed the pistol at Vandercook's feet and pulled the trigger. The deafening explosion brought all three men out of their blankets, Vandercook screaming in surprise and pain.

"That's for killing my dog!" Ben shouted. "Now git over into that sagebrush."

Vandercook's two companions scurried for the sagebrush.

"You too!" Ben roared, cocking the pistol and pointing it at Vandercook.

"I can't," the deputy whimpered. "My foot." There was a big red hole in one of his stockinged feet.

"Crawl. Or so help me I'll put a hole in your other foot."

Vandercook began crawling after his companions as Ben backed quickly towards the three horses. Without taking his eyes off the men, who were beginning to shout threats in his direction, Ben untied all three horses. He leapt upon one, holding the lead rope to the second. He assumed the third would follow the other two and it did as Ben rode his horse into a draw and out of sight.

"Damn," Ben growled when Stella met him at the mouth of the little canyon where she had spent the night.

"What's the matter?" she asked as she rode alongside, leading the black horse.

"Forgot my boots," he said. Stella began to laugh as they urged their horses towards Grantsville at a full gallop.

Chapter 20

. . . The whole institution (Mormon Church) is but a vast commercial, political machine, with polygamy as the cement of the nefarious system.

—Salt Lake Tribune, March 8, 1901

When Ben and Stella finally slowed the horses to a fast walk, Stella became more talkative than she had been the day before.

"I heard a shot," she said.

"Plugged Vandercook in the foot."

"Has it occurred to you that you may be starting something where a lot of people could get hurt?" she said.

"Has it occurred to you that a lot of people have already been hurt?" Ben countered. "Besides, Vandercook shot my dog. Had it coming."

"What are you going to do now?" she asked.

"Keep from getting caught. Just keep on the move. Maybe make a little more trouble for the skunks."

"Don't know what I'm going to do," she said. "Probably can't hide at the Woolleys' place anymore. Wish I wasn't pregnant."

"Can you go back to your husband?" Ben asked. "Didn't you say he lived in Salt Lake?"

"I can't go there. If they catch me he'll go to jail."

"How can you be so sure?"

"I lived in the same house with his first wife, Mary. If I turn up pregnant, that's proof of polygamy or cohabitation.

Men have gone to jail on less evidence than that.''

''Do you love your husband?'' Ben asked.

''What does that have to do with anything?'' Stella responded, obviously not liking the question.

''Just wondered,'' Ben said. ''He's the one who got you in this mess. Seems he ought to be taking care of you.''

''If he does he'll go to jail.''

''So he cuts you loose to fend for yourself.''

''He can't just go to jail. He has another wife and children.''

''Do you love him?'' Ben repeated.

''Yes,'' she said. ''Angus is a good man.''

''Angus,'' said Ben slowly, deliberately, as if tasting the man's name. ''How old is he?''

''I don't see where that's any business of yours,'' Stella said, looking ahead.

''Must be pretty old,'' Ben laughed. ''Sixty? Maybe seventy?''

''I'm beginning to wish you hadn't rescued me from Owen,'' Stella snapped. ''He may have tied my hands to the saddle, but he was a lot more pleasant than you.''

''Eighty?''

''Fifty-one,'' she conceded.

''Why?'' Ben asked.

''Because he was born in 1835, and if you subtract that from 1886, you come up with fifty-one.''

''That isn't what I meant. Why did you marry him?''

''It was the will of the Lord.''

''Who told you that?''

''You're beginning to sound like the skunks.''

''My father has two wives,'' Ben offered, ''in a marriage that seems natural and right. But both women are about the same age as my father. In your case it seems different, like it's not right, if you know what I mean.''

Stella was silent for a long time.

''I'm seventeen,'' she began. ''There were several young men in Taylorsville—that's where I grew up—that I really liked. At first I didn't want to marry Angus, but when my father told me Angus had asked for me and when I prayed about it, I just felt it was the right thing to do. Angus is a good man. He has a big farm. His wife and children love him. I guess I just couldn't say no."

"Did you try?"

"No."

"Now you're pregnant and on your own."

"Not exactly. A lot of people have been helping me, like the Woolleys in Grantsville," Stella said. "But now that the deputies found me there I can't go back."

"That's where we're headed."

"But I can't stay."

"What are you going to do?"

"Can I come with you?"

"I'm an outlaw," Ben said, looking over at Stella. "These horses, except for your paint, are stolen. Horse thieves are hanged."

"I'm an outlaw too," she said.

"Not the kind that gets hanged."

About midday the wind began to blow, bringing with it more snow flurries. Ben and Stella sought shelter between two large boulders. Ben made a fire over which they began to roast the last of the deer meat.

"Why don't you want me to come with you?" Stella asked.

"I can think of three good reasons."

"Go on—name them."

"First, you're a woman."

"But that can have its advantages," Stella said. "If you're traveling with a woman, you'll appear less suspicious to authorities."

"Two, you're pregnant."

"I'll concede that. What's the third reason?"

"You're not like me," he said.

"What do you mean?"

"Until they were killed, my best friends were a dog named Dix and a horse named Sonny. I'm a loner. Never enjoyed being around people very much, especially strangers and women. They make me stutter."

"I haven't noticed any stuttering the past few days."

"I know. Something happened when my horse died. I'm not sure what. Somehow the stuttering went away, along with my fear of deputies and bears."

Ben told her about his confrontation with the bear when it had tried to get to Sonny.

"After that I haven't been afraid of anything, not even Owen and Vandercook," Ben said. "If the devil himself walked up right now I'd just stand up and piss on him."

"I don't like it when you talk crude like that."

"If God really does exist up there in the heavens somewhere," Ben continued, "I know one thing for sure. He doesn't go out of his way to meddle in the affairs of men. A meddling God wouldn't have let Patrick, Dix, and Sonny die the way they did. You can bet God's just going to sit back and watch every Mormon in the territory go to prison—unless someone stands up and fights back. That's going to be me, I suppose."

"And you don't think I can help," she said.

"You're too soft."

"You haven't heard me complaining, riding these horses all day yesterday and today."

"No, but we haven't been pushing. If the deputies were after us, it'd be a different story."

"What makes you think you've got a monopoly on toughness or hardship?" Stella said, standing up. "I've had my share of Gethsemane too. Do you have any idea what it's like being 17, attractive, the object of every young man's fancy, then to be married off to a 51-year-old farmer nearly old enough to be your grandfather? His first wife is jealous of you. She hates you, though she smiles when he's around. But she's the boss over you, and when he's gone she works you like a slave, giving you all the dirty jobs, especially on the days after he's spent the night with you. Then you get pregnant and know in a few years you'll be an old woman, that your youth will be gone without your ever having fully tasted it. I know what it's like to cry all night, feeling like my heart is going to burst. You're not the only person in the world to be toughened by pain."

Stella dropped back to the ground, exhausted, her anger

spent. Neither she nor Ben said anything for what seemed a long time. They sat cross-legged on opposite sides of the fire, Ben stirring the red coals with a stick.

"I know a cabin where they could never find me or you," Ben offered.

"Does that mean you'll take me with you?" Stella said.

"If you can pass the test."

"What test?"

"I'm running from the law. You've got to prove to me you can keep a cool head when things get tough, that you'll do whatever I say, no matter how hard."

"Okay. What do you want me to do?"

"Just stay where you are and keep looking at me."

"That's no test."

"No matter what I do. Just stay put until I tell you to move. Think you can do that?"

"Sure."

"We'll see," said Ben, removing a big .45 cartridge from his belt, eyeing it carefully, rolling it back and forth between his thumb and forefinger.

"Remember, whatever I do, don't move," he warned.

She nodded.

Ben and Stella were looking into each other's faces. Without glancing down, Ben tossed the cartridge into the fire.

"That's stupid," Stella said, continuing to look at Ben, her jaw set, her eyes unblinking. Ben said nothing.

"Will it explode?" she asked.

Ben didn't answer. He just looked at her.

"Was that a .45 cartridge?" she asked, her voice almost a whisper.

Ben remained silent.

"Is it worth it? One of us losing an eye, or getting shot through the heart?"

Ben remained silent.

Stella and Ben waited out the long seconds, continuing to look into each other's eyes, each daring the other to remain next to the fire.

The bullet exploded, showering hot coals in every direction, the split casing whining off into space. Trying to appear calm, Stella brushed the coals from her lap. Ben stood up, facing east.

"About a ten-day ride from here to the cabin, I guess," he said, "if the pass isn't snowed in. Maybe we can reach Grantsville by tonight."

"Let's get going," Stella said. The cold wind was still blowing, but she was ready to travel.

Chapter 21

Resolved that it is the duty of Congress to enact such laws as shall promptly and effectually suppress the system of polygamy within our territories; and divorce the political from the ecclesiastical power of the so-called Mormon church; and that the laws so enacted should be rigidly enforced by the civil authorities, if possible, and by the military if need be.

—Republican Party Platform, 1884

Upon reaching Grantsville, Stella didn't waste any time telling everyone how Ben had wounded the two deputies and taken their horses. The news spread throughout the community. By the time they were ready to leave the next day, they had been showered with gifts—ammunition, food, clothing, a pack saddle—even a new pair of boots for Ben.

The entire community turned out to wave and cheer as Ben and Stella rode out of town. Anti-polygamy harassment had been intense. Local men—good men—were in prison. Finally, someone was fighting back. Ben was a hero, a modern Robin Hood who had rescued a maiden in distress from the clutches of a wicked sheriff.

As they approached the edge of town, Ben and Stella rode side by side, Ben leading a loaded pack horse and two others. He had tried to sell two of the horses, but since they were stolen, no one would take them.

"Young man, I want to talk to you," called a man from the front of one of the last homes, a white frame house with a well-tended yard, lined on both sides by poplar trees. The man, in his late forties, had the look of a storekeeper or banker. An otherwise sedate and comfortable-looking man, he now had an earnest, even worried, look about him. Ben handed the lead rope to Stella and rode over to see what the man wanted.

"I hear you are taking the young woman to a mountain hideaway where she can have her baby in peace," the man said.

"That seems to be the plan," Ben responded carefully.

"Will you take my daughter with you?"

"What?" Ben asked, not sure he had heard the man correctly.

"She's a plural wife on the run, just like the Smoot woman," he explained, nodding towards Stella. "Expecting, too. Things too hot in Salt Lake so she came home. The same deputies you took these horses from were here day before yesterday looking for her. Hid her in the pigpen. They'll be back, so she can't stay. Will you take her with you?"

"Already got one too many," Ben said coolly, wanting to be on his way.

"With two, you'll be free to leave the cabin," the man argued persuasively, like he was selling a wagonload of fresh smoked hams. "They'll keep each other company, take care of each other, deliver each other's babies. Or do you know how to deliver babies?"

Ben felt like swearing but didn't, marveling how life could get so complicated so fast. Just a few days ago he and Sonny were alone in the mountains with no other plan than to live away from people. Now he had five horses and a pregnant woman to take care of, and another closing in quickly.

"I'm an outlaw. You'd trust your daughter with me?" Ben challenged.

"You're Dan Storm's son," the man said. "He's a good man; I'm sure you are too. Please take her with you. She has relatives in Springville. You can leave her there, if you wish. I'll give you money."

"How far along is she? Can she ride a horse?" Ben asked.

"Five months. She can ride and cook and sew. Won't slow you down."

Ben looked over at Stella, then back at the man.

"Throw a saddle on one of the ponies," Ben said, nodding towards the horses behind Stella. "One set of saddle bags, a bedroll, and the clothes on her back. That's all. If she's ready in ten minutes she can come with us."

The man charged towards Stella, spooking the horses she was holding. He took the lead rope to a tall sorrel, pulling it towards his barn.

"My name's James Hurren," he shouted as he hurried past Ben. "My daughter's Priscilla."

Ben turned his horse back to the center of the street, where Stella was waiting.

"What's happening?" she asked as he rode up.

"Got company," he said without enthusiasm.

"What?"

"Priscilla Hurren's coming with us. Pregnant and running from the law, just like you."

Stella bent forward, reaching out and putting her hand on Ben's, trying to look him in the eye.

"You're really wonderful, Ben. Do you know that?"

Ben looked away, feeling a blush creep up his neck.

Ten minutes later Mr. Hurren led the sorrel, saddled and loaded with saddle bags and bedroll, into the street. There was still no sign of Priscilla.

Walking up to Ben, Mr. Hurren handed the young man a purse containing coins. Ben accepted it without thanks and put it in his coat pocket.

"There's one more thing," the man said reluctantly, sensing Ben's irritation.

"Don't tell me your neighbor has a pregnant daughter that needs hiding out too," Ben warned.

"Oh no," Mr. Hurren laughed. "Nothing like that. You see, Priscilla's got a dog, a husky-wolf cross. Got him off a ship in San Francisco. The dog's licked every dog in the valley—killed a few wolves and coyotes too. Best sheep dog you ever saw. Take him along and nobody'll bother the girls."

"Call him and let me look at him," Ben said.

"Can't," the man said.

"Why not?"

"Unless we're working sheep, the dog doesn't obey me—only Priscilla. He's kind of a loner, but he's a good watchdog. He's out back, and he'll join us when Priscilla comes out."

A few minutes later, Priscilla Hurren marched out the front door, her strides long and confident. Her long brown hair was neatly brushed and hanging loose about her shoulders. She was wearing a long blue coat that looked new, and brown riding pants, the kind English noblemen wore when they chased foxes. Her chin was high, her eyes intense but not unfriendly. She was much older than Stella, maybe 30. Matronly Mrs. Hurren trotted behind her daughter, carrying a heavy picnic basket.

A bewildered Ben wondered what he was getting into. After brief introductions and goodbyes, Priscilla placed her foot in the stirrup and swung into the saddle, maintaining control with the reins as she did so. It was apparent she knew how to handle a horse.

Mrs. Hurren handed Ben the picnic basket, explaining hurriedly that it contained cold chicken, fresh baked bread, butter, currant jam, apple pie, boiled eggs, pickles and apples. Ben was just turning his horse east towards the Oquirrh Mountains when he saw a gray wolf-dog racing towards the horses.

"What's the dog's name?" he asked.

"Lobo," Priscilla said.

Ben swung out of his saddle, dropping to one knee.

"Come here, Lobo. Come."

About a pace away from Ben, the dog froze, its eyes glaring. When Ben reached out to pet the dog, its ears fell back against its head, its lips curling up to expose long white fangs. There was a rumble, a sort of deep chortling in its chest. Ben withdrew his hand, stood up and swung into the saddle. He liked the dog.

"Let's go," he said, urging his horse into an easy gallop towards the snow-capped Oquirrh Mountains. Lobo loped easily at his side, and the women followed.

Chapter 22

Not polygamy but the power of the Priesthood is the real danger. . . .

When the anti-slavery agitation was at its height, popular feeling at the north was exercised chiefly with the immoral quality of slavery as an institution. Yet the great war of the Rebellion, by which slavery was overthrown, turned on an altogether different issue, the question, namely, of political sovereignty. . . .

Popular judgement is today repeating the same blunder in the matter of Mormonism. Attention is fastened upon a single aspect of Mormonism, the revolting immorality of polygamy, and this conspicuous offensive part is mistaken for the whole just as the conspicuous barbarism of slavery was mistaken for the whole of Southern policy. . . . If they persist in this mistake the country will one day have another rude and terrible awakening. It will be discovered all at once that the essential principle of Mormonism is not polygamy at all but the ambition of an ecclesiastical hierarchy to wield sovereignty; to rule the souls and lives of its subjects with absolute authority, unrestrained by any civil power. . . .

There need be no hesitation about hastening the conflict over this question. The sooner it is made and decided, the better. The boldest course that Congress could take would be the best one.

—The Springfield (Mass.) Union
Reprinted in the Salt Lake Tribune
February 15, 1885

Priscilla wasn't an easy woman to get to know. Though she talked freely about trivial matters with Ben and Stella, she was very guarded about personal information. She was careful not to reveal anything about the man she was married to. She admitted to having two children who were being taken care of by "the other wives." But who those wives were, where they lived, or who the husband and father was, was information she guarded carefully.

Ben figured Priscilla was probably the wife of one of the general authorities of the church, possibly one of those in the underground. Priscilla was intelligent, articulate, beautiful—the kind of woman Ben figured would marry a general authority. She was a woman who seemed able to take everything in stride—the sleeping out, the outdoor cooking, the riding, the cold. She was a strong woman capable of warmth and friendliness, who knew how to maintain confidences. Priscilla reminded Ben of his mother, Caroline.

Lobo was even harder to get to know. Mostly he kept his distance, loping back and forth a hundred yards or so in front of the horses. Several times during the day he had caught a rabbit, chewed on it for a while, then returned to his self-appointed place in front. He seemed to accept Ben's leadership, but would not come near Ben, even when the party stopped for a break. At those times Lobo would accept scraps tossed to him by Priscilla, but not from Ben or Stella.

"Why's the dog so unfriendly?" Ben asked when he and Priscilla were riding side by side.

"I don't know," she said. "He's always been that way. Maybe he was beaten as a pup."

"Is he mean? Does he bite people?" Ben asked.

"He's chewed up a couple of strangers, and one Indian that came begging. But he's never touched a woman or a child. An eight-year-old boy took after him with a stick once outside the church. I saw it from a distance and thought Lobo would tear into the boy, but the dog only trotted out of reach. He's smart."

"I like him," Ben said.

"Kindred spirits, perhaps," Priscilla offered.

"Would you consider selling him to me?" Ben ventured.

"Only if you can get him to like you. I wouldn't sell him, but I'd give him to you."

"Why would you just give him to me?"

"He doesn't belong with me. I'm a woman raising a family. I don't get out much. He's a born wanderer, wasting his life away lying at my door. He needs to be out traveling, on the move. That's his nature."

"Mine too," Ben said. "Just wish he'd quit catching those rabbits. Then maybe he'd let me feed him. It'll be hard to win him over without him wanting food from me."

"When you drop me off at Springville, if you can get him to go with you, he's yours," Priscilla said.

Earlier Ben had agreed to take her to John Jex, her mother's brother, in Springville. Priscilla didn't think the authorities would find her there, at least not for a while. Ben was thinking of leaving Stella there too, if he could get Jex to take her in. Then Ben would be free to do as he pleased.

The first night, they camped at a place Priscilla recognized as Soldier Canyon, where a tiny stream flowed westward out of the Oquirrh Mountains.

Upon leaving Grantsville, Ben had decided that the safest way to reach Springville was to avoid Salt Lake and northern Utah Valley by traveling south along the west side of the Oquirrh Mountains and around the southern end of Utah Lake.

As soon as they had picketed the horses and wolfed down a cold supper from the picnic basket, Priscilla and Lobo went for a walk. She said she wanted to be alone for a while.

"Something you said the other day has been bothering me," Ben said to Stella as he was gathering sticks and brush to start a fire. The sky had cleared and the night was going to be cold.

"When you told me about marrying this Smoot fellow," he continued, "you said you had approached the matter prayerfully and felt right about it."

"I did," she said.

"But a few minutes later you were describing the marriage as your Gethsemane. I don't understand."

"I did feel right about the marriage," Stella offered.

"But something came up later that changed my mind." She paused.

"Do you want to tell me about it?" Ben asked.

"I don't think so," she said. "Not yet."

"After what we've been through together the last few days," Ben said, "I feel like we're friends. Because I like you, I would like to know." Ben was amazed that he wasn't stuttering. "But if it's something very personal or private," he continued, "I'll understand if you don't want to say any more."

Ben dropped to one knee, struck a wooden match against a rock, and ignited the pile of fixings he had prepared for the fire. Lowering his face close to the ground, he puffed gently into the smoldering twigs. The fire grew brighter as Ben gently laid on more pieces of wood, each piece bigger than the one before it.

It wasn't until the fire was burning brightly and Ben had returned to a sitting position that Stella rose to her feet. "I'll tell you," she said, hands on her hips, facing a surprised Ben. "You may not like it, a good Mormon boy like you. But you say you're my friend, so I'll tell you."

Ben looked into her face. Stella's clear eyes were wide and intense, reflecting the dancing fire. She looked like she was ready to fight, like she feared nothing. She was no longer the timid, frightened girl Ben had rescued from Owen.

"Remember how I told you about Angus's first wife, Mary?"

Ben nodded.

"She has a daughter named Amy, only sixteen when I married Angus. We were friends. When I married Angus I was looking forward to being in the same house with Amy. We laughed a lot when we were together."

Stella paused, swallowing hard, like it wasn't going to be easy to get out the next sentence.

"Go ahead," Ben said.

"Two weeks after I married Angus, Amy was married to my father."

"You didn't like that?"

"I would expect a question like that from a man. "Of

course I objected. She was just a child.''

''She didn't want to do it?''

''She went along about like I did. But from then on things were different.''

''What do you mean?''

''Up until that time I had viewed Angus and my father as wise, spiritual men—in the same class as Jesus or the Prophet. But after Amy's marriage I couldn't get the idea out of my head that they were just two sex-hungry men who made a secret deal to swap daughters so each could get a new young wife.''

''That's terrible,'' Ben said.

''You bet it is,'' she said, ''and the more I thought about it, the more convinced I became that that was exactly what had happened. It was like my eyes were opened.''

''Why did the other wives—your mother and Mary—go along with it?''

''I asked my mother.''

''What'd she say?''

''She just cried.''

''Why didn't you go to the authorities?''

''And put my own father in jail? And what about my brothers and sisters, and Mary's children? I couldn't do that.''

''Did you say anything to your father or Angus?''

''Are you kidding? Both of them believe they were inspired to do it. Neither has missed a family prayer or church meeting since the weddings.''

''Do you blame the Church?''

''Of course not. Five years ago this could never have happened. The Church leaders and the community would not have stood for it. Everything was in the open then. Now it's different. Because of the persecutions, everything is secret. Nobody knows who is married to whom. You know, the great Utah guessing game. There are marriages taking place where the only ones who know are the man and woman involved. No written records are kept. Everything is confusion, and the leaders are underground where they can't do anything about it. I hate polygamy; I hope the church abandons it.''

"When this is all over, will you go back to Angus?" Ben asked.

"Not if I don't have to."

"What will you do?"

Stella was calmer now, having finally let out what had been kept inside her too long. She sat down next to Ben and gazed into the fire.

"Three days ago I couldn't have answered that question."

"What are you thinking now?"

"I propose you and I go to California and start a new life together." Both were still looking into the fire.

"As man and wife?" Ben asked, startled.

"Yes."

Ben started laughing.

"What's so funny?"

"My mother used to try to get me to dance at the church dances. Never did. You're proposing to a fellow who's never even danced with a girl, to say nothing of . . ."

"Let me tell you, marriage isn't that big a deal," Stella interrupted.

"Maybe not for you, married to Angus, but for me it would be a very big deal," Ben said.

Stella looked over at Ben, who was gazing into the fire.

"You want to know something?" she asked.

"What?"

"The mighty gunfighter is blushing."

Ben stood up and turned away, looking into the night. He saw the two yellow eyes of Lobo about twenty yards from the fire. That meant Priscilla was returning.

Ben dropped to one knee and held out his hand.

"Come here, boy," he called in a gentle voice.

The dog didn't move.

Chapter 23

I have talked with some of the brethren, and we feel that if relief does not soon apear, our community will be scattered and the great work crushed.
—GEORGE Q. CANNON, 1888

There was a lot of talk of California the next two days, mostly a result of questions from Stella. Priscilla had been there on two occasions, and was willing to tell all she knew. Ben kept pretty much to himself, pondering Stella's proposal. Marriage had been the furthest thing from his mind.

Stella had caught Ben totally off guard. Though he liked Stella, he was not in love with her—at least not yet. He had begun to feel quite comfortable around Stella, but now she made him nervous. He needed time and distance before he could seriously consider marriage. On the other hand, the thought of going to California was a fascinating one, especially now that the law was after him. The idea of getting away from all the conflict was enticing.

Priscilla told Ben about California's mild winters, the majestic mountains, beautiful rivers, vast fertile valleys with scattered farms, the growing, prospering cities, and the ocean—the beautiful blue Pacific, the largest ocean in the world. She made California sound like a wonderful place.

Stella was ready to go immediately, but Ben had to think about it. As exciting as California sounded, he felt that even though he might go there sometime in the future, now was not the time. He still had unfinished business in Utah. What that business was, he wasn't sure. It was just a feeling, but a strong one.

"Do you think we'll make Springville tonight?" Priscilla asked as they worked their way around the south end of West Mountain. It was mid-morning of the fourth day, and Ben hadn't been pushing hard because Stella had been ill in the mornings. Priscilla, on the other hand, was feeling fine.

"Hope so," Ben said.

Lobo, chasing a big jackrabbit, had just headed off to the south as they approached a house-size boulder they had seen many miles back. It appeared that beyond the boulder they would have an excellent view of the valley.

Riding past the big rock, they were in sudden view of three people—a man, a woman, and an Indian—reclining around a small, smokeless campfire about 30 feet away. The huge boulder had prevented Ben and the women from seeing the camp earlier. Beyond the people, on the windswept hillside, two horses and a large gray mule had stopped grazing to look at the new arrivals.

Ben saw the man reaching for the gun on his hip and responded in kind. A moment later two Colt pistols were pointed at each other. Neither man pulled the trigger.

"Put that pistol away," the man ordered.

"Who are you?" Ben asked, not lowering his pistol.

"Deputy U.S. Marshal Jed Gibson."

"I think it would be better if you put your pistol down," Ben said, his pistol steady.

"Who are you?" the deputy asked, slowly standing up, keeping his pistol pointed at Ben.

"Ever hear of Ben Storm?"

"The kid who shot Owen and Vandercook?"

"That's right," Ben said, "and I'll plug you too if you don't put that pistol down right now."

The Indian and the woman scooted away from the nervous lawman, who looked this way and that like he expected reinforcements to arrive at any moment. Then he looked back at Ben as though he had made a decision.

"I'm not putting this gun down. I'm on official business

of the United States Government, and these are my prisoners. You're under arrest.''

''Nobody's going to take me prisoner,'' Ben said, his voice calm and deliberate. ''Shoot away. We'll die together.''

''No!'' Priscilla screamed at the deputy. ''You'll die if you try to shoot him.''

''Why's that?'' the deputy asked, not taking his eyes off Ben.

''Because I have a gun too, and I'll shoot you through the heart if you pull the trigger. Might do it anyway if you don't put that gun down.''

Ben and the deputy looked over at Priscilla, who was holding a small silver-barreled pistol out in front of her. She had it aimed directly at the deputy. Her elbows were locked. The hammer was cocked. It appeared she knew what she was doing. Her hands were steady, and her aim appeared accurate.

The deputy looked back at Ben and slowly lowered his gun.

''Drop it,'' Ben ordered. The deputy obeyed.

Ben dismounted and walked over to the deputy, picked up the pistol, and slipped it into his belt.

''You're going to pay for this!''

''If I were you I'd keep my mouth shut,'' Stella warned. ''I saw him shoot Owen. He enjoyed it.''

Ben made the deputy walk over to the big rock and sit facing it.

The woman walked up to Ben and held out her hands. They were tied in front of her. She was a big-boned woman in her late twenties or early thirties. Her hair was black and stringy, her dirty face flat and round like the bottom of a large frying pan. Her small mouth was curled down in an exaggerated frown, like a child trying to stop crying. She was wearing a filthy gray dress and oversized men's boots with the right sole coming loose.

Ben pulled out his knife and cut her hands free. She looked down, rubbing her sore wrists.

''Did he treat you badly?'' Ben asked. ''You look terrible.''

"To men I have always looked terrible," she said, beginning to smile.

"That isn't what I. . . ."

"I know," she said. "No. He just caught me last night. I've been hiding like a rat in a hole for a week. That's why I look so bad. Name's Madge Johnson. Pleased to meet you, Mr. Storm." She reached out and shook Ben's hand.

Stella and Priscilla dismounted and came over to Madge, helping her clean up with a handkerchief and water from a canteen.

"Why did the deputy arrest you?" Priscilla asked.

"The usual," Madge said matter-of-factly.

"You're a plural wife? They want to make you testify against your husband?" Priscilla asked.

Madge nodded.

"You're not pregnant, are you?" Ben asked.

"That's kind of a personal question coming from a stranger," Madge said.

"Sorry. It just seems that everybody the law's after is pregnant. Thought you might be too."

"The Indian isn't," Madge said, "but I am, and will be for another three months."

"Do you want to come with us?" Priscilla asked.

"Sure," Madge said. "Don't want to go with him."

"Is that okay?" Priscilla asked, turning to Ben.

Ben didn't like what was happening, but how could he say no. "Sure," he said.

"What about the Injun?" Ben asked, noting that the Indian had wandered over to a cedar tree and was looking off to the east. His hands were tied too, but behind his back. There were chains on his ankles, allowing him to take only tiny steps.

"Some men brought him into camp last night," Madge explained. "Asked Gibson to take him to Salt Lake. I think they're going to hang him. He hasn't said a word. I don't know if he speaks English."

The Indian was tall, with broad shoulders, but he wasn't young. There were streaks of gray in his long black hair. He had pock marks on his neck and cheeks. He wore elkskin leggings and a blue army coat without any buttons, even on the sleeves.

"Let's just leave him with the deputy," Stella offered.

"What did the Indian do to get arrested?" Ben asked, loud enough for Gibson to hear him.

"Don't let that old buck go," warned the deputy.

"What'd he do?" Ben asked.

"Stole a whole herd of cattle out of Santaquin. Drove them out in the desert where some Injuns were camped. Killed four head before the owners could fetch 'em back. He'll hang for it."

Ben walked over to the Indian, who continued to look off to the east.

"What do they call you?" Ben asked.

The Indian ignored him.

"Can you speak English?"

Again, no response.

Ben returned to the women.

"Should we let them hang him?" Ben asked.

"I don't want him coming with us," Stella said.

"We could just let him go," Priscilla said. "Hate to see a man hang, even if he did steal some cows."

"Do you know the Injun's name?" Ben asked the deputy. "Or his tribe?"

"A thievin' Ute," the deputy said. "Not from these parts. From the east, I think. They call him Flat Nose George."

"Give me the key to the chains," Ben said.

"He'll scalp and rape the women," the deputy warned.

"Give me the key," Ben said. The deputy handed it over. Ben unlocked the Indian's feet and cut his hands free. The old Indian just looked at Ben, saying nothing. His back was straight, his jaw firm, his eyes steady.

Ben placed his hands on the Indian's shoulders. "You buried my brother in the salt springs. Thank you. Dan Storm is my father. The black Indian Ike is my friend."

Flat Nose George nodded that he understood, then said, "Me get horses." He turned and walked towards the grazing animals.

"Which way?" Priscilla asked when everyone but Gibson was mounted. Flat Nose George was riding the big gray mule.

"You'll hang if you take my horse," Gibson warned.

"I've heard that before," Ben said. "Owen and Vandercook made the same promise. Since I have only one neck, I suppose it doesn't matter how many horses I steal. I'll take good care of it for you."

"You'll pay for this."

"By the way," Ben said in parting, "if you don't want to get shot in the foot like Owen and Vandercook, you should wait until tomorrow before following us into the valley."

Gibson said nothing as Ben, the three women, the big Indian, the two pack horses, and the dog started eastward into Utah Valley.

"Go on ahead. I'll catch up," Ben said when they had gone about a hundred yards. He turned his horse around and galloped back to the camp. Fifteen minutes later he returned.

"You didn't shoot him, did you?" Priscilla asked cautiously.

"Did you hear any shots?" Ben asked. There hadn't been any.

"I know what he did," Stella said.

"What?" Priscilla demanded. Ben was silent.

"He made the poor man take off his boots and throw them in the fire," Stella said with confidence.

Both women looked at Ben, who acknowledged that Stella had guessed correctly.

Chapter 24

These scoundrels here must be removed—if there's any way to do it. They're trying to repeat the persecution of Missouri and Illinois. They want to despoil us of our heritage—of our families. I'm sick of being hunted like a wild beast. I've done no harm to them or theirs. Why can't they leave us alone to live our religion and obey the commandments of God and build up Zion?
—GEORGE Q. CANNON, 1888

It was nearly midnight when Ben and his party reached John Jex's red brick home on First East in Springville. Jex was a prosperous man, owning several businesses in Springville and Spanish Fork. There was a large barn behind the house.

Flat Nose George and Lobo stayed in the barn with the horses and mule, while Ben and the women entered the kitchen, where the shades were drawn so as not to attract attention. The women were more interested in bathing than sleeping, and began immediately to heat water on the stove. Jex's first wife, Anna, helped them, all the while fussing like a mother hen. The oldest son took food to the barn for the Indian and dog.

While the women busied themselves with bathing in the next room, Ben sat at the big kitchen table with John Jex, enjoying a late supper of bread and milk, green onions, cheese and buttermilk. Jex—a man in his mid 40's with a thin, wiry frame and lots of black whiskers—was eager to speak with Ben.

"Your reputation has preceded you," he said.

"What?" Ben mumbled, his mouth full of cheese.

"Everyone in the territory is talking about the Mormon Robin Hood who shot two deputies to free a damsel in distress."

"News travels fast," Ben said.

Jex stared at Ben, shaking his head in amazement.

"Want to see what the papers are saying about you?" he asked.

Ben nodded. Jex went into another room and returned a minute later with two newspapers in hand, the most recent issues of the *Deseret News* and the *Salt Lake Tribune.*

"Here, read the *Trib* article first—top right," Jex said, handing the paper to Ben.

Upon seeing the headline, Ben stopped chewing. He read the entire story without looking up.

Killer Mormon Opens Fire on U.S. Marshals, Abducts Woman

by Harry Chew

This Monday past, two deputy U.S. marshals were ambushed and shot by Ben Storm, 18, of American Fork. Both incidents occurred in the west desert about a day's ride southwest of Grantsville. The two seriously wounded deputies are Charles Owen and Oscar Vandercook, both of Salt Lake. Both were shot in the foot in unprovoked early morning attacks, their boots destroyed, and their horses stolen.

In the first attack, against Deputy Owen, Salt Lake resident Stella Smoot, 18, was abducted by Storm. A four-county search is underway to locate the pregnant woman. Deputy Owen was escorting Smoot to Salt Lake, where she was to testify in court.

"This is horrible," Ben said, beginning to laugh. "It wasn't that way at all." He resumed his reading, finding more to make him laugh.

"We are very concerned for Smoot's safety and well-being," Owen told the Tribune. "We have reason to believe Storm will harm her physically. Anyone knowing anything about Miss Smoot's or Storm's whereabouts should contact authorities immediately."

U.S. Marshal Sam Gilson said his office is offering a $1,000 reward for information leading to the arrest of Ben Storm, who was last seen riding a tall black gelding belonging to Deputy Owen. "No man, woman or horse in this territory is safe until this mad dog is behind bars," added Gilson.

See the next issue of the Tribune for more details on these unprovoked attacks of terror.

"Now read this," Jex said, handing Ben the *Deseret News* story.

"I hope it's better than the other," Ben said. He looked down at the *Deseret News* headline, also on the front page.

Mormon Robin Hood Rescues Woman, Wounds Abductor

by John Nicholson

When Deputy U.S. Marshal Charles Owen arrested Stella Smoot, 18, in the desert west of Grantsville last weekend, he had no idea anyone would challenge his authority when he attempted to bring her back to Salt Lake to testify against her husband in an unconstitutional court of law.

But that's exactly what happened this past Monday morning when Ben Storm, 18, of American Fork bravely rode into Owen's camp and demanded he release the prisoner. Owen drew his pistol and began to shoot at Storm, who without concern for his own safety held his ground and returned the fire, wounding Owen in the foot before disarming the deputy and freeing Mrs. Smoot. To prevent pursuit, Storm relieved the swearing deputy of his boots and horse.

When three more deputies, led by Oscar Vandercook of

Salt Lake, attempted to recapture the woman, there was another gun battle in which Vandercook was wounded, also in the foot. Again, to prevent pursuit, Storm relieved the men of their boots and horses.

Throughout the territory Mormons are cheering Ben Storm, whom many are calling a modern Robin Hood.

"It's about time someone stood up to these unjust persecutions which the courts of the United States are pouring down upon an innocent people who want only to live their religion," said an LDS Church leader in an unofficial capacity.

"It's a good thing Storm stepped in when he did," said another. "We have reason to believe some of the deputies, including Owen, have been involved in forceful sexual indiscretions with female captives."

While an official statement from Church leaders was not available at press time—the leaders being underground to avoid unjust arrest for trying to obey their God—it is the feeling in Salt Lake that Church members everywhere should offer assistance where possible to young Storm for his heroic defense of their cause.

"It wasn't that way either," Ben said, "but you don't mind the lies so much when they make you look good." He resumed eating while rereading the articles.

"What are you going to do now?" Jex asked.

"Promised the women I'd take them to a secret hideaway where they could have their babies in peace. We'll be on our way before morning."

"Do you need anything?"

"Could you spare a couple of pack saddles for the extra horses? We could use some food, blankets, bullets, and even some oilcloth to patch up the hideout against the winter.

"I'll get on it right away," said Jex. "I'll have to run down to the store. Everything will be ready by daylight."

"Thanks."

"Is Priscilla going with you, or staying here?"

"She was planning to stay here," Ben explained, "but after pulling a gun on Gibson, she wants to get as far from the settlements as possible. They might put a price on her head. If they did she would feel like she couldn't trust anyone. Never know what even good people will do if there's a reward involved."

"Do you want to tell me where you're taking them?"

"I don't know," Ben said, looking Jex in the eye. The man was a Mormon, a polygamist, Priscilla's uncle. But could he keep a secret? Ben didn't know.

"If I knew where you were I could send out supplies in the spring. Maybe one of the husbands will want to visit his wife, send help. Maybe your father will want to reach you. In these troubled times, sometimes getting a message through becomes very urgent. I can't help you if I don't know where you are."

"Tell you what I'll do," Ben said after thinking a minute.

"Do you know who Priscilla is married to?"

"Yes," Jex said cautiously.

"She won't tell me," Ben said. "Let's make a deal. If you'll tell me who her husband is, I'll tell you where my hideout is."

"Can't do that," Jex said. "That's a confidence I can't break."

"We're on the same side," Ben said. "Tell me."

Jex remained silent.

"Is he a general authority?" Ben asked.

"You can catch a little sleep on the bench," Jex said. "I'll start getting those supplies ready." He turned and started for the door.

"Wait a minute," Ben said. "I suppose if you can keep that secret, you can do the same with the whereabouts of my hideout. I'll tell you—if you'll do me a personal favor."

"What's that?" Jex asked, returning to the table.

"Next time you go to Salt Lake, will you stop off in American Fork and tell my folks what really happened to those deputies?"

"Sure," Jex smiled through his black whiskers. "That's a promise."

Chapter 25

In order to fasten the semblance of guilt upon men accused of this offense (unlawful cohabitation), women are arrested and forcibly taken before sixteen men and plied with questions that no decent woman can hear without a blush.... If they decline to answer, they are imprisoned in the penitentiary as though they were criminals. . . .

But this is not all. In defiance of law and the usages of courts for ages, the legal (first) wife is now compelled to submit to the same indignities. . . .

We also direct your attention to the outrages perpetuated by rough and brutal deputy marshals, who watch around our dooryards, peer into our bedroom windows, ply little children with questions about their parents, and, when hunting their prey, burst into people's domiciles and terrorize the innocent. . . .

—Memorial to the U.S. Congress by Utah women, 1886

Ben had mixed feelings about the approaching snowstorm. On the one hand, he had wanted to get over the pass before the winter snows closed in. On the other, he was so tired from the incessant travel and lack of sleep that he welcomed the heavy snows, which would not only prevent his party from forging ahead but would also slow pursuers, if there were any. Heavy snow meant time for a much-needed rest, especially for the pregnant women. With the long, high pass ahead, and nearly a week's travel beyond that to his hideout, a good rest was not only welcomed, but necessary.

There were plenty of blankets in the pack saddles, and a big piece of canvas that would provide adequate protection against the falling snow. The party's rest would be a comfortable one.

It was late afternoon, the first day out of Springville, and Ben figured they were at least 20 miles from town, a comfortable distance with snows coming to cover their tracks and slow pursuit.

Ben had been leading the way most of the day, keeping a sharp eye out for other travelers. Once, when a train had passed, the party had moved behind some rocks so no one would see them. The new Denver and Rio Grande Railroad used the pass too.

The three women rode together behind Ben. Further back, Flat Nose George followed on his big gray mule, leading the two fully loaded pack horses. Lobo went where he pleased, sometimes in the lead, sometimes beside Priscilla, sometimes falling behind to check out Flat Nose George and the pack animals.

The only other travelers they encountered, except for the train, were two big sixes, freight wagons pulled by six-horse teams. The wagons had left Provo two days earlier, loaded with supplies and bound for the new town of Price.

Ben didn't know how long Flat Nose George would accompany them because the big Indian didn't say much, not even when questioned. But there was something about the Indian that Ben liked, something that told him the Indian was a friend who could be depended on when times were hard—maybe not in the white man's ways, but in the ways of the wilderness. He was a man who knew what to do on the trail. As far as Ben was concerned, Flat Nose George could travel with them as long as he wished, perhaps all the way to the hideout.

Ben was familiar with Spanish Fork Canyon, having traveled it a number of times with his father and brothers on hunting expeditions. He knew a small side canyon not very far ahead where they could camp near a spring out of sight of the main trail. He had camped there before. His father called it Hard Horse Canyon. The name had something to do with some unusual rock formations near the mouth.

The big snowflakes grew larger and larger, and were soon falling so thick that it was impossible to see more than a hundred yards ahead. Still, Ben didn't have any trouble finding the rock formations signaling the entrance to the canyon, and the snow would cover their tracks into the canyon.

It was nearly dark when they reached the spring. While Flat Nose George picketed the horses, Ben ran a line between two stout juniper trees. After pulling it as tight as he could, he stretched the big canvas over it to form a tent. He rolled big rocks along the edge of the canvas to hold it in place. The women helped bring the gear inside, standing the saddles upright at both ends to block out the snow and wind. They spread the saddle blankets out on the new snow to make a floor.

Ben was too tired to build a fire. Everyone was more tired than hungry, anyway. After chewing wearily on cold beef and rolls that John Jex had given them, they all rolled up in dry blankets and settled down for the night as the snow continued to fall. Within a few minutes everyone was asleep, even Lobo, who found a dry spot between Priscilla and Flat Nose George.

Ben was the first one up the next morning, and he found the snow up to his knees as he crawled from the shelter. He looked up at a partly cloudy sky, the clouds moving eastward before a cool, westerly breeze. It was going to be a pleasant day. He climbed the nearest hill where it appeared he could get a decent view of the main road, both behind them and where it led up to the pass.

Except for a solitary doe tiptoeing along the opposite hillside, there was no sign of life. The snow-blanketed land was white and clean, empty of man, and still. Beautiful. It was a good time to be alone, a good time to think. Ben wondered if he had done the right thing bringing three pregnant women into the wilderness at the beginning of winter. There were other pregnant plural wives doing just fine, hiding in settlements where there were plenty of civilized comforts, food, shelter, even doctors. There was nothing except a small cabin where Ben was taking these women.

Ben wondered why they wanted to come with him in the first place, why they trusted him. All he had done was show a little spunk by shooting two deputies in the foot. He didn't know much; he was just a kid, and a socially backward one at that. This whole adventure seemed so crazy at times.

And what about Stella wanting to marry him and run off to California? That was even crazier. He wasn't ready for marriage at all—especially with a $1,000 reward on his head. He wondered if he would ever want to marry as long as the law was after him.

Looking back to the west, Ben wondered about his people, the Mormons, frustrated and unhappy, trying only to live their religion while the United States Government was determined to stop them. The leaders were either in jail or on the underground. People were drifting, making mistakes.

How would it all end? Would the government give up and leave the Mormons alone? Hardly. Would the Mormons pull up stakes like they had in Far West and Nauvoo, and move on to a place like Canada or Mexico, where they might be left alone? Would the conflict die down, or flare up with more people getting shot, maybe even killed? Would the Mormons buckle under, telling their God that polygamy was just too tough a law to follow? Was the government pressure too much for a people to bear? He didn't think the church would buckle under. Pressure from governments wouldn't change the laws of God. God was above governments.

Maybe things would change during the winter, by the time the women had had their babies. Ben knew only one thing for sure. After what had happened to his brother, his dog and his horse, he knew that if war broke out between the Mormons and the government, he would be in the middle of it. If men like Owen and Vandercook continued to push the Mormons around, they would pay dearly. He would see to it.

Catching a movement out of the corner of his eye, Ben saw Lobo charging up the hill, throwing the soft new powder in every direction. Though not very affectionate, the dog hadn't been any trouble and Ben had a hunch Lobo would be a fearless ally in a confrontation. Ben was eager to make friends. He still hadn't petted the dog.

When Lobo reached him, Ben said a few kind words, then turned and headed further up the ridge, Lobo following close behind. Not close enough to reach out and touch, but closer than he had ever been before.

When Ben returned to camp, he could hear talking inside the shelter. The women were awake.

"Who's hungry for a big breakfast of pancakes and bacon?" Ben called cheerfully. "I'll get the fire started."

Priscilla was the first to come out of the tent. Ben could tell by the sober look on her face that something was wrong.

"We've got to talk," she said, wading forcefully through the snow until she was face to face with Ben.

"That Indian has got to go," she said, hands on hips.

"What Indian?" Ben asked innocently.

"You know who. Flat Nose George."

"What's wrong?"

"You've got a traveling maternity ward here, being chased by the law, winter coming on, babies to deliver. There's no place for a drunken, irresponsible savage."

While she was speaking Flat Nose George crawled out of the tent, a bottle of whiskey in his hand. Standing to his full height, he removed the cork from the bottle and took a deep drink. He held the bottle out to Ben.

"No thanks," Ben said. George then turned to Lobo, who had been standing beside the closest juniper tree, and extended the bottle towards the dog. Lobo trotted up to the Indian and sneezed when he got a whiff of the drink. Goerge, after taking another quick snort, returned the cork to its proper place, dropped to one knee, and began petting the dog.

"Now do you see what I'm talking about?" Priscilla asked. "He has to go, and now." She was talking loud enough for Flat Nose George to hear every word.

"He's petting the dog," Ben said, astonished.

"He's getting drunk," Priscilla snapped back.

"Your uncle must have given him the bottle," Ben said.

"Well, I don't think any of the women are safe. A drunken Indian is capable of anything, even rape and murder. He's got to go."

Flat Nose George stood up, removed the cork, and took another drink. His hand was steady. He looked over at Priscilla and Ben.

"Me go," he said, then belched. Ben guessed the insult was for Priscilla's benefit, evidence he had heard every word. George picked up his rawhide bridle and began walking towards the mule. His gait was steady. Lobo was at his side.

"He's an excellent tracker and scout," Ben said, hoping to soften Priscilla. "He's a good hand with the stock. He can hunt and bring us meat. He'll be a good lookout, even handy with a gun, if the law gets onto us. Bet he even knows how to deliver babies."

The comment about the babies was the wrong thing to say.

"If you think for one moment that drunken savage is going to lay a hand on one of us . . ." Priscilla warned.

"Who's going to lead the pack horses when we hit the trail again?" Ben demanded, finally getting angry too.

"There are three of us. Plenty of help."

"Tomorrow George will be sober. The three of you will still be pregnant," Ben said.

Stella and Madge crawled out of the tent.

"Do you two want George to go too?" Ben asked.

They nodded they did.

Ben had had enough of this irrational conversation. He crawled under the canvas and pulled out George's saddle and some of the supplies. He helped George saddle the mule.

"Injun no hurt squaws," was the only thing Flat Nose George said.

"I know," Ben said, "but they're scared of you. That bottle really got them going."

Without saying goodbye, shaking hands, or even nodding farewell, Flat Nose George climbed upon the big mule, the bottle still in his hand. He pulled the mule's head around and started down the canyon towards the road. Lobo was at his side.

"Lobo, come here!" Priscilla shouted. The dog stopped, looked back at his mistress, then turned and bounded through the deep snow after the Indian.

"Craziest thing I ever saw," Ben said, taking off his hat and scratching the side of his head.

Priscilla continued to yell after the dog, but Lobo ignored her.

"Stop!" Ben yelled. He ran through the snow to catch up with the big mule. "I want you to stay," he said when he was alongside. George stopped the mule and looked at Ben, but didn't say anything. "Don't pay any attention to the squaws," Ben said. "I need your help." After a minute, the Indian turned the mule around and followed Ben back to camp.

"He's not going to stay," Priscilla warned.

Ben walked up to her. They were standing face to face. Ben returned his hat to his head, pulling it down tight like he was getting ready to ride a wild horse.

"Any man that can win over Lobo that fast has got to have some good in him," he said.

She started to say something, but he cut her off.

"I guess I'm kind of like that dog of yours," he said. "Something inside tells me this here Indian is the kind of hand I ought to be traveling with, so I aim to do it. The dog and I are in agreement."

Ben looked over at Stella and Madge, making sure they heard him.

"Me, the Injun, and the dog are going to a hideout about a week's journey from here, a place where the deputies will never find us. We're going to keep out of sight for a while, maybe the whole winter, until things cool off, or until I can't stand being away any longer. The three of you are welcome to come along." Ben paused. The women were listening. He couldn't tell if Flat Nose George was or not.

"But if any or all of you don't like traveling with me or my friends," Ben continued, "you are free to leave. I'll give a horse and plenty of supplies to anyone who wants to go back. It's only a day's ride back to Springville. Ladies, you are free to do as you please."

"You're saying you think the Indian is more important than we are," Priscilla said, a pouting, defensive look on her face.

"No," Ben said calmly. "I'm saying that where we're going the Indian will be a good hand to have along, and that sending him away is a stupid, narrow-minded, irrational thing to do. I'm in charge here and he's going to stay."

Priscilla turned and stomped back to the tent. Madge walked up to the big mule and held out her hand. "Like to warm my tummy before I start cooking the pancakes and bacon," she said.

Ben couldn't be sure, but it looked like there was a hint of a smile on the face of Flat Nose George as he handed Madge the bottle.

Chapter 26

It is alleged that we are in danger of perverting the nation's morals. . . .

There are now in the city (Salt Lake) some six brothels, forty tap rooms, a number of gambling houses, pool tables, and other disreputable concerns—all run by non-Mormons.

It is a remarkable fact that in all these years since the introduction of polygamy among us, not one gentile has ever entered it through our agency. Those who are corrupt have easier methods which are furnished and approved by the professed Christian world. . . .

If in thirty-four years not one gentile has adopted polygamy, how many years will it take to demoralize the fifty-five millions of the United States?

—First Presidency epistle read in General Conference and published in the Deseret News, 1886

Crossing Soldier Summit in the new snow wasn't as hard as Ben thought it would be. While there was as much as four feet of snow in places on top of the summit, it was soft with no crust to break. The traveling was easy as long as everyone stayed single file. The only animal really having to exert itself was the horse in the lead, the one breaking trail.

At first they changed the lead horse every half hour, so no one animal would do more than its share of the hard work. But when Flat Nose George's big gray mule finally got a turn at breaking trail, he not only seemed to like it, he was tireless, mile after mile. They left him in the lead, getting over the pass almost as fast as if there had been no snow at all.

"Sure glad we have that mule along," Ben yelled to Priscilla as they followed the Price River out of the pass. She didn't respond.

Dropping out of the high country into the Price River Valley, Ben was careful to make a big circle around the little railroad town of Price. He avoided farms and cabins too, thinking the fewer people who saw his caravan of pregnant women, the better. Thanks to Jex they had plenty of supplies, so there was no need to stop.

The party followed the Price River through desert country where the previous storm had dropped little more than a skiff of snow, and that was mostly melted now. To the east was the Beckworth Plateau, a huge table of land mass that unknown geological forces had pushed skyward, leaving a long, jagged skyline of irregular cliffs that looked like a long, crooked row of tightly stacked books. The first explorers had called the place Castle Valley. Some of the local sheepherders called the formation the Book Cliffs.

Four days after leaving the snow, the party reached the Green River. The day was gray and wintery, a bitter wind sweeping down from the north.

"But it's not green," Stella said when she saw the brown water.

"It's green up north where it crosses the Oregon Trail," Ben responded, amused by Stella's reaction. "I suppose that's where they named it."

"It looks so cold and dirty," Priscilla said. "Do we have to cross it?"

"Not if we go downstream to the railroad crossing," Ben said. "George and I will push the horses across while you women walk across the trestle."

They rode downstream, the wind at their backs, until they came to the trestle, a powerful structure of huge pine beams over which the iron tracks crossed. While a horse could not cross because of the separations between the ties, it was a simple matter to walk across on foot.

On the west bank near the tracks were two shacks made from discarded railroad ties. Several Chinamen in blue pajamas stepped outside to see who was coming, but the wind forced a quick retreat back inside.

The Chinese had been brought in to work on the railroad. Some had stayed behind after the construction was complete, some had gone into mining and freighting, and others worked in stores and restaurants.

The women dismounted and started across the trestle, walking on the upwind side, leaning into the bitter wind that tugged disrespectfully at their full dresses. Ben led the way into the water, the Indian herding the horses from beind. There was only a short space where they needed to swim, so neither George nor Ben got out of the saddle to be pulled through the water, the easiest way to cross a long stretch of deep water. For the hundredth time since Hard Horse Canyon, Ben was glad the Indian was along. Getting all those horses across the river by himself would have been much more difficult.

Had the wind not suddenly stopped, Ben probably would not have heard the scream. Had the wind not suddenly stopped, there probably would not have been a scream. It was Priscilla, who had been leaning into the wind, walking along the edge of the trestle, when the wind stopped pushing against her and she momentarily lost her balance. Her arms and legs flailed wildly as she did a somersault and entered the deepest part of the river with a dull splash, Lobo leaping in after her. "Can't swim!" she cried as she flailed about. In panic she grabbed Lobo, pulling him under.

The other women were screaming. Ben frantically tried to turn his horse around and into the other horses, now plunging to get up the muddy bank. The Chinamen were charging out of their huts to see what was wrong.

The only person showing any degree of calmness was Flat Nose George, still in the deepest part of the stream, astride the big gray mule as it swam towards Ben—about 30 feet upstream from Priscilla and Lobo.

An observer might have guessed that Flat Nose George wasn't even aware the woman had fallen in, except that, without even looking towards her, he calmly reached out and pulled the mule's head downstream, forcing the animal to stay in the deep water, and headed right for Priscilla.

The long, powerful legs of the mule soon had Flat Nose George within reach of the now hysterical woman. Leaning over in the saddle and reaching out with his long arm, the Indian surprised everyone. He didn't grab the woman, but the dog, jerking Lobo roughly out of Priscilla's grasp, pulling the dog sideways over his saddle, then pushing the dog towards shore. Priscilla didn't sink, there still being plenty of bubbles under her petticoats.

Gasping for air, Lobo began swimming for shore. That's when George finally reached out and grabbed Priscilla's hand, letting her trail alongside as the big mule churned towards shallow water.

As soon as Ben saw that George had things under control, he turned his horse toward the bank. When he reached dry ground, he dismounted and began gathering dry cottonwood and willow limbs for a fire. The north wind had resumed in full force, and Priscilla would need a blazing fire as much as she had needed the Indian's hand.

As soon as the fire was burning, Ben and Flat Nose George went off to gather the wandering horses, while Stella and Madge got Priscilla out of her wet clothes and wrapped her in dry blankets. When that was accomplished, the Chinamen returned to their shacks.

With the horses picketed out to graze, Ben and George, both wet from the waist down, returned to the fire to warm up. A subdued Priscilla, wrapped in a green wool blanket, was standing with her back to the fire.

"You all right?" Ben asked, walking up beside her. She nodded that she was. The Indian sat down on a cottonwood log, stretching his hands and feet towards the fire.

Without a word Priscilla walked over to the Indian and sat down beside him, reaching out for his arm and holding it in her lap.

"I'm sorry about wanting you to leave," she said, looking at his face as he continued to stare straight ahead. "I'm glad you didn't."

With his free hand, George reached behind the log for his now half-full bottle of whiskey and offered it to Priscilla.

"No thank you," she said politely. Nor did she move away when Flat Nose George removed the cork and took a deep swallow.

The next morning they continued in an easterly direction along the railroad tracks until they were out of sight of the Chinese. Then Ben led everyone up a draw to the north, being careful to keep in the bottom where no one could see them. An hour later they were following the Green River upstream.

"Is this the hideout?" Madge asked when they spotted a stone cabin surrounded by big cottonwood trees.

"No," Ben said, "but it looks just like the one we're going to stay in. The cabins were built by sheepherders. Sometimes used in the summer, but seldom in the winter. Tomorrow night we'll be at the hideout. Be surprised if we see anyone else all winter."

It was the first time the women had slept under a roof in over a week. There were even some straw mattresses in the cabin. After a hot meal of beans and ham, the women and Ben lazed around, talking about their new home. As tired as they were after a long day on the trail, and even though it was getting late, the anticipation of reaching their destination the next day was something to stay awake for—except for Flat Nose George and Lobo, who had made their beds on the front steps and were already fast asleep.

Chapter 27

New Year's Day but I do not despond. If I were here for a crime I would consider this part of my life literally wasted, but as it is I rejoice.

—From the prison journal of polygamist LEVI SAVAGE, January 1, 1888

"How many wives ye got?" the big-bellied guard asked through his drooping handlebar mustache. He was standing straight, hands on hips, watching Sam Storm change into the standard uniform provided all the prisoners at the federal prison in Detroit, Michigan. Storm had arrived from Utah on the train an hour earlier. The paperwork already completed, the guard had brought Storm to the prison commisary for his clothing, blanket and bucket. Storm didn't answer the question.

"You're already in prison. Won't hurt to tell now. How many?"

Sam finished buttoning up his shirt, still not answering the question.

"Smart guy, huh? I can fix that," the guard said, grinning. "Instead of putting you in a cell with another Mormon, I'll just toss you in the hole with the perverts. You'll learn to answer my questions."

Sam looked at the guard, wondering if the man was bluffing, wondering if the guard really had the authority to determine where he would stay in the prison. Sharing a cell with a fellow Mormon was certainly more desirable than being thrown into an unknown hole with strangers who had unnatural sexual preferences.

"How many wives?" the guard repeated.

Sam looked around as if to make sure no one else was listening.

"Enough so I never get a good night's sleep."

The guard howled, his eyes rolling high at the ceiling.

"Had to take a nap every afteroon so I could get through the nights," Sam lied. The guard howled a second time.

Sam finished buttoning his shirt and pulled it straight, looking the guard square in the eye as if he were about to take a belt of whiskey. "Fourteen," he said.

Staring at Sam, the guard swallowed hard, his big, hairy mouth gaping wide as if he had just watched the Mormon swallow a two-pound toad, live and whole.

"Actually," Sam said, starting to enjoy the spoof, "I'm kind of looking forward to a stay in the penitentiary. Need time to rest, get my strength back. Need a lot of strength when I get out of here. Be going home to 14 wives."

The big guard howled a third time, slapping his thighs. Finally, getting control of himself, he handed Sam a blanket and a rusty tin bucket, and pointed towards the door.

A minute later the guard was leading Sam down the stone walkway in Cell Block B, a gloomy pigpen of a place. Each cell opening was covered with a thick grate—strips of iron riveted crossways on each other, hinges on one side, big locks on the other.

Grimy faces of men and boys—some jeering, some laughing, some angry, others sad—peered through the grate squares. Many were smoking dirty, black pipes. Sam could smell the smoke, and suddenly he felt like he was drowning in a heavy man-musk of sweat, urine, feces, and tobacco smoke. It made him sick. Sam was amazed that the guard and the men looking at him through the grates didn't seem to notice the strangling stench.

As dark and gloomy as it was in the hallway, the cells were even darker. It was impossible to see more than a few feet beyond the grate doors. Even at midday the cells were dark—too dark to read or sew or do anything useful. There were no windows in the cells. The only light came from two dirty skylights over the hallway.

Sam fought the urge to run, to break out, to get away. It hurt to the very core of his soul to think he was going to stay in this place. His pigs lived better than this. This was no place for a man, especially a man who was not a criminal. He was here for trying to live his religion. He had violated no one's rights. He had not stolen from, cheated, nor hurt anyone. It was so wrong, so unjust. He was glad Kathryn couldn't see him now. He would never tell her what this place was really like. And he was afraid the worst was yet to come.

"Here we are, Number 23," the guard said, stopping in front of one of the black grate doors and putting a big key into the massive lock.

"Moron Hess will be your cellmate," the guard said. "He's been on a hunger strike for three days. Maybe you can talk some sense into him. My name's Oz. Keep yer nose clean, and there won't be no trouble."

Sam walked into the cell, stopping as the door clanked shut behind him. The click of the closing lock thundered through his head like a cannon shot, leaving him with a trapped, helpless feeling. He put down his bucket and blanket, slowly looking around as his eyes adjusted to the semi-darkness.

Along the side of the cell were two wooden cots barely two feet wide. There was a blanket on one, nothing on the other. At the back of the cell was a small wooden table. The other man's bucket, covered with a piece of wrinkled brown oilcloth, was under it. The words "Christ Comes!" and "Freedom and Justice for All" were smeared on the wall in blood.

The other prisoner was seated on the floor. He was an older man with a white beard, his knees drawn up close against his chest, his arms resting on his knees. He bore a remarkable resemblance to round-faced George Q. Cannon of the First Presidency. The man wore wrinkled prison denims like those Sam had just received. On the man's head was a remarkably well-kept black hat, a round-topped bowler.

"The name's Sam Storm," Sam said, reaching out to shake the man's hand. "That your blood on the wall?"

"Nope," the man said. "Randolph made the ultimate sacrifice for those inscriptions. Blood atonement, I call it."

"Where's Randolph now?" Sam asked.

"Dead. In the bucket."

"I don't understand."

"Randolph is . . . or I suppose was, a rat. Been after him for a month. Finally caught him day before yesterday. Felt bad, him dying such a useless death. So I twisted his head off and wrote something important on the wall. What do you think? Did I give some meaning to the poor devil's death?"

"I don't know," Sam said, marveling at what prison could do to a man. He wondered what it would do to him. He would fight. He wouldn't let it get to him.

"My name's Moroni Hess," the man said. "Please excuse me for not standing up. Not much strength in this old man today."

"The guard said you're on a hunger strike," Sam said.

"Shows how little he knows."

"You're eating, then?"

"No, but I'm not on a hunger strike."

"I don't understand."

"I'm fasting. A big difference, you know."

"What are you fasting for?"

"Not for the benefit of the jailers, that's for sure. First, tell me how you got here."

Sam sat down beside Moroni and told him the whole story—how he had married Lydia, his arrest and trial, and how Lydia had betrayed him. He told about his trip to Detroit on the train, and the horrible news he had received as he departed, that his wife Kathryn had lost her unborn baby, her only child in 16 years of marriage. The trauma of the trial and riding back and forth between jails in open wagons were probably the cause. But it hurt too much to talk about that.

"How did you get here?" Sam asked.

"About the same as you," Moroni said, " 'cept I almost got the judge in Provo to let me go. Told him my first wife,

Mary, was in the cemetery. The judge could see my second wife, Judy, sitting in the courtroom. He couldn't understand why they arrested me if my first wife was in the cemetery.

"Then this skunk takes a note up to the bench and hands it to the judge. It explains that Mary is at the cemetery just like I said, but she's not dead, only living in a tent there. That did it. The judge smashed down his gavel and gave me three years. He said normally he'd give an old man only two years, but since I was a patriarch he was going to give me three. So here I am."

"Tell me why you're fasting," Sam said.

Moroni looked over at Sam, trying to judge if this newcomer was ready for the truth.

"Sure you want to know?"

"Yes."

"So the glory, the honor, the intelligence, and the power of the priesthood will distill on my soul as the dew from heaven." Moroni's voice was suddenly strong and forceful. He was looking straight ahead through the cell door. "Tonight I am going to raise my right arm to the square and command the walls of this prison to crumble."

He looked over at Sam. "Do you believe me? Do you believe it will happen?"

"I hope it will happen," Sam responded. "With all my heart I hope it will happen."

Chapter 28

. . . and the earth shook mightily, and the walls of the prison were rent in twain, so that they fell to the earth. . . . And Alma and Amulek came forth out of the prison, and they were not hurt; for the Lord had granted unto them power, according to their faith, which was in Christ. And they straightway came forth out of the prison; and they were loosed from their bands; and the prison had fallen to the earth, and every soul within the walls thereof, save it were Alma and Amulek, was slain; and they straightway came forth into the city.

—Alma 14: 27-28, The Book of Mormon

"Would you like to join me in the true order of prayer?" Moroni asked.

"This is not a sacred place," Sam said. "Don't know if we should bring anything sacred into this vile hole."

"Maybe you're right," Moroni said thoughtfully. "Will you join me in a more regular kind of prayer?"

"I'd be honored," Sam said.

It was dark and the last prison lantern had been turned out long ago. A full moon shining against the dirty skylights offered just enough light to keep the men from bumping into large objects.

Even though Sam and Moroni had not retired to their cots, they were wrapped in blankets to keep warm against the cold December night. There was one woodburning stove for the entire building, and except for sunny afternoons, the building was always cold in winter.

Moroni moved the little table to the middle of the cell, then dropped to his knees, placing his forearms across the table.

"Please join me," he said.

Sam knelt on the opposite side of the table, placing his forearms on the table too. Moroni placed his rough old hands over Sam's. Sam felt something harder than skin and very smooth in one of Moroni's hands.

"What's in your hand?" he asked.

"My seerstone. Sometimes when it's dark I can see things in it. Maybe it will help us tonight. Joseph Smith said every man should have a seerstone."

"Is it like those Joseph used to translate the gold plates?" Sam asked.

"No," said Moroni, "I think those were clear, like diamonds. Mine's light brown in color, with white lines crossing it. Tomorrow when there's light you can look at it."

"What kind of things do you see in it?" Sam asked.

"Sometimes I can see my wives and families back home, what they're doing, how they're getting along. But we can talk more about that tomorrow. Let's pray."

While Sam bowed his head, Moroni lifted his face towards heaven. "Our Father in Heaven, two of thy servants kneel before thee this cold winter night in humble supplication."

There was a pause while Moroni gathered his thoughts.

"Falsely arrested, falsely tried and falsely sentenced, we are kneeling in this filthy prison two thousand miles from our homes and loved ones. Thou knowest our cause is just, our imprisonment unjust.

"We belong back home, caring for our loved ones, building the kingdom, serving thee as upright, honorable, and free men.

"Thou knowest the desires of our hearts. Thou knowest why we need to get out of this place."

Ben felt the old man's hands tighten their grip. Through them he could feel a growing tension in the old man, an increasing intensity that was reflected in Moroni's voice as he continued to pray.

"Father, you know about Alma and Amulek in the Book of Mormon, how they were beaten, then bound and cast into prison without food, water or clothing. Because they were thy righteous servants, the prison walls came tumbling down and they walked out free men.

"We, thy servants, humbly ask thee to help us do that here tonight. When we command the walls to fall, please be with us in power and glory, so the walls will obey. In the name of Jesus Christ, amen."

"Amen," Sam said.

Slowly, Moroni stood up. Without another word he pushed the table back to its proper place against the wall. Sam remained on his knees, watching through the dim light as Moroni raised his right hand to the square and turned to face the stone wall at the back of the cell.

"In the name of Jesus Christ, and with the power of the holy priesthood I bear," he said in a powerful, confident voice, "I command the walls of this prison to crumble, the mortar to turn to dust, the stones to crack, and the whole dirty mess to come crashing down on the heads of the wicked!"

Sam listened and looked about. The silence was complete. As much as he yearned to hear the rumbling of falling stones, there was nothing.

"I command the walls to fall," Moroni ordered, his voice louder. Still, nothing happened. Moroni stood motionless, silent, feet apart, arm to the square.

"It didn't work," he said finally, his voice meek and broken.

"I wonder why," Sam asked.

"Not enough faith, I suppose. Thought three days of fasting would be enough. Guess it wasn't."

"I guess not," Sam said.

"Maybe you should try it," Moroni said, his subdued voice showing a little more enthusiasm.

"What makes you think my faith would be any stronger than yours? I've never fasted three days."

"Try it."

"Don't know if I'm worthy."

"Do you pay tithes and offerings?"

"Yes."

"Do you pray?"

"Yes."

"Do you believe the Book of Mormon is the word of God, that Alma and Amulek walked out of that prison after the walls had tumbled down?"

"Yes."

"Have you ever committed fornication or adultery?"

"No."

"Then try it. Maybe your faith is stronger, even without the fasting."

Sam got to his feet and walked over to the wall. Fighting off the inclination to feel foolish, he raised his right arm to the square. He began to open his mouth, but no words would come out.

"Go ahead and say it," Moroni ordered. "Show the Lord that you have faith in him, that you can command the walls of this awful place to fall."

"In the name of Jesus Christ," Sam began slowly, "and with the power of the priesthood . . . " He paused. "I order this wall to fall to pieces, right now!"

Nothing happened. Moroni didn't move or say a word.

"Damn it—fall!" Sam shouted.

Nothing happened.

After a while Sam walked over to his cot and sat down.

"Are you going to continue fasting?" he asked.

"No," Moroni said, crawling over to his cot. "Got to think this through, got to figure out why the walls didn't fall. What did we do wrong?"

"I don't know," Sam said. "Maybe we don't have it as tough as we think. Maybe it was a lot worse for Alma and Amulek. Didn't you say they were without food, water and clothing, that they were tied up and beaten too?"

"That's what the book says."

"If that's what it takes to break down walls, don't know if I want any part of it."

"You may not have any choice."

Sam rolled up tight in his blanket, hoping to get some

sleep before morning. He was so tired, and he missed Kathryn.

Chapter 29

Thursday, February 3, 1887. Fast day. Had a very interesting meeting at the wardhouse. Bishop Driggs did not expect to meet the ward soon again in that capacity. Would likely be in the pen for co-hab before the month was out. He spoke very feelingly to the people, giving counsel and instructions.

Thursday, 17. Evening at ward meeting in school house. Quite a number spoke their feelings about the bishop going to the pen, myself among the number.

Friday, 18. Our bishop Appolas G. Driggs and others went to the pen today.

—Samuel W. Richards' journal

"Chow time!" bellowed the guard shortly after daylight the next morning. All the doors in Cell Block B were unlocked and the inmates marched single file to the dining hall, a block building near the south outer wall of the prison.

Inside the dining hall were three rows of long tables set with rusty tin plates and cups. There were no knives or forks, but there were spoons at about half the places.

"The plates and cups are dirty," Sam said as he and Moroni seated themselves at one of the long tables.

"The prisoners from Cell Block A just finished. We'll eat from the same plates and cups, then the men from C will eat from ours. Tonight everything gets washed up so the A men get clean plates again in the morning," explained Moroni.

Ben noticed that some of the men had pulled flat pieces of wood from their pockets. Others picked up the dirty spoons.

Sam and Moroni were without utensils.

As soon as everyone was seated, five or six trustees and three guards brought in two large tubs full of steaming food. The first one contained beans; the second, black coffee.

The men with the beans led the way, going down each aisle and dumping a ladleful of beans on each plate. The men with the coffee followed.

The beans tasted good to Sam. There was no meat, but plenty of salt. Because he didn't have a spoon, he held the plate up to his mouth and began drinking down the beans, occasionally pushing them into his mouth with a forefinger. Though he would have been reluctant to admit it, Sam was enjoying his first meal at the prison. It didn't matter that his satisfaction was more a function of intense hunger than the quality of the food.

By the time the coffee tub came by, Sam was feeling so well he decided to ask a question of the guard handling the ladle. The guard was a big, unshaven man, very muscular, with uncombed red hair and bloodshot eyes. A heavy drinker, figured Sam.

"I don't like coffee," Sam said. "Do you think I could go out and get some water?"

From the way the guard stopped serving, looking in amazement at the new prisoner, Sam knew he had made a big mistake.

"Coffee's fine," Sam said, holding out his cup. The guard did not fill the cup. It was too late.

"The new inmate doesn't like our coffee!" shouted the guard to his companions. "Any sarsparilla in the kitchen?" Everyone laughed, including the inmates.

"No!" shouted one of the other guards, "but ask him if he'd like a cold lemonade, with just a tiny shot of whiskey in it." Everyone in the room roared.

"How about some warm pee from Mrs. Hooper's chamber pot?" shouted the first guard. Mrs. Hooper was the warden's wife. The laughter continued.

"Coffee's fine," Sam said, when it had quieted enough for the guard to hear him.

Finally the guard filled Sam's cup, then continued down

the aisle. Sam set the cup of coffee beside his plate, not drinking any.

A few minutes later, after all the food was served, Sam suddenly became aware of someone standing behind him. He turned to find the same guard who had filled his cup.

No longer laughing, the guard reached around Sam and picked up the still-full cup of coffee.

"Maybe our coffee doesn't have enough flavor for you," the guard said, loud enough for all to hear. Everyone in the room, guards and inmates alike, turned towards Sam, who knew he'd better be careful.

"The coffee's fine," Sam said.

"Then why aren't you drinking it?" the guard asked.

"Saving it for last," Sam lied. "Always save the best part for last."

"Be glad to give it more flavor for you," the guard offered.

"No thanks," Sam said, reaching for the cup. "Just fine the way it is."

"A lump of sugar?" the guard asked, holding the cup away from Sam's reach.

"No thanks."

"How about this?" the guard asked, bringing the cup to his chin and spitting in it. He handed the cup back to Sam.

"Drink," the guard ordered.

"Better do as he says," Moroni said. "A lot worse things can happen to a man around here than drinking spit."

Sam stood up, looking the guard in the eye. Sam didn't have any trouble recognizing true meanness in the bloodshot eyes. Still, he wasn't about to drink the man's spit.

"Changed my mind," Sam said. "Don't like your coffee after all." Some of the inmates cheered at Sam's courage.

"Drink," the guard said.

Sam drew the cup towards his face as if he were going to drink or at least sniff the brew. Then, without warning, his hand shot forward, throwing the entire contents of the cup into the guard's face.

Sam stepped back, anticipating the need to defend himself.

The guard did nothing but smile.

"Glad you did that," he said. "By the time I get through with you, you'll love prison coffee, even if it's pissed in."

Sam waited, ready to fight. The guard continued to grin. Without warning, another cup, half full of coffee, hit the guard in the chest. Then a plate of beans. One of the other guards yelled as he was struck with a full cup. Plates and cups were flying in every direction, the room erupting with cursing and yelling. The guards began to swing their sticks, mixing blood with the spilled beans and coffee.

The riot ended almost as quickly as it had begun; the men marched outside, many holding injured arms and heads. One man had a broken arm, and several were bleeding profusely from noses and mouths.

Instead of returning to Cell Block B, the men were marched to the outdoor showers behind the dining hall and ordered to strip and wash. For the regularly scheduled weekly showers on Friday afternoons, a big boiler was fired up so the men could wash in warm water. Not so today. It became clear that the guards intended to wash the men who were splattered with beans and coffee.

It was a cold December morning with a stiff breeze off Lake Huron. Nobody wanted to strip and shower in cold water, but there was no choice. One by one the men slipped out of their soiled uniforms, tossed them into a big tub, and jumped in and out of the cold showers. Not until everyone was wet were they allowed to return single file to Cell Block B, wearing only their shoes. They were not given towels or dry clothing. The guards marched the naked, shivering men around the yard a few times, in no hurry to get them back to their cells.

"Next time drink the spit," one blue-lipped man said to Sam.

"I'm with you," another said. "You got grit."

When the prisoners were finally allowed to return to their cells and wrap their freezing bodies in dry blankets, Sam found himself alone. Moroni had been marched to another cell in another part of the building.

As Sam paced back and forth, wrapped tightly in his

blanket, he felt a grim satisfaction at having thrown the coffee in the guard's face. Still, he didn't fool himself by thinking the cold shower and losing Moroni as a cellmate were the extent of the guard's revenge. There would be more. How much more, he had no idea.

Chapter 30

I thank the Lord that I was considered worthy to be one of the number that was imprisoned for maintaining one of the pure principles of the everlasting gospel, even the principle of celestial marriage.
—JOHN LEE JONES

It wasn't accidental that the door to Cell Block B was left open that night. Nor was it accidental that the stove was allowed to burn out.

No one slept. With the door open, the stove out, and without clothing, every man spent the night pacing back and forth, wrapped tightly in his threadbare blanket to keep from shivering.

Immediately after daylight, relief arrived, and the men were issued clean, dry uniforms. Wrapped in blankets, the otherwise naked men waited eagerly at the cell doors.

The basket didn't stop at Sam's door, however.

"Sorry," said the guard as he wheeled past. "Wolfstein said your clothes got lost at the laundry. Maybe we'll find them tomorrow." As Sam had already learned, Rudolf Wolfstein was the name of the big red-haired guard Sam had thrown the coffee on.

When it was time to go to the dining hall, Sam's door was unlocked along with the others, but when he tried to step outside, wrapped only in his blanket, he was stopped by the guard.

"Sorry, blankets aren't allowed outside the cells," said

the guard. "If you want to eat, you'll have to leave the blanket behind."

Sam resisted the temptation to remain in his cell, missing half his daily food allotment. He desperately needed food. Pacing his cell all night in freezing temperatures had seriously drained his energy reserves.

He tossed his blanket on the cot and, stark naked except for his shoes, followed the guard into the hallway, where he joined the other prisoners on their way to the dining hall. There were no jeering remarks about his nakedness, at least not from the prisoners. Everyone knew Sam was being punished. Throwing the coffee into the guard's face had earned their respect.

On this particular morning, each man received a cup of broth and two boiled potatoes with the skins on. Without a word, Sam wolfed down every morsel. There was very little talking in the dining hall, as everyone was equally starved and weary from the sleepless night. The prisoners only wanted to get back to their cells, where with food in their stomachs and the warmth of the recently returned uniforms, they hoped to get some sleep. Even if the door continued to be left open, the daytime temperatures would keep the heat up enough to allow sleep. These were Sam's thoughts, too.

Wolfstein didn't make any more trouble for Sam during breakfast, but when Sam returned to his cell, his blanket was gone. No clothes. No blanket. Even if they closed the door and lit the stove, the temperature would not get above 50 or 60 degrees. But the door remained open, the stove without fire. While the other men tried to sleep, Sam paced back and forth in his cell, wearing nothing but his shoes.

At first Sam thought he would catch cold, then possibly pneumonia. But he didn't. He paced back and forth until he was too weary to continue, then he let himself collapse on his cot until he woke up shivering. Then he would resume his pacing.

At first his naps were short—five or ten minutes, at most. But his body adapted and he began to sleep longer and longer until he could sleep deeply and soundly several hours, even at night when the temperatures inside the cell block dropped close to freezing. With nothing to keep him warm, Sam was amazed at how well he learned to sleep and how quickly his body adapted. With time, he would wake up feeling rested and refreshed, ready to resume his incessant pacing, the only way to keep warm when he wasn't sleeping.

He was a wolverine in a cage, pacing back and forth, back and forth, hour after hour, day after day. The only escapes were the occasional naps and the twice-a-day trips to the dining hall.

With time, however, Sam realized he was fighting a losing battle. While his naked body adapted amazingly well to the cold temperatures, he realized he was burning more energy than he was taking in at the prison meals. Upon entering the prison there had been very little fat on his body. Now there was none, and the reserve energies his body was demanding were coming from muscle and other tissues. His arms and legs were getting thin. His stomach had a gaunt, caved-in look. His ribs became more clearly defined every day. His once powerful neck was becoming little more than a stem. While his chest and back seemed to be growing more hair—possibly a reaction to the cold, much like a horse or dog grows a thicker coat in the winter—the hair on his head was beginning to shed, with more falling out every day.

Sam knew what the problem was. The message from his gaunt stomach came through loud and clear. He wasn't getting enough food. He knew that if this regimen continued, he would die.

Other prisoners noticed his worsening condition and tried to slip him an extra crust of bread, a few beans, or part of a potato. But they had to be careful. Once when Wolfstein caught a man giving Sam a slice of apple, the man was cut to half rations for three days.

Whenever coffee, always black without sweetening or cream, was served with the food, Wolfstein made a point of spitting in Sam's cup, saying he was flavoring the coffee. While Sam did not throw any more coffee on Wolfstein, neither did he drink it.

With time Sam realized that he was in a battle of pride with Wolfstein. To drink or not to drink the coffee with the spit in it was the contest. What bothered Sam the most was that the other prisoners were suffering in part as a result of the conflict. While the guards had begun to light an occasional fire in the woodstove, they made no effort to keep it going all the time, particularly on cold nights when most of the time the door was still left open. Sam didn't like the thought of his problem bringing misery to the other men. But at least they had uniforms and blankets.

The inmates of Cell Block B polarized into two groups. The first was those who wanted Sam to drink the spit-flavored coffee in the hope the doors would close and the stove would stay lit. Whenever Sam had an opportunity to speak with Moroni, on the way to or from the dining hall, the old patriarch always told him to drink the coffee and get it over with. "You are no good to anyone dead," the old man would say. "Don't need to prove anything to Wolfstein, anyway. He's worthless, but as long as he holds the keys, a gun, and the soup ladle, you just do as he says, biding your time, maintaining your strength, waiting for the opportunity to go home. That's all that's important here."

The other group was composed of those who encouraged Sam to hold out regardless of the consequences. These were the ones who said, "Don't let Wolfstein win, or next week he'll be doing it to someone else. When spring comes you will have whipped the bastard." These were the men who tried to slip Sam pieces of food, who encouraged him by saying that Detroit sometimes had early springs. Once spring arrived the punishment would be ineffective. Wolfstein would have been beaten by a man in chains.

Late on a particularly cold night, as Sam was pacing back and forth in his cell, a voice called to him from the next cell.

"Storm, here's a midnight snack."

A hand appeared in the dim starlight, tossing something into his cell. Sam hurried over to pick it up, his mouth already watering, thinking he had been blessed with a crust of bread. Tears of gratitude filled his eyes. He was so hungry, and his stomach had been growling for what seemed like hours.

But this time it was not a crust of bread. It was too soft, almost furry. And warm. A freshly killed chicken?

No. It was not a chicken, but a rat, a big gray one, still warm. Someone had caught it in their cell and had passed it on to the hungriest man in Cell Block B.

At first Sam was repulsed at the idea of eating a rat. What diseases might it carry? But as he resumed pacing, kneading the warm, lifeless body between his hands, he estimated that perhaps the small body carried a quarter pound of meat or so. He hadn't had that much meat in weeks. Meat was meat. A starving man couldn't be too selective. He supposed there was as much food value in rat as beef—perhaps more. It was a rodent, and he had eaten plenty of rabbits. Rodent meat could be very tasty and nourishing.

Still, Sam wasn't ready to eat a rat. Maybe if he had a fire and could roast it. But there was no way to cook it, and the thought of eating raw rat—well, Sam didn't think he was that hungry. Or was he?

A week earlier he had tried to eat a cockroach. It hadn't been so bad crunching through the crusty outer shell, but when the soft insides had oozed onto his tongue, he had had to spit the roach out.

A rat would be better than a cockroach—taste more like foods he was used to. If only he had a fire, and salt and pepper.

After pacing back and forth for another hour or so, Sam began to think that maybe it wouldn't hurt to just taste the rat, to see if he could handle the rodent meat. After all, he was starving. Spring was still a couple of months away. He feared he wouldn't be able to hold out that long with only prison fare. He needed extra food. There were more rats where this one came from. Some of the prisoners would catch them for him. Perhaps the rats would enable him to hang on, to defeat Wolfstein.

But how did one skin a rat? He didn't have a knife or anything sharp—only his teeth. Holding his breath, Sam bit into the rat's soft underbelly, taking care to tear the skin without disemboweling the creature. That accomplished, he used his fingers to pull off the entire skin in one piece.

Carefully, he then disemboweled the animal over his waste bucket, saving the skin. In the event he began to eat rats on a regular basis, eventually he would have enough of the little furry hides to make a warm shirt.

Knowing it would be light soon and that the better he could see it, the harder the rat would be to swallow, Sam bit into one of the thighs, tearing away as big a piece as possible.

At first he thought he would just swallow without chewing, but then changed his mind. That was a mistake. The stringy flesh had more flavor than he had figured on. Kind of a ripe skunk taste, he thought. The more he chewed, the more apprehensive he became about swallowing. His stomach was beginning to growl and churn. There was a dry, heavy feeling in his throat. He was getting sick.

Sam reached for his bucket. There was enough light now for him to see the rat entrails in the bottom, mixed with his own waste. He might have stood the putrid sight alone, but such ugliness combined with an equally ugly smell was more than he could bear. Sam began to retch uncontrollably into the bucket.

When finished, exhausted from the dry heaves, he threw the rest of the rat and the skin into the bucket. As hungry as he was, he was not hungry enough to eat raw rat meat and figured he never would be.

Maybe Moroni was right. Maybe he was too proud. Wolfstein didn't matter, except that he was standing in the way of Sam's return to Utah. Kathryn, and being with her, were the things that mattered. No more would he let his pride distract him from a much more important objective, that of getting out of this place and returning to Kathryn. He decided to drink the coffee. Wolfstein had won, and it didn't really matter. Why, then, did he feel like crying?

The next morning Sam spaced his entry into the dining hall so as to sit next to Moroni.

"I'm going to drink his coffee today," Sam whispered when they were seated.

"It's the right thing to do."

"Why?" Sam said, figuring he already knew what

Moroni would say, but wanting to keep the conversation going and keep his mind off the humiliating thing he was about to do.

"Because we've got to get you strong for the journey back to Salt Lake. I'm getting you out of here."

That wasn't what Sam expected to hear, but before he could ask Moroni to explain, the guards were coming down the aisle with breakfast—boiled brown rice with a slice of pork, and black coffee. As usual, Wolfstein was ladling out the coffee.

As had become the custom, the guard made a special ceremony of filling Sam's cup and spitting in it. Then he placed the cup on the table in front of Sam, who acted his usual self, staring straight ahead, doing nothing. Not expecting anything different, Wolfstein moved on to the next group of cups.

"Wolfstein," Sam called, standing up, holding the steaming cup towards the burly guard. Wolfstein turned around, glaring, expecting an insult that would force him to dole out more punishment on this stupid Mormon.

"A toast to your good health," Sam said, smiling. The room was silent. Every head was turned towards Sam, some of the eyes glancing nervously at the guard.

Slowly Sam raised the cup to his lips and swallowed deeply. "Mmm," he said. "Just like Mother used to make, but more flavor. Sir, you may spit in my coffee any day." Raising the cup to his lips once again, Sam swallowed the entire contents.

Some of the inmates cheered; others booed and hissed. Wolfstein grinned over what he figured was a hard-earned victory. Sam sat back down at the table and began wolfing down his rice. The rest of the men soon quieted down and resumed eating.

As they were filing out of the hall, no one noticed that the cup in front of Moroni's plate was still full.

"Would you have done it if I hadn't switched cups with you?" Moroni whispered.

"Yes," Sam said.

Chapter 31

Those who are convicted invariably regard themselves and are regarded by the Church as martyrs. When one is convicted, the usual announcement in the organ of the Church is that he has been convicted of "living with his wives" or of "living his religion!" Those eminent in the Church who have been convicted of sexual crimes (cohabitation or polygamy), on emerging from the penitentiary, have in some instances been met at the prison doors by brass bands and a procession with banners, escorted to their homes to be toasted, extolled, and feasted as though it were the conclusion of some brilliant and honorable achievement, rather than the expiration of a sentence, an expiation for a crime committed against the laws of the country. . . .

It is not regarded as any disgrace by the Mormons of Utah to have served a term in the penitentiary for any of the sexual crimes prohibited by the laws of Congress. On the contrary it is regarded as a badge of merit, and as entitling the persons so convicted to promotion in the Church, as has been the case in some instances.

—Message and Documents, Department of Interior, 1889-90, 3:184

Later in the day a guard delivered a clean uniform and blanket to Sam's cell. Sam never thought he would feel so grateful at being allowed to put on a prison uniform. He held the blanket in his arms for hours, not wanting to let it out of his grasp. He was looking forward to a glorious night of sleep and rest.

A fire was even built in the woodstove, and the outer door was kept closed. For the first time in weeks, the cell block was bearable. It felt so good to be warm, to not have to pace incessantly. Sam marveled at how luxurious one could feel sitting in a warm room.

But the best event of the entire day occurred after the evening meal. Moroni was allowed to return.

It was wonderful to sit back and talk to someone. The lonely, endless hours of pacing had ended. Conversation with Moroni tasted as good as beefsteak.

Sam and Moroni had a good laugh over switching the coffee cups and made an oath not to tell any of the other prisoners. They couldn't chance word getting back to Wolfstein.

"At breakfast," Sam said, "you were starting to say something about us getting out of here."

"Got the key in my pocket," Moroni whispered, reaching into his trousers.

"The key to this cell?" Sam asked.

"The key to getting out of this prison," Moroni said, pulling his hand out of his pocket, reaching towards Sam with a closed fist and finally opening it, palm up. There was no key, only a brown rock crisscrossed with white lines.

"Are you joking?" Sam asked.

"No," Moroni said. "This is my seerstone and it's going to get us out of here."

"I suppose you're going to throw it at the walls and like a cannonball it's going to knock them down."

"Don't mock sacred things," Moroni warned.

"I'm sorry," Sam said. "It's just that for a minute I thought you had something. . . ." He paused, not sure how to finish the sentence without further insulting Moroni.

"You don't believe much in seerstones, do you?" the old man said.

"If you want an honest answer, I don't, except for translating old records, maybe. Never seen one work."

"Let me tell you something. We possibly wouldn't even have the restored church today if it weren't for stones like this. Joseph Smith was using seerstones long before the Book of Mormon was translated or the church was organized," Moroni explained.

"The way I got the story, Joseph was first shown how the stones work by a man from Dartmouth College who looked at his stone in a hat. The old man could see things underground, like running water for wells. He even saw buried treasures. Joseph looked into the hat and saw the location of his own seerstone. With the help of his brothers, he dug it up. Joseph joined with some other men who were using stones, and they entered into an agreement to help each other find buried treasures.

"As they began finding treasures, they also found that the treasures were guarded by spirits—sometimes evil ones. Treasures would disappear. Tools would be lost. Holes would fill mysteriously with water. Strange things were always happening. Joseph and his friends began dabbling in white magic to bring the spirits under control so they could get the buried treasures. There's even one story of a spirit in the form of a white salamander or toad guarding one of the locations. Don't know if I believe that.

"One thing led to another and Joseph began having spiritual manifestations. He found the gold records from which the Book of Mormon was translated. Having received a divine calling, he could not share the gold plates with his treasure-seeking comrades. They became angry and came after Joseph."

"Wait a minute," Sam said. "Why haven't I heard any of this before?"

"You have, but not the whole story. The whole story brought nothing but persecution on the heads of Joseph and his followers. The way I understand it, about 1838 a watered down version of the origins of Mormonism was published. While not the whole story, it was generally accurate and much more palatable to protestant America.

"But when you know the whole story, you find seerstones like this in a central role. Joseph said every man should have a seerstone. All the early brethren did. Ask any of the old-timers still around if they have a seerstone. You'll be surprised how many of them do."

"But how's that rock going to help get us out of here?" Sam asked.

"I'm not sure yet," Moroni said, "but some things are happening, and I have a feeling they are going to work out to our benefit."

"What do you mean?"

"Remember the fat guard, Oz, the man with the long mustache?"

"Sure," Sam said. "He checked me in the first day."

"A week ago he saw me looking into my hat at the stone and asked what I was doing. I told him a little about the stone, and he asked if I could see anything about him. I looked for a minute, then told him his wife needed him."

"What did you see?" Sam asked.

"I didn't really see anything. Just had a feeling his wife was in some kind of trouble."

"What happened?"

"He went home and found the woman with another man. A big fight broke out. Oz sent them packing."

"And?"

"Oz is now a firm believer in the rock."

"And that's going to get us out of here?"

"Just might," Moroni said, a puzzled look on his face, "but I'm not sure how just yet."

"Any ideas?"

"Oz has heard some of the stories about Joseph's treasure-hunting adventures and the gold plates. He's got it in his head that this seerstone and I are going to locate him a buried treasure."

"Can you do it?"

"Never found treasure before, but I told him I would try."

"What kind of things do you see in the stone?"

"Usually just common things like how my wives and families are getting along. If one of my children gets hurt, I usually see that."

"Seriously?"

"Of course."

"Can you see how my wife Kathryn is getting along?"

"I can try," Moroni said, removing the black hat from his head, turning it upside down, and dropping the stone inside.

He asked Sam where Kathryn was likely to be staying, if she worked in a business, how many brothers and sisters she had. Sam answered all his questions.

Moroni sat on the edge of his cot, placing the hat between his knees. He then bent forward, placing his face over the hat opening, peering intently at the stone. He didn't move or say anything for several minutes.

"She has long, black hair," Moroni said, still looking into the hat. Sam couldn't remember telling Moroni what she looked like. He didn't think he had.

"She's sitting by a window. Outside there are trees."

"That would be our front room," Sam said.

"She's writing, perhaps a letter to you."

"Yes, she would do that. Is there anyone else in the room?"

"Can't see anyone. She looks very sad. She's been crying. She lost her baby."

"You'd better not be spoofing me," Sam threatened.

Moroni looked up from the hat, a surprised look on his face.

"Why would I do that?"

"I don't know," Sam said. "I only know that Kathryn has no living children and that almost getting this one, then losing it, has been hard. She needs me."

"I'm sorry," Moroni said. There was a surety in his voice that Sam didn't miss. Something inside Sam told him the old patriarch wasn't playing with him, that the old man's spiritual gifts were real.

"I've got to get out of here," Sam said.

"You will in a few years," said a strange voice through the cell door. Sam spun to face the stranger. It was Oz, the fat guard.

"Your friend will get out too," Oz continued, "but before old Moron leaves, him and me are going to use that peep stone to find us a buried treasure."

Chapter 32

Wednesday, August 4 (1886), at 6 in the morning, in company with Jas Moyle, passed through the gates a free man. Exchanged my convict garb for my own clothes. Met my sons, Frank and Clarence and Orson Romney. Put my things in the shop wagon. Jumped in the buggy with Frank and drove to town. It was a most lovely sight after five months confinement. Arrived home in time for breakfast. Had a joyful meeting with my family, and after dinner went to the shop and went to work.
—Journal of George Hamilton Taylor

"I see something that might be gold," Moroni said, some hesitation in his voice. He was sitting cross-legged next to the cell door, his hat in his lap as he peered at the seerstone. The big guard Oz was pacing back and forth outside the door like he was the one in jail.

"I see a lot of gold bars," Moroni said.

"What are they in?" Oz demanded.

"The container is dark and rough," Moroni continued without looking up. "Perhaps old wood, but I think it's stone."

"Where is it?"

"Can't really tell," Moroni said. He was much calmer than Oz. "Looks like there are stones around the box and dirt—no, mud. Yes. I know where it is."

"Where?"

"Underground. It's buried."

"But where?"

Moroni didn't answer for several minutes, still looking into the hat and occasionally turning it to the right, then to the left. Oz continued to pace back and forth, repeating "Where's it buried?" every few seconds.

"Best I can figure," Moroni finally responded, "is that it's around here somewhere. Perhaps in Detroit, but not very far away. I've never done this before. I'm not sure I can locate the exact spot. It's beginning to fade. My eyes are getting tired."

"How many? How many?"

"How many what?"

"How many bars are in the box?"

"Oh. Let's see. Six side by side across the top. Three lengthwise in front of the six. That's nine to a layer. It looks like either five or six layers. That would be 45 or 54 bars."

"Wow," Oz exclaimed. "That would be hundreds of pounds. How big are the bars?"

"I can't tell," Moroni said. "They could be four or five inches long, or maybe only two or three. There's just no way to tell. I can't see anything of a known size to compare them with. The bars are getting dimmer and dimmer; I can hardly see them now." He withdrew his face from the hat, straightening his back and rubbing his eyes.

"What good is that peep stone if you can't tell where stuff is?" Oz asked, obviously irritated that Moroni couldn't give him any detail as to the location of the treasure.

"Patience," Moroni said. "You don't turn spiritual gifts on and off. They only come a piece at a time, precept upon precept, if at all."

"What's that supposed to mean? You're not going to find the gold?"

"Not necessarily. I saw more today than yesterday. More yesterday than last week. Seems to be a matter of focus. I can see very well up close, but as I try to draw back to see where the treasure is, things get out of focus. With time, maybe, I'll master that. Then we'll know where it is."

"I'll be back tomorrow," Oz said.

"He'd probably be able to concentrate better," Sam

said, "if he wasn't so hungry all the time. Bring a loaf of bread with you tomorrow."

"Do you really think that would help?" the guard asked.

"No doubt about it," Sam said, winking secretly at Moroni.

"I don't know if bread would give me as much strength as a good piece of meat, like a roast chicken or a side of beef ribs," Moroni said, taking the cue.

"If you hadn't tipped me off about my wife, I'd think you was working me for a free meal," Oz said.

"You've got to give Moroni a good reason to want to find the gold for you," Sam said. "Besides freedom, there's no better way to a prisoner's heart than through his stomach. You know a prisoner would do almost anything for some good food. Here's your chance to put Moroni in your debt. If you bring him enough food he just might give you the whole treasure and not take any for himself."

"See you tomorrow," Oz said as he lumbered off.

"What are you trying to do?" Sam asked when Oz was out of earshot.

"Get us a decent meal," Moroni smiled.

"No, I mean with the stone and all this talk about treasure. You really don't see any gold in that hat, do you?"

"You still don't believe in the visionary power of seerstones, do you?"

"You don't expect me to believe all this talk about gold bars being stashed in a stone box around here somewhere."

"Oz believes it."

"Oz is a fool."

"You really think so?"

"Yes, but not fool enough to take you out of this prison looking for buried treasure, if that's what you're trying to set him up for."

"No," Moroni said simply.

"Then what are you trying to do?"

Before Moroni had a chance to answer, a key turned in the big lock, and another guard announced it was time for breakfast. The morning fare consisted of lumpy cornmeal mush without milk, and black, unsweetened tea.

"I'm half tempted to spit in your cup again just to make sure you learned your lesson," Wolfstein said as he filled Sam's cup.

"You do and I'll throw it in your face," Sam thought, but he held his tongue. Instead he said, "I only want to get along, sir. If you spit in it, I'll drink it. Don't want any trouble, sir."

Wolfstein looked at Sam a second, then handed him the cup. He did not spit in it.

"Good attitude, prisoner. I don't want any trouble either."

"Then why did you spit in it in the first place?" Sam thought as Wolfstein moved down the aisle.

Why had the bully backed off when he knew he had Sam right where he wanted him, subdued and willing to drink spit?

Sam wondered if because of the recent conflict he had won a little respect for himself and made Wolfstein reluctant to set him off again. In drinking the coffee Sam had ended the conflict without Wolfstein losing face. Maybe next time it would be different. Wolfstein wasn't about to find out.

Sam wondered if Wolfstein had noticed the switched cups. It was possible, but he wasn't about to ask. All he knew was that the conflict had ended, and that the bully Wolfstein no longer wanted to spit in his cup. That was enough.

The next morning as Oz waddled down the aisle towards Moroni's cell, he carried what looked like a rolled up blanket under his arm. He was whistling quietly as if nothing was out of the ordinary.

"Here's the clean blanket I promised," he said, loud enough for the other guards to hear. He unlocked the cell and after tossing the blanket inside quickly closed the door and locked it.

"Can't stay now," he said, his voice much softer, "but I'll be back in a couple of hours to see how the peep stone is working today." He turned and disappeared.

Sam and Moroni could hardly believe their good luck. Unfolding the blanket, they found an entire loaf of fresh baked bread, two whole roasted chickens, and a flask of apple juice. Not a word was spoken as they gulped down every last morsel.

"When he comes back, what are you going to see in the hat?" Sam asked.

"Don't know," Moroni said. "That's up to the stone, you unbeliever."

Chapter 33

The "Mormon problem" claimed wide attention in the public press, from which came varied interpretations and suggestions for its solutions. From New England, home of Radical Republicans who had played leading roles in the southern reconstruction, came warnings that the Utah situation threatened repetition of the tragic events of the 1860's (Civil War).

—GUSTIVE O. LARSON

"The Americanization of Utah for Statehood"

"I can see now that it's about 20 feet below the surface," Moroni said, looking into his hat. Just outside the cell, Oz was holding onto the grate with both hands, his face pushed tightly against one of the square openings.

Sam was sitting at the back of the cell, finishing off the last of the cinnamon rolls and milk, keeping his eye on a cold piece of pork he was going to work on next.

"The surface of the ground is smooth," Moroni continued. "No bushes or trees or grass, just well-packed dirt and gravel, perhaps a place where people walk."

"Where is it?" asked an excited Oz. There was a white square on his face from pushing it against the opening.

"Patience," Moroni cautioned in a calm voice without looking up. "Hmm. I see a stone wall—a tall stone wall—about ten feet away. And there's a gray block building on the other side of the hole."

"Any signs or lettering on the building or wall?" Oz asked.

Sam had eaten the meat off the piece of pork and was now gnawing on the bone.

"No signs or street numbers. Nothing like that," Moroni answered. "But the building and wall look strangely familiar. I've seen them before."

"Not in Salt Lake?" Oz asked.

"I don't think so. It's got to be a lot closer than that, but I can't be sure."

Oz let go of the door and started pacing.

"I don't think we're ever going to find it," he said.

"Oh, ye of little faith."

"Well, if we haven't figured out the exact location by tomorrow, I'm not bringing any more food," Oz threatened.

"I've been seeing a little more each day," Moroni said. "I think by tomorrow we might have the exact spot."

"You'd better."

"Some ham and potato salad might help," Sam suggested.

Without responding, Oz marched off down the hall.

The next day Moroni went right to work. While Sam enjoyed the potato salad and ham, the old patriarch seated himself on the floor by the door, placed his hat between his knees, dropped in the stone, then leaned forward and placed his face against the hat opening.

"I know where it is," he said after only a few seconds.

"Near the prison?" Oz asked.

"No, it's not *near* the prison," Moroni said.

"It isn't?" Oz said, disappointed.

"No," Moroni whispered, looking up from the hat. "It's in the prison yard."

"No!" Oz exclaimed. Sam stopped chewing.

"Remember the building I described?" Moroni asked.

Oz nodded.

"It's the prison dining hall. About midway along the back outside wall, halfway to the outer wall."

"About 20 feet down," Oz said.

"Maybe 22 feet," Moroni added.

Without another word, Oz ran towards the outer door

and disappeared.

"You're going to have one very angry guard on your hands," Sam said. "He'll probably throw you in that hole and cover you up before he's through."

"You don't have any faith in me at all, do you?"

"Don't see any sense in all this buried treasure business."

"You enjoyed the food, didn't you?"

"Of course."

"Trust me, then."

The next evening as Sam and Moroni entered the dining hall, they dropped out of line to peek around the corner of the building, where they saw some large, wide boards covering the ground about midway along the back wall, between the dining hall and the outer prison wall.

During the meal they noticed that all the guards, including Oz and Wolfstein, had mud on their boots—not a normal situation, there being gravel walkways around the prison yard.

"Hope you enjoyed all that good food," Sam whispered. "Unless you come up with something fast, they'll kill you. Maybe me too."

"How deep do you suppose they are?" Moroni asked.

"Probably only a couple of feet. Ground's awful rocky around here. May take them three or four days, maybe even a week to get down 20 feet. After that we're in trouble."

"And if they find the gold?"

"If they do, they won't share it with us or let us go. Might give you another chicken. Looks like we lose either way."

"I don't think so," Moroni said. "When they get down about ten feet, how are they going to get in and out of the hole?"

"They'll probably have to bring in a ladder," Sam said.

"That's what I was thinking."

Chapter 34

The days between indictment by the grand jury and almost certain sentencing, following a brief trial, were precious ones for cohabs caught in the widespread legal net. Personal affairs could be set in order and arrangements made for care of the family during the breadwinner's absence. In this he usually found substantial neighborly assistance which represented church policy. The Brethren on the underground relayed instructions through stake presidents and ward bishops that "the families of those brethren who are imprisoned and those who have been compelled to flee should be looked after."

—GUSTIVE O. LARSON

"The Americanization of Utah for Statehood"

Two days later when Sam and Moroni left their cell for the evening meal, their loose-fitting uniforms were bulkier than usual, but no one noticed. And the condition wasn't because of overindulging on Oz's food. The big guard, after finding the location of the treasure, had not brought any more food.

Before going to the dining hall, Sam and Moroni had slipped out of their uniforms, wrapped the blankets tightly around their bodies, and climbed back into the loose-fitting uniforms. There was a two-fold purpose for wrapping in blankets. In the event they succeeded in getting over the wall, the blankets would help keep them warm during the cold winter night. Just as important, the blankets, once removed from under the uniforms and wrapped Indian-style around the outside, would cover the attention-getting black and white stripes.

As the prisoners hurried into the dining hall, Sam and Moroni slipped out of sight around the corner of the building. Sure enough, one end of a ladder was extending from the hole.

They backed up against the building, breathlessly considering their opportunity for freedom. It was nearly dark.

"Have you given much thought as to how we might get away once we get outside the wall?" Sam whispered.

"Since I was the one who got us the ladder," Moroni said, "I thought you might take the responsibility of keeping us from getting caught once we get out."

"We won't have much time," Sam said. "After supper the prisoners will be marched around the yard, then returned to their cells. That's when the guards will discover we're missing. We have an hour at most."

"Ready to try it?" Moroni asked.

"Kind of like kissing your sweetheart for the first time," Sam said. "No matter how much you want to do it, and no matter how much you've thought about doing it, it's still hard to muster the courage."

"What do you think they'll do to us if they nab us outside the wall?" Moroni asked, staring straight ahead at the ladder.

"Hope we never find out," Sam said, suddenly leaping forward towards the ladder, Moroni close behind. Trying to be as quiet as possible, they pulled the ladder from the hole, leaned it up against the wall, and began climbing, Sam in the lead.

The ladder wasn't quite long enough to reach the top of the wall, so Sam had to stand on the top rung and pull himself up with his hands. Once Moroni was up, Sam reached down and carefully pulled the ladder up and over the wall, slowly lowering it down the other side. By placing the ladder on the outside, it would take longer for the guards to figure out Sam and Moroni were outside the prison walls.

"I wonder how the guards will explain that hole to the

warden,'' Sam said as he worked the ladder into position for their descent.

''Or the ladder,'' Moroni snickered. ''The warden will want to know how it got in the yard.''

''Oz and Wolfstein might end up in our cell,'' Sam said as he placed his foot on the top rung of the ladder. Both could hardly keep from laughing as they descended to the ground. After sliding the ladder under some low-hanging tree branches where it would be hard to see, they jerked their blankets out from under their uniforms. With the blankets draped over their shoulders to cover the stripes of their uniforms, they began running south across the frozen fields. Fortunately there was no snow on the ground.

''Got about another half hour,'' Sam puffed when they stopped to catch their breath. They had covered perhaps two miles. ''Hope they spend an hour or so looking inside the prison before they come outside.''

Moroni was so winded he didn't say anything. Leaning forward with his hands on his knees, he was fighting for all the oxygen he could get. That's when Sam saw the horses.

Four of them were nibbling at the frozen turf in a large field fenced with barbed wire. Had there not been a full moon in the clear winter sky, he would not have seen them.

Removing his blanket, Sam tore two narrow strips off one end. ''Wait here,'' he said, handing his blanket to Moroni. He crawled between the wires, explaining, ''If I can catch you a horse, you won't have to run anymore.''

''Stealing horses is against the law,'' Moroni protested. Like most Mormons sent to prison on cohabitation charges, he didn't consider himself a criminal.

''So is breaking out of prison,'' Sam said. ''After you do so much, you just have to keep going.'' Moroni offered no further protest.

Sam walked towards the horses, speaking to them in a soft voice. When they saw him coming, they snorted and began galloping away. But they stopped after a short distance, facing Sam, ears forward, heads high. It was as though they'd suddenly realized he was just a man and didn't mean them any harm. A tall bay mare stepped forward, thinking perhaps this stranger had a treat for her. Under his breath, Sam thanked the Lord for his good fortune. The horses—at least the big bay—were broke and had been handled gently enough to make them easy to catch in an open pasture.

Sam stopped walking, still talking to the horses. The bay mare continued towards him, her confidence increasing at every step. Two steps away, she stopped. Inching forward, still talking, Sam reached out slowly with his right hand and began stroking the mare on the neck, very gently at first, but firmer as she continued to stand still. Slowly he reached under her neck with his left hand, holding one end of the blanket strip. Reaching over the top of her neck with his right hand, he grabbed the blanket end and drew it towards him. He tied a quick knot; the mare was his. After rubbing his hands over her neck, shoulders, back and hind quarters, he was satisfied she was no wild horse. He led her towards Moroni, the other horses following curiously behind.

After handing the mare's tether to Moroni, Sam caught another horse, a buckskin gelding.

"How will we get them through the fence?" Moroni asked, taking the lead rope to the second horse too. "I think the only gate is over by the house."

"Don't want to go over there," Sam said. There were lights in the windows of the home, and because it was still early in the evening, there was a good chance someone would be moving around the yard doing chores.

"We'll jump them," Sam said. He tore another strip from his blanket and began wrapping it around the top two strands of barbed wire, midway between two fenceposts. He pulled the blanket tighter and tighter until the two wires were almost touching.

After securing the blanket ends in a tight knot, Sam moved the horses to where the wires were pulled closest together. Trying the bay mare first, Sam got behind her and began to twist her tail as Moroni pulled on the lead rope from the other side of the fence. At first she balked, digging in. She didn't like the increasing pain in her tail. Moroni wouldn't let her move her head to either side. Over the fence was the only way to get away from the tail twisting. Dropping back on her hind quarters, the mare half reared and lunged forward, clearing the wires by at least a foot. With the bay mare leading the way, the buckskin didn't need as much coaxing. The moment Sam touched his tail, he reared and jumped.

With both animals outside the fence, Sam removed the blanket strip from the wires and stuffed it inside his uniform. Next he removed the blanket strip from the mare's neck, ran one end through her mouth, tied it snugly around her lower jaw, and tossed the free end over her neck.

"That's the way the Indians do it," Sam said as he helped Moroni onto the horse. A minute later Sam had secured the other blanket strip to the buckskin's lower jaw and had leapt upon the gelding's back.

Urging their animals into an easy trot, Sam and Moroni headed south along a deserted lane.

Chapter 35

As was the case with other Mormons in my position, our offense was not looked upon even by non-Mormons acquainted with the circumstances as containing the element of crime; but our incarceration was in fact an imprisonment for conscience's sake. . . . A term in the penitentiary under those conditions and at that time, while a severe hardship, especially upon one in my state of health, was by no means a moral disgrace, since those who had to endure it were of the better class of men, whose uprightness, honor, integrity, and sincerity were beyond question in the community where their lives were an open book.
—JAMES S. BROWN
"Life of a Pioneer"

"My knees are killing me," Moroni complained after he and Sam had been riding about three hours. It was nearly midnight, and they were traveling through a sparsely wooded area with few farm houses, most of them totally dark by now. When dogs barked, Sam and Moroni just continued their pace as if they were normal travelers.

Both men slipped to the ground, continuing to lead their horses in a southerly direction. That's when Sam saw the darkened farmhouse with drying laundry still hanging out on a long clothesline.

"Looks to me like somebody left out a change of clothes for us," he said. A minute later Sam was crawling along a split rail fence towards the house. Moroni stayed behind with the horses, rubbing his aching knees.

Sam waited several minutes at the edge of the yard, watching for any sign of a dog. None appeared, so he crept forward and removed two shirts and two pairs of trousers from the line. A few minutes later he and Moroni slipped out of their stripes and into their chilled, partially frozen new clothes.

Sam stuffed their striped uniforms into some thick bushes growing along a small creek. Even with their blankets wrapped around their shoulders, both were shivering, so they led the horses for a mile or two to warm up. Upon remounting, they changed their direction from south to west. After considerable discussion they decided to go to Chicago, a journey they thought would take about a week. In Chicago the plan was to sell the horses for enough money to buy train tickets to Utah.

Though Moroni continued to be bothered by his knees, he rarely complained as the horses trotted westward throughout the night. Having changed out of their prison garb, he and Sam weren't so worried about being seen. Still, as the dawn approached they discussed leaving the road and taking cover before daytime travelers began appearing on the road. Besides, they were bone weary. In the warmer daytime hours, sleeping would be easier. They were hungry too but, having no money, they weren't sure what they were going to do about that.

In a mostly uninhabited area near what they figured was the Ohio border, they left the lonely road and headed at an angle into what appeared to be thickening timber. Their plan was to find an isolated clearing where they could stretch out in the morning sun and sleep without fear of being discovered.

Just when Sam and Moroni thought they were far enough from the road to be safe, they suddenly came upon a woman chopping furiously at the ground with a pick. Beside her on the ground was a shovel. She was a young woman, perhaps in her early 20's, with long, uncombed black hair brushing loosely across her face as she hacked intently at the ground. She was wearing a man's coat over a long, pink dress. There were overshoes on her feet, but no gloves on her hands, nor did she have a bonnet.

She was so intent at her task that she did not see Sam and Moroni ride from the trees. Sam's first inclination was to make a hasty retreat before the woman discovered them, but before he could turn his horse around, Moroni spoke to the woman.

"That hole would be a lot easier to dig in the afternoon when the ground isn't frozen," he said, tipping his hat when the woman looked up.

Sam thought she had a pretty face—or at least it would have been under normal circumstances. As it was, the woman's eyes were red, possibly from rubbing or crying, and her nose was running from the cold. She had a hurt look on her face that did not go away when she looked up at the two strangers.

"My man can't wait until afternoon," she said coldly.

"I don't understand," Moroni said.

"Passed away yesterday and I've got to get him in the ground."

"Why clear out here?" Moroni asked.

"Cabin's right over there," she said, pointing through the trees to a small but new cabin Sam and Moroni hadn't seen earlier. There was no smoke coming from the chimney.

"This was a favorite spot of his," she said. "We used to have picnics here."

"We'll help you," Moroni said, slipping down from his horse and reaching for the shovel. "I'm Moroni Hess and this is Sam Storm. We hold the holy priesthood of God and will give your man a proper burial."

Sam looked away, biting his lip, wondering why Moroni didn't have enough sense to make up some phony names. Next thing, he would tell her how he and Sam had just broken out of the federal prison at Detroit—unless Sam told her something else first.

"On our way back to Chicago," he said, slipping down from his horse. "Had business in Detroit. Some men stole our saddles and supplies last evening. That's why we're riding bareback."

''Thanks,'' she said, handing Sam the pick. Her mood was warming.

''I'm Ramona Kelly. Henry had a green tree fall on him day before yesterday.''

''You don't have any neighbors or a minister to help out?'' Moroni asked.

''Just moved here last month from Pennsylvania. Hardly know anyone. Closest neighbors are six miles away. I just didn't feel like leaving him.''

Moroni shoveled the dirt out of the growing hole as Sam picked the soil loose. They worked fast, becoming warm with the effort, and soon had to shed their blanket wraps. When they were finished, they walked Ramona back to the cabin.

''Didn't build a fire last night,'' she explained. ''Didn't know when I'd be able to bury him, and didn't want him to start smelling.''

''Want to bury him now?'' Sam asked as they entered the two-room cabin. The body was not in the front room with the table and woodstove. Sam guessed the man was in the next room.

''Yes,'' she answered, ''as soon as possible.''

''He's a big man,'' Moroni said when they entered the next room and saw the body stretched out the entire length of the bed. He was wrapped in a patchwork blanket.

''The grave's a long way away,'' Moroni said. ''How were you going to get him there? You couldn't carry him by yourself.''

''Got two mules,'' she said. ''Figured to drag him.''

''You're a resourceful woman,'' Sam said.

''Do the best I can.''

Sam bent over to take hold of the body. Ramona put her hand on his arm. ''Please—not yet,'' she said. ''Let me look at him one more time.'' Sam and Moroni backed away as Ramona slowly pulled the corner of the blanket away from her man's whiskered face. Cocking her head slightly to one side, she affectionately drew her hand down over his forehead and made sure his eyelids were closed all the way. The face was pale, almost blue, especially above the brow, where a hat had always shielded him from the sun. Ramona leaned forward and gave her man one last kiss on the lips. Tears were running down her cheeks and Moroni's too.

Moroni helped Sam lift the stiff body onto his shoulders. As soon as it was balanced, Sam turned and headed for the door. The body was heavy, and if he was going to make it all the way to the grave without a rest, there was no time to lose.

"Do you have a Bible?" Moroni asked.

"No," Ramona said. They followed Sam out the door and down the path to the grave, where Sam lowered the body to the ground. He and Moroni jumped into the hole, then gently lowered the body to its final resting place.

After they climbed out of the hole, Moroni removed his hat and bowed his head.

"May I offer the prayer?" he asked. Ramona nodded as she and Sam lowered their heads and closed their eyes.

"Our Father in Heaven," Moroni began, a slight tremble in his voice. "We gather here this winter day to dedicate this piece of earth as the final resting place for Henry Kelly, a young man who brought his bride to this beautiful place to start a new life. Their hopes and dreams of a lifetime together were shattered by a falling tree. It isn't fair, Lord, and I don't know how it can be right." He paused.

"But we accept thy will in all things," he said, his voice becoming meek, "and dedicate, consecrate, and set apart this piece of ground as the final resting place for Henry Kelly in the hope he will come forth in the first resurrection to be reunited with this good woman who was his companion and helpmeet. And Lord, we ask thee to watch over this woman as she seeks new direction in life. We, thy servants, will stand by, ready to provide whatever she needs. . . ."

Sam didn't hear the rest of the prayer, wondering what the consequences would be of Moroni's promise to help this woman. They were 40, perhaps 50, miles from the Detroit prison. Search parties would be looking for them, and now Moroni was promising the Lord they would take care of Ramona Kelly.

Chapter 36

Joseph (Smith) had a stone which was dug from the well of Mason Chase, twenty-four feet from the surface. In this stone he could see many things to my certain knowledge.
—MARTIN HARRIS

When Moroni finished his prayer, Ramona was the first to shovel dirt on her husband. Sam and Moroni finished the job.

They returned to the cabin, where Ramona agreed to let Sam fix a breakfast of pancakes, bacon, and eggs. All were hungry, and very tired. There was little conversation during breakfast.

After the meal, Ramona thanked Moroni once again for the fine prayer he had said over Henry's grave, then retired to the bedroom for much-needed sleep while Sam and Moroni stretched out on the living room floor beside the woodstove, using their prison blankets for mattresses. Before going to sleep, Sam went outside and moved the buckskin and bay to a remote meadow where they could not been seen from the cabin. In the event someone came by, he didn't want the horses raising suspicion. When he returned to the cabin, Moroni was already snoring.

Sam was awakened by voices in mid-afternoon. A greatly refreshed Ramona and Moroni were seated at the plank table, talking quietly.

"It contained over $60 and I just can't find it anywhere," she was telling Moroni.

"We'd make you a loan, but we don't have any money either," Moroni said.

"It was the last of our savings," Ramona continued. "Plenty to get me back home to Ma and Pa in New York, but I just can't find it. Henry was so afraid someone might steal the money box that he just hid it too well."

"You didn't think to ask him about it before he died?" Moroni asked.

"No. I thought it was under a board in the chicken pen. That was where we first hid it. But Henry had been doing some work in there, and apparently moved it without telling me. I just don't have any idea where it might be. I've looked everywhere."

"We'll see if we can help you find it," Sam said, sitting up. Sam, Moroni, and Ramona spent the next hour searching every inch of the chicken pen, the shed where the harnesses and wagon were kept, the cabin, and the neighboring woods. They looked everywhere without success.

When they returned to the cabin, a subdued Ramona began fixing supper. Sam and Moroni were seated at the table, conversing quietly.

"After supper we should be on our way," Sam said.

"We can't leave this woman alone, her man hardly cold in the ground."

"We can't stay," Sam said. "Got to put more miles between us and that prison."

"I think we're less likely to be discovered here than out on the road," Moroni protested. "Everyone will be on the lookout for us. Let's stay hidden for a few days, until the search slows down."

"I don't like staying in any one place too long. It's too risky."

"Then go," Moroni said. "I'm staying. I promised the Lord I'd help this woman out of her trouble, and that's what I intend to do."

Sam had no intention of leaving the man who was responsible for getting him out of prison, so he reluctantly agreed to stay for a day or two.

"What was your business in Detroit?" Ramona asked

when she returned to the table with a steaming platter of ham and fried potatoes.

"Business with the government," Moroni said. Sam was getting nervous, wondering what the old patriarch would say next. The old man wouldn't lie to the woman.

"I train and sell horses to the Army," Sam said, pleased that he had come up with a truthful statement too, one that hopefully would put an end to the questions.

"Oh," Ramona said, obviously pleased. "Then you might be interested in buying my mules."

"We were robbed of all our money," Sam explained.

"But when you get back to Chicago you could get some more. I don't have any pressing appointments. I could wait."

"I told you we were going to Chicago and that is correct," Sam explained carefully, "but our real home is Salt Lake City. We couldn't go there and back just to buy two mules, but we might be able to help you sell them."

"That would be wonderful," she said. "Then I would have enough train fare to get home." So Sam and Moroni agreed to help Ramona sell her mules.

"You wouldn't be Mormons, would you?" she asked, after they had been eating for a while.

"Yes ma'am," Moroni said proudly.

"Polygamists?" she asked.

"I have two lovely wives," Moroni answered, not hesitating to admit he was breaking the law.

"And you?" she asked, looking at Sam.

"I only have one wife," he said. Lydia wasn't really a wife, not after how she had turned on him in court. Besides, they had never consummated the marriage. To Sam, the sealing to Lydia had been annulled before it had become real.

For the next hour, Moroni talked freely about his two wives, how well they got along with each other, how much he missed them, and what a happy reunion they would all have upon his return. Ramona seemed to like listening to Moroni, but Sam didn't. The old man talked too much and made him nervous. Moroni didn't seem worried about getting caught.

It was almost dark when they heard the neigh of a horse off in the woods. Sam was the first one out of his chair, hurrying to the little window. Two riders were less than a quarter of a mile away and approaching quickly.

"Riders coming," Sam warned as he began to clear the dishes from the table.

"What are you doing?" Ramona asked.

"Don't want them to know we're here," Sam said.

"Why not?" the woman asked.

Sam knew he was trapped and was surprised Moroni was keeping his mouth shut. He didn't see any way out of the situation except to tell Ramona the truth, then hope she would not turn them in.

"We escaped from the Detroit prison yesterday," Sam said, looking Ramona in the eye, worried how she would take the news. Without taking her eyes from Sam, she pushed her stool back and stood up.

"Are you really Mormons?" she asked.

Sam and Moroni both said yes.

"You were in prison for practicing polygamy?"

"That's right," they said.

"Get in the bedroom," she said. "I won't turn you in." She turned and quickly hid the remainder of the dishes under the sink.

A moment later there was a knock at the door. Sam and Moroni couldn't see the faces when Ramona opened the outside door, but when one of the visitors asked, "Ma'am, may we talk to your husband?" Sam instantly recognized the voice of prison guard Rudolf Wolfstein.

Chapter 37

In the year 1822, I was engaged in digging a well. I employed Alvin and Joseph Smith to assist me. . . . After digging about twenty feet below the surface of the earth, we discovered a singularly appearing stone, which excited my curiosity. I brought it to the top of the well, and as we were examining it, Joseph put it into his hat, and then his face into the top of his hat. . . . The next morning he came to me and wished to obtain the stone, alleging that he could see in it; but I told him I did not wish to part with it on account of it being a curiosity, but would lend it. . . .

In April, 1830, I again asked Hiram for the stone which he had borrowed off me; he told me I should not have it, for Joseph made use of it in translating his Bible.

—WILLARD CHASE

"Ma'am, with your husband gone and two convicts on the loose, you shouldn't be here alone," Wolfstein cautioned as he and his companion seated themselves at the plank table. Ramona had already told them about her husband's death and that she hadn't seen any convicts. Sam and Moroni were listening from the next room, their ears against the door.

"Isn't there a neighbor you could stay with until we catch them?" Wolfstein asked.

"Are they dangerous?" Ramona asked innocently.

"Very dangerous."

"Are they murderers?"

"No, they are Mormons." There was a finality in his voice, as if nothing more needed to be said.

"How does that make them dangerous?" Ramona asked.

Wolfstein looked over at his companion.

"Mormons believe in polygamy," he said, as if it were a great revelation.

"I know that," Ramona said, getting annoyed. "How does that make them dangerous?"

"Because you're a single woman, alone, and would be a prime target for their perversions if they knew you were here."

"What would they do to me?" she asked, her voice once again innocent.

"Try to force you to become a plural wife and go with them to Utah," he said carefully, as if he were afraid to offend Ramona's sensibilities.

"Heaven forbid," she said mockingly. "What would they do if I refused?"

"Take a Danite oath and slit your throat."

"I think I'll go stay with the neighbors like you suggested," Ramona offered. "I have some hot water on the stove. Would you like a cup of tea before you leave?"

"Thank you, ma'am," Wolfstein said. "It's mighty cold out today. That would be very kind of you." Ramona got up from the table, checked the water on the stove, and removed the last two clean cups from the cupboard.

"Got another cup in the next room," she said. "Be back shortly."

Upon entering the bedroom, she smiled teasingly at Sam and Moroni, who were standing nervously behind the door. She retrieved a red metal cup from a box in the corner and was almost to the door when Sam motioned for her to stop. He reached out and took the cup from her. Holding it up to his lips, he very quietly spit in it. Ramona was both surprised and disgusted.

"For Wolfstein," Sam whispered, handing the cup back to her. She looked questioningly at Sam. "For Wolfstein," he whispered again with determination. Ramona shrugged her shoulders, opened the door, and re-entered the front room.

"Is rosehip tea all right?" she asked as she poured the boiling water into three cups.

"I'll drink anything," Wolfstein said, "as long as it's hot and has a little sugar in it."

Behind the door, Sam and Moroni exchanged smiles.

Ramona returned to the table with three steaming cups, two white and one red. She gave the red one to Wolfstein, a white one to his companion, then sat down to sip tea with the two guards.

"Best rose tea I ever drank," Wolfstein said.

"Thank you," Ramona said, smiling.

Before leaving, Wolfstein reminded her to go to the neighbors until the Mormons were behind bars again. He promised to stop by the next time he was in the area.

When the deputies were out of sight, Sam and Moroni ventured from the bedroom.

" 'I'll drink anything as long as it's hot,' " Sam mimicked, " 'and has a little sugar. . . .' "

"And some spit in it," interrupted Ramona. They all laughed.

" 'Best rose tea I ever drank,' " added Moroni. They laughed again.

This was the first time Sam and Moroni had seen Ramona relax and enjoy herself. Though she was still mourning the death of her husband, it was good to see a smile on her face.

Ramona rinsed out the cups and made some fresh rosehip tea.

"Ramona, what are you going to do?" Sam asked, deciding it was time to get serious. Ramona, in no hurry to answer, sipped carefully at her hot tea.

"Think I'll go home to the folks," she finally said. "Help them on the farm a while, then start over. Maybe find another man. Perhaps it's a good thing Henry and I didn't have any children."

"How will you get home? Your folks live in New York, don't they?"

"Yes," she said. "Guess I'll just hitch up the mules and drive home. Only problem is I don't have any money, not a penny."

"What do you need money for?" Moroni asked.

"Tolls to get across the rivers, grease for the axles, shoes for the mules, a place to stay at night. It's too cold to sleep in the wagon. Besides, I'm alone. Maybe I can sell some of my personal belongings along the way."

While she was talking, Moroni got up from the table and walked over to the door, where his hat was hanging on a peg. Hat in hand, he returned to the table and placed the hat in front of him. Reaching into his pocket, he pulled out the seerstone.

"What are you doing?" Sam asked.

"Going to find her money box," the old man said, dropping the stone into the hat, leaning forward and covering the opening with his face.

"What's he doing?" Ramona asked Sam.

"Trying to find your money."

"In his hat?"

"No. Sometimes he can see things in the stone. He's trying to see the location of your money box."

"Are you serious?"

"I don't know if I am," Sam said, "but he is."

"Has it worked before?"

"He says it has."

With his face over the hat opening, Moroni seemingly did not hear any of the conversation between Sam and Ramona.

Sam told Ramona about Joseph Smith finding and using a seerstone, and how it helped translate the Book of Mormon from golden plates found in a stone box on a hill in New York. Ramona had heard about the golden bible before, but never the seerstone. She was politely curious, not wanting to offend the old man who was merely trying to do her a favor.

"No wonder we couldn't find it," Moroni said, finally raising his face and looking enthusiastically at Sam and Ramona. "Henry didn't hide it around the house or shed. It's out in the woods."

Neither Sam nor Ramona said a word.

"Unbelievers," Moroni scolded, goodwill still in his voice. "You'll see." He pushed his chair back, put on his coat, and stepped outside.

"Do you want the lantern?" Ramona called after him.

"I've seen the exact spot. Don't need any lantern," Moroni said confidently and disappeared into the night.

"Want to place any bets?" Sam asked. Ramona just laughed.

"Impossible," she said.

A few minutes later Moroni pushed the door open. He was grinning, and under his left arm was a gray metal box.

"I believe this is your money box," he said, dropping the box onto the table.

"It is!" Ramona gasped.

"Are you sure you didn't find it this afternoon," Sam asked, "and just wait until now so you could show off your stone?"

"Oh ye of little faith," Moroni chastized.

Ramona opened the box, which contained a marriage license and silver dollars. She began stacking the coins in piles of ten each until they were all counted.

"Sixty-seven dollars," she said. "More than enough to see me home." She pushed one of the piles of ten towards Moroni, another towards Sam. "You'll need money too. It's a long way to Salt Lake."

"The Lord will provide for us," Moroni said, pushing the money back.

"Yes," Ramona said, pushing the money back to him, "and he is doing it through me. I wouldn't have any money if it weren't for you."

"Thank you," Moroni said meekly as he put the ten silver coins in his pockets.

"Are you sure?" Sam asked.

"I'm sure," she said.

"I saw something else in the stone," Moroni said as Sam pocketed his silver dollars.

"What?" Ramona asked. Sam remained silent, wondering what Moroni was going to come up with next.

"I saw you, Ramona, happy and content in Salt Lake City."

"No," she laughed. "It must have been someone else—someone who looks like me."

"No, it was you," Moroni insisted. "Come with us to Salt Lake."

"Absolutely not!" This time it was Sam speaking. "We're escaped convicts, and if she were caught with us, she'd go to jail."

"What would I do in Salt Lake?" Ramona asked, her voice soft, seemingly ignoring Sam's emphatic remarks.

"Marry a good man and raise a family," Moroni said.

"Do you have anyone in mind?" she asked.

"Sure do." Moroni said.

"Who?"

"Sam Storm."

Sam and Ramona looked at each other, a hint of blush on both faces.

"He already has a wife," Ramona said without thinking.

"That's not a problem in Mormon country," Moroni said. They laughed.

"I think you should go home to your parents," Sam said, "and read the Book of Mormon. Then, if you believe it's true, let us know and we'll help you get to Utah."

"I'll do that."

"Sure you don't want to come with us now?" Moroni asked.

"I'm sure," she said with finality.

Ramona helped Sam and Moroni prepare a satchel of food. She also insisted they take her husband's gloves, a hat, and several pairs of socks.

Sam and Moroni each gave Ramona a hug, thanked her for the supplies and money, and wished her good luck on her trip. She stood in the open doorway, smiling and waving as they disappeared into the night, hoping to cover another 40 or 50 miles before daybreak.

Chapter 38

The great tabernacle was filled with waves of sound as the "amens" of the congregation burst out. The shout of men going into battle was no more stirring than the closing words of this memorable conference. . . . Acquainted though I am with displays of Oriental fanaticism and western revivalism, I set this Mormon enthusiasm on one side, as being altogether of a different character; for it not only astonishes by its fervor, but commands respect by its sincere sobriety.... The very simplicity of this great gathering of country folk was striking in the extreme, and significant from first to last of a power that should hardly be trifled with by sentimental legislation.

—PHIL ROBINSON of the New York World,
describing General Conference in the Tabernacle
after passage of the Edmunds Bill in 1882

Madge was the first to go into labor. With Priscilla and Stella to care for her, no one anticipated any problems. The three women were comfortable in Ben's stone hideway near a small stream that meandered towards the Green River. Ben and Flat Nose George kept the women supplied with meat, mostly deer and elk, and lump coal from a nearby vein that surfaced in the edge of a cliff. While the three women shared the cabin, Ben and Flat Nose George lived in a canvas tepee the Indian had made from materials provided by John Jex.

It was late December when Madge's pains began. With it being her first child and her not knowing what to expect, she was not overly alarmed.

It was a gray morning with snow beginning to fall. Ben had been off hunting since before daybreak. Flat Nose George had not yet emerged from the tepee. Though Stella and Priscilla were not experienced in the art of midwifery, both had been around enough births to know the basics. After making Madge as comfortable as possibly on a crude grass mattress, they proceeded to heat water and assemble a neat pile of recently washed rags for keeping things clean and to tie off the umbilical cord.

"I didn't think it would hurt so much," Madge moaned when she had been in labor well past the mid-day mark. Priscilla and Stella were getting worried. Ben was still in the hills and, barely more than a boy, there was little he could do anyway.

"Get George," Madge cried, limp and relaxed after another siege of labor. Her black hair was damp with perspiration.

"Can't have a man in the cabin while you're in this condition," Priscilla said nervously. Two kettles of water had already boiled away. The fire to keep the water boiling had created so much heat that the cabin's only window was wide open, even with the snow falling outside.

"Maybe he's got more of that painkiller, the firewater," Madge gasped as a new wave of pains cut off her breath. Without waiting for Priscilla to say anything, Stella rushed out the door to find Flat Nose George.

The old Indian was in the tepee, crouched cross-legged in front of the fire, staring blankly into the flames. When Stella told him Madge was in labor and wanted some firewater, he said he didn't have any but had something that would be better for her. Removing a leather pouch from his saddle bag, he followed Stella to the cabin.

Taking a quick look at Madge, George moved to the stove and sprinkled some light green leaves and stems into the boiling water. A minute later he poured some of the brew into a cup, cooled it with some cold water, and took it over to Madge, who was between labor pains. Propping her head up with his arm, George began pouring the steaming brew into her mouth.

No sooner had he begun than Madge began coughing and spitting the drink all over her bedclothes.

"What are you trying to do, poison me?" she screamed.

"Drink," was Flat Nose George's only reaction, bringing the cup back to her lips.

"Too bitter," she said, trying to push the cup away. But he was stronger than she was. Finally she gave in to his persistence, holding her breath while she swallowed several times. George put the cup down when she began a new wave of labor pains.

"Time to have baby," he said to Priscilla.

"Excellent observation," she said sarcastically.

"Time to have baby," he repeated, as if he expected Priscilla to do something she wasn't already doing.

"What do you want me to do?" Priscilla asked, irritated at being told what to do by a man, and an Indian at that. This was women's work.

"Can't have baby here," George said.

"Well, she's not going outside to have it in the snow. Is that what you make your squaws do?"

"Don't mean outside," he said, realizing the white women were content to let Madge just lie there on the mattress until she pushed the baby out.

"Baby needs help," he said, getting up and heading for the door. Neither Stella nor Priscilla said anything. Madge was writhing in pain.

A minute later George returned with a rope and tied one end to a piñon rafter. He grabbed a large piece of kindling wood, which he tied crossways through the rope with three half-hitches about five feet off the floor. Then he turned to Priscilla and Stella.

"Madge too tired," he said. "Can't push hard. Mother Earth must help."

Priscilla and Stella had no idea what George was talking about, but when he took Madge by the arm to help her to her feet, they both hurried alongside to help. Even though they didn't know what George wanted to do, they responded to his confidence. He seemed so sure that Mother Earth could help, whatever that meant.

Upon reaching the dangling rope, George got Madge to grab the stick with both hands and hang, her knees barely touching the floor.

"Get down on floor and help baby out," he said to Priscilla. Now she understood. By Mother Earth helping, he meant gravity. With Madge now hanging in an upright position, the force of gravity would help pull the baby down. Priscilla dropped to her knees, lifting Madge's nightgown. George retired to a chair to watch.

"It's coming!" Priscilla screamed. She was leaning forward, both arms under Madge. Stella was on her knees on the other side. When Priscilla straightened up, still on her knees, she was holding a blue baby. Stella worked quickly, tying off the umbilical cord and cutting it with a knife. The baby began to cry. Madge let go of the stick and collapsed to the floor, exhausted and relieved. George and Stella helped her back to her mattress while Priscilla wiped the baby clean and wrapped it in a blanket.

"It's a boy," Priscilla said, placing the infant in his mother's arms.

"What are you going to name him?" Stella asked.

"George," Madge said weakly, looking up at the Indian.

Flat Nose George was grinning.

Chapter 39

There never was a time probably in our history when the Latter-day Saints needed more than they do at present the assistance which God has promised.
—Mormon Church First Presidency
December 2, 1889

It was the middle of a moonless night, and a bitter north wind was sweeping down off the stone bluffs when Ben heard the cry. He sat upright, still wrapped in his buffalo robe, shaking his head to consciousness, pushing away the sleep. Across the fire from him George was still sleeping soundly. Ben could hear the deep breathing. He could also hear the flapping of the tepee canvas in the cold wind, but that was not what had awakened him. The small tepee fire between him and George had burned out, nothing remaining but a dull, barely visible orange glow.

The cry had sounded human, but Ben couldn't be sure. Perhaps it had been a wolf or a coyote. Still, he was used to their cries and wasn't usually awakened by them.

He still wasn't sure if the cry was real or something from his already forgotten dreams. Then it occurred to him the cry might have come from the cabin. But it wasn't the sound a baby would make. Perhaps something was wrong with one of the women.

It wasn't until Ben slipped into his coat that he noticed Lobo was missing. The big wolf dog usually spent his nights curled up just inside the tepee entrance.

"Lobo, come here," Ben called as he slipped his boots on. The dog did not come.

Ben crawled outside into the blackness, holding his coat tight against the bitter wind. The cabin's only window was black.

Ben pounded on the door. There was no immediate answer. Finally a sleepy Stella pulled back the bolt and opened the door just enough to hear what was wanted.

"Is something wrong?" Ben asked. "Did someone cry out?"

"No," Stella said. "Do you want to come in?"

"No. Heard a cry. Just checking. Is Lobo inside?"

"No. Haven't seen him."

"I'll check down by the stream," Ben said, turning into the wind. Stella closed the door and bolted it tight.

Without a moon, Ben could see very little. Upon reaching the flat, graveled stream bed, he called again for the dog, waiting, listening. Except for the howl of the wind and the gurgling of the ice-clogged water, he could hear nothing. He began to shiver from the cold.

He was just turning to return to the tepee when he heard the unmistakable splashing of feet in water downstream. Not the galloping sound of a horse, but a wolf or dog. "Lobo," he called once more.

A few seconds later the big dog was at his side, panting from a fast run. When Ben reached down to pet the dog, Lobo stepped away, not towards the tepee or cabin, but downstream, in the same direction he had just come from.

"Come," Ben said, "let's go back to the tepee." He turned towards the tepee and began walking. When the dog refused to follow, Ben realized there must be something downstream that was worrying the dog. He turned and walked towards Lobo, who in turn spun and ran downstream. Ben followed as fast as he could, occasionally stumbling in the blackness. He continued to listen for the cry to repeat itself, but heard nothing.

Ben hadn't gone more than a few hundred yards when he heard the dog bark behind him and off to one side. In the darkness he hadn't noticed where the dog had left the flat stream bed to head up onto a sagebrush flat. Ben hurried towards the sound of the bark.

He finally located Lobo at the base of a huge boulder, barking and yapping as he danced about. Ben wished he had brought a lantern. The dog's behavior told him something was at the base of the boulder, but it was too dark to see.

Ben dropped to his knees, cautiously feeling in front of him. He touched something cold, like a piece of wet canvas. He felt further. It was frozen clothing. He touched a cool, unconscious face. No whiskers. Long hair. It was a woman. He moved one hand along the rough, frozen clothing. He thought he could feel a heartbeat. Her stomach was flat. At least she wasn't pregnant. He picked up the unconscious woman and hurried back to the cabin, Lobo leading the way.

Without putting the woman down, Ben kicked against the cabin door. When Stella pulled back the bolt, he pushed inside. "Light some candles," he ordered. "This woman's unconscious. Got to get her warm, get her out of these frozen clothes." Priscilla and Madge crawled out from under their warm blankets and helped Stella undress the woman while Ben lit the candles.

A minute later the unconscious woman was stretched out on one of the grass mattresses under a pile of blankets. Stella and Priscilla were under the blankets too, pressing their bodies against the woman in an effort to share their body heat with her. Madge was busy at the stove, heating up some soup.

The unconscious woman was young, no more than twenty. She had long hair, strawberry in color, like a sorrel horse. Neither Ben nor any of the women recognized her.

When the soup was hot, Stella and Priscilla held up the woman's head while Madge began pouring the steaming broth into her mouth.

"Drink," Madge ordered in a loud, firm voice. Coughing weakly, still unconscious, the woman began to swallow. Her eyes remained closed.

With nothing more to do, Ben returned to the tepee, rolled up in his buffalo robe, and went back to sleep.

The next thing he remembered, he was awakened by

George stirring up the fire. It was light outside. Ben waited until he could feel the warmth against his face before sitting up and slipping on his boots. While he was doing that, George was arranging two green sticks across the fire, upon which he balanced a partially cooked side of venison ribs. Ben told him about the half-frozen woman he and Lobo had found during the night, and how he had carried the unconscious body back to the cabin.

"Think I'll see how she's doing before I join you for breakfast," Ben said as he crawled outside.

"How is she?" he asked as he entered the cabin. He could see the woman under a pile of blankets, apparently still unconscious. The other three women were up and dressed. Madge was nursing her new baby.

"She's sleeping," Priscilla said. "She's breathing deeply. There's no temperature or coughing. We've gotten soup down her a couple of times. Think she just needs more sleep to get her strength back."

"Any idea who she is?"

"No. She hasn't talked at all."

"Let me know if she wakes up," Ben said, returning to the tepee.

George tossed the first rib to Lobo, cut one off for Ben, then one for himself. Neither man spoke as each gnawed on the juicy, smoke-flavored meat. Ben was just finishing his third rib when he heard the cabin door swing open.

"She's awake," Stella called.

After wiping the grease from their hands and faces, Ben and George hurried to the cabin. When they entered, the new woman was seated at the table, sipping a cup of broth. She looked a little pale, but otherwise normal. She looked up at Ben.

"This is the young man who saved my life?" she asked of the other women, not taking her eyes off Ben.

"Ben Storm," Stella said, "I'm pleased to introduce you to Nellie Russell."

"Thank you for saving my life."

"Pleased to meet you," Ben said. He couldn't recall having heard her name before. "Why are you here?"

"I'm a reporter for the *Anti-Polygamy Standard,* the *Salt Lake Tribune,* and several Eastern newspapers," she said, an official note in her voice. The women gasped. "I've come to interview the notorious Mormon Robin Hood, the reckless young man who shot two deputies in the foot while helping pregnant plural wives escape the law."

While flattered at being compared to Robin Hood, Ben was disturbed by Nellie's boldness. She didn't sound like a woman who had been at the edge of death a few hours earlier. But even more, he was disturbed that she had found the hideout. If she knew where it was, others probably knew too. Maybe the cabin was no longer safe.

"Who else knows you're here?" Ben asked.

"I don't think it would be wise to tell you that," she said.

"Hell of a way to talk to the man who just saved your life," Ben thought. "You're not welcome here," he said.

"As soon as I've interviewed you, I'll be returning to Salt Lake."

"You'll be doing neither," Ben said, turning and heading out the door.

Chapter 40

The time is coming swiftly when there is going to be surrender.
—The Salt Lake Tribune, February 18, 1883

Nellie followed Ben out of the cabin. She was wearing a yellow dress belonging to Priscilla, because her own dress, along with her undergarments, was hanging on a rope to dry.

"I'm sorry for being so rude," she said. "I just want to ask you a few questions."

Ben didn't answer as he slipped inside the tepee. She crawled in after him. "I promise I'll write a fair story."

"Who knows you're here?" Ben asked a second time.

"I would feel safer if you didn't know that," she said, making herself comfortable on George's buffalo robe, across the fire from Ben.

"I've got two pregnant women and a mother with a brand new baby in that cabin," Ben said, looking her in the eye. "The women are wanted by the law. It's winter. New storms pass over every few days. Those women and the baby shouldn't be out in the weather, but they're not going to jail, either. If half the deputies in Salt Lake are following you up this canyon, I've got to know."

"Don't worry, nobody's following me," she said.

"Why should I believe you?"

Nellie explained that the *Tribune* had received a tip from a spy in Springville who said David Butler and Grace

Woolley had left that town by way of Spanish Fork Canyon to join Ben Storm and the pregnant plural wives somewhere near the Green River crossing. That was all the informer knew.

Against the advice of Harry Chew, who preferred Nellie limit her interviewing to deputies Owen and Vandercook, Nellie got on the train for Price and Green River.

After spending a day in and around Price and failing to find anyone who had seen a white man and an Indian with three pregnant women, she caught the next train heading east. She persuaded the train to stop at the Green River crossing so she could question the Chinese who were living in the shacks by the trestle.

When the Chinese said they had seen Ben, the Indian, and three women at the crossing about a month earlier, and that they had headed north along the river, she waved the train on without her. The Chinese said a man and a woman had gotten off the train the day before and had headed north along the east bank of the river. Nellie was sure they were Butler and Woolley. After purchasing some food and a blanket from the Chinese, she crossed the trestle and headed north, eventually finding Ben's trail. Most of the horse and mule tracks had been washed away, but seven horses had left enough droppings for her to follow without difficulty.

"I passed David and Grace at the first cabin, the one by the river," she explained. "They didn't see me, though I suppose when they started out again they saw my tracks. I thought maybe I would get a better interview if I reached you first. I kept thinking it wasn't much further, so I just kept going. By the time the storm hit, about the middle of the third day, my food was almost gone, and I was out of matches. My blanket became wet, and I was soaked all over. I knew I couldn't make it back. I didn't want to go to David for help."

"Why not?" Ben asked.

She explained how she had come to Utah from England to marry David Butler, and how she had broken off the engagement when he had greeted her with another wife at the train station.

"It was a horrible surprise," she said. "I wasn't about to become his second wife. I don't want anything more to do with the man. He didn't tell me about the other wife before I left England.

"So I just kept following your trail. When it got dark at the end of the third day, I didn't have the strength to continue or go back. I couldn't build a fire. I knew I would die if I didn't get help. There was nothing else I could do, so I just screamed as loud as I could and lay down to die. That's when you found me, I suppose, though I can't remember. Nobody knows where I am, except maybe the Chinese. And they just know a general direction."

"How do I know you're telling me the truth?" Ben asked.

"You saved my life. I wouldn't help send you to jail."

"I wish I could believe you."

"I'll write my story here and let you read it. You'll see how fair I can be. There'll be none of the mad-dog, 'bloody killer on the loose' hogwash."

"I read one of the *Tribune* articles about me," Ben said. "It wasn't accurate. It was slanted against me."

"Help me write a fair story," she pleaded.

"Then the *Trib* wouldn't print it," Ben scoffed.

"Yes they would," she said. "Just let me ask you a few questions."

"You'll leave me alone if I let you ask a few questions?" Ben said, suddenly smiling.

"That's a promise."

"Think carefully what you want to ask. I'll only answer three," he warned.

"Oh, thank you."

"Tell me when you're ready to begin," he said.

The conversation ceased for a moment while Nellie gathered her thoughts. She was looking into the fire. Ben was looking at her.

"I'm ready," she said, looking up at him. "Are you sure you won't answer more than three questions?"

"Just three," Ben said, moving his right hand to his cartridge belt and removing two 30-caliber rifle bullets. With the bullets between his thumb and forefinger he reached out across the fire, as if handing them to Nellie. Then, without warning, he dropped both bullets into the fire. Stella had passed the bullet test. He wondered if Nellie would do as well.

"Won't they explode?" she asked in surprise.

"Yup."

"Isn't that dangerous?" she asked.

"Yup." Ben rolled over backwards and pulled his buffalo robe up to shield him from the coming explosions. Following his cue, Nellie rolled back too, pulling up George's robe as the first bullet exploded. The casing zinged against one of the tepee poles and fell to the ground. The second one thumped against the canvas.

"What did you do that for?" she demanded angrily, as she pulled the buffalo robe away from her face.

"That's the third one," Ben said as he began to crawl outside.

"Where are you going?" she demanded. "What about my questions?"

"Only promised to answer three, and I've done that," he said as he walked down to the stream, Lobo trotting ahead.

Chapter 41

We did not reveal celestial marriage. We cannot withdraw or renounce it. God revealed it, and He has promised to maintain it, and to bless those who obey it. Whatever fate, then, may threaten us, there is but one course for men of God to take; that is, to keep inviolate the holy covenants they have made in the presence of God and angels.

—First Presidency Epistle, 1885

Ben wasn't sure what he was going to do with Nellie Russell. He couldn't just let her walk back to the Green River crossing and catch a train to Salt Lake. She would write about the hideout. The authorities would find out where it was and waste no time in going after the man who had shot two deputies in the foot and burned their boots.

As Ben saw it, he had two alternatives. He could let Nellie go, then move the women and baby to a new hideout, an unsafe and difficult undertaking in the middle of winter, or he could keep Nellie around as a hostage until spring, in which case kidnapping would probably be added to the charges against him.

With the time approaching for Priscilla and Stella to have their babies, it didn't seem prudent to attempt to move them, and with Madge's baby so young, it didn't seem like a good idea taking it out in the weather. No, the women and baby would stay right where they were, and so would Nellie.

But how could he keep her? He couldn't tie her up all

winter. With the stone cabin the only building around, he couldn't lock her up. He couldn't watch her all the time, not with coal to get and game to shoot. It wasn't practical for him and George to keep constant watch on her day and night.

As Ben wandered along the small stream, Lobo running back and forth through the sagebrush, looking for a rabbit, Ben began to formulate a plan whereby he could make Nellie Russell his captive and prevent her escape. He turned and headed back to the cabin.

First, he told George of his intentions to move the horses several miles upstream, above a point where the men could build a log barrier to keep the animals from returning to the cabin on their own. Then he marched unannounced into the cabin.

"Take off your shoes," he said to Nellie.

"Why?" Nellie asked, making no move to obey.

"Give me your shoes," he said, his voice quiet but firm, "or I'll take you down and remove them myself."

"You wouldn't do that!"

"Yes he would, honey," Madge warned.

"What do you want her shoes for?" Priscilla asked.

Ben didn't take his eyes off Nellie, who was still making no effort to remove her shoes. "The shoes," he said, taking a deliberate step towards her.

Nellie looked at the other women, hoping to rally support for her resistance to what she thought was an unreasonable demand. She had no idea why he wanted her shoes, but the fact that this bold young man demanded she hand them over was sufficient reason, as far as she was concerned, not to do it.

"Never wrassled with a woman before," Ben said, slipping out of his coat and letting it fall to the floor, all the time keeping his eyes on Nellie.

Finding no support from the other women, Nellie stepped back, feeling very cornered, still not wanting to give up her shoes and puzzled as to why he wanted them.

"Tell me why you want them," she said, her voice sounding like she was about to cry. Her own weakness made her angry. "You just barge in here and demand my shoes like you can just have whatever you want, like a spoiled child. No 'please,' no reason. Well, I won't give them to you."

"I'll give you a reason," Ben said, still calm. "Without shoes you won't be walking out of here to tell the law where these women and I are hiding out."

"I'll give you my word that I won't tell the law where you are, but I'll write my story."

"Please, the shoes," Ben said, holding out his hand.

"This is a free country!" she cried. "I have done nothing to deserve imprisonment. You have no right to detain me. I can come and go as I please."

"But you'll do it barefooted," Ben said, suddenly lunging forward, reaching down to grab her feet.

Nellie was not slow to react, falling back against the wall, striking out with her right foot and kicking as hard as she could. Ben caught the foot in mid-air. Falling to the floor, she kicked at him with the other foot, which he caught in his other hand. With an ankle in each hand, he pinned her tightly against the floor. The hem of her dress was up to her neck. Roughly Ben removed the shoes, then rolled away.

When he looked back at her, he was blushing. Nellie's face was red too, as she quickly pulled her dress down about her ankles. While her clothes were drying on the line, the other women had given her a dress to wear, but no undergarments.

Ben turned away, quickly gathering the rest of the shoes in the cabin.

"What do you want with our shoes?" Madge demanded.

"Nellie could borrow them in the middle of the night," Ben explained.

"But, without shoes, how can we go to the outhouse?" Priscilla asked.

'Very quickly," Ben responded as he disappeared out the door.

Chapter 42

Thou shalt not commit adultery; and he that committeth adultery, and repenteth not, shall be cast out.
—Doctrine & Covenants 42:24

"I don't think I really fell in love with her until after they said I couldn't marry her," David Butler said cautiously. He and Ben were stretched out on a huge flat rock at the end of a long ridge, overlooking the winding valley with the tiny stream and the stone cabin. It was one of those clear, sunny winter afternoons when there is more spring than winter in the air. The sun was warm in a deep blue, windless sky, having already melted all the snow from the south-facing slopes and most of the flat places too. A few crusty patches of white remained on the shady north slopes.

David Butler and a very weary Grace Woolley had arrived on foot the same afternoon Ben had taken the shoes from the women. Ben had immediately recognized Butler as the lawyer who had defended his brother, Sam, in court. Butler was an ally, though Ben didn't like how easily the attorney had found the hideout.

Ben hadn't met Grace before, but had heard about the Mormon pro-polygamy activist through newspaper reports and community gossip. But the woman Ben met was not the aggressive, articulate, fiery zealot he had always imagined Grace Woolley to be. She had a weary, downcast look about her. Ben couldn't put his finger on it, but he sensed the heaviness of her step was more than weariness from four days on the trail.

And she was pregnant, though not yet beginning to show. That was why David Butler had brought her to Ben. The law was after her in an effort to put David, the enthusiastic Mormon defender, behind bars. She needed a safe, quiet place to have her baby. Through John Jex, Butler had learned the location of the hideout.

"I don't know how safe she'll be here," Ben said. "Look how easy you found the cabin. That woman reporter followed you without a hitch, and I wonder how long it will be until a posse comes riding up the canyon."

"All over the territory, women are having their babies in caves, barns and cellars," Butler said. "No place is safe for the pregnant plural wife, but I figured this place was best because you are here."

"I don't need your flattery."

"I didn't mean a shallow compliment. All over, our people are frightened, hiding, and scrambling for safety they can't find. Church leaders are hiding too, to stay out of jail. It's almost panic. And right in the middle of it all, you stand up and say no, pull out your gun, shoot two deputies in the foot, and burn their boots. You're a modern David."

"That doesn't make me a David."

"But what you did has been good for the people. It's given them hope. Good news to talk about. A chance to laugh again. You shooting those deputies was like a beam of light shining under a very dark cloud. Grace is very low and needs to stand in that light."

"You said they wouldn't let you marry her. So she's not your plural wife?" Ben asked.

"No."

Ben was confused. David had brought Grace to the hideout to have a baby. He had naturally assumed the two were married, at least secretly in a plural relationship. Now David was saying they weren't. Ben wasn't sure how to proceed with the conversation. Finally, he asked, "Who is she married to?"

"Nobody." There was a long silence. Ben wasn't sure it was his place to ask any more questions. On the other hand, if Grace was going to be left in his care, maybe he should know the circumstances that caused Butler to bring her to him.

"She's expecting. There's a father."

"Me," David said. There was emotion in his voice. "We've both been excommunicated from the Church for adultery."

Ben hadn't expected this. Butler was one of the prominent young men in the Church, a defender of the faith in the courtroom, respected by everyone. His wife Alice was a good woman from a prominent family.

And Grace. A Mormon zealot if ever there were one. Standing up for polygamy—in the streets, the courtrooms, the newspapers. A faithful defender of the faith too. Now both were on the outside.

"Then why's the law after her if she's not your plural wife?"

"Under the Edmunds-Tucker Law, adultery's a felony. The authorities would notice her pregnancy when she starts to show. I have been seen with her, at night, the two of us alone. If they caught her and made her testify, I'd go to jail."

"What will you do?" Ben asked. "Are you going back?"

"Yes. With Grace out of reach, I'll be safe to continue my work. I still have some cases, though some of the Church authorities are no longer having me defend them. I can't stay here more than a day or two."

"Why wouldn't they let you marry her?" Ben asked.

"For our own good," he said, laughing bitterly. "So we could continue defending the faith without fear of arrest."

Ben thought about asking how it had happened, but decided against it, figuring it was probably none of his business. But David continued.

"I thought it was all over when President George Q. Cannon would not give his permission," David said in a faraway voice, more like he was talking to himself than to Ben.

"After the meeting in Centerville where my request to take her as a plural wife was rejected, I took her back to Salt Lake. It was late, near midnight. It was a quiet ride, neither of us saying very much. I suppose both of us were wondering what might have been, what might have happened between us. Now it was over, me back to defending cohabs, her heading up more rallies.

"But things could never really be the same again. In those few moments during the ride to Centerville, when we had talked of love, of possible marriage—even a polygamous one—something had happened that couldn't be reversed, couldn't be forgotten.

"As we drove back to Salt Lake that night, under the silver light of a three-quarter moon, she looked more beautiful than ever before. I was angry with myself. I had never considered myself in the ranks of those who are irrationally attracted to forbidden fruit, but that is the way it was that night.

"I was angry with Grace for looking so beautiful. I was angry with Alice for suggesting the arrangement in the first place. I was angry with the brethren for rejecting my request to take her as a plural wife. I was angry with myself for not being able to let things return to the way they were.

"Suddenly I was aware of horses approaching from the rear. It was Deputy Vandercook and two of his skunk friends. Probably got wind of the night meetings going on in Centerville and were checking carriages on the road for suspicious circumstances.

"Vandercook ordered me to stop, and when I did, he immediately recognized me. He knew Grace too. You should have seen the big grin on his face, like a hog that had just found an apple in a manure pile.

"Said he always suspected Grace, as handsome as she was, had to be hitched to some polyg, but never figured it was me. Not high enough in the Church. Grace didn't say anything, and neither did I. We both knew it wouldn't do any good to argue.

"When Vandercook said he was going to take us in, I felt trapped, like I had to do something. I just slapped the old horse on the rump and away we flew, Vandercook and his skunk friends chasing us. I knew men who had gone to prison on less evidence than they had on me and Grace. I had to get her into hiding where she couldn't be made to testify. I figured it'd be best for me to lay low for a while too, until things cooled off."

"You can't outrun mounted riders with a buggy," Ben said.

"I know," David said, "but I knew where I could get some help, even in the middle of the night. I headed for Temple Square."

Ben grinned in anticipation of what he thought David would say next. With the temple still under construction, Mormon men were living in tents and cabins at the construction site. These weren't the local Salt Lake men, but workers who came from distant communities throughout the territory to help finish the temple. Away from the tempering influence of their wives and to a man angry over the polygamy persecutions, these workmen could present formidable opposition to anyone attempting to harass a polygamist.

"We approached Temple Square at a full gallop. We made a complete loop past the tents where the men were staying, continuing all the way around Temple Square. Grace was yelling 'Help, skunks!' as loud as she could. By the time we were coming past the tents the second time, sleepy men in long underwear were stumbling about, gathering chunks of granite, residue from the huge stones being shaped for the temple.

"As we raced by, the men pelted Vandercook and his friends with the sharp rocks. Vandercook's horse bolted away from the rock throwers, causing the deputy to lose his seat and fall to the ground. When he tried to run after his horse, he was stopped by a horde of workers who, as I learned later, insisted the deputy lie down while they tended his wounds. They apologized for hitting his horse with the rocks, saying they had been trying to hit the carriage but had missed.

"By the time Vandercook and his companions had wrestled themselves free of the overly helpful Mormons, Grace and I were gone. Knowing it wouldn't be safe to go to her place or mine, and knowing officers would soon be watching for us on all the main roads, I took her to a barn on Seventh East, where I thought we would be safe until we figured out what to do. That's where it happened.''

Ben was sitting with his arms wrapped around his knees, looking out across the valley. He said nothing to encourage or discourage David in telling his story. If David wanted to tell him everything that had happened, that was all right with Ben. David continued.

''We drove the carriage inside the barn, out of sight, and closed the doors. We didn't unhitch the horses, just removed their bridles and gave them some hay. Then Grace and I crawled into the loft, at the front where we could watch the road through the cracks.

''It was a cold November night. Without blankets, it seemed only natural to sit close to each other, sharing each other's warmth. I put my arms around her. We didn't talk about what was happening. We didn't decide to do anything.

''I kissed her, and it could have ended there, I suppose, but she kissed me back. The warmth of her body was like a magnet, pulling me to her with a force that grew so strong I couldn't resist. In the dark we sinned.''

Ben looked over at David, who was now looking away across thc valley. His eyes were moist. He paused, fighting for control of his emotions. Ben waited for him to continue.

''When it was over I wanted to blame anyone but myself. First, President Cannon for refusing to let us marry. Then Vandercook for trying to arrest us, causing us to come to the barn. I even blamed Grace for letting me kiss her, for kissing me back. Grace was quiet, speaking only when spoken to, the rest of the night. I felt horrible, overwhelmed by the consequences of what must follow.

''We went into hiding at various homes in the Salt Lake Valley. I didn't see her for several weeks. We both confessed to the church authorities. A court was held. Both of us lost our membership.

''It wasn't until after we were excommunicated that Grace told me she was pregnant. We were walking away from President Angus Cannon's office. She said it coldly, matter-of-factly. That's the way she has been ever since that night in the barn. I wish she would cry. She won't. I wish she would get angry with me. She won't. I wish she would talk about it. She won't. I'm worried about her.

"After I leave, maybe you can get her to talk to you. Maybe she'll open up to the other women. She's holding a lot of hurt and guilt inside. She's got to let it out. Being around me doesn't seem to help. After I leave, maybe she'll let it out. Please try to talk to her, to get her to talk to you."

"I will," Ben promised.

"I pray every night that God will speak from heaven and order his prophets to give up polygamy," David said, his voice suddenly stronger. "Too many good men are in prison. Too many good women have broken hearts. Too many children are confused. There's too much hate, jealousy, and suspicion. More bad than good is coming of it."

Without warning, David began to smile—a cynical, bitter smile.

"And the next victim will be John Jex, your friend in Springville."

"Why's that?" asked Ben.

"When I was passing through last week he was busy courting himself a new wife."

"How can you be so sure he'll get in trouble?" Ben asked. "John is a careful man, very discreet."

"It's the woman he's courting. No way to avoid trouble."

"Who is she?" Ben asked.

"Can't you guess?"

"No."

"Would you believe Lydia?"

"You don't mean Sam's wife?"

"None other. She's divorced your brother and has John Jex following her around like she was the last woman on earth."

"Someone should talk to him."

"I have."

"And he wouldn't listen?"

"Of course not."

"I don't understand," Ben said.

"You know Lydia, what she looks like."

"Very beautiful."

"That's an understatement. She's a ravishing queen with more sexuality than a hundred ordinary women combined. A woman like Lydia looks at a man, smiles, throws back her shoulders—and the poor devil's got a revelation that she's to be his next wife. She's a black widow, a siren, and when a man like Jex gets her under his skin, no amount of talking can put any sense in his head. That black-haired beauty just keeps spreading her poison.

"As I said before," David continued, as he and Ben rose to their feet and started back to camp, "I pray every night that the Lord will put a stop to polygamy. But I don't suppose he hears my prayers anymore, now that I've committed adultery and been excommunicated." Ben didn't respond.

Chapter 43

The principle of plural marriage, against which the main force of the opposition is being hurled, has been a divine institution from before the foundation of the world.
—Deseret News editorial
April 6, 1885

As soon as David left the next morning, Ben headed up the canyon with George to help bring down two deer the Indian had shot the day before. Lobo accompanied them. With five women, two men and a dog to feed, they needed plenty of meat. Deer, elk, and even mountain sheep were plentiful in the area during winter months. In the warmer months the animals migrated to the higher altitudes to the east.

The deer were several miles up a side canyon, in the middle of a sagebrush plateau. After slicing a hole between the sixth and seventh ribs on both animals, Ben and George lifted one onto each saddle, slipping the saddle horn in the hole between the ribs to hold the deer in place. After securing the feet to each side of the cinch, they began leading their heavily laden horses back to camp.

They hadn't gone far when George stopped in some shoulder-high brush. "Squaw bush," he said. "Good tea for squaws having babies." He proceeded to gather a pocketful of the leaves that had not yet fallen to the ground. These were the same leaves Flat Nose George had used in making the tea for Madge. He told Ben the new babies came out faster and easier if the women drank tea made from the squaw bush leaves. He didn't know why.

About half a mile from camp they noticed Nellie running towards them. Something was wrong. By the time she reached them, she was too out of breath to speak. Ben noticed her feet. With the shoes hidden, she had wrapped rags around them. "Grace, gone," was all she could get out. Ben and George hurried back to camp, Nellie following close behind.

"Which way did she go?" Ben asked as he entered the cabin. No one knew. Grace, wearing a white dress and a gray shawl, had gone to the outhouse and had not returned. She had been gone several hours.

"She's been so quiet," Priscilla said. "She wouldn't open up and talk to us more than the necessary yeses and no's. She's troubled. You'd better find her, and quick."

Ben ran down to the creek bottom. No tracks led downstream, the direction David had taken. No tracks led upstream, either. Ben ran past the cabin to the trail that led up to the cliffs, the same trail he and Flat Nose George followed to get the coal. He hadn't gone more than a few feet along the trail when he spotted the unmistakable track of a barefooted woman. Then another. She was going up to the cliffs.

Ben ran up the trail. Even though the past few days had been warm and sunny, the nighttime temperatures were below freezing. Without a blanket or fire, Grace would probably not last the night. He had to find her before dark. He couldn't figure out why she had gone up the trail. It did not lead anywhere except up to the cliffs. Ben whistled for Lobo. The dog could help find her if her tracks became difficult to follow. By the time Ben reached the top of the first bluff, Lobo was at his side. Ben stopped for a minute to catch his breath.

He looked in every direction but could see no sign of Grace. Her tracks continued up the gentle slope towards a steep ridge. Whenever Ben stopped to make sure he was still on her trail, Lobo would run circles around him, sensing the urgency of the chase, but not yet sure what they were chasing.

They hadn't gone far when Ben spotted something gray

up ahead. He ran to it. It was not Grace, just her shawl, discarded carelessly on the ground. It appeared she had become hot during the climb and had removed the shawl to cool off. Foolish. She would need it as soon as she found herself in the afternoon shadows. Ben picked up the shawl and urged Lobo to sniff it.

Timidly the dog stepped forward, his nose outstretched towards the gray cloth. The smell of Grace was on the cloth. It was the same scent the dog had found on the trail they had been following. Suddenly, he understood. Ben was trying to find the woman who had preceded them up the mountain, the same woman who had been wearing the shawl. Lobo took the lead with Ben jogging behind.

Soon they were on a narrow deer trail winding up into the steep red cliffs. At a point where the trail went right around a rocky corner, Lobo started picking his way onto the upper reaches of a sheer cliff to the left. Ben could see no tracks in the trail, so he followed the dog.

Ben hadn't gone far when he spotted Grace as she could go out on a thin ledge near the top of the 200-foot cliff. She didn't see Ben or the dog. Standing in the late afternoon sun, the cool breeze tossing her black hair lightly across her face, she was looking straight ahead at the horizon.

Ben looked down at the jagged boulder pile below. He knew why she was out on the ledge. Calling Lobo back, he remembered his own confrontation with death a few months earlier. Instead of the poisonous dog bane plant, she had selected a fall from a cliff to end it all.

Ben began working his way along the edge of the cliff towards Grace. He moved cautiously, not wanting to startle her as she continued to stare blankly into space.

It was Lobo's bark that finally caught Grace's attention, letting her know she had visitors. Ben was only a dozen feet away when she turned and saw him.

'Don't come any closer,'' she warned. Her voice sounded calm and strong, not like a woman about to throw her life away. ''One more step towards me, and I'll jump.'' Ben stopped.

''Don't do it,'' Ben said.

At first, she didn't respond. She was just looking at Ben to see if he would try to get any closer. He stayed where he was.

"Go away. Leave me alone."

"Let me take you back to the cabin," Ben said.

"I'm not going back."

"It'll be cold soon. You'll freeze," Ben said, not sure why he was talking about the weather, except that perhaps a change of subject might buy time for her destructive mood to pass.

"The man I gave my body to has deserted me. The church I gave my life to has excommunicated me. I don't have anything else to live for." She was still speaking in a cool, calm voice.

"What about the baby inside you?" Ben asked.

"Do you know what they call a baby born out of wedlock?" There was emotion in her voice now. Anger.

"No," Ben said innocently.

"Bastards. I'm carrying a little bastard. When I step forward I'll be doing us both a favor. I don't want to have a little bastard, and I don't think it wants to be born one, either."

"It's not as bad as you make it," Ben said soothingly.

"I thought that at first, too," she said. "I couldn't figure out how anything that felt so right, so good and natural, could be so evil. But it is. I've sinned and ruined my life."

"You're not evil."

"How do you know?" she asked, again angry. "Have you ever committed adultery?"

"No, but I've tried to take my life—much like you are doing."

"Apparently you failed. How were you going to do it?" she asked.

Ben told her about the dog bane and how he tried to smoke it. How he sat in front of the fire all night, trying to muster the courage to smoke the poison, and how he just couldn't bring himself to do it.

"Do you think I'll do it?" she asked.

"I hope not," Ben said.

"Do you think I have the courage to do it?"

"I hope not."

"I think I do," she said coldly, looking down at her feet. "All I have to do is step forward about six inches and it's all over. It's that simple. Just one step forward."

Ben didn't answer. He was wondering what chance there would be to hurry to her and take her by the arm. He was much stronger than Grace. But the ledge was no more than a foot wide, with no firm places for holding on. If she fought him, they would both fall to the rocks below. Ben was beginning to believe she really intended to kill herself. She didn't seem afraid. She wasn't crying.

"It's just not fair," she said.

"What isn't fair?" Ben asked, wanting to prolong the conversation.

"I've spent the last two years of my life defending the God-given institution of celestial marriage. But when I ask to partake myself, they turn me down. It isn't fair."

"Who says life has to be fair?" Ben said, beginning to feel some anger himself. "I don't know anyone who has had a fair shake all the way through. That isn't the way it is."

"Then I don't want any more of it!" she screamed.

"Things will work out better than you think," Ben said, trying to calm her down.

"I don't believe . . ."

Suddenly she was gone. No warning. No scream. Ben looked down in time to see her limp body float downward onto the rocks. It didn't bounce. It just stopped. There was no sound or movement.

Ben didn't move for a long time. He wondered if things might have been different had he stayed in camp that morning instead of going after the deer with George. David had asked Ben to talk with her. He shouldn't have waited. He wondered why she had been able to take her life when he had not. Was she braver, stronger, perhaps more desperate? He didn't know.

Who was responsible for her death? Ben, for not getting to her in time? Grace, for taking that last desperate step? David, for what he had done to her? The Lord, for asking the people to live polygamy? Or those who persecuted the Mormons for polygamy, not allowing a free people to practice their religion? Regardless of who was at fault, Grace was a victim, a casualty of the turbulent times. When would it end? Who would be the next victim?

Lobo yelped impatiently. The sun was going down, and it was time to leave. Ben worked his way back to the trail, but he didn't return directly to the cabin. He and the dog worked their way down the rugged cliff to the lifeless form in the white dress.

"She will have a proper burial," Ben said as he bent down to pick up the broken body. As he stood upright, the limp body in his arms, the warm blood trickled from her mouth onto his forearm. Lobo pointed his nose upward into the evening breeze and howled.

Chapter 44

Sponsored by the respective chairmen of the Senate and House judiciary committees, it (Edmunds-Tucker bill of 1887) aimed not only at plugging the loopholes in the Edmunds Law of 1882 but included provisions to destroy the Mormon Church politically and economically.
—GUSTIVE O. LARSON,
"The Americanization of Utah for Statehood"

It was after dark when Ben knocked the front door of the cabin, Grace's lifeless form in his arms.

"No!" Stella cried as she opened the door, the light from the lantern shining out on Ben and Grace. "Is she alive?"

"No," Ben said, stepping into the cabin, gently depositing the body on Stella's cot. George, having heard Ben come into camp, followed him into the cabin, closing the door against the night chill.

"Fell off a cliff," Ben said. "Died instantly."

"Suicide?" Madge asked, standing by the stove, holding her sleeping baby close against her breast.

"Can't be sure if she slipped or did it on purpose," Ben responded as he seated himself wearily on the edge of the cot. "Talked about killing herself when I found her, but it happened so fast I can't be sure she did it on purpose."

"Should we bury her here?" Priscilla asked, walking up to the cot to get a closer look at Grace.

"Yes," said Ben. He couldn't just throw her over a horse and take her to Salt Lake. "When you get her cleaned up,

I'll take her outside. We'll bury her in the morning."

"I can't believe it," Stella cried. "She was so beautiful, so brave, so smart. How could she do it? Why?" Ben didn't answer. Stella began to cry. Priscilla, Madge and Flat Nose George just stared at the body.

Ben turned towards the door, then stopped. He suddenly looked back towards the women, a look of concern on his face.

"Where's Nellie?" he asked, an edge to his voice.

None of them would look him in the eye. Madge spoke first.

"She left while you were looking for Grace. Said she was going back to Salt Lake."

"She didn't have any shoes," Ben said.

"She had rags on her feet," Madge returned. "She took a blanket with her."

"Why didn't you tell George?"

"Five in one cabin is too many," Priscilla offered. "She promised not to tell anyone where we are."

"And you believed her?" Ben asked, annoyed and disappointed the women hadn't trusted his judgment, hadn't supported his decision to keep Nellie with them through the winter.

"I'm going to bring her back," Ben said, turning and marching out the door, George following close behind.

"How you find her in the dark?" the Indian asked as Ben saddled both horses, one for himself and the other to bring Nellie home on.

"Should reach the mouth of the canyon by daylight," he said. "If I don't find any tracks there, I'll work back until I find her. If she's gone further than that, I shouldn't be far behind. Can't take any chances on her getting to the trestle."

A few minutes later, Lobo at his side, Ben rode down the dark canyon. He didn't mind losing a night's sleep. After what had happened to Grace, he wouldn't have slept anyway.

As he rode along, letting the horse pick its way in the dark, Ben wondered what Grace's spirit was doing. Had it really left her body and not been snuffed out on the rocks? Was she in some kind of spirit prison or paradise? Was she with loved ones who had passed on before? Was she being punished for her sin? Was what she had done as serious on the other side as it had been in mortality? Was she happier or sadder now that she was dead? Could she see ahead? Did she now know what was in store for her friends and the Church? Did she know how the polygamy persecutions would end? Would the Church be victorious, with the government backing off? Or would the church back off, giving up a divine principle under pressure?

There were so many things Ben didn't know. He wondered how other people could be so sure about the world beyond death when they had never seen or visited the other side. He only knew one thing for sure. When he thought of Grace Woolley there was a great sadness in his heart. There always would be. Her death was tragic and unnecessary.

He also wondered how he would describe Grace's death to David Butler. Should he tell David what she had said about being deserted by the man she loved? Perhaps not. There had been enough suffering already.

When Ben reached the Green River it was still dark and there was no sign of Nellie. He dismounted and stretched out on the soft, dry sand, waiting for the dawn when he could look for tracks. Sleep was still far away, so he listened to the soothing sound of the water as it churned over the huge boulders. Occasionally he could hear the muffled thumping of a boulder being pushed along the rocky bottom.

Lobo snuggled up next to him, the first time the dog had ever done that. Weeks of hunting, bringing in meat and coal and hiking the hills together, had finally won the dog's confidence. Lobo now spent more time with Ben than with Priscilla. A change had taken place. Lobo was Ben's dog now, not Priscilla's, or even George's, though the Indian had been the first to win the animal's confidence. It wasn't that Priscilla had officially given the dog to Ben. She had not. Lobo had decided for himself that Ben was now his master. The dog was still polite and even friendly at times towards Priscilla, but if she and Ben were to take separate paths, the dog would follow Ben instead of his former mistress.

At first light Ben led the horses away from the river towards the mountain, looking for Nellie's tracks. He half-believed he had passed her in the night and would have to head back the way he had come, but right at the very edge of the hill, along a deer and sheep trail, he found fresh smudges that he guessed were made by someone with feet wrapped in rags.

Ben swung up on his black gelding, the same one he had taken from Owen, and trotted downstream, leaning over just enough to keep the tracks in view. Lobo loped ahead.

Lobo was the first to find Nellie, wrapped tightly in her blanket, half buried in the soft white sand, shivering from the cold in a restless half-sleep that had just come upon her after a long, sleepless night. Because her face was buried in the blanket, and because she was near a noisy rapid, she did not hear or see Ben's approach.

Nellie sat up with a jerk when Lobo began to pull at the blanket. She didn't look ready for visitors, her strawberry hair twisted and knotted, white sand sifting down over her shoulders. There were smudges of dirt on her tired, startled face, probably the result of falling during her midnight hike. There was a large bruise, half-covered with a fresh scab, on her left jaw.

"I'm not going back with you," she said as soon as she saw Ben.

"I don't want to take you any more than you want to go," he said in a tired voice. "You can get on the horse and let me lead you back, or I'll tie you across the saddle. The choice is yours."

"You can't do this to me," she cried. "This is a free country. I have my rights. I can come and go as I please, and you can't stop me."

Ben didn't feel like fighting, much less arguing. People wasted too much of life in conflict with each other. Life was too precious, too valuable, to waste by arguing.

"I brought some fresh meat," Ben said, changing the subject. "You look hungry. Can I cook you some breakfast?"

Nellie just looked at him. She didn't want to argue either, and the hunger pangs were gnawing away at her insides. She was hungry, very hungry.

"Yes, I would like some breakfast," she said politely. "Then I would like to continue on my way to the railroad crossing."

Ben debated for a few seconds whether or not to respond to the challenge or just ignore it and fix breakfast. He decided on the latter.

"Did you find Grace?" she asked, as Ben began building a fire.

He stopped what he was doing and looked up at her.

"Yes, I found her."

"And? Why did she leave?"

"She's dead."

"No!" Nellie exclaimed, putting her hand to her mouth.

"Killed herself. Jumped off a cliff."

"But why?"

"She just wanted out, I suppose, and had the grit to do it. Not like the rest of us. Guilt and rejection probably helped her along."

"Where's her body?"

"At the cabin. We were going to bury her this morning, but I had to come after you. Suppose we'll do it when you and I return."

Neither spoke for a while as Ben handed Nellie a sharpened stick and a fist-sized chunk of deer meat. They began roasting the meat over the fire, occasionally biting off outside pieces as the meat began to cook.

"I figured you'd find me," she said. "What I can't figure out is how you got so far ahead of me. Must have pushed the horses hard. I was really surprised when I saw the light of your fire so far down the canyon."

Ben stopped chewing.

"You saw the light of my fire?" he asked.

"Sure, down the canyon."

"I didn't build a fire last night, and I wasn't down the canyon ahead of you."

Nellie stopped chewing too.

"Where?" asked Ben, standing up.

She pointed to a spot about a mile away where the cliffs pushed close to the water's edge. Suddenly she was sorry she had said anything, thinking perhaps she was closer to help than she had supposed. Similar thoughts were going through Ben's mind.

Should he leave Nellie tied up with the horses while he walked downstream to check out the newcomers, or take her with him? Suddenly she jumped to her feet and started running towards the cliffs where she had seen the reflection of the fire. She began calling for help, but the sound of her voice was swallowed up by the thunder of the rapids.

In the soft sand, she couldn't go very fast, and the rags on her feet didn't provide adequate traction. Ben caught up with her quickly, wrestling her onto the sand. He put his palm over her mouth when she tried to scream again. She struggled for a moment, then relaxed, too tired to fight anymore.

Ben couldn't help but compare the feel of this live woman with the dead one he had held in his arms just a few hours earlier. Life was so precious, so beautiful. The warmth, her body against his, felt so good. He just wanted to forget about the people who had built the fire, bury his head between Nellie's full breasts, close his eyes and hold her close forever.

He looked into her blue eyes, wondering if she was feeling what he felt. She spit at him.

Ben jumped up, dragging her by the arm towards the horses. Grabbing a rope, he tied her hands behind her back, then to a small cottonwood tree after he had pushed her down into a sitting position. He reached for the hem of her dress, brushing her foot aside when she tried to kick him. He tore off a long strip of fabric, which he tied over her mouth. With the roar of the rapids her voice wouldn't carry far, but he wasn't going to take any chances. After tying the horses in the thick willows where they could not be seen from the trail, he headed towards the cliffs where Nellie had seen the light of a campfire.

Chapter 45

Not polygamy but the power of the Priesthood is the real danger. . . .
—Springfield (Mass.) Union
Reprinted in the Salt Lake Tribune,
February 15, 1885

Ben hadn't gone more than a hundred yards when he heard the unmistakable clacking of a rock tumbling over other rocks. He darted sideways into a thick clump of sagebrush and dropped to his knees. He drew his pistol, cocked back the hammer, and waited.

Ben didn't have to wait long. A minute later two men walked into view. They were looking down at the trail, apparently following tracks. The tracks couldn't be Nellie's. She hadn't gone that far.

Ben recognized one of the men—Jed Gibson, the deputy who had arrested Flat Nose George and Madge. The big deputy had a new pair of boots, replacing the pair Ben had burned. Ben didn't recognize the other man, small and thin with large black eyes and a mouth like a prune. He was much older than Gibson. Ben wondered why only two deputies were seeking his hideout, and why they were on foot. This was no ordinary posse.

The men were only ten feet away, still looking down at the trail, when Ben stood up and ordered them to reach for the sky. Gibson recognized Ben immediately and began to swear.

"Knew we should have gone for help before trying to follow the tracks," he said to the other man.

"How come there's only two of you?" Ben asked.

"The rest are around the bend. Be here shortly," the stranger said.

"If that were true, you wouldn't be telling me," Ben said. "What are you doing here?" he asked Gibson. "Tell me or I'll burn those new boots."

Gibson explained that he and Shank, his companion, had just taken a prisoner to Denver on the train and were coming home. When the train was waved to a stop at the Green River crossing, they noticed that it was David Butler who was doing the waving. They already knew Ben was hiding somewhere in the area, so Gibson suggested they sneak off the train and, in the hope of finding Ben's hideout, try to backtrack Butler's trail while the tracks were still fresh. If they found the hideout, they would return for reinforcements.

At gunpoint, Ben marched Gibson and Shank up the trail to Nellie and the horses. Tying their hands behind their backs, Ben made them sit down where he could tie them to trees.

"We didn't know you had a woman prisoner," Gibson said.

"You'll probably hang for kidnapping a woman," Shank added.

Ben didn't respond and neither did Nellie, her mouth still gagged with the strip of cloth. Ben was wondering what to do with the two deputies. Had he captured Owen and Vandercook, he would have been tempted to shoot them. But not Gibson and Shank, two harmless clowns. They didn't have enough cunning or poison in them to deserve killing, he thought. Still, he couldn't let them go to bring back a possee, nor could he take them back as prisoners. He had one prisoner too many already in Nellie. It would be impossible for him and George to keep constant watch on the two men too. There was no place to lock them up.

Gibson and Shank wouldn't stop their incessant talking, so Ben tore two more strips of fabric from Nellie's dress and gagged them too. As before, she tried to kick him but was unsuccessful.

With all three prisoners silenced, Ben sat cross-legged in front of them. The only sound was the roar of the nearby rapids. For a long time Ben didn't say anything, just stared at the two men and wondered what to do with them.

"The simplest thing," he finally said, "would be to shoot the both of you and throw the bodies in the river." He looked down at his pistol and spun the cylinder. Shank's eyes were big as fifty-cent pieces. Gibson's eyes were closed, like he was praying.

"But I don't want to kill either one of you," he continued. "At least not yet. Still, I can't let you go, because you'd bring back a posse." Both men shook their heads emphatically, but Ben knew they were only lying to save their necks.

"I could rip your tongues out," he suggested. "Then you couldn't tell anyone where you found me." Both prisoners shook their heads vigorously.

"But even without your tongues you could lead them here," Ben continued. "You couldn't do that if I gouged your eyes out, but I don't want to do that either."

Ben got up and walked over to the river, wondering what he might do with the two men. In front of him was a huge pile of cottonwood logs that looked like dinosaur bones. Sam idly wondered how far they had come before the spring runoff had deposited them on the sandy beach. He also wondered how far they might have gone had they not been washed up on the sand. He knew the Green River joined the Colorado about a hundred miles downstream, and that the Colorado dumped into the Gulf of California. He didn't know of any towns along the river, though he figured there might be a cabin or two at Lee's Ferry.

Suddenly he had an idea—send the deputies to the Gulf of California. Build a raft and set them adrift with their hands and feet tied. Once they passed the Green River crossing where the Chinamen lived, if they got ashore it would take them weeks if not months to find their way back to Salt Lake. Ben had heard stories of how rough the river became inside the Grand Canyon. If God wanted them to live, they would find a way. If not, they would die, but Ben would not be the one who killed them—at least not directly.

Ben wasn't sure he could defend his logic, but in the absence of any other reasonable alternative, he felt he ought to go ahead and do it.

He wrestled four of the biggest logs from the pile and rolled them down to the water. After returning to the horses and obtaining the remainder of the rope, he lashed the logs together as tightly as possible to withstand the fierce rapids.

It was early afternoon when Ben removed the gags not just from the two deputies, but from Nellie as well. He gave them a drink of water from his canteen and a few pieces of cold deer meat.

"What are you going to do with us?" Shank asked, his mouth still full as he chewed on the meat.

"Turn you into sailors," Ben said, smiling. Gibson and Shank gave each other worried looks.

Ben untied the knots that bound his prisoners to the trees, leaving their hands tied behind their backs. He released Nellie from her tree so she could follow, but her hands remained tied behind her back. He helped his prisoners to their feet and marched them down to the river.

Shank and Gibson both stopped when they saw the raft.

"No! I can't swim," Gibson cried.

"Me neither," Shank added.

"Try to see my side of this mess," Ben insisted. "I can't take the two of you to my hideout, and I can't just let you go. Don't want to kill you, so the next best thing is to just set you adrift. Even if you get ashore at Lee's Ferry, it'll be many weeks before you're back in Salt Lake. By then I'll have a new hideout."

"But we'll drown," Gibson protested.

"Not if you stay on the raft."

"Are you going to untie us?" Shank asked.

"Nope," Ben said. "That'd make it too easy. I'm hoping it'll take you a hundred miles or so to get your hands free, hopefully before you enter the whitewater of the Grand Canyon."

Ben turned and inched the crude raft into the water until it was floating freely, held to shore by a rope tied to a small bush. He then waved for the two frightened deputies to climb aboard. Ben wasn't in any hurry to send them on their way. He just wanted to make sure the raft would bear their weight. He didn't want them reaching the trestle before dark, and he didn't want anyone at the crossing or any of the Chinamen to see them float by.

"You can't do this!" Nellie cried, unable to remain silent any longer.

"I'm listening, if you have a better idea," Ben said calmly.

"Just let them go. Make them promise not to tell where they saw you."

"Can't do that," Ben said. "They would tell."

"You might as well shoot them," she said. "Either way they'll die, making you a murderer."

Instead of answering, Ben turned and helped the two deputies onto the raft. The logs were about two-thirds submerged. Ben figured the raft would work just fine, at least in smooth water. How it would do in rapids, he had no idea.

"This is foolishness," Nellie cried. "I won't let you do it."

"How are you going to stop me?" Ben asked.

"I don't know, but I'll find a way."

"I'm tempted to put you on the raft with them," Ben said.

"You wouldn't!"

"Keep talking and see."

"I'd certainly prefer their company to yours," she cried.

Without another word, Ben took Nellie in his arms, her hands still tied behind her back, and waded into the thigh-deep water, dropping her roughly onto the raft. The logs were now nearly three-fourths submerged. Nellie glared back at Ben, who was looking up at the afternoon sun now casting long shadows off the western cliffs. In a few minutes the beach would be in shadow.

"Might as well get you on your way," Ben said. "Be dark by the time you reach the trestle. The Chinamen won't see you."

Ben tied Gibson's and Shank's hands to the bindings that held the logs together. "If you get in shallow water, I wouldn't want you just wading ashore," he explained.

"The raft would have a lot better chance of making it if it didn't have a third person on board," Ben said to Nellie.

"He's right," Shank said. "You'd better get off and go with him." Gibson nodded his agreement.

Had Ben been the only one trying to get her off the raft, Nellie might have refused, but with both deputies wanting her off, she swallowed her pride, slipped into the water, and waded ashore. She didn't look at Ben, nor did she speak to him.

Without further ceremony, Ben replaced the gags on the two men so they couldn't call out to the Chinamen, then pushed the raft out into the current. He didn't speak to the deputies, nor did they try to mumble to him, though both nodded to Nellie, who began to cry.

Upon catching the swift current in the middle of the stream, the crude raft glided effortlessly into the first rapid. Bobbing up and down like a bucking horse, it plunged ahead. Though both men were splashed upon, they glided safely through to the swift, smooth water below, soon disappearing around a bend.

Ben retrieved the horses, helped Nellie onto hers without untying her hands, and headed back to the cabin. Nellie didn't speak a single word to Ben the entire distance.

Chapter 46

The provisions of the Edmunds Law of 1882, which denied the right to vote, serve on juries, and hold public office to a large number of Mormons who did not practice polygamy, evidenced a growing concept that because polygamy was an evil practiced by the Church, it followed that the entire institution was an evil to be legislated against. This view assumed fullest expression in the Edmunds-Tucker bill, which not only denied basic American rights to the innocent but went to the extreme of destroying the Church to which they belonged and took possession of its property.
—GUSTIVE O. LARSON,
"The Americanization of Utah for Statehood"

Digging Grace Woolley's grave was not an easy task. It wasn't that the red ground was rocky or frozen, but the lack of a shovel that made the task so difficult. The work consisted of loosening the soil three or four inches at a time with digging sticks, then scooping the dirt out by hand.

Ben, George and Madge had been at the task about an hour and were about half finished when Nellie joined them.

"I'd like to help," she said. She didn't look at Ben, nor he at her.

He moved over as she stepped into the hole and dropped to her knees, helping him scoop out the last of the loose dirt before Madge and George climbed in for another round with the digging sticks.

Ben thought of asking Nellie why she had come out to

help. He knew she hadn't done it for his benefit. He knew, too, that Nellie had known Grace before either had come to the cabin. Even though their convictions had led them in opposite directions, Nellie and Grace had seemed to share a mutual respect, even liking. Perhaps that was why she wanted to help, Ben guessed.

He had to keep reminding himself that Nellie was an enemy who would turn him in, testify against him in court, and slander him in published articles if she could. Ben was annoyed at his reaction to her being close to him. He was too aware of her breathing, the smoothness of her skin, the curve of her hip, the swell of her breasts under her shirt. Though she was an enemy, everything about her fascinated him. He couldn't understand how a woman on her knees scraping dirt out of a hole could look so good to him. He wished she would go back to the cabin, but was glad when she didn't.

When Madge and George stepped into the hole to loosen another layer of soil, Ben and Nellie climbed out and waited. Still, no words passed between them. Flat Nose George and Madge chatted back and forth like they were lifetime friends. After having her baby, Madge had regained her strength quickly and had begun to spend more and more time outside with George, sometimes helping with the chores, other times merely strolling along the stream bed or just lounging around the tepee fire. Madge and George had become fast friends. More and more, it was George who was holding and playing with her baby.

When the hole was about five feet deep, Ben and George returned to the cabin to get the body and the other women. Grace was wrapped in a clean gray blanket. Her body felt somewhat lighter to Ben.

After setting the body beside the hole, Ben and George climbed in, then carefully lowered Grace to her final resting place.

Nellie was holding a handkerchief to her face, unsuccessfully trying to control her emotions. Stella was fighting back tears too. Priscilla and Madge appeared calm and controlled.

When Ben and George crawled out of the hole, everyone

gathered close in a tight circle around the grave, looking down at the gray blanket.

"Since we don't have a preacher," Ben began, without looking up, "I think it would be appropriate if each of us said a few words before we say a prayer and cover her up. If someone is ready to speak, go ahead."

There was silence for a few moments. Priscilla was the first to speak.

"Grace Woolley lived and died," she began in a steady voice, "for a sacred sisterhood of women who uphold each other and their husbands, who know their children are not born in sin. I hope somehow her death was not in vain, that thousands and thousands more will be able to live the principle of celestial marriage. I pray for the day when young women throughout Zion will not have to watch in dismay as all the men worth marrying are taken, one at a time, forcing those poor leftover girls to settle for unworthy pigs. I pray for a day when the best men are free to marry all the best women, as many as may be available, leaving the pigs to root with the whores. Then Grace Woolley will not have died in vain."

"Amen," Madge said. The rest remained silent.

"I didn't know her," Stella said. "All I know is that she was sad, so sad you could see hurt in her eyes. I just wish she could have found a better way to end the sadness. I don't know what else to say. I didn't know her."

Madge was the next to speak.

"I didn't know Grace either," she began slowly, gathering her thoughts, "except that she was a brave woman. The Bible says the Lord loved David, even after he committed adultery. The Lord loved David because he was the only man in Israel brave enough to stand up to Goliath. Grace was about the only woman in Zion brave enough to stand up to the authorities and defend polygamy, even though she didn't do it herself and wasn't allowed to. She was brave enough to give herself to the man she loved when she knew her Church would cast her out for it. And when she felt abandoned by her Church and the man she loved, she had the courage to end it all by stepping off a cliff. If the Lord loved

David for his courage, he loves Grace too. I don't condemn her, and I hope the Lord doesn't either."

"None of us knew Grace very well," Ben began without hesitation, "but we are all very sad at her passing. Why? Because it is such a waste to see a beautiful, articulate, kind girl cold and lifeless in a damn hole in the ground." He paused, his face and neck turning red. The muscles in his tight jaw were twitching. His fists were clenched.

"She didn't deserve this end," he continued. "It's not her fault. This innocent girl is dead because evil men are trying to wrassle economic and political power from a small church, using polygamy as their excuse for doing it. Those devils will answer to God for the death of Grace Woolley, and they will pay dearly in the eternal fires of hell."

"Amen," everyone said together, except Nellie.

"Grace is dead," Nellie said, her voice loud and harsh, full of emotion, "because the men running her church were not content with one wife and figured out how to convince young women that it was all right to give themselves to church leaders who were already married. Of course, Christian people everywhere rose up in protest, resulting in the present conflict. But they're not the ones who killed this poor woman. It was the church that let its men take plural wives."

For the first time that day, Ben glared at Nellie. She returned the look, not backing down an inch. Ben was amazed more than anything at his own feelings. A half hour earlier he was so drawn to the woman he wished it had taken longer to dig the grave. Now all he wanted to do was blacken her eyes.

He was about to offer a rebuttal to her statement when Flat Nose George reminded him, and Nellie too, that the purpose of the gathering was not to argue religion, politics, or polygamy, but to bury a poor woman who had fallen off a cliff. The old Indian stepped up to the edge of the hole and with a swipe of his boot, pushed some loose red dirt onto the gray blanket.

"Not yet," Madge said. "First we must have a prayer."

Ben stepped forward, bowed his head, and began to pray.

Chapter 47

The local (Salt Lake) crusaders evidently had in mind Gentile minority rule instead of Mormon ecclesiastical domination. They wanted political control in Utah and appealed for public and federal government support through charges against the Mormons, ranging from murder to treason. But most convenient for them was the charge of immorality, as they kept the polygamy issue in the forefront of their campaigning.

—GUSTIVE O. LARSON,
"The Americanization of Utah for Statehood"

As the winter months passed Ben often wondered what had happened to Gibson and Shank. Sometimes he had dreams in which he saw the raft shatter on a huge boulder, the men's hands still tied behind their backs as they disappeared beneath the white water.

Still, Ben and George kept a close watch on the approach to the cabin. Even if Gibson and Shank hadn't made it back to Salt Lake, too many other people knew the location of the hideout. David Butler and John Jex wouldn't go to the authorities to betray Ben, George, and the women. That wasn't the concern. It was that something might accidentally be found out. So Ben and George watched and waited while the time of delivery for Priscilla and Stella grew closer and closer.

Priscilla was the first to deliver her baby, a fat little girl. There were no complications as George forced Priscilla to swallow cup after cup of a bitter tea made from wild raspberry leaves and squaw bush. Madge performed the delivery.

Winter passed. The snow at the lower elevations melted, and the snowpack at the head of the canyons began to melt too, the brown runoff nearly tripling the size of the small stream. Though the nights were still cold, the grass began to turn green and the first of the wild violets and dandelions began to show their colors. Stella's time for delivery was drawing close.

Ben grew increasingly restless. Though the cabin had been a safe refuge during the winter, he had an uneasy feeling that he had kept the women there long enough. It was time to be moving, though he wasn't sure why or where. Something was wrong, and he didn't know what it was. He would sometimes wake up in the middle of the night, a knot in his stomach. He spent hours high on the ridges, restlessly watching the canyon floor through which unwelcome riders might approach the hideout. He kept his gun loaded and one of his horses saddled, even at night. Flat Nose George and the women didn't share Ben's concern.

Then one morning Nellie was gone. Ben's not giving the women their shoes back did not stop her now. Going without shoes for several months had toughened the women's feet and, with the approach of warmer weather, Nellie no longer needed shoes, especially not in the smooth sand of the wash. Her barefoot tracks were leading downstream towards the Green River.

Leaving Flat Nose George behind to keep an eye on things, Ben leapt upon the black gelding and headed down the wash, Lobo at his side. Ben pushed the horse into a fast trot, hoping to close the gap as quickly as possible.

Ben followed Nellie's tracks for about a mile before they disappeared into a sagebrush flat. Making no attempt to follow the exact trail, Ben just continued along the wash, figuring he'd run into the tracks again further downstream. He didn't.

After riding about two or three miles without further sign of Nellie's tracks, Ben stopped. Something was wrong. Approaching a place where sheer white cliffs from both sides of the canyon narrowed to a gap less than fifty yards wide, Ben dismounted, carefully examining the ground between the two cliffs. Confident Nellie had not passed that way, he began working back the way he had come, riding the horse back and forth across the sagebrush flats, searching for tracks.

Not finding anything, he eventually returned to the spot in the sandy wash where he had last seen her tracks. Dismounting, Ben followed them into the sagebrush. In the soft spring soil, the soft, round impressions of Nellie's bare feet were easy to follow. Lobo ran back and forth enthusiastically, but otherwise offered no assistance.

The trail gradually veered downstream away from the wash, eventually disappearing onto a bench of white sandstone. Ben hurried to the other side of the bench, carefully searching the soil where the stone surface ended. He found nothing.

He was sitting on a rock, wondering why he couldn't find the tracks, when it occurred to him that perhaps Nellie was trying not only to hide her trail, but also to trick Ben into thinking she had gone downstream when she intended something entirely different.

Ben hurried back to where the tracks had disappeared onto the stone surface. This time he worked his way up the hill. He hadn't gone far when he spotted Nellie's tracks heading back towards the camp, just further uphill from the wash. He got back on his horse. The tracks were easy to follow.

The trail led past the cabin and tepee. Ben didn't see anyone outside as he rode by.

Eventually the trail re-entered the wash. After starting a false trail to get him to think she was headed for the Green River, Nellie had circled back and was now headed upstream. Though it was a long way away, maybe 30 miles, Ben figured she was probably headed for Little Creek, a tiny trading post where a few Indians and sheepherders stayed. Flat Nose George had mentioned the place a few days earlier. What Nellie probably didn't know was that there was a high, long mountain pass to go over where there would still be a lot of snow. Ben hurried his pace. In the damp sand, the tracks were easy to follow, even on horseback.

Occasionally the trail disappeared on rock surfaces, but always reappeared on the upstream side. Nellie's direction was consistent now.

Ben was amazed at how far the trail continued. Nellie must have left early in the night and walked a good part of it and the day too. He had lost a lot of time figuring out what she was up to, so he still hadn't caught up with her as darkness began to fall. Not far ahead, he could see where the winding, sandy canyon bottom suddenly ended, and the trail began a steep, rocky climb to the alpine snow fields above. He stopped for the night, deciding not to risk passing her in the dark and possibly alerting her to his presence. Ben didn't build a fire; instead, he just chewed on some jerky from his saddle bags and wrapped himself in his damp saddle blanket.

Ben was almost asleep when he noticed firelight reflected off a huge boulder not more than half a mile up the trail. He smiled to himself. Nellie either didn't think she was being followed, or she was simply too cold to spend the night without a fire.

Saddling the horse and leading it behind him, Ben crept up the trail, keeping Lobo at his side. It was Nellie, all right, huddled over a tiny fire, rubbing her sore feet. Except for the clothes on her back, all she had was a white bonnet and a bag with some food and matches.

She didn't notice Ben until he was nearly upon her. She looked towards him, but didn't bother to stand. Her feet were too sore.

"You can't keep me prisoner anymore!" she cried. "I'm going home, and I won't let you stop me. Kill me if you must, but I'm not going back with you." She looked back at the fire and continued rubbing her feet.

"Mind if I share the fire with you?" Ben asked. She didn't answer. He didn't ask again, leading his horse to the nearest tree and tying it up. He removed the saddle and returned to the fire, offering Nellie a strip of jerky. She ignored him.

He sat down across the fire from her. Neither spoke.

"All right," Ben said, after a while. "You can go home. I won't stop you. I'll even give you a horse."

"I don't believe you," she said, looking up at him for the first time.

"Tomorrow we'll go back to the cabin. I'll give you your shoes back, plus a horse and saddle. You can leave for Green River whenever you want."

"You aren't worried about me telling where you are?"

"We'll move. Been here too long anyway. Got to find a new hideaway that nobody knows about. Might as well do it now."

"How do I know you're not just saying all this to get me to return willingly with you? Why won't you just let me take your horse and keep going to Willow Creek?"

"Two reasons," Ben said. "One, there's too much snow up on the pass, even if you are on a horse. Might not be able to get through. Two, this is the horse I took from Owen after he slit open the belly of an old friend. This horse reminds me of why I'm here. As long as I have this black, I won't get soft on men like Owen, who've got coming whatever I might want to do to them."

"Like those two men you tied up and sent to their deaths on the river?"

"That's right," Ben said.

"If you're lying about letting me go you'll be sorry," she warned.

"I'm not lying," Ben said. No further words passed between them, not even when Ben offered her his saddle blanket for warmth, which she accepted. While she wrapped it around her shoulders, Ben wandered towards the outer ring of the firelight, gathering firewood. That was when he heard the cry.

At first he thought it was a coyote or wolf, but it wasn't. The cry was less shrill, more full, very human—yet too shrill to be that of a man. Carried on the evening breezes, the cry was not clear and sharp but Ben knew he heard it. It seemed to be coming from a plateau to the south, somewhere beyond a hillside forest of aspen and pine trees.

"Did you hear that cry?" Ben asked when he returned to

the fire with an armload of firewood.

"A wolf, wasn't it?" Nellie responded.

"I didn't think it was shrill enough. Maybe we'll hear it again." After placing three or four limbs on the fire, Ben sat down cross-legged across from Nellie. Neither spoke, both looking into the fire and listening.

The second time they heard the cry, it was more clear. Rather than the long, mournful cry of a wolf, it had more urgency, more desperation, though the pitch and sound were similar.

"Not a wolf," Ben said.

"Could it be a child?" Nellie asked.

"Don't see how it could," Ben said. "Nobody lives up here. George said Indians come through hunting in the warmer months, but not now. Couldn't be a child."

They continued to hear the cry at irregular intervals. There was something both chilling and terrifying in the sound.

"I think we should go see what it is," Nellie said.

"Probably won't get any sleep if we don't," Ben said.

Nellie wrapped her feet in some rags she had been carrying in her sack, then with the horse blanket still wrapped around her, she followed Ben into the darkness.

He moved slowly at first, but as their eyes adjusted to the dark, he walked faster and faster, eventually finding what appeared to be a game trail leading up through a grove of aspens towards the sound of the cry. The sound was getting weaker, or the source was moving further away. They hurried up the trail.

By the time they reached the top of the hill, the cry had stopped completely. They waited, both catching their breath, cooling down, listening.

"Do you think we should go back?" Nellie asked.

"If we do, the cry will probably start again about the time we reach camp," Ben said. "Let's wait awhile."

They found a protected hollow under the leaning trunks of some large aspens where the snow had already melted. They crawled in, stretching out side by side, sharing the blanket. Neither spoke.

Eventually Nellie drifted into a weary slumber. Having not slept the previous night, she was more tired than Ben. He looked up at the stars, wondering at the strangeness of sharing his warmth and saddle blanket with a woman who would send him to jail if she got the chance. He wouldn't give her that chance.

He remembered his promise earlier that evening to let her go home. He would miss her, even though she was the enemy. Keeping an eye on her had been a challenge. The debates, the arguments for and against polygamy, had been stimulating. He liked this hostage and he wished she were an ally instead of an enemy. Eventually he dozed too. Hours passed.

Suddenly the cry resumed, louder and more frequent than before. It did sound like a crying child, but it couldn't be.

Ben shook Nellie. Instantly she was on her feet, facing the direction from which the sound was coming. They hurried forward. Occasionally, as the breeze shifted directions, they made adjustments in their course. They were getting closer. Then the crying stopped.

They continued forward slowly to the edge of another aspen grove.

"I smell something dead," Nellie said.

"Me too," Ben said, stopping, reaching out and grabbing what appeared to be a little tree about as big around as an arm. When he tried to shake it, three other trees about the same size shook too. They formed a rectangle and appeared to be supporting a large black bundle about a foot above Ben's head.

"What is it?" Nellie whispered.

"I think we're in an Indian burial ground," Sam said, whispering too. "These poles are holding up a body."

"What about the cry?" Nellie asked.

"Do you believe in ghosts?"

"Be serious," Nellie scolded. "What's making the sound?"

"I don't know. Let's wait until we hear it again."

It wasn't until the darkness began to fade into a gray

dawn that they again heard the cry. It was weaker now, less steady, but close. Ben and Nellie hurried forward, guessing it couldn't be very far away now.

And it wasn't. Reaching the top of a gentle swell, they spotted another burial rack, with four poles supporting a body wrapped in a dark buffalo robe.

"They wouldn't have buried someone alive," Nellie ventured.

"I don't think so," Ben said. Nellie stopped, reaching out and placing her hand on Ben's arm, causing him to stop too.

"Look, it's moving," she said.

"Must be the wind," Ben said. The body atop the poles was swaying slightly.

"The wind isn't blowing," Nellie said.

They moved closer. The body continued to sway. Sagebrush prevented them from seeing the ground at the base of the poles.

"It has to be a child," Nellie cried when they heard the cry again. She ran forward, Ben at her heels.

When they reached the poles, neither understood what they saw, at least not at first. Nellie had been right. The cries were coming from a child, a shivering Indian boy, perhaps six or seven years old. He was fully clothed, his back on the ground, directly underneath the elevated body. One of the boy's legs was in the air, held up by a leather thong attached to one of the crosspoles above. The boy's foot pulling on the thong had caused the body to sway.

Upon seeing Nellie and Ben, the boy made a feeble attempt to scramble free but was unable to, his right foot being held three feet above the ground by the thong. That's when Ben and Nellie noticed the dried blood on his hands.

Ben rushed forward, drawing his knife from its sheath, slicing the thong in two and allowing the boy's foot to fall to the ground. Ben dropped to his knees. The boy's eyes were wide with fear as Ben took him into his arms. As Nellie handed Ben the blanket, she saw tears streaming down Ben's cheeks.

"What is it?" she asked softly. "What's going on?"

"I've heard about this," Ben choked, hardly able to talk.

"About what?"

Ben wrapped the boy in the blanket, being careful not to touch the injured hands and attempting to comfort the child with a tearful smile. Ben stood up, the boy still in his arms.

"Some tribes believe the cries of a child will keep evil spirits away from a fresh grave, giving the dead person's spirit time to get away to the happy hunting ground or wherever dead Indians go."

"You're serious?"

"They hurt the child so it will cry, but not bad enough to kill it. Then they tie it close to the grave so it can't get away. The child will cry for three or four days and eventually die."

"I've never heard of anything so cruel."

"Me neither," Ben said.

"What's wrong with his hands?" Nellie asked.

"Looks like they tied his leg up so he couldn't get away, then smashed his hands with a rock so he couldn't untie the knots where the thong was tied to his leg."

"What should we do with him?"

"Get him back to camp, give him some water and food, then see what we can do about the hands." Nellie followed close behind as Ben hurried back to camp, the boy in his arms.

Chapter 48

Sir, we cannot indirectly legislate for the purpose of destroying any religion, whether false or true. We cannot take away its chartered rights which have been given to it by law, selecting it as one out of many to the end that it may be destroyed, without violating not only the principles of the Constitution, but the essential principles of the religion of Christ.
—SENATOR WILSON CALL, Florida
Congressional Record, 1886, 17:507

"I think all the Indians involved should be arrested and sent to prison," Nellie said. It was late that same afternoon. She was holding the sleeping boy in the saddle in front of her while Ben led the horse down the sandy wash towards the cabin. While the boy's hands were bruised and swollen, he could still move his fingers, though not without pain. With time, it appeared the hands would heal.

When Ben and Nellie arrived back at camp with the boy, he gulped down half a quart of cold water and began to chew ravenously on a strip of deer jerky. After cleaning and wrapping his hands, they began the journey back to the cabin. After filling his belly with meat and taking several long pulls from the canteen, the boy had fallen asleep. Nellie had her arms around him to prevent him from falling from the horse, and the gentle rocking helped keep him in a deep sleep.

"They were just practicing their religion," Ben said in response to Nellie's comment about sending the Indians to jail for hurting the child.

"Don't tell me you don't see anything wrong with what they did," she argued.

"That's not the point," Ben said. "I'm just saying that perhaps we shouldn't be too quick to judge a group of Indians for practicing their religion. They broke the boy's hands and tied him up believing his cries would keep evil spirits away from the Indian who died. What gives us the right to interfere?"

"I forgot how cold-hearted you are," she said.

"You're avoiding my question," Ben said patiently. "What gives us the right to step between an Indian and his customs?"

"This boy gives us the right," she said quietly so as not to awaken the child. "You saw how he was tied to that grave, left to cry until he died. You saw how they smashed his little hands. How can you even suggest that decent people look the other way and allow this kind of cruelty to continue?"

"Are you saying that Indians shouldn't be allowed to practice religious traditions that hurt innocent people who don't share those same religious views?"

"That's what I'm saying."

"Then you're a hypocrite," Ben concluded.

"I have no idea what you are talking about."

"You and your friends are just like the Indians who tied this boy to the grave."

"You don't know what you're saying."

"Because you have a religious belief that a man should have only one wife, you are bent on crushing an entire people who believe differently. Hundreds of pregnant women are in hiding. Hundreds of good men are in jail. Not criminals, but law-abiding men and women. Why? Because their religious beliefs concerning marriage are different than yours. Why does your belief in monogamous marriage give you the right to hound good men and women to the ends of the earth? You and your kind are no different than the Indians who smashed this child's hands and tied him to that grave."

Nellie just looked at Ben, saying nothing. His face was red with anger.

"If polygamy could be stopped by smashing the hands of Mormon children and tying them to graves, you and your friends would do it," he continued. "Chaste women are running from your officers and having babies in caves. Honorable men are rotting in your cold prison cells. Children are without parents to care for them. All because of a stupid religious belief shared by you and your friends that a man should not be allowed to love and care for more than one woman. You, your friends, and those Indians are alike, forcing innocent people to suffer because of your religious beliefs."

Ben waited for Nellie to respond. She didn't, at least not at first.

When she did speak, she was smiling. This irritated Ben.

"You're very persuasive. You ought to consider becoming a lawyer," she said.

"Don't change the subject," he answered. "We were talking about your hypocrisy, not my future profession."

"You are more persuasive than David Butler. Have you ever thought about becoming an attorney?"

"Outlaws don't go to law school," he said sarcastically. "You and your monogamous friends, in trying to shove your views on marriage down the throats of the Mormons, have made me an outlaw."

"And a magnificent one at that," she said.

Ben couldn't figure out why she wouldn't argue with him. Maybe she wanted something from him.

"What do you want?" he asked.

"I don't want to argue with you anymore."

"I got you in a corner, didn't I? So now you don't want to continue the discussion."

"I'm not so sure you have me cornered," she said. "I suppose I could bring up Priscilla's situation, a 15-year-old girl being married to an old man. She'll be a widow by the time she's 25. I suppose it could be argued that that is a form of tying a child to the grave."

"But . . ." Ben began. Nellie cut him off.

"I don't want to argue with you anymore."

"I wasn't aware there was any other way to communicate with you,'' Ben said. ''If you don't want to argue, what do you want to do?''

''Just talk.''

''Why the sudden change?'' he asked, softening.

''Seeing that boy tied to a grave,'' she began slowly, ''left there to die. People shouldn't treat each other like that.''

''What about the people who made three pregnant women spend this past winter in a cabin away from their husbands and families?''

''That's wrong too.'' She pulled the Indian child closer to her, stroking the top of his head as if he were a kitten or a puppy.

''People are too easily hurt,'' she said. ''There's not enough kindness, not enough caring for others. Too many people are hurting each other as though life isn't worth anything.''

''You're sounding like Jesus,'' Ben said, not intending to be funny.

''I feel sad,'' she said. ''So sad I can hardly keep from crying. Like if I don't do something to help stop the meanness in the world, I'll shrivel up and die.''

''I feel sad too,'' Ben said, ''but I also feel mad. Mormons aren't getting a fair shake. There is no justice for them. I want to fight back. . . .''

Still walking backwards, Ben suddenly tripped on a rock and fell on his back. Nellie began to laugh, and Ben threw a handful of sand at her. The boy awakened, beginning to cry. Nellie held him close, trying to comfort him, as Ben picked up the reins and resumed leading the horse down the wash, this time facing forward, so he could see where he was going.

Chapter 49

It is the duty of the government to strip this conspiracy (Mormon Church) of all political power; take the government of the territory into its own hands, and demolish the conspiracy. Polygamy would die with the trunk upon which it grows and bears its baleful fruit. To annihilate a thing in detail is agony long drawn out. The monster's vitals should be punctured first, and dissolution speedily follows. Nothing short of a legislative commission, and possibly a military government for Utah, will ever effectively eradicate the real Mormon evil and redeem Utah from the theocratic yoke of its masters.

—"The Mormon Conspiracy"
Booklet published by the Salt Lake Tribune, 1885

Ben, Nellie, and the Indian boy were approaching the cabin about mid-morning the following day when they saw the billowing gray-white pillar of smoke contrasted sharply against the blue sky.

Ben helped Nellie and the boy down from the horse, then leapt upon the animal's back and galloped towards the smoke, Lobo racing at his heels. Upon reaching the top of a brushy rise about half a mile upstream from the cabin, Ben jerked the horse to a sudden halt. The smoke was coming from the cabin as he had supposed. While the stone walls were still standing, the roof was nearly gone.

At first Ben thought the fire was an accident—the result, perhaps, of an overheated stove. But when he saw the bare tepee poles, he knew there had been a raid on the camp. The canvas had been ripped from the poles, something only an attacker would do.

Ben held his horse still for several minutes and scanned the horizon, the draw beyond the canyon, and the hillsides. He could see no sign of life, not even a grazing horse. Slowly and cautiously, gun in hand, he approached the smoldering cabin.

Everyone—Priscilla, Stella, Madge, George, and the two babies—was gone. Everything of value was gone too—the saddles, food, blankets, ropes, the axe, even the canvas tepee cover. Horse and boot tracks were everywhere. From the departing tracks down the sandy wash, Ben figured there had been at least a dozen horses and perhaps as many riders.

Near the tepee poles Ben dropped to one knee, pushing his finger into a small circle of black mud. When he saw the red smeared on the nearest clump of sagebrush, he knew the mud had not been made by water or urine mixed with the red soil, but by blood.

Ben stood up, turning slowly and searching for anything out of the ordinary. He scanned the nearby hills, the horizon, the sagebrush and the ground in front of him.

That's when Lobo brought it to him. At first, it looked like a leather pouch. Then maybe a piece of flesh. There was blood on it.

Ben took one more careful look over his shoulder and down the canyon before bending over to see what the dog had brought him. It was a large, brown left hand. Flat Nose George. A strand of long white sinew moved in and out across a shattered bone when Ben moved the fingers. Ben felt both sick and angry. He also felt sad, discouraged and drained—like everything he had done to give the women a safe haven had been a waste. George had lost a hand and was dead, perhaps.

Tucking the hand under his belt, Ben moved in circles, hoping he wouldn't find a body, but knowing he had to look. That's when he heard someone calling his name.

"Ben?" It was a female voice.

A dark head slowly rose above the sagebrush about 30

yards away. It was Madge. As she stood up, Ben could see the baby in her arms.

As they hurried towards each other, Madge was crying. "They cut off his hand," she sobbed. "They just cut it off."

"Who?" Ben asked.

"Deputies," she explained when she stopped in front of Ben. "They were trying to make him tell where you had gone. When he wouldn't, they just pulled out his hand and chopped it off. It all happened so fast.

"Stella tied a rag around the bleeding stump. That's when Priscilla told them you had gone downstream towards the Green River after Nellie."

"Where's George?" Ben asked.

"They took him with them to jail."

"Why did they leave you?"

"When they were getting ready to leave, I just walked off in the brush and laid down."

"Little George didn't cry?"

"I let him nurse. He was hungry."

"Why didn't you go with them? They wouldn't have harmed you or the baby."

"They cut his hand off," she cried. "I had to find you, tell you what happened. We must help George."

Ben had the urge to get on the horse and go after the posse. Not burdened with the woman and baby, he could probably catch up with them before they reached the river. But he couldn't leave Madge and her baby, and Nellie and the Indian boy were waiting for him a short distance up the canyon. He figured the rest of the horses he had stolen were still in the side canyon. He could use them to get the women and children to a safe haven somewhere, then he would go after George.

"What should we do with this?" Ben asked, removing the hand from his belt.

Madge, cradling her sleeping infant in one arm, reached out with the other to take the hand. She kissed it gently, then held it tightly against her tear-stained cheek.

"I suppose we ought to bury it," she said, fighting to keep control of her voice.

"No," Ben said, after a brief pause. "I want to keep it as an ugly reminder. Don't want to forget what they did to Flat Nose George, or what they have done to all of us."

"Won't it rot and begin to smell?" she asked.

"Not if we salt it good and hang it in the sun to dry."

"I think George would approve," she said, lifting her chin and throwing back her shoulders. Madge handed the hand back to Ben, who placed it once again in his belt. After helping Madge onto the horse and handing her the infant, Ben headed upstream to where he had left Nellie and the Indian boy.

Chapter 50

God has established his kingdom; he has rolled back that cloud that has overspread the moral horizon of the world. He has opened the heavens, revealed the fullness of the everlasting gospel, organized his kingdom according to the pattern that exists in the heavens; and he has placed certain keys, powers and oracles in our midst; and we are the people of God, we are his government.
—JOHN TAYLOR
August 30, 1857

After establishing a camp under a sandstone ledge where Madge, her baby, the Indian boy and Nellie would be as comfortable as possible, Ben headed for the side canyon where he and George had wintered the rest of the horses.

Ben didn't expect to find any sign of horses in the lower part of the canyon. He and George had blocked the trail where it passed along the edge of a sheer cliff about 30 feet above the sandy bottom, and travel in the bottom was blocked by huge boulders. By placing dead cedars further up across the trail, Ben and George had built a barrier to prevent their horses from coming back down the canyon. The horses had been left above the barrier most of the winter.

After he'd passed the cliff, Ben began to see hoofprints and old droppings, but it wasn't until he had gone four or five miles further that he saw the first horse. Two more were a short distance away. Herding them into a small box canyon, Ben cornered the animals, managing to get ropes on two of them. He headed back down the canyon, figuring the free horse would follow the other two. It did.

Ben hadn't gone far when he noticed something he had missed on the way up. Near the base of a gnarled old piñon pine that had been lightning struck years ago, he saw honeybees crawling in and out of an opening.

With his mouth already beginning to water, Ben tied up the three horses and took a closer look. Only a few of the earliest wildflowers were in bloom; still, the bees were busy gathering the wild sweetness. Ben could hear the humming of thousands of bees inside the tree.

Getting as close as he dared, he dropped to one knee and brushed together a pile of dry pine needles. Seconds later he was piling dry twigs of increasing size on a growing fire. When the flames were several feet high he started throwing on grass and green leaves, creating thick billows of white smoke around the bee tree.

Ben waited until he felt confident the bees were sufficiently stunned not to bother him, then took a deep breath and approached the tree, his hunting knife in hand. Reaching quickly inside the tree, he cut free a large chunk of honeycomb dripping with golden honey. Setting it on the grass away from the smoke, he went back for a second and third piece.

Cleaning out one of his saddle bags, Ben made a nest of clean, green grass inside, which he filled with the chunks of honeycomb, holding back the largest to satisfy his craving for sweets as he returned to camp. With honeycomb and reins in one hand and the lead rope in the other, he resumed his journey down the canyon.

It was dark when Ben reached the narrow trail along the cliff. He was riding the black gelding, leading one horse with one more tied to its tail. Lobo was out in front. The fourth horse was following without a rope, further back. The narrow trail was dangerous enough in broad daylight, but in the dark it was treacherous. The sheer dropoff was just inches to the left of where the horses were walking. The slope on the right was too steep, and the rocks were too loose to provide any kind of secure footing.

Right when Ben was at the narrowest, most treacherous part of the trail, the horse that had been following on its own suddenly decided to catch up with the others at a full gallop.

"Whoa!" Ben shouted in a loud voice when he heard its rapid advance, accompanied by the clattering of loose rocks falling over the steep edge and striking the boulders and sand below. The echo of Ben's voice, thundering hooves, and clattering rocks was bouncing back and forth across the steep, narrow canyon.

Ben could tell by the sound of the hooves that the approaching horse was not slowing down. He couldn't turn to the right or left, and the trail was too narrow to urge his horse into a trot or gallop. He couldn't be sure if the approaching horse would suddenly stop, plow into the rear of the last horse, or try to go around on the steep uphill side.

In the sparse light, Ben turned to watch. Rather than slowing down, the horse seemed to be gaining speed. It was almost upon them, and showing no signs of stopping.

Ben stepped out of the saddle on the right, uphill side, yelling "Whoa" at the approaching horse and waving his arms, trying not to startle any more than necessary the two animals secured by lead ropes.

Instead of plowing into the other horses, the running horse tried to go around them to the right on the uphill side. Finding footing difficult in the loose rock, it turned straight up the mountain. But the hill was too steep to go very far, and soon the horse was sliding back down the hill, headed straight for Ben's black gelding, which was standing precariously on the edge of the cliff.

Ben waved and yelled, accomplishing nothing. Leaning back on its hindquarters, the horse was sliding out of control, being preceded by a wave of loose rocks. Sensing he ought to just get out of the way, Ben instead scrambled into the horse's path, hoping somehow his presence would cause it to turn or stop. He was ready to push and shove if necessary.

As the animal met Ben in a shower of hooves and rocks, the ground began to move as he and the horse gained speed towards the narrow trail and sheer dropoff. The black gelding lunged forward to get out of the way, and the other two horses pushed back to allow Ben, the horse, and the loose rocks to pass in front of them.

The horse, instinctively spinning and scrambling for footing, was the first to reach the trail. It might have succeeded in gaining its footing had Ben not tumbled into its hindquarter. Both the horse and Ben suddenly disappeared into the darkness below.

The stars had not yet begun to fade when Nellie became aware of something tugging on her blanket. The fire had gone out long ago, but it wasn't too dark for her to recognize Lobo.

"What is it, boy?" she asked, suddenly alert. She hadn't been aroused from a deep sleep, but from one of many short naps that had made up a very restless night. It had been harder to sleep soundly with Ben gone. She had been more aware of every sound, every distant cry of a coyote or wolf. Occasionally she thought she heard approaching footsteps, perhaps those of hostile Indians.

Nellie found herself thinking back on the previous night and how soundly she had slept knowing Ben was near. Though she had never been on friendly terms with Ben because he was keeping her hostage against her will, she had to acknowledge how she had grown dependent on him and his protection. She didn't feel safe with him gone. She missed him and wished he were rolled up in a blanket across the fire from her, perhaps even next to her. As she thought about that, her sleepiness seemed to vanish, at least for a while, until eventually she began to doze, even if only for a few minutes at a time.

When she sat up to speak to Lobo, he let go of the blanket and ran off into the night, yelping back at her. She slipped on her shoes and stood up. The dog continued to yelp, a short distance off in the darkness.

"What's going on?" asked a sleepy Madge, sitting up in her blanket.

"I think Lobo may want me to follow him," Nellie said. "Something may have happened to Ben."

"Go ahead," Madge said. "I'll stay with the children."

Nellie stepped forward, then stopped.

"Do you think I should wait until daylight?" she asked. She felt afraid, not only of what she might find, but of what might find her. She remembered Flat Nose George telling about the bears in the canyon where they were keeping the horses.

"I'd go now," Madge said. "He might be hurt."

"But I've never been up there before. There might be cliffs, quicksand, or who knows what else that I wouldn't see in the dark."

"Lobo will be with you," Madge said firmly. "If you are afraid, I'll go. You can stay with the children."

On the one hand, Nellie felt relieved that Madge had offered to go. That's what she had been trying to get the older woman to do. What she couldn't understand was why she couldn't bring herself to say, "All right, you go with the dog. I'll stay with the children."

If Ben was in trouble, she wanted to go, had to go. If someone had told her a few hours earlier how she would feel at this moment, she would have laughed.

"No, I'll go," Nellie said, swallowing deeply. A few seconds later she disappeared into the darkness.

Chapter 51

How strange it is, that a matter of comparatively so small consequence to the nation as polygamy is, should have served as the sole means for many years to hold in check this diabolical conspiracy for the founding of a theocratic empire in the very heart of the greatest and freest republic the world has ever known!
—"The Mormon Conspiracy"
Booklet published by the Salt Lake Tribune, 1885

Ben was dreaming. He was no longer a man, but a wooden doll stretched out on the floor of the workshop belonging to Gepetto, the old man who had made the wooden boy Pinocchio in the story Ben had heard many times as a child. The old man was on his knees, grasping a wood rasp with both hands, filing away at Ben's face.

"Nose too long, lips too fat," the old man said as he ran the rasp slowly back and forth across Ben's nose and mouth. The rasp made a rough, scratching sensation that felt good rather than painful to Ben.

"Fingers too fat," Gepetto said, suddenly removing the rasp from the face and beginning to work on the fingers. Again the sensation was a pleasant one for Ben. The only unpleasant sensation was Gepetto's breath. It was rank, like a can of fishing worms that had been left in the sun too long. Ben wanted to turn his head to the side but couldn't. He was made of wood and couldn't move.

After a while Gepetto left the fingers and resumed work

on the mouth and nose. The smell of his breath was becoming more unbearable with each brush of the rasp.

Ben felt like he would suffocate or perhaps strangle from the stench if he didn't move. He focused all his energy on turning his head, straining with all his might.

He didn't succeed. But as he relaxed from his efforts, feeling the rasp scratching away at his mouth, he noticed a strange unevenness on the surface beneath him. He wasn't on a workshop floor, but on cold, lumpy sand. Damp sand. The rasping continued on his mouth and nose, still feeling good.

Ben realized he was not in Gepetto's shop. He wasn't a wooden doll, either. That had been a dream. But he could still feel the rasping sensation, regular and rough, against his nose and mouth. And the rotten worm smell was bad enough to make him want to retch.

Ben strained to open his eyes, finally succeeding but seeing nothing but blackness. The rasping continued. The smell seemed to penetrate to the inside of his stomach.

His mind was confusion. Nothing was clear. He tried to focus his thoughts on remembering what he was doing before he lost consciousness and where he might be. Gradually it began to come back to him—his body slamming onto wet sand and rocks, the tumble from the narrow trail into black space, the horse sliding down the hill towards him, the sweet honey he had enjoyed so much, the bee tree, catching the horses in the canyon where Flat Nose George said there were many bears. . . .

Suddenly Ben knew what was happening to him. A bear was licking the honey from his face and hands. Earlier the bear had probably been eating from the rotting carcass of a winter-killed deer or elk. That explained the smell.

Ben's mind was clear now, though he felt paralyzed with fear. In spite of the incessant licking by the bear's wet, rough tongue, Ben's mouth felt dry. Slowly, he moved his right hand towards his hip until he could feel the butt of his sheath knife. If he stabbed the bear would it become angry and attack him? If he startled it by screaming and yelling, would he frighten it away, or would it attack? If he held still, pretending to be dead, would it eventually leave when the honey was gone, or would it begin eating him?

Slowly Ben inched his fingers around the butt of the knife. Even more slowly, he drew it from the sheath. The bear was licking around his nose now.

Ben didn't want to use the knife if he didn't have to. In the darkness, he wasn't sure exactly where the bear was standing. If he lunged and missed, or only wounded the bear in a non-fatal spot like its front shoulder, it might not give him a second chance to stab again.

Ben decided to wait, as hard as that was, to see what the bear would do when the honey was gone. He would gamble that it would leave. If it decided to try some of Ben's flesh, that's when he would strike with the knife.

Ben's lips and nose were raw before the animal lifted its head to sniff around. Ben wished he could tell it where the bee tree was, where it could find a lot more honey.

The sky was no longer black, but gray with early dawn. Ben could now see the black hulk beside him, though not in detail. The bear seemed bigger than normal, though Ben still couldn't be sure if it was a black bear or a grizzly.

It lowered its head again, this time sniffing instead of licking. It sniffed his neck and chest, then stomach. When it pushed its wet, cold nose between his legs and up into his genitals, Ben tightened his grip on the knife handle but otherwise remained motionless.

Slowly the bear pulled its nose away, then without warning, grabbed Ben's thigh between its powerful jaws. He felt the teeth penetrating his flesh.

Screaming with all the fury he could muster, Ben sat up, plunging the knife into the bear's neck. The startled animal lunged back, but did not let go of Ben's thigh. It jerked its head from side to side, tossing Ben back and forth like a rag doll. He plunged the knife into the neck a second time. Still the bear did not let go of the leg. Instead, it growled through its locked jaws.

Ben was beginning to think the bear would never let go when suddenly a gray streak from his left slammed into the bear's neck. There was a loud snarl as white teeth sank into the dark hide, ripping and tearing. It was Lobo.

The bear let go of Ben, turning all its attention and fury on the wolf-dog. Ben rolled free as the bear caught the dog with its paw, sending Lobo sprawling across the wet sand. In an instant the dog was back, snapping and snarling. Lobo was darting in and out, nipping here and there while deftly avoiding the huge paws. Lobo gradually took the fight away from his master. Ben began throwing rocks at the bear, which soon turned and ran up the canyon.

When Lobo returned, Ben was on his back, holding the injured leg in the air, pressing against the wounded area in an effort to stop the blood spurting in pulses between his fingers. His leg and hands were covered with blood.

"Lobo, come here," called an unsure woman's voice from down the canyon. It was Nellie. The dog looked towards the sound, but remained beside Ben, who yelled, "Up here, under the cliff. Hurry."

Chapter 52

We have been persecuted and robbed long enough, and in the name of Israel's God we will be free!
—JOHN TAYLOR
September 13, 1857

By the time Nellie reached Ben he was lying in a pool of his own blood, unable to stop the bleeding in his leg. A few feet away lay a dead horse. Nellie acted quickly. As a reporter in Scotland she had covered train wrecks and factory cave-ins, frequently interviewing doctors as they worked. She knew what to do with a severed artery.

She tore a strip of fabric from the hem of her dress, wrapping it loosely around his leg just above the bleeding wound and finally tying both ends in a knot. Grabbing a stick off the ground, she slipped it under the strip of cloth and began twisting the bandage tighter and tighter until the bleeding slowed to a trickle.

"Hold this," she ordered, nodding for Ben to grab the stick so it wouldn't unwind when she let go. He obeyed without comment. Unable to stop the bleeding himself, he was content to let Nellie tell him what to do.

She was on her knees in the blood-soaked sand, not seeming to notice her dress was soaking up the redness. She leaned over the wound, her long red hair covering her face. Working quickly, she tore several long threads from her dress; then, working her fingers deep into the wound, she found the ripped artery and tied it off with the threads.

"There," she said when she was finished. She pushed Ben's hand away from the stick and loosened it several turns. While there was still some bleeding in the wound, the spurting had stopped.

Nellie hurried back to where she had tied the loose horses earlier. She needed a horse to carry Ben back to camp. Feeling weak and sick, he stretched out on the cool sand and closed his eyes. Lobo stood guard beside him, ready should the bear return.

By the time Nellie helped Ben onto the black gelding and began leading him back to camp, he was so weak he could hardly stay in the saddle. His face was white except for a smear of blood on his left cheek. The injured leg was beginning to swell. He had no appetite. Upon reaching camp, he just let go and fell to the ground in an unconscious heap.

Nellie and Madge made Ben as comfortable as possible on the dry white sand beneath the ledge. While Nellie went back to get the rest of the horses, Madge and the Indian boy picked handfuls of the soft green yarrow leaves growing along the edge of the cliffs. After crushing the leaves into a moist pulp by rubbing them back and forth between her palms, Madge packed the wound. She had been taught that yarrow stopped infection and bleeding. Unconscious, Ben didn't feel any pain as she pushed the green pulp deep into his flesh.

By the time Nellie returned, it was almost dark, and Ben had not awakened, though his slumber was becoming restless. The leg continued to swell, and his face had turned to a pink flush. His temperature was going up.

Ben did not regain consciousness that night. The women forced him to swallow a few sips of water, but he had not eaten since the accident.

"Maybe one of us should try to find a doctor," Madge suggested as the sky began to turn gray with the approaching day. "There might be one in Green River."

It was decided Madge would go for help, taking her baby with her on the black horse. Nellie and the boy would stay to care for Ben. They guessed it would take Madge at least a day to get to Green River, and an equal amount of time for the doctor to return—that is, if she could find a doctor.

By the time the sun spread its golden rays over the eastern mountains, Madge had disappeared down the canyon. Nellie sat beside Ben, caressing his hot forehead with a cool, damp rag. Occasionally she would speak to him, asking how he felt or if he wanted anything. He didn't answer, though he continued to toss restlessly about.

Occasionally Nellie would look down towards the trickle of water in the bottom of the wash where the Indian boy was playing. He had recovered quickly from his ordeal. Though still careful with his injured hands, he was no longer content to sit and do nothing. He was still shy and didn't like being talked to in English, but he no longer seemed afraid of his new benefactors.

Nellie wondered what the boy's name was and if he would ever be able to tell her. She wondered if she should give him a new one. If Ben died, she would call him Ben. But Ben wouldn't die. He was too strong, too healthy. Even more important, there was a quality about Ben that Nellie couldn't put her finger on. He had held her against her will, in violation of the law. He had set two deputies adrift on the Green River and shot others in the feet and stolen their horses. Still, there was something good about Ben, a feeling that he had something important to do, that he had a mission to accomplish and couldn't be stopped by a fall from a cliff or a bite from a bear. Ben was chosen for something. Nellie wasn't sure what it was. It was just a feeling, but a strong one.

The stretch of sand beneath the overhanging cliff became warm in the afternoon sun. Even though it was early spring, with patches of snow above the cliffs, the south-facing overhang, protected from the cool afternoon breezes that danced across the tops of the cliffs, became unusually warm as the sun shone brightly through a cloudless blue sky.

Nellie removed Ben's shirt to help lower his temperature. As she ran the cool, wet rag across his chest, she couldn't help but admire his perfectly proportioned body—smooth, white skin stretched tightly across firm muscles. There was no fat. It seemed wrong for a body so healthy and strong to be unconscious and helpless.

Once, as she pushed the wet rag across his chest onto his abdomen, the rag bunched up under her palm, allowing her fingers to touch his wet skin. The first time, she quickly spread the rag back out to cover all the skin beneath her palm and fingers. But the second time, she let the rag remain in a clump, allowing her fingertips to stroke the smooth skin. The result was a warm, tingling sensation passing up her arm and into her body.

She looked over at the Indian boy, who was busy with a pile of stones, then downstream to see if Madge was returning. Of course she wasn't. Nellie realized she was feeling guilty for touching Ben and she wasn't sure why. She only knew she would be embarrassed if anyone saw her, saw through her and knew she liked it.

Suddenly angry with herself and her feelings, Nellie stood up and began walking upstream. Ben would just have to be hot for a while. But she wasn't gone long, and when she returned, she took little care to make sure the wet rag stayed beneath her palm. Occasionally she ran the cooling rag over the wound to shoo away the first of the spring flies, which seemed determined to get inside. While the swelling had not gone away, it didn't seem to be getting any worse.

In the middle of the night, Ben's temperature finally broke. Nellie awoke with a start, not sure what had disturbed her. The cool night breeze was pushing down from the snowy mountains to the east, chilling everything in its path.

Reaching over to Ben in the darkness, Nellie touched him. The skin on his chest was no longer hot and wet with perspiration, but dry and cool with goosebumps. She could feel him shivering and hear the chattering of his teeth.

Pushing back her blanket, she pushed close to him, pressing her body against his in an effort to share her warmth, then pulling her blanket around the two of them. His teeth stopped chattering, then the shivering stopped. Ben seemed to be drifting into a deep, comfortable sleep. She decided she preferred the chills to the temperature. At least she could do something about the chills.

The morning sun was just rising over the eastern cliffs

when Nellie noticed that Ben had regained consciousness. She was bent over the fire, cooking some chunks of horse meat on pointed sticks, when she looked up to see him staring at her.

"You're conscious," she said simply.

"Yes," he said, "thanks to you."

"Madge and I were worried about you," she said, looking back down at the meat, not understanding why she felt timid before his stare. She wished she had taken time to wash her face and brush her hair.

"Where's Madge?" he asked. She told him how Madge had left in search of a doctor.

"How long was I out? What happened?"

Nellie told him everything—how he and one of the horses had fallen off the cliff, how Lobo had gone for help and chased off the bear, how she had tied off the severed artery and brought him back to camp on the black gelding, how he had been unconscious for nearly 40 hours.

"You sure know how to cure the chills," he said matter-of-factly when she had finished talking.

"How long have you been conscious?" Nellie demanded, a hint of anger in her voice, her face suddenly red.

"Since before you decided to put a stop to my chills," he said bluntly.

"Why didn't you tell me you were conscious?" she cried.

"Afraid you might pull away," he said honestly.

She stood up, turning her back to him, walking towards the stream, wanting to be out of his sight. She was angry, wanting to hurt him with words that she couldn't bring herself to say because they were lies, wanting to kick him in the injured leg but knowing she couldn't. She wanted to cry, but at the same time felt better than she had felt in years. She was confused, except for one lingering thought that seemed to overshadow everything else. She was in love with Ben Storm.

Chapter 53

But that it (Mormonism) could be dealt with by legislation there can be no doubt, if the government and the Nation would wake up to the fact that Mormonism is a conspiracy, whatever else it may be, to establish an independent theocratic empire in America. Polygamy is as nothing in comparison with Mormonism as a whole. It is a great mistake to regard this crime as the sole objection to the system.

—"The Mormon Conspiracy"
Booklet published by the Salt Lake Tribune, 1885

Another day passed with no sign of Madge or a doctor. Ben was still weak, but was now eating and drinking. His temperature was back to normal. Even the swelling in the leg had come down some, though the smell—the stench of rotten flesh and mildew—was getting worse.

Nellie had just returned from picking more yarrow in preparation for cleaning the wound and making a fresh dressing. Ben had resigned himself to letting her work on the wound, knowing it would be painful.

The Indian boy and Lobo were playing near the creek—the boy throwing a stick up the bank, the dog retrieving it. A cool breeze was blowing off the mountain, a pleasant contrast to the warmth of the sun-warmed cliffs.

Carefully Nellie began pulling out the blood-soaked sprigs of yarrow, gently applying moisture where they were stuck to dry flesh. Ben was on his back, his elbows holding his shoulders up so he could watch. He acted as if the pain were bearable, but Nellie could tell from the occasional twitch of his cheek and the perspiration on his forehead that her work was bringing him pain.

It was Nellie who finally cried out as she removed the last large wad of yarrow. It was not a cry of pain, but one of surprise. As she removed the wad, three white worms with black heads quickly wiggled deeper into the wound.

"Looks like the flies laid some eggs," Ben responded as Lobo and the boy ran up to see what had alarmed Nellie. "I've heard maggots will clean up a bad wound."

"Whether they do or not, we're getting them out of there," Nellie said firmly. "I'll not have worms eating you up."

She placed the damp wad of old yarrow back over the wound where the maggots had been, in the hopes that when it was covered again, they would return to the surface. While waiting for them, Nellie fashioned a pair of tweezers from a green willow stick. Lobo and the boy stayed close, curious about what she was doing.

With the tweezers poised a few inches above the wound, Nellie jerked away the dressing, quickly clamping down on a fat maggot before it could follow its companions into the flesh. Victoriously, Nellie held it up for all to see before releasing it on a flat rock beside her.

Lobo stepped forward to sniff the white worm as the boy quickly picked it up and popped it into his mouth. "No!" screamed Nellie. "Spit that out!"

Even though the boy hadn't been around white people long enough to understand their language, he knew the meaning of the word "no."

Reluctantly the boy spit the still wiggling worm onto his palm and handed it back to Nellie, expecting her to pop it in her mouth.

To the boy's amazement, she dropped it on the ground and crushed it in the dirt beneath her foot. Not understanding this strange white woman, the boy shrugged his shoulders and returned to the creek where he had been playing. Lobo followed.

Nellie bent back over the wound in search of a second maggot.

"Why didn't you let him eat it?" Ben asked.

"What?" she asked, looking up from her task.

"Why didn't you let him eat it?" he repeated.

"Because it was a maggot," she said, astonished Ben would ask a question with such an obvious answer.

"That's not a reason," he said, grinning.

"Reason enough for me," she responded, looking back down at her work, quickly removing the yarrow wad and trying to grab another worm.

"Some Indians eat grubs, caterpillars, even grasshoppers," Ben explained. "Lots of vitamins and minerals. You may have denied the boy what he thinks is a real treat."

"You really think so?" she asked with pretended innocence, looking into his eyes.

"Very likely," he responded, looking back at her. Previously, Ben had always considered Nellie a threat because of the things she might write about him and his church. Today he looked at her differently. It wasn't just that she had saved his life by tying off the spurting artery and doctoring him while he was unconscious. He felt drawn to this woman by an unwavering force. She looked better to him all the time. He couldn't forget her drawing close to him that cold night to share her warmth with him. In fact, he found himself wondering how he might fake another set of chills so the experience could be repeated.

"Close your eyes," she ordered.

By now Ben was used to taking orders from Nellie concerning his health, so without thinking he closed his eyes. No sooner had he done so than he felt something small and moist being pushed between his lips. It wiggled.

"By switch!" he hollered, spitting out the maggot and reaching for Nellie, who had already darted out of reach.

"Lots of vitamins and minerals," she mimicked.

When Ben tried to stand to go after her, a searing pain ripped through the entire length of his wounded thigh, causing him to collapse. Nellie was laughing, and in spite of the pain, Ben laughed with her.

Chapter 54

Profoundly grateful to our God for his kindness to us in permitting us to have a name and a place among his people, and to be the bearers of his everlasting priesthood, we are determined with his help to press forward with increased diligence and zeal in doing our part towards the carrying on of his purposes and works.

—General epistle to the Saints from
John Taylor and George Q. Cannon, April 4, 1885

The boy was playing on the hill above the camp when he saw the approaching riders—two men on fast-walking horses, not more than half a mile away. The boy ran down the hill, interrupting Ben and Nellie's conversation, anxiously pointing in the direction of the two riders.

Ben was a lot stronger now. The fever was gone, as were the maggots, and the leg was healing though he still had difficulty placing weight on it. Ben grabbed his rifle and the three of them scampered behind the nearest big rock on the uphill side of the camp. The boy was holding Lobo by the collar. The horses were grazing out of sight upstream from the camp.

No sooner were they in place than the two men rode into view. Nellie and Ben were looking for something—perhaps a medical bag—to indicate one of the men might be the doctor Madge wanted to send back. There was nothing.

Without warning, Ben leaned his rifle against the rock and stood up in full view of the two riders.

"Big brother!" Ben shouted, his hand on Nellie's shoulder for balance as he tried to keep his weight off the injured leg. Ben recognized his older brother, Sam, who was supposed to be in prison in Detroit. He didn't recognize the older man with the white beard and little black hat.

"Brought you a little venison," Sam shouted, patting the side of a freshly killed doe stretched across the front of his saddle.

After introductions were made and everyone had a good look at Ben's wound, Sam and Moroni went to work cleaning and skinning the deer. Later that night, as dripping chunks of fresh venison were roasting over the fire, Sam and Moroni told of their escape from the Detroit prison and their journey back to Utah. They had found out from their families that there were prices on their heads, and after spending a few days with their wives and deciding it would be too risky to stay in the Salt Lake area, they had decided to try to find Ben and his outlaw band.

Upon hearing that, Ben laughed. "The rest of my band—one old Indian—was arrested last week," he explained. "At least, most of him was arrested. They left part behind." He showed Sam and Moroni Flat Nose George's hand, which was dry and somewhat shriveled from days in the sun.

Sam and Moroni had run into Madge at Green River, where she was having no success finding a doctor. She had told Sam and Moroni where they could find Ben, and they had given her train fare back to Springville, seeing no need for her to return to the camp.

When Sam and Moroni finished the story of their travels, Ben told them his story, beginning with Kathryn's arrest and the confrontation with Vandercook, up to and including Grace Woolley's suicide.

"She was so sad," Nellie added. "We should have guessed she might try something like that."

While the exchange of information was taking place, Nellie was sitting close to Ben. Sam noticed that their shoulders were touching.

"Everything is sad these days," Moroni said, "with

Church leaders on the underground and hundreds of polygamists in jail. The U.S. Marshal even has a 'for rent' sign on the turtle."

"The turtle?" Nellie asked.

"Tabernacle," Sam explained. "Where the Mormons meet on Temple Square. The roof is shaped like a turtle."

"Why does the marshal have anything to do with the tabernacle?" Ben asked.

"The new Edmunds-Tucker law has made the old Edmunds law enforceable—the part about a church that teaches polygamy not being allowed to have more than $50,000 in assets. In addition to the tabernacle and the entire temple block, Marshal Dyer has confiscated the historian's office, the general tithing office, President Taylor's home, the Guardo House, and about 30,000 sheep belonging to the Church."

"They can't just take all that," Ben protested. "It's not right."

"But it's legal," Moroni responded.

"What about all the meetinghouses?" Nellie asked.

"Church acted fast and got most of the titles transferred into the names of various Church leaders," Moroni explained.

"What are the leaders going to do about it?" Ben asked.

"They're in hiding, dodging the law and not doing much of anything except keeping out of jail," Sam explained.

"President Taylor married himself a new wife in December," Moroni added, a slight chuckle in his voice.

"You're joking," Nellie said. "He must be seventy years old."

"Seventy-eight," Moroni said.

"That's disgusting," Nellie responded.

"That depends on your point of view," Moroni argued. "To a man my age it is anything but disgusting, but to a young woman on the outside—I can see why you might feel that way."

"What should we do?" Ben asked, changing the subject.

"Let's eat," Moroni said.

"What should we *do* about this whole mess?" Ben persisted.

"I don't know," Sam said.

"Can't stay here," Ben said. "Now that they know about the place, deputies could be dropping in at any time."

"Dad's still in Canada. We could go there," Sam suggested.

"Some are going to Mexico," Moroni added.

"You could go back to Salt Lake and turn yourselves in," Nellie said. All three men looked at her soberly.

"If I was sent back to that cold prison in Detroit, I'd never return home alive," Moroni said, a coldness in his voice that hadn't been there before.

"You have broken the law," Nellie said, her voice cold too. "You have a debt to pay."

"If caring for the women who married me and bore my children is breaking the law," he said, "then I am indeed a criminal. But I have done no wrong."

"Breaking the law is wrong," Nellie insisted.

"Trying to crush a people for trying to live their religion is wrong!" Moroni shouted.

"Your arguing is a waste of time," Sam interrupted. "What you are talking about has been discussed and rediscussed until it makes me sick. Everything's been said and resaid a thousand times. The question is no longer *if* polygamy is right or wrong. The Mormons believe in it. The rest of the United States doesn't. Any further discussion is a waste of time and energy."

"So what do we do?" Nellie asked nastily.

"Now you've hit upon it," Sam said, "as Ben did a few minutes ago. What *do* we do?

"I see two alternatives," Ben said, addressing Sam. Moroni and Nellie were still glaring at each other, apparently thinking of things to say to continue their argument, but obviously feeling restrained by the forcefulness of Sam's objection.

"Giving ourselves up and going to jail is not an alternative as far as I am concerned," Ben continued. "We are not criminals. Stupid men in Washington passing a law to make our religion illegal doesn't make us criminals."

"What are the alternatives?" Sam asked, wanting Ben to

get to the point.

"First," Ben explained without hesitation, "we can get out of here, go to Canada or Mexico, and start over where they will leave us alone."

"Is that what you want to do?" Nellie asked Ben.

"No," he said. "My home is here. I want to stay, but the law won't let me."

"Not as long as you support polygamy," Nellie said.

"You forget. Polygamy is part of the religion I grew up with. You can't just forget your religion and your upbringing because a new law is passed," Ben explained.

"What's the second alternative?" Sam asked.

"Stay and fight. Strap on the guns and let the world know there are some Mormons who have had enough of politics. If they persist in chasing our church leaders, confiscating our church property, dragging virtuous women into court to make them look like whores, and throwing good men in jail, then by hell they are going to have to answer for it!"

"How?" Sam asked.

"Blow up their prisons, burn their courthouses, derail their trains and fill their ballot boxes with wet cow manure."

"But that will just make them more angry," Nellie said, trying to add some moderation to Ben's violent talk. "The pressure on the church would become more intense."

"How could it?" Ben asked. "The church is on its knees, its leaders in hiding, its property confiscated, its best men in jail. How could it get worse? Being passive hasn't done any good in the past. It's time some of us got a little starch in our spines and let them know we will not stand for any more!"

"I'm with you, Ben," Sam said.

"You can count me in too," Moroni added.

"Don't look at me that way," Nellie said when Ben glanced over at her. "You can count me out."

"You misunderstood," Ben said, laughing. "I was looking at you for a totally different reason."

"What?" she asked.

"Personal—we'll talk later."

"When should we go?" Sam asked.

"The leg needs a couple more days," Ben said, "then we

can travel to Salt Lake. We'll let the whole world know the Mormons have been pushed too far."

"Amen," said Moroni.

Chapter 55

We do not know that the people of the United States will ever be aroused to the treason of the whole Mormon system, until it shall be forced upon their attention through a civil war....
—Salt Lake Tribune editorial
October 9, 1886

"I want you to know I am totally opposed to what you are about to do," Nellie said later that same night, as she and Ben walked along the sandy, moonlit wash. Ben was limping with the help of a crutch Sam had fashioned for him from a chokecherry limb. The reflection of the moonlight on the sand gave them plenty of light to see their way.

"I know you're against it," Ben responded. "That's why I wanted to talk with you alone."

"To try to change my mind?"

"No, just wondering how things will be between you and me after we leave here."

"It's one thing to save pregnant women from being dragged off to jail. But it's something else to lead a band of outlaws into Salt Lake City, bent on destroying property and disrupting government business. We're not talking about a crime against society, but declaring war on the United States. I don't think you are aware of the consequences. I don't think things will ever be the same again between you and me."

"My people have no fair recourse in the law. There's no

choice left but to go outside it.''

''You could do nothing. Let the church leaders defend their church.''

''They're old men. Wise, but old.''

''And you're young. Not even 20. And not so wise.''

''I can't stand by and see my people stomped into the dirt. I'd rather fight.''

''What makes you think you can take on the whole United States government by yourself?''

''Others will join me.''

''Are you sure?''

''I'm not yet 20 and have never led men into battle. I don't know why other men will join and follow me. I just believe they will.''

''Maybe some will die.''

''There are things worse than death.''

''What about us?''

Ben stopped. Discussing the decision to fight the anti-Mormons was easier than discussing for the first time in his life a romantic relationship with a woman.

''We'll take you with us,'' he said slowly, skirting her question. ''At least as far as the closest train stop. From there you'll be on your own.''

''Will I see you again?''

''In jail, maybe.''

''Stop it,'' she said. ''This last week I thought something was happening between you and me.''

''I thought the same thing,'' he ventured.

''So what happens next? I want to know.'' She wasn't so cautious.

''I'm going to Salt Lake to raise all the hell I can.''

''What am I supposed to do?''

''Write about it. Tell the real story why people like me and my brother are fighting back.''

''I don't like polygamy. I won't have a hand in supporting it.''

''Nobody's asking you to do anything but be fair and tell the truth. You don't have to believe in polygamy to do that.''

''What about us?''

"You can send letters to my father's place in American Fork. They'll get to me. I'll try to visit you. No promises. I don't know what's going to happen. When it's all over, maybe things can be better for you and me."

Nellie turned and started walking back to camp.

"Wait," Ben said. "Come back."

"What else is there to talk about?" she asked, stopping, waiting for him to catch up with her. He put his hand on her shoulder.

"You saved my life," he said.

"I'd have done the same for any man who had been hurt like that." Her voice was cold, distant.

"Nellie, I love you," he said.

"You're three years younger than I am. And you believe in polygamy."

"I still love you, and I think you feel the same way about me."

"How can you be sure?"

Ben let his crutch fall to the ground. With a hand on each of her shoulders he pulled her close to him, gently kissing her above the right eye, then above the left. Nellie pushed back, grinning.

"Have you ever kissed a woman before?" she asked.

"No," Ben said, an innocence in his voice that couldn't be questioned.

"I'll bet you've kissed horses before."

"Sure," Ben said, like that was the most natural thing in the world.

"Above the eyes?"

"Mostly on the nose."

"I'll show you how to kiss a woman," she said, suddenly throwing her arms around his neck and pulling his mouth down on hers. He responded by wrapping his arms around her and pulling her firmly against him. It was a long kiss.

"Are you sure you have to go to Salt Lake," she gasped, finally pulling her head back to catch her breath.

"I'm sure."

"Oh, how I wish I didn't love you so, but I do."

"You ruined it," he said.

"Ruined what?"

"I'll never enjoy kissing a horse again." Her laugh was cut short as he began to kiss her again.

Chapter 56

. . . They tried to give him (horse) medicine but could not succeed. The horse lay on his side with his forefoot over his ear, but Reuben Strong said he believed there was breath in him yet, and proposed to lay hands upon him. Some present doubted whether it was right to lay hands on a horse; Elder Hall replied the Prophet Joel has said that in the last days the Lord would pour out his spirit upon all flesh and thus satisfied the brethren. Elders William Hall, Reuben R. Strong, Lluellen Mantle, Joseph Camplin, Martin Potter and one more laid hands on the horse and commanded the unclean and foul spirits of every name and nature to depart and go to the gentiles at Warsaw and trouble the saints no more, when the horse rolled twice over in great distress, sprang to his feet, squealed, vomited and purged, and the next morning was harnessed to a load of about twelve hundred weight and performed his part as usual.

—Brigham Young's Iowa Journal
Saturday, March 14, 1846

It was early morning when Moroni, Ben, and Sam reached the top of the ridge. Nellie and the boy, hand in hand, were trailing behind.

Moroni was in charge this morning. He removed his black hat as Ben and Sam gathered around. His white hair and beard glistened like new wool in the morning sun. His blue eyes sparkled as he looked beyond the ridge at the surrounding mountains and valleys—a rugged, wild country.

"This is the kind of place Moses would have picked," he said.

"Why's that?" Sam asked.

"When Moses sought God he went to the tops of the mountains. He wandered into the most remote wildernesses. So did Enoch, John the Baptist, Jeremiah, and Elijah. They went to the places where other men didn't go, where perhaps no man had ever set foot before. This looks like that kind of place. I feel like we are standing on holy ground."

"You still haven't explained why we've come up here," Nellie said, out of breath from the climb.

"Moroni's going to give us a blessing before we head out for Salt Lake," Ben explained, his voice almost a whisper, taking Moroni's lead that they were indeed on holy ground requiring reverence and reserve in speech and actions.

"Oh, I see," Nellie said, her voice still loud, her speech still interrupted by deep breaths as she continued to catch her breath after the steep climb. "He's going to turn your outlaw raid into a religious crusade."

"We shouldn't have let her come," Moroni said to Ben and Sam. "We should have left her behind. We are on God's errand and there's no place for a gentile heckler among us. She must leave."

"Nellie, I think you ought to go back to camp," Ben said. "We'd rather do this out of range of your critical eye."

"I'm sorry," she said, her voice suddenly soft and subdued, thinking under her breath that she didn't want to miss this for anything. "I apologize for making light of your blessings."

"I don't want her to stay," Moroni said, mumbling something about throwing pearls before swine.

"I'll be quiet," Nellie promised, not responding to his bait to get her in another argument.

"Let her stay," Ben said. "Her tongue is sharp, but her heart is in the right place."

"All right," Moroni said after a long pause. "But not a word."

Nellie nodded her humble agreement.

"You'd better cover your head and face," Moroni advised.

Nellie resisted the urge to demand an explanation as she tied a scarf over her hair, pulling part of it forward over her face. Then she seated herself on a patch of new grass, pulling the child down beside her.

Ben thought she looked silly with part of the scarf over her face, but resisted the urge to laugh or tease. This was no time for frivolity.

Moroni motioned for Ben to be seated on a flat rock. He then moved behind Ben, placing both his hands on Ben's head. Sam was to one side, his hands on Moroni's.

All three men bowed their heads and closed their eyes as Moroni began the blessing. Nellie and the child watched quietly from their patch of grass. A slight breeze drifting down from the snow-capped mountains to the east was cool, but the morning sun was warm.

Moroni began the blessing in the usual manner, addressing Ben by name and mentioning the priesthood which gave him authority and power to bless and curse.

"As David of old slew Goliath to deliver Israel from the Phillistines," Moroni continued, "so are you, Ben Storm, called to deliver Israel from the evil designs of ambitious politicians, crooked judges, and the lies of the *Salt Lake Tribune.*" Moroni paused, taking a deep breath and resuming the blessing in a louder voice with more intensity.

"As you become anxiously engaged in delivering this people from the very clutches of Satan, the Lord God of Israel will strengthen your arm as he did the arms of Samson, David, Ammon, and Mormon. Be faithful and diligent in this calling and the blessings of heaven will distill upon your head as the early morning dew. At the sound of your voice the hosts of Israel will gather to battle, and your enemies will quake.

"And as you step forth to deliver Israel, the angels of heaven with the means available to them will gather about to protect you from harm. The Lord will open your mind so you will know what to do. He will put words in your mouth that will inspire the armies of Israel to obey your every command.

"And I promise you, Ben Storm, that as you are faithful

the Lord will clear the way before you, lay your enemies to waste, curse them that curse you, bless them that bless you, and one day when you finally lay down your sword, the Lord will pour out upon your head the blessings of heaven, more than you can receive—of success, fame, properties, families, wives and children, in this world and the world to come. To this end I bless you with strength in the mind, sinews, and loins forever and ever."

Moroni continued for a few more minutes, his voice growing quieter and quieter until he finally closed in the name of Jesus Christ. Ben stood up, and the three men soberly shook hands. Then Sam sat down on the rock, Ben and Moroni laying hands on his head as Moroni gave a second blessing, similar in content to the one he had given Ben. When this blessing was finished, after a second round of handshaking Moroni seated himself on the rock while Sam delivered the blessing, again similar to the two earlier ones. Nellie listened carefully, trying to remember all that was said, making special note of the promise in Ben's blessing that he would have more than one wife.

When Sam finished with Moroni's blessing, the old man stood up, shook hands with Sam and Ben, then looked over at Nellie and the boy.

"While we're at it, might as well give the lad a name and blessing," he said, motioning for the boy to come to him.

"It's all right," Ben said when Nellie, a look of concern on her face, began to reach out to stop the boy.

A minute later the three men had their hands on the boy's head as Moroni gave him the name of Abinadi, a fiery Book of Mormon prophet, and blessed the boy with health and strength and a mission to take the gospel to the Lamanites or Indians so they could "become a white and delightsome people." The boy didn't understand what was said, but quickly learned his new name with a little coaching from Ben and Moroni after the blessing was over.

Once that was accomplished, everyone walked in silence back down the mountain to camp, Moroni leading the way.

Nellie had a hundred questions she wanted to ask, but because of the sober, silent mood of the men, she decided to wait for a better time. She had felt the intensity of the blessings. There was no doubt in her mind that Ben, Sam, and Moroni believed God had a hand, not only in what had just transpired on the mountain, but in their future activities as they headed for Salt Lake.

Nellie didn't know whether or not there was divine involvement in the blessings, but she did know the men believed there was and that they had a mandate from God to go to Salt Lake and cause trouble for the non-Mormons. How far they would go, she didn't know. The words of the blessings indicated fighting and killing. Were those words symbolic or literal? Either way, she intended to find out. She would be riding at least part of the way with them. When the fireworks began, she would report it, if she could find anyone to print her stories. She was determined not to be a pawn for the anti-Mormon *Tribune,* nor would she be a defender of polygamy. She would write about what she observed, as truthfully and fairly as possible. She had no idea who would run those kinds of stories. Hopefully there was an editor somewhere who didn't have an ax to grind.

Chapter 57

. . . The gathering of one creed into one body is dangerous to the liberty of citizens, and inimical to our institutions, while the assumption of divine right to rule and the attempt to put it into practice is the real evil now existing in Utah; and the thing that alone threatens the peace, good order and happiness of the Pacific States and territories.
—"The Mormon Conspiracy"
A booklet published by the Salt Lake Tribune, 1885

As the travelers approached the railroad tracks just east of where they crossed the Green River, a deer bolted from the willows, bouncing up the trail. Ben raised his rifle to his shoulder, dropping the animal with the first shot.

"What'd you do that for?" Sam asked. "We still have plenty of meat left from the deer I killed."

"Just thinking about those Chinamen," Ben said, returning the rifle to the scabbard. "We had a pretty quiet winter up at the cabin. Can't help but feel those Chinamen knew we were there but didn't tell anyone. Thought they might like a little fresh venison to cook with their rice."

A half hour later they were swimming the river just above the railroad trestle. The deer was lashed across one of the pack horses. With warmer weather and the absence of pregnant women, this crossing was easier than when they had done it the previous winter. The river was not yet swollen with spring runoff.

Ben led the pack horse to the top of the rise where the two

little shacks were located, dismounted, and began untying the deer as three chattering Chinamen in blue pajamas trotted outside to see what was happening. At first they seemed alarmed, like they were in some kind of trouble with the white man, but when Ben slipped the deer to the ground, motioning for them to help themselves, the three men grinned with delight. Nellie, Sam, Moroni, and Abinadi arrived at the top of the ridge just in time to join in the celebration, which consisted of the Chinamen refusing to let Ben leave after giving them such a wonderful gift. One tried to give Ben a pan, another a blue army coat. Politely, Ben declined. Still, they couldn't let him go unrewarded.

Finally one of the Chinamen led Ben into one of the little shacks. Ben whistled his surprise. "Ought to see all the stuff in here!" he shouted through the open door.

A minute later he emerged grinning, a wooden box in his hands. Printed in black ink across the front of the box was the word "Explosives."

"They gave me 15 sticks of dynamite, along with caps and fuses," Ben explained as he found a place for the box on the gentler of the two pack horses.

Though the Chinamen wanted Ben and his companions to stay for dinner, Ben insisted they must leave. "Much business in Salt Lake," he explained.

"What are you going to do with all that dynamite?" Nellie asked when they were once again traveling.

"I'm not really sure," Ben said. "Maybe we'll find a spot for it in the *Trib* office. Your friend Harry Chew would get a bang out of that."

Sam and Moroni laughed at Ben's bad humor, but not Nellie.

"When will I see you again?" Nellie asked as she dismounted beside the train depot in Price. Ben reached out and took her reins. Sam, Moroni, and Abinadi were waiting in a grove of trees several miles from town. It was an hour or two before dawn.

"I have your address," he whispered. "I'll come and see you in a week or two, if you promise not to have deputies waiting for me."

"You know I wouldn't do that."

"What are you going to say when they ask how you got away?"

"That you let me go. I think that's enough. Truthful, too."

"And if they ask where I am?"

"I'll tell them you're on the loose, and that every deputy in the territory had better be on the lookout for you if he doesn't want his horse stolen or his foot shot."

"We'll leave Abinadi with John Jex in Springville. You can see him there whenever you want. He'll have a good home."

"I'll miss you," she said, moving closer to his horse. He bent over and kissed her gently on the lips. Their hands touched for a brief moment before he spun the horse around and galloped into the night.

Four nights later Ben, Sam, and Moroni were camped in a protected clump of oakbrush near the top of Traverse Ridge, the hills extending westward from the Wasatch Mountains to separate Utah Valley from the Salt Lake Valley. From the hill above their camp they could look down on the entire Salt Lake Valley. After a brief stop at the Storm ranch where Kathryn was staying with Caroline and Sarah—Dan was still in Canada—they followed the old wagon road up Hog Hollow to the top of the ridge.

From the hill above their camp they watched the sun go down over the Salt Lake Valley. They were trying to decide how to begin their campaign against the anti-Mormons. Moroni's first suggestion was to send out word through the underground that they were raising an army to drive every anti-Mormon gentile from the territory.

"The difference between you and me," Ben said, "is that you want to fight like a bull while I would rather fight like a fox. I'm afraid if we get a bunch of people in the open, guns blazing, a lot of men will die."

"How do you want to begin?" Sam asked.

"Since we've got all this dynamite, I thought we might blow up the prison at Sugarhouse. Lots of good Mormons in there, and a one-handed Indian. Let's get them out. Maybe that'll be the beginning of our army."

"Sounds like a good plan to me," Sam said. "What do you think, Moroni?"

The old man removed his hat, turned it upside down, and carefully placed his seerstone in the bottom. Bending over until his face covered the opening, Moroni concentrated on his stone for several minutes.

"See anything?" Sam asked.

"No," Moroni said after a while, "but I feel good about going to the prison first. The Lord delivered the deer into our hands, which got us the dynamite. Back in Detroit I wanted more than anything in the world to make the prison walls crumble. I couldn't do it by raising my arm to the square and shouting, so it looks like the Lord has given me some dynamite in place of the faith I lack. Yes, I feel good about the prison."

"It's settled, then," Sam said.

Chapter 58

To judge by the epistle put forth by the first presidency of the Mormon Church at the present conference, the church must be on its last legs. It (the letter) is strong in no feature except its vindictiveness, and even in that it has a sound like the bark of a toothless dog.

—Salt Lake Tribune editorial
October 9, 1886

"Looks as solid as the temple," Moroni said as he, Sam, and Ben rode east past the front of the federal prison at Sugarhouse.

"Made from the same granite, quarried up Little Cottonwood," Sam added.

"I didn't know the walls were so high" was Ben's comment.

"Not sure the dynamite will shoot a hole through that wall," Sam said. "And even if it did, how would we get Flat Nose George out? Can't be positive he's in there. Maybe he's at Park City."

As they passed the north gate, they slowed the horses to let a guard and prisoner pass in front of them, the latter dressed in a black and white zebra suit. The guard was a heavy slug of a man, with a bushy black beard covering much of his face.

Continuing on their way, Ben and Sam looked back over their shoulders to see where the guard was taking his prisoner. They entered a very unusual restaurant. According to the crude letters above the door, it was called "The Ball and Chain." The poles supporting the porch roof were painted in black and white horizontal stripes.

"Looks like the prisoners get to go out to dinner once in a while," Moroni commented. "If we wait long enough, maybe they'll bring Flat Nose George out. It would be easy getting him away from one guard."

"Think we need to experiment with the dynamite," Sam said, "and find out what it'll do. Got to know that before we can come up with a plan."

"What do you suggest?" Ben asked.

'Tonight, let's set off two sticks. Slip one under the bottom of the east gate, and another anywhere up against the wall. That will give us an idea what we're up against."

"Certainly liven things up at the prison," Moroni said, chuckling.

Later that night, not long after dark, Moroni staggered up to the east gate and knocked at the little window. When the face of a guard appeared at the window, Moroni, his words slurred, demanded to see the warden. He was leaning against the gate, using both hands to support himself.

"Get lost, you old drunk," the guard growled, "or you'll be setting up house inside these walls." Moroni belched, loud enough for Ben and Sam to hear him from across the street. Removing his hands from the gate, Moroni began to stagger, falling carelessly to the ground.

"If the warden won't see me, then I'll go to the governor," he slurred.

"You do that," the guard said.

Moroni wanderered off to the west, falling one more time near the prison wall.

It was well past midnight when Sam and Moroni appeared from between two buildings about a quarter of a mile east of the prison.

"Sure you put the one with the long fuse under the gate?" Sam whispered.

"I'm sure," Moroni assured him. "But don't waste any time getting on your horse."

Sam set off at a brisk walk down the road past the prison gate. Moroni disappeared into the darkness of an alley.

When Sam was even with the gate, he walked over to it, dropped to one knee, struck a wooden match on one of the iron hinges, and lit the fuse to the stick of dynamite Moroni had wedged beneath the gate earlier in the evening.

Sam then ran to the next stick of dynamite at the base of the wall, lit it, and ran west past the corner of the prison to where Ben was holding the horses in the shadows of a large tree.

"Halt!" ordered a guard from the top of the wall. Sam ignored the voice, leapt into the saddle, and he and Ben galloped into the night.

A few seconds later, an explosion at the base of the right half of the gate sent dirt and splintered wood flying in every direction, lifting the same side of the huge gate from its hinges and sending it crashing to the ground. Shouting could be heard from inside the prison.

No sooner had the shattered gate come to rest than the second charge went off, resulting again in a huge cloud of dust and dirt but very little granite. When the dust settled, there was a hole by the wall and some powder marks on the granite, but no significant damage.

The next day as workmen were replacing the right half of the gate, Sam and Ben rode by, assessing the damage. Lobo followed. Since Moroni had shown himself to the guard the night before, they thought it best he keep from sight.

"If we blow up anything, looks like it'll have to be a gate," Sam said.

"There are three of them," Ben added. "I like the one on the west."

"Ought to suit our plan just fine."

They rode to the front of "The Ball and Chain," dismounted, and tied their horses to the hitching rail. Lobo followed them inside. They seated themselves at a table in the corner and ordered two plates of pork chops, turnip greens, and mashed potatoes. Lobo made himself comfortable under the table. There was no waiter—just a white-hatted cook who hollered from the kitchen to find out what they wanted. Sam and Ben were the only customers in the restaurant.

When the cook brought the food, the same black-bearded guard they had seen the day before entered the room, a black and white striped prisoner in tow. They seated themselves at a table, also ordering the pork chops, greens, and potatoes.

"That's our man," Sam whispered. He was referring to the prisoner, a kind-looking, well-fed man in his late forties. With his large, rough hands and sun-bronzed cheeks beneath a white brow, the prisoner looked like a farmer. "Polygamist, I guess," continued Sam. "Do you think he knows Flat Nose George?"

"You find out while I distract the guard. Don't forget—tomorrow night at nine at the west gate."

Ben was looking around for a means of distraction when the cook walked in from the kitchen and handed plates of food to the guard and the prisoner. The prisoner gave the cook 30 cents to cover both meals.

"Looks like the guard has a profitable arrangement. Takes the prisoners out for meals, and he gets fed too," whispered Sam to Ben.

"This pig meat's old and cold, not fit fer a dog," the guard growled, loud enough for everyone to hear, including the cook.

"Then don't eat it," yelled the cook from the kitchen. "But ya don't git yer money back."

"Not fit fer a dog," repeated the guard, taking another bite.

Seeing his opportunity, Ben stood up and walked over to the table where the guard and the old man were seated. Before the guard even noticed, Ben picked up Black Beard's plate and headed towards the door.

"What do you think you're doing?" the surprised guard demanded.

Ben didn't answer at first. He just dropped to one knee and whistled for Lobo. The dog obeyed and Ben rewarded him with the guard's pork chop. "Is too fit fer a dog," Ben said.

The guard came out of his chair so fast it fell over

backwards, clattering loudly as it hit the floor. By the time Black Beard reached his plate, Lobo had finished off the meat portion of the chop and was grinding away at the bone with his rear teeth.

"A man could die over something like this," the guard growled, glaring at Ben, his fists clenched. Over the guard's shoulder Ben could see Sam talking to the prisoner.

"Man killed over a pork chop," Ben taunted. "Never heard of such a thing."

"Yes, over a pork chop," the guard repeated, stepping back with one leg into a fighting stance, knees partly bent, fists in front of him like a prizefighter beginning a new round. Ben still had the plate in his hand.

"Ever see a man with his throat ripped out?" Ben asked.

"What?" The guard was less sure of himself.

"Touch me and Lobo here will go for yours, fast."

The guard looked down at Lobo, who had dropped the bone. His upper lip was curled up, his ears were back, and there was a gurgling sound coming from his throat.

The guard was reluctant to proceed. He had tangled with big dogs before and had fought and defeated more than his share of hard men. But he was hesitant to take on this rude young man and his dog at the same time.

Black Beard resisted the urge to put a hand over his soft throat as he looked at Lobo's ugly white fangs. But the guard wasn't going to back away, either. He was too proud for that.

Ben was the next to speak, following a long silence.

"Perhaps I made a mistake. The dog was hungry. The cook will bring you another chop. I'll pay for it." Without taking his eyes off the guard, Ben reached into his pocket and placed 15 cents on the nearest table.

Grunting his disgust and relief at the same time, the guard picked up the money and returned to his table, where the prisoner was innocently filling his mouth with greens. Sam had already departed, joining Ben and Lobo on the way out the door.

"He's a polygamist, all right," Sam said when they were mounted and riding away. "Name's Billy Parkin. From

Bountiful. Knows Flat Nose George and says the arm is healing fine. He agreed to warn the prisoners and tell George to head for the west gate when the fireworks begin.''

The next evening at nine, Ben and Sam rode along the south wall of the prison, which also served as the rear wall of the main cell block. They were leading a third horse. Suddenly the quiet of the night was shattered by the not too distant sound of rifle fire. Bullets began ricocheting off the nearest guard tower, sending the guard scampering for cover. Ben struck a match and Sam held out a bottle of kerosene with a cloth wick extending from its mouth. As soon as the first wick caught fire, Ben and Sam took more bottles from their saddle bags, lit them, and threw them onto the prison roof. The bottles shattered, and the kerosene burst into brilliant flames that spread over the roof. After they had thrown four or five bottles, Ben and Sam galloped out of sight, then carefully circled back to the west gate.

Inside they could hear the guards shouting orders and men screaming to be let out. The roaring flames turned night into day as the shingles began burning with the kerosene.

When it became obvious from all the yelling that many of the prisoners were in the yard outside the cell block, Ben ran up to the west gate and slipped a stick of dynamite beneath it, the fuse already burning.

This time the entire gate was blown from its hinges. Ben and Sam waited in the shadows across the street, mounted on their horses and ready to pick up their friend.

Men in striped suits began gathering at the gate. There were no guards yet. The prisoners stopped in front of the opening, unsure, like they were afraid they might be shot if they ventured outside. The guards had left the towers, but the prisoners did not know it. Ben and Sam waited, their horses prancing about, caught up in the excitement of the evening.

Finally one of the prisoners began picking his way over the shattered gate. He was dressed like the others, but he was different with his high cheekbones, bronze skin, and long black hair. One sleeve was empty.

Ben and Sam headed for the gate at a full gallop. Even with one hand missing, George had no trouble swinging into the saddle. Ben handed him the reins and the threesome galloped away. Other prisoners emerged from the west gate and disappeared into dark lanes and alleys like frightened cockroaches. The clanging of fire engines could be heard in the distance.

Chapter 59

(In the First Presidency epistle) the United States court is designated as an "altar of hate," . . . the reason is that the court will not take the word of . . . a Mormon woman that she has not lived at all with her fraction of a husband for three years, when she has on her knee a howling evidence that she is lying.
—Salt Lake Tribune editorial
October 9, 1886

Nobody really planned to go to Molly Skinner's house on West Temple where she managed her crew of soiled doves. It just happened that way.

They had stopped a mile or so from the prison to let Flat Nose George change out of his stripes. That's when the posse saw them.

It was in the downtown area, just before dawn, that the posse finally made a wrong turn at a blind corner, giving Ben, Sam, Moroni, and George a few minutes to let their jaded horses catch their wind. They knew the chase would resume again if they weren't quick to get off the streets. That's when Moroni spotted a tiny livery stable owned by a distant relative. Quickly they found their way inside, closing the big door to the street. Still rubbing the sleep from his eyes, the relative, a balding rabbit of a man, reluctantly agreed to keep the horses, but insisted his house wasn't big enough, or his stable private enough, to hide three men and an Indian.

That's when Sam remembered Molly Skinner's place was just around the corner. Sixteen years earlier, Molly had financed Sam's and Lance Claw's boyhood adventure, a firewater-selling expedition to the Shoshone Indians.

"That's the last place in the world they would look for Mormons on the run," he explained to Ben and Moroni. "Besides, she likes Indians. Lance worshipped the lady. She'll welcome Flat Nose George with open arms. We'll just stay a couple of days, then head for the hills."

Ben was easier to convince than Moroni.

"I'm a patriarch of the church," he said. "I can't go in a place like that."

"That's the beauty of it," Sam argued. "They would never look for a Mormon patriarch at Molly's."

"I don't know."

"You're also an escaped convict," Sam reminded him. "You know where you'll go if they catch you."

Reluctantly, Moroni agreed to hide out at Molly's. It was still dark as they hurried behind the buildings to Molly's side door.

A minute later the four men were seated on a long purple sofa in Molly's office. Except for the sofa and the silk curtains, the office looked like any other prosperous business or law office. In the center was a huge mahogany desk cluttered with correspondence, official-looking papers, and open books. Except for several tasteful paintings, the walls were lined with bookshelves filled with books. Many were law books.

"I remember you," Molly said to Sam after she had ushered him and his friends into her office. "I loaned you and that Indian boy $300 and you paid it back. What was his name?"

"Lance."

"How is he?"

"Running with a band of Paiutes along the Humboldt somewhere."

Molly looked about the same as Sam remembered, only with a few more wrinkles and a little more gray in her hair. Her sorrel hair was a little shorter.

"Still studying the law, I see," Sam said, nodding towards an open law book on the desk.

"Knowing the law makes a big difference in my business. What can I do for you?"

Sam explained their predicament and how they had broken Flat Nose George out of prison.

"You set the prison on fire?" Molly asked.

"And blew off the north and west gates," Ben added.

"I suppose I'd be in a lot of trouble if the law found out I was hiding you here," she said.

"I suppose you would," Sam responded.

"What makes you think I won't turn you in? Why did you come here?"

"I've been here before," Sam said confidently. "You have a soft spot in your heart for people in trouble, especially Indians. Thought you would put us up for a few days until it's safe to leave town."

"I suppose I might," she said coolly. "I like what you're doing to defend polygamy."

"You what?" Moroni demanded, unable to hold his tongue.

"I'm in favor of polygamy," she said matter-of-factly.

"Why?" Moroni asked.

"Good for business," she explained. "Keeps the supply of single women to a minimum. With no available women around, more men come here. All six brothels in Salt Lake are prospering, and I'm sure polygamy has something to do with that."

"I'll be damned," Moroni said. Sam looked at him in surprise, never having heard the old man swear before.

"Also," Molly added, "the new anti-polygamy laws make adultery a felony. Those laws don't just affect the Mormon Church, but me too. Not only does the new law make polygamists felons, but my customers too. That's bad for business."

"I'll be damned," Moroni said a second time.

"Follow me," Molly said, standing up. "I'm sure you're exhausted. I'll show you where you can stay."

"Do you have somewhere secret and private?" Ben asked.

"Everything around here is secret and private and very discreet," she said. "Preferred customers demand discretion. It's our trademark."

The four tired men followed Molly up a stairway and down a dimly lighted hallway. A brightly-colored Persian carpet covered the oak floor, and the walls were covered with a flower-patterned wallpaper that looked like silk. Molly stopped in front of a full-length painting of a woman bathing in a tree-lined mountain stream. Ben, Sam, and George had a good look while Moroni turned away. Taking hold of the edge of the picture frame, Molly opened it like a door, leading the men into a secret room decorated like the hallway. There was one bed, and a small window overlooking the side alley.

"You'll be safe here," she said. "I'll have two cots and some food sent up. If there's anything else you want, just pull on this cord two times." She pointed to a green rope tied to one of the bedposts and extending downward through a hole in the floor.

"I'll see that you get the newspapers and all the latest gossip," Molly said as she turned to leave. "Here, we learn much of the news before it ever gets in the papers."

"I can believe that," Sam said as Molly disappeared through the secret door.

It was Moroni who discovered the unique position of their room. In the early evening, after hearing a tapping on the door below the window, Moroni moved a chair to the window and, parting the curtains slightly, began watching the alley to see who was coming and going.

"Brother Page!" he gasped, spinning away from the window, a look of disbelief on his face. "I blessed that man that he would be a stalwart in church. What's he doing here?"

Flat Nose George remained stretched out on the bed while Sam and Ben joined Moroni at the window to see whom they might recognize.

After several strange faces, Sam and Ben simultaneously recognized Oscar Vandercook, the deputy who had arrested

Kathryn and whom Ben had shot in the foot.

"He's still limping," Ben whispered proudly as the big deputy approached the door.

Ben became even more interested in a later visitor. Moroni announced that *Tribune* editor Harry Chew was coming down the alley. Ben had never met the man, but he knew from what Nellie had said that the editor had a romantic interest in her. Chew seemed in a hurry, almost trotting up the alley. Stopping in front of the door, he looked up and down the alley, then tapped lightly on the door. A few seconds later he disappeared inside.

Later on the traffic in the alley became less compelling than the sounds coming through the walls—the laughter and teasing of women, gruff mumbling of men's voices, the shattering of drinking glasses, drunken boasting, the squeaking of bedsprings. Flat Nose George was the only one who got a good night's sleep.

The next morning, Sam pulled twice on the green rope. A few minutes later when Molly arrived, Sam got right down to business. He asked her if she really wanted polygamy to continue.

"I meant what I said," she responded.

"You can help," Sam said.

"How?"

"First, get a message to Brigham Hampton that I need to see him here today. He's head of detectives at the Salt Lake Police Department. Then get me a brace and bit that'll make a hole about as big as a dime."

"What are you going to do?" she asked.

"I'll explain it all when you get Brigham here. All I can say now," he said, grabbing her by both shoulders and kissing her on the cheek, "is that you are going to be instrumental in setting back the anti-polygamy crusade a hundred years."

"I'll have your Deputy Hampton and brace and bit here within the hour," she said in parting.

"I have a feeling you'll be visiting Nellie soon," Sam said to Ben, "to give her the hottest story of her career."

Chapter 60

This writer might . . . have felt as did the Democrats who went from here to Idaho and who drafted for Idaho men the test-oath, and explained to them that polygamy was but the filthy cement in the Mormon structure, that the greater evil was the accursed Priesthood rule which puts a clamp upon the brains and souls of men and leaves them in a little while as morally and intellectually deformed and dwarfed as is the Chinese woman's foot.

—Salt Lake Tribune editorial
October 12, 1886

Two weeks later Nellie's article appeared in the *Deseret News.* All Salt Lake was in an uproar, the anti-Mormons howling "foul," the Mormons roaring with delight at seeing the tables turned on their enemies.

The article announced that Salt Lake City police officer Brigham Hampton had arrested U.S. Deputy Marshal Oscar Vandercook on the charges of lewd and lascivious cohabitation and resorting to houses of ill repute. The next day, Hampton arrested bigger game—U.S. Assistant Prosecuting Attorney Samuel H. Lewis.

The article said the evidence leading to the arrests was obtained by undercover detectives stationed in sporting houses where they could peer through small holes drilled in the walls. The article went on to say that Hampton was preparing indictments from a list of more than a hundred men of substance and position who had served on juries, issued warrants, and held other public positions, including some of the most prominent in the territory. Most of the men on the list were married, said the article.

It also indicated there would probably be limited coverage of the scandal in the *Tribune* because editor Harry Chew was on the list with charges pending, and would likely be so busy keeping himslf out of jail that he would be hampered in his usual editorializing.

The story went on to predict a landslide of wrecked careers, broken families, disgrace, and scandal. Nellie added that even if all one hundred men went to prison, there would still be a lot more Mormons penalized by the law than non-Mormons. Nearly a thousand Mormons had been sent to jail since passage of the Edmunds Law. The arrests by Hampton, while not balancing the scales of justice, were at least a move toward equality.

While the non-Mormons scrambled to avoid scandal, the Mormons read Nellie's story with delight and celebrated. Brigham Hampton was the hero of the day.

Probably the most sensational spinoff of the scandal was the near fatal shooting of *Tribune* editor Harry Chew by his fiancée, Lydia, a former plural wife of Patrick O'Riley. As a result of the shooting, Chew was in critical condition in Deseret Hospital, with gunshot wounds to the chest and groin, and Lydia was in the city jail.

The celebration ended as quickly as it had begun. Judge Charles Zane crushed the prosecution by granting a motion by Assistant U.S. Attorney C.S. Varian to dismiss the cases on grounds the evidence was gained by entrapment. "I would not believe such scoundrels on oath," Varian said of eyewitnesses who patronized houses of ill repute to gather their evidence, "even in the high court of heaven itself."

Judge Zane concurred.

Mormons were furious. Judge Zane responded by pouring more salt on their wounds by ordering the arrest of Brigham Hampton on the charge of conspiracy. He was tried before a gentile jury and sentenced to one year in prison.

"The legal system of the United States is a mockery of justice," bellowed Moroni after reading the *Tribune* article describing Hampton's trial and resulting sentence. He slammed the paper down on the table.

They had left Molly's shortly before Hampton arrested Vandercook, and had been hiding in a barn belonging to one of Moroni's friends in Taylorsville. They had decided against leaving town, not wanting to miss all the excitement as Hampton arrested the non-Mormon adulterers. Now the tables had been turned.

It was late afternoon, on a warm spring day when a man feels like he ought to be outside working in the soil, breaking sod and planting new crops. Sam, Ben, Moroni, and George had been cooped up in the barn for days, living on the anticipated excitement of Hampton's victory. That was gone now, and nobody wanted to stay in the barn another minute.

"What should we do?" Sam asked. "I've sat around long enough." "Me too," Ben said, picking up the paper and scanning it restlessly.

"We can't just leave," Moroni said. "We have to do something."

"Listen to this," Ben said, holding up the *Tribune*. He was looking at an editorial on page 2.

" 'John the Revelator has lost a big part of his flock,' " he began reading. " 'A total of 20,419 bleating Mormon sheep are no longer in the clutches of the Mormon hierarchy, having been turned over by the Church welfare department to the U.S. Marshal, who said these lambs will never be fleeced again by the Mormon leaders. The sheep were herded in from several valley welfare farms last Thursday and turned over to the U.S. Marshal.

" 'According to Judge Charles Zane, the sheep will be sold at public auction this coming Saturday at 1 p.m. at the Seventh East estray compound. Interested bidders may inspect the sheep in the large pasture just east of the Jordan River where it passes under South Temple. Proceeds from the sale will help defray additional legal and law enforcement costs incurred by the federal government in recent months in its efforts to enforce the Edmunds-Tucker Act. The sheep have already been sheared, and the wool removed from over their eyes, a condition much needed by the rest of the Mormon flock.' "

Ben threw the paper down and walked over to a window. "We can do something about those sheep," he said calmly.

"Like scatter them to hell and back," Sam responded.

"The article said they would be sold at the Seventh East estray compound day after tomorrow," Moroni said. "Maybe some of them could get lost before then."

At dusk Ben, Sam, Moroni, George, and Lobo headed north towards the sheep pasture, staying on the less traveled side roads as much as possible.

There were just a couple of dogs with the sheep. The only sign of human life was a light in the window of a tiny board shack on the east bank of the Jordan River. Knowing they couldn't get away with much sneaking around with dogs about, the men rode right up to the front of the shack and dismounted, guns ready. To their surprise, no one emerged to greet them.

Sam knocked.

A moment later the door was opened by a thin, hatless cowboy. Immediately the man's eyes locked on Ben, who was grinning broadly as he cocked back the hammer on his pistol.

"You know each other?" Sam asked.

"Yup," Ben said, as the cowboy slowly raised his hands above his head. "Name's Shank. One of the deputies I set adrift on the Green River. Looks like he made it through the rapids."

Sam and Ben pushed their way inside, where Gibson was stretched out on a canvas cot, his eyes closed.

"That's the other one," Ben said. "Don't know when I've been so glad to see two men. Thought I'd killed them. Feels good to know I didn't."

Ben pulled Gibson's feet off the cot, letting them fall to the floor. Gibson sat up with a start, immediately recognizing Ben as he, too, raised his hands high over his head.

"Tell us about your Green River float trip," Ben ordered.

Gibson and Shank looked at each other. Gibson spoke first.

"Got untied the second day, a long way past the Chinamen's huts. Just kept going till we reached Lee's Ferry. By then the raft was all broke up. We was just hanging on to a couple of logs. Nearly starved to death."

"Glad you made it through," Ben said, sounding genuinely sincere.

"What do you want?" Gibson demanded.

"The sheep," Moroni said.

"We're still deputies," Shank whined. "You'll leave us alone if you know what's good for you."

"Want me to shoot 'em?" George asked.

"I've got a better idea," Sam said and whispered something in Ben's ear.

"No," Ben said. "If you only knew how much my conscience has bothered me, how much I've worried about these two."

"You wouldn't dare," Shank yelled, suddenly realizing what Ben and Sam were talking about.

Half an hour later Sam pushed the raft into the river. Bound and gagged, Shank and Gibson floated towards the Great Salt Lake.

"Someone will find them come morning," Sam said. "In the meantime, they won't be around to cause us any trouble over the sheep."

With Shank and Gibson floating down the river, the dogs eagerly joined in to help when Ben sent Lobo out to gather the sheep. An hour later, South Temple was clogged with sheep, heading east towards downtown Salt Lake.

It was after midnight when they reached the edge of the city. Several times along the way, people asked where they were going in the middle of the night with so many sheep. The answer was simple. They were taking the sheep to the Seventh East estray compound, where the sheep were to be sold. They were going at night so as not to obstruct daytime traffic.

It was several hours past midnight when Ben walked up the steps of the *Tribune* office and knocked loudly on the locked door. No one responded, not even a guard. Ben kicked in the door, grabbed the nearest sheep by the ear, and dragged it through the doorway; others followed as Lobo nipped at their heels. Moroni lit a gas lamp so they could see what they were doing as they packed over 600 sheep into the *Tribune* offices.

It was Flat Nose George who discovered the big drums of printer's ink and began pouring the black goo onto the floor. It was so slippery many of the sheep lost their footing temporarily, their wool soaking up the ink. They became walking paint brushes once they regained their footing, and millions of black tracks were made throughout the building and all over the piles of formerly clean white paper.

Lobo was pushing a thousand sheep up the steps to Judge Zane's courtroom when a posse of over a dozen armed men appeared to catch the sheep rustlers. They raced around the corner at full gallop, plunging headlong into a sea of bleating sheep. The first three or four horses went down, the sheep pressing closely around them. The remaining horses held back, their riders trying desperately to push them through the flock. The progress was so slow that by the time they reached the courthouse, the rustlers were long gone.

At daybreak Ben and his gang were back at the barn, tired but feeling good knowing they had ruined the marshal's sheep sale by scattering sheep throughout Salt Lake while destroying the *Tribune* offices.

After sleeping most of the morning, everyone gathered around the wooden table to discuss what they might do next.

"That sheep thing makes me feel more like a teenage prankster than a defender of the faith," Moroni said. "We've given the editorial writers something fun and interesting to write about. But really, did we do any good for the cause? I think not."

No one argued with Moroni, not even Ben. They had come to Salt Lake to help deliver the Mormons from the jaws of persecution, and the best thing they had come up with was a monstrous prank involving 20,000 sheep. Sure, they had disrupted a public sale of church property, but as soon as the sheep were rounded up, there would be another. The

Tribune certainly wouldn't back off in its campaign against the Mormons. If anything, the paper would become more antagonistic as a result of having to clean up a million black tracks and green pellets.

"What should we do now?" asked Sam. "Put an ad in the paper and raise an army?"

"I used to think that was the answer," Moroni said, his head in his hands, "but I just don't know anymore."

"Me find Madge and little George," Flat Nose George said. "Go elk hunting tonight." He began to make preparations to leave, tying up his bedroll and packing his saddle bags.

No one offered any objections to George's leaving. At least someone knew what he wanted to do.

"I need to spend some time with Kathryn," Sam said. "She's never really gotten over losing her baby and my marrying Lydia. We need time together, without hounding from the law. Think I'll take her to Canada. I'll go with Flat Nose George as far as American Fork. If you come up with any great ideas and need my help, let me know."

"Guess I'll go home too," Moroni said. "Miss my wives and children. I pray to God they won't catch me and send me back to prison."

"Well, I'm not going to walk away from this," Ben said. He was standing by the window, looking outside.

"What are you going to do?" Sam asked.

"Guess I'll go see the prophet," he said after a long pause. "If anyone can untangle this mess, he's the one. He should know what's going to happen, what we ought to be doing. If he doesn't care, then I'll walk away from it too. But I think he cares. I think God cares. The prophet ought to have some answers."

"Ought to," Sam said.

"Good luck," Moroni said. "They've got him hid pretty good, but if you start sniffing around Centerville and Kaysville, I think you'll find him."

Ben returned to his bunk and joined the others in rolling up blankets and packing saddle bags. That night everyone went his separate way.

Chapter 61

The persecutions will increase in hardship until the Mormon power shall finally be broken. They have exhausted the whole gamut of falsehood, perjury, misrepresentation, hypocrisy and double dealing. The mask is now stripped off and the Nation is seeing more and more clearly what Mormonism as practiced means, and the men of this Nation will not have it so.

—Salt Lake Tribune editorial
October 14, 1886

Ben waited until after dark to head north to Centerville, where he hoped to begin his search for President Taylor. He was traveling one of the less traveled roads west of the main road through north Salt Lake when he heard men's voices up ahead. In the moonlight he could see the silhouettes of three approaching riders. Quickly he turned his horse onto a lane, hiding behind a row of box elder trees. There were no lights to indicate there were any homes nearby. He waited as the voices grew closer and louder. Ben could hear hoofbeats, indicating the men were on horseback.

"Things'll be a lot easier for you if you'll admit the prison fire or the sheep theft," said one of the voices, the first clear statement Ben could understand as they rode past.

Looking through the branches of the trees, Ben could see three riders. One had his hands tied behind his back, and his horse was being led by one of the others.

"I have witnesses to prove I was in Bountiful the night of

the prison fire and the night the sheep were stolen."

"Listen, Parish. Lying witnesses won't save you this time," growled the third rider. The voice was familiar to Ben. He had heard it before.

Ben eased his horse back onto the road, but instead of heading north, he turned south, following the three men. The man called Parish was in need of help. Sensing trouble, Lobo stayed at Ben's side.

"I have ways to make men like you talk," said the familiar voice.

"What can I say?" Parish pleaded. "I have done nothing to deserve this."

"We'll see." The three horses stopped. So did Ben, about thirty yards back.

"This is your last chance," the familiar voice said. Ben could see the silhouettes of the three riders against the distant lights of the city. The rider with the familiar voice was tall and thin. Suddenly Ben remembered the voice. It was Deputy Charles Owen, the man who had slit open Sonny, and the first deputy Ben had shot in the foot.

"I have nothing to confess," Parish said. Owen dismounted, fishing a piece of rope from his saddle bag.

"What are you going to do?" Parish asked.

"Since you have no faith in the due process of the law," Owen said, "I thought you might like me to turn you loose and give your God a chance to intervene directly on your behalf."

"What are you going to do?" Parish demanded.

"Nothing I haven't done before. Hold your damn foot still." It appeared Owen was pushing Parish's foot through the stirrup.

"Now the rope goes around your pony's flanks," Owen said. "When I jerk it tight, we'll see how good you can ride and whether or not God thinks your life is worth saving—unless you'd rather confess to the prison fire or the sheep rustling."

"I tell you I didn't do either."

"Then let God in heaven be your judge." Owen placed the rope over the hindquarters of Parish's horse.

"That'll make him buck," Parish cried. "My foot's stuck in the stirrup."

"You've got the general idea," the other man said.

"If I confess to something I didn't do, you'll take my foot out of the stirrup?"

"A little late for that," Owen said icily. "Gone to too much trouble already. Cohabs like you are costing the government too much money. We'll just jerk this here rope tight and let God be your judge. He can save you if he wants to." Owen reached under the horse for the free end of the rope. Parish was quiet.

Ben remembered what he had heard about Dan and Ike finding Patrick's horse out in the west desert, the foot still in the stirrup. Ben remembered his father telling him the foot had been pushed through the stirrup by someone, that Pat's hands had been tied behind his back as he was dragged to death behind the horse.

"Owen, let go of that rope," Ben ordered, allowing his horse to step forward. The three men looked back, startled at Ben's approach.

"Who's there?" Owen demanded.

"Brother to the last man you did this to."

"Listen here," growled Owen. "We're on official business of the United States Government. You get the hell out of here, whoever you are."

"If the rope isn't off that horse's back in three seconds I'll shoot you in the other foot," Ben said as his horse continued to walk towards the three men.

"Other foot?" Owen asked, suddenly remembering where he had heard the stranger's voice before. 'It's the Storm kid, the one who shot me, stole my horse, and burned my boots."

Owen jerked the rope from the back of Parish's horse, at the same time flipping the lead rope over the animal's neck. It bolted forward, beginning to gallop away. But when it noticed the other horses weren't following, it slowed to a walk, turned around, and trotted back to the other horses, a frightened Parish keeping his seat.

"If you two don't reach for the sky right now I'm going

to start shooting,'' Ben said. Everyone could hear the click as he cocked back the hammer on his pistol. While the one deputy obeyed, Owen hesitated. ''You fire a gun and Parish's horse will bolt,'' he said.

Not waiting for a standoff to develop, Ben rode in close and, drawing his knife, cut Parish's hands free. He handed the man a cocked rifle with orders to keep it pointed at the second deputy.

Owen finally raised his hands above his head. Ben dismounted and, while keeping his pistol aimed at Owen, helped Parish get his boot off so he could get his foot out of the stirrup.

''That's my black horse you're riding,'' Owen said.

''Tell me how my brother died and I'll give the horse back to you,'' Ben said.

''I didn't know your brother was dead. Last I heard he broke out of the federal prison in Detroit.''

''That's Sam. I'm talking about Pat—Dr. Patrick O'Riley.''

''I don't know anything about that,'' Owen said, too quickly to satisfy Ben.

''Did Pat beg you not to force his foot through the stirrup?''

Owen didn't respond.

''What did Pat say when you cinched up the rope around his horse's flanks?''

''Didn't cinch up a rope around the horse's flanks,'' Owen said defensively.

''Why not?'' Ben asked, wondering what he was going to do now he knew Owen was involved in Pat's death.

''We didn't do it on purpose,'' Owen said. ''We were just bringing the doc back to stand trial, hands tied behind his back. We pushed one foot through the stirrup just so he'd be afraid to try anything. That sorrel was jumpy, got scared by a badger. The doc lost his seat. The horse went crazy, jerked away. We couldn't catch it, even with it dragging the doc. Went through places we couldn't even ride. We gave up trying when we knew he was dead.''

''How do I know you didn't do it on purpose?'' Ben asked.

"Because there was no rope on the horse's flanks. You lied about that, didn't you?"

"Yes," Ben admitted. "I think you're telling the truth, so I won't kill you here in the middle of the road."

"I want the black gelding back."

"You can have it," said Ben, "but first we're going to tie up your partner." With Parish's rifle still pointed at him, the other deputy dismounted so Ben could tie his hands behind his back. Ben pushed the man to the ground so Parish could remove his boots, which he tied to the man's saddle.

Next Ben bound Owen's hands behind his back.

"What are you going to do?" Owen demanded. "I'm a deputy U.S. marshal."

"Here's your horse," Ben said, leading the black gelding forward. "Get on."

"I can't. My hands are tied."

"Parish will help you." Parish helped Owen get on the horse.

"Where are we going?" Owen asked.

"*We* are not going anywhere," Ben said, quickly grabbing Owen's foot and forcing it through the stirrup until the stirrup was dangling loosely about his ankle.

"Parish," Ben said, "if you have a place to hide, I suggest you get on your way. You don't want to be a party to what's going to happen next." Parish didn't waste any time getting on his horse and galloping off to the north.

Ben picked up the loose rope, which had fallen to the ground.

"Please don't tie his flanks," Owen pleaded. "It was an accident with the doc—honest, it was."

"It was no accident with Parish. If I hadn't come along, you'd have killed the man."

"But he set the prison on fire and run off all those sheep."

"I know he didn't," Ben said as he tied up the reins of the black gelding so they wouldn't drag on the ground. Then he removed his bedroll and saddle bags from behind Owen.

"I believe you when you say Pat's death was an accident," Ben said. "Still, you admit to pushing his foot through the stirrup. Pat wasn't a good horseman, and you knew it."

"How would I know that?"

"And Parish would have been killed," Ben said, not bothering to repond to Owen's comment, "had I not come along and stopped you from putting on the flank cinch. The horse would have bucked him off with his foot through the stirrup. You're no good, Owen."

"I'm not a polygamist."

"Just as you told Parish his fate was in the hands of God, so is yours now," Ben said, slapping the black gelding on the rump with the loose rope. The gelding lurched forward into a full gallop, the other horse at its side. Both horses disappeared into the blackness, heading south towards Salt Lake City.

When the galloping horses could no longer be seen or heard, Ben turned to the barefooted deputy.

"Have you heard from Gibson or Shank since the sheep ruckus?"

"What?" the deputy asked.

"Gibson and Shank—the deputies who were guarding the sheep. Where are they?"

"Disappeared with the sheep."

"Last I saw them, they were on a raft with their hands tied, floating down the Jordan River into the Great Salt Lake. When you get untied tomorrow, better send a search party to look for them."

"I will," the deputy promised.

After throwing the saddle bags and bedroll over the saddle on the remaining horse, Ben leapt upon its back and headed north in search of Mormon Church president John Taylor.

Chapter 62

We should be strictly honest, one with another, and with all men; let our word always be as good as our bond; avoid all ostentation of pride and vanity; and be meek, lowly, and humble; be full of integrity and honor; and deal justly and righteously with all men; and have the fear and love of God continually before us, and seek for the comforting influence of the Holy Ghost to dwell with us.
—From John Taylor's last letter to his wives and children prior to his death

It was at John Woolley's place in Centerville that Ben learned where President Taylor was hiding. News of the run-in with Owen had preceded Ben through Parish. Still, no one wanted to tell Ben where the president was—at least, not at first. But as Ben answered their questions concerning his confrontations with Owen and Vandercook, it was John Woolley who finally decided that maybe the prophet would like to see Ben. All doubts were removed when Ben told them how he and his friends pushed the sheep into the *Tribune* offices after kicking in the door. He showed them Lobo, the dog that had made it possible. They were even more excited when he told how he, Sam, and Moroni had engineered the prison escape for Flat Nose George by starting the fire and blowing up the west gate.

Late the next day Ben rode northeast along Bluff Road, the main route connecting Salt Lake to Ogden. At Kaysville he turned west towards the marshes bordering the Great Salt

Lake, the late afternoon sun in his eyes. His destination was the two-story adobe home of Thomas Roueche, mayor of Kaysville. Near the home was a pond where Roueche had dammed up Kays Creek 30 years earlier when he had settled the area. The Roueche family had moved out of their home to make room for the prophet and his aides. The Roueches were living in the old log cabin they had built when settling the area.

As Ben approached the front gate, he was stopped by Sam Bateman, the prophet's personal bodyguard. Ben introduced himself, saying he wanted to see the prophet.

"What makes you think you can just ride in here and get an audience with the living prophet?" Bateman asked.

"Thought he might be willing to see me for a few minutes."

"There are thousands of people who would pay a lot of money for an audience with the prophet, including the U.S. Marshal, who has a $300 reward offered for information leading to the capture of John Taylor. Do you really think that with a reward on his head he'd be staying in a place like this right next to the main road?"

"That's what they told me at Woolleys' place in Centerville."

"Well, they were wrong. He left here day before yesterday."

"Where did he go?" Ben asked, turning in the saddle, looking back towards the mountains.

"That's not public information," Bateman said.

"Well, I'm not exactly the public," Ben responded, turning back to face the guard.

"Look, why don't you stay for supper? Too late to get anywhere tonight, anyway."

Ben didn't like being put off, but he was hungry. After an almost steady diet of jerky, dried apples, and old bread, a home-cooked meal sounded good. He hadn't had any good food since leaving Molly's.

"You can turn your horse in the front pasture and let him get a belly full of grass while you're filling yours," Bateman added. Ben dismounted, removed the saddle, and turned the horse into the pasture.

After washing up, Ben found himself seated at a large oak table with eight or nine other people, mostly men. But they weren't hired men or farmers. Three were well armed like Bateman, probably guards. The other men—perhaps clerks or scribes—were dressed in Sunday clothes, white shirts and collars.

From the Church-oriented conversation, Ben gathered he was sharing a meal with President Taylor's staff. Why hadn't they left with the prophet? Maybe he hadn't left. Maybe Bateman had lied.

Ben's suspicions were confirmed when the youngest and prettiest of the women present, Josephine Roueche, excused herself from the table, taking a modest plate of food up the stairs to one of the bedrooms. Josephine was tall and slender, a pretty woman with dark hair and eyes, in her late 20's. As Ben's eyes followed the woman up the stairs, he became aware that Bateman was watching him.

Sam remembered something Moroni had said about the prophet marrying a new wife the previous December on his 78th birthday. Ben wondered if Josephine might be the one.

The meal consisted of roast pork with new potatoes and peas from the garden. Most of the men generously poured a white cream sauce over everything on their plates. There was plenty of cold buttermilk to drink. Ben hadn't eaten so well in a long time and didn't waste any time filling his mouth.

But he had a hard time getting full, because Bateman asked him so many questions that required answering. The guard wanted to know everything about Ben's confrontation with Owen and Vandercook and taking the pregnant women to the hidden mountain retreat. Ben was surprised how much Bateman knew. The guard even asked how Flat Nose George was getting along without one of his hands.

After Ben had been answering questions for what seemed an hour, somehow managing to get his fill of pork and vegetables, Bateman turned to one of the other guards and told the man to tell the "boss" that Ben Storm, the boy who shot the deputies in the foot, wanted to see him. The guard pushed back his chair and headed up the stairs, two steps at a time.

"The boss?" Ben asked, sure it was the prophet but wanting Bateman to say it.

"Can't be too careful when you're guarding the prophet of God," Bateman explained. "Had to make sure you weren't a spy."

A second later the room became silent. Heads turned towards the top of the stairs. Josephine was guiding a tall, silver-haired man towards the stairway. Though slightly bent and taking only small steps, there was a strong, confident air about him. His blue eyes were alert and clear.

Ben had seen the prophet before, in conference as a boy. He remembered the time the prophet stood up and with one bold statement wiped away all the debts owed the Perpetual Immigration Fund by foreign immigrants too poor to pay. Weeping with gratitude, thousands of foreigners had pushed towards the pulpit, deeply grateful to the man who had removed a heavy burden from their shoulders. Ben remembered what his father had said about John Taylor always writing, preaching and defending the kingdom—even in the middle of the persecutions. A man powerful with words. Always able to see to the heart of matters, not easily fooled or deceived. Still, a prayerful, humble man, even in his old age. Yet still bold enough to marry a new plural wife when the whole world was condemning the Mormons for polygamy.

Carefully Josephine guided the prophet down the stairs while everyone watched. He moved slowly but deliberately, one step at a time. Ben felt his heart ache with compassion for this great man. How did he feel, being weak and old, running from the law at a time when the church was on its knees, its very breath being sucked away by political and social pressures? How did it feel to see one's strength and vitality being smothered by old age when the Church needed strong, vital leadership? How did it feel to be away from wives and children, knowing he might never see them again even though they were only a short distance away in Salt Lake?

"I want to shake the hand of the man who shot Chuck Owen in the foot," Taylor said when he reached the bottom of the stairs. Ben stood up and walked over to the prophet, taking the old hand in his young, strong one. Ben felt firmness and warmth in the hand as he looked into the old man's eyes.

"Tell me, young man, did he holler?"

"Like a pup that had been stepped on by a horse," Ben answered.

"That does my heart good," grinned the prophet. "I hope the Lord will forgive me for taking delight in another man's pain."

"I bet he will," Bateman added loudly from across the room.

"Young man, will you share an evening walk with me?" the prophet asked.

"I'd be honored," Ben said, turning with Taylor towards the door.

"Too risky, boss," Bateman said. "Don't know who might see you or what young deputy might be hiding in the marshes wanting to become a hero."

"With Ben Storm at my side, I'll be quite safe," Taylor said, continuing towards the door. Ben felt his heart swell with pride. He thought back when he had cowered before Vandercook and Owen. So much had happened since then, especially within himself. The prophet's confidence was justified. If something happened, Ben would maintain a calm mind and would fight—even die, if necessary—defending the prophet. Besides, both Lobo and Bateman would probably tag along, too.

"I like to walk at dusk," Taylor said as they stepped off the porch. "Can't be seen from the road, yet light enough to see where you're putting your feet." Ben didn't say anything, content to listen to the prophet.

"It did me a world of good when you plugged those deputies and rescued those women," said Taylor. Ben told him about his recent run-in with Owen, the rescue of Parish, the prison escape, and how they had run off with the marshal's sheep. The president wanted to hear every detail, and Ben was glad to comply.

"It makes me feel young again to listen to your adventures," Taylor said. "Your boldness in defending the kingdom gives me strength."

"Thank you," Ben said.

"You see," Taylor continued, "sometimes I feel like I am all alone in defending the principle. Even President Cannon wants a compromise. You stood up and fought back like I have been doing. You make me feel like I am not alone. But this very night, Cannon, Richards, and others are meeting in Salt Lake with legislators drafting a proposed constitution for Utah that would ban polygamy forever."

"Church leaders are involved in that?" Ben asked in surprise.

"Yes. They say the church can't survive unless Utah becomes a state and is able to govern itself. That will never happen as long as polygamy is allowed. They say once we get statehood, we can interpret the law any way we want, even to the point of not enforcing anti-polygamy laws. I disagree. If we back down, even a little, I fear the whole dam we have been doggedly preserving will wash away. I fear we will incur the wrath of Almighty God by abandoning one of his most sacred laws."

Ben looked over his shoulder. Bateman and a companion were following, rifles over their shoulders, about 50 yards back.

"We have a generation of Saints who no longer understand. We have a generation of people willing to sacrifice an eternal kingdom for friendship with the gentiles. I don't fear the deputies, judges, and presidents. I fear the Saints who are too eager to get along with the world.

"Do you think those deputies, judges, and *Trib* writers could put a halt to polygamy if as a whole the Saints were determined to live it? Never. Men like you would lead our militia, and the forces of hell—even Satan's armies—would quake with fear. But that's not the case. We are not united. We are not determined. We are not converted to the fulness of the everlasting gospel. As a people we are divided and scrambling for concessions that will make our enemies our friends. But do you know what worries me the most?"

"I have no idea," Ben said as they turned and headed back to the house.

"That maybe Cannon and the others are right," he said. "That to avoid total destruction of the Church, concessions have to be made. If so, I want no part of it. I will be gone soon, so they can do their compromising and conceding without me. I want no part of such business, and God knows it."

"What should I do?" Ben asked.

"You'd like to stand by my side and fight, wouldn't you?"

"Yes, sir," Ben said.

"Some bitter battles will be fought the next few years, but they won't be fought with guns and swords. They'll be in judges' chambers, courtrooms, the pages of newspapers, in the halls of Congress. No place for you there, young man."

"What would you have me do?"

"Do you have a girl?"

"Yes," Ben said, surprised at the nature of the question.

"Marry her. Go to Mexico. Many of our best people are going there, and Canada too. Raise a houseful of children who fear God and, like their father, will stand up and fight for right and truth. And if it works out, take a second or third wife, if it won't break the heart of your first love. That's what you should do, young man. Don't stay around here where you risk spending the best years of your life in a prison. Go to Mexico.

"I am going somewhere better than Mexico," he continued, his voice quieter. "I am going soon, rejoicing at meeting loved ones who have gone before me, but sad, so very sad, that I am leaving the Saints during such troubled times. I pray continually that those after me do not offend Almighty God."

Josephine met them at the back steps. She offered her hand to the prophet, who started with her towards the door. Just as they entered, he stopped, turning towards Ben. Even in the dim lantern light, Ben could see the tears welling in the old man's eyes.

"They've put us under the rule of carpetbaggers," he began, so much emotion in his voice he could hardly get the words out. "They've taken away our vote, confiscated our property, hounded our leaders to the ends of the earth, and locked our best men in jail. I defy them to do more. I will not turn from my God." He paused, swallowing hard, not taking his eyes off Ben.

"But when the Saints say they have had enough, that they want to compromise, make a deal with the carpetbaggers, then I weep. Maybe Cannon is right when he says we need to try harder to get along with the rest of the country. Still, I wonder if I have failed, and think perhaps it is time to die."

Hanging onto the woman's arm, the prophet turned and entered the house. Ben never saw him again.

"I can put you up in the barn if you like," Bateman said.

Ben turned and looked at the guard.

"No thanks," Ben said finally. "I think I'll be moving on to Salt Lake. There's a young lady there, a writer. The prophet wanted me to talk to her."

"No," Bateman said. "He's not going to do it again!"

It took Ben a few seconds to figure out what Bateman was getting at. He finally saw the humor in what the guard said, but did not laugh.

"No," Ben said. "President Taylor doesn't want another wife. I'll be talking to her for me, not for him."

Epilogue

Inasmuch as laws have been enacted by Congress forbidding plural marriages, which laws have been pronounced constitutional by the court of last resort, I hereby declare my intention to submit to those laws, and to use my influence with the members of the Church over which I preside to have them do likewise. . . . And now I publicly declare that my advice to the Latter-day Saints is to refrain from contracting any marriage forbidden by the law of the land.
—Mormon Church President Wilford Woodruff, from the 1890 Manifesto

by Dan Storm

John Taylor died July 25, 1887, shortly after my return from Canada. Three days after his death the people of Utah voted overwhelmingly in favor of a proposed constitution that would prohibit polygamy forever in Utah.

Three years later the new president of the Church, Wilford Woodruff, issued a manifesto in which the Mormon Church agreed to stop the practice of polygamy. While the Church allowed more secret plural marriages to be performed, mostly in Mexico and Canada, the practice eventually halted, at least for the main body of the Church.

In 1896 Utah finally became a state, its new constitution forbidding polygamy forever.

Harry Chew recovered from his gunshot wounds and continued writing for the *Tribune*, but his editorials lost their former bite. With polygamy under the carpet and statehood obtained, the *Tribune* lost much of its vindictiveness and—even in the eyes of many devout Mormons—became a respectable newspaper.

Lydia, after her release from jail, moved to the East with funds provided by John Jex. She was never heard from again.

Gibson and Shank were found in the tall marsh grass where the Jordan River empties into the Great Salt Lake. With their hands still tied, they were very thirsty and sunburned, but otherwise all right. Both turned in their badges.

Deputy Charles Owen managed to stay in the saddle until rescued by Mormon dairyman Jake Smith, who was bringing a load of milk to Salt Lake. He spotted the black gelding just as it was getting light. While Owen continued to chase cohabs, there was never another report of him pushing anyone's foot through a stirrup.

When Ben told me about Owen's confession concerning Patrick's death and how the runaway was not deliberate, I backed away from my personal vow for revenge, accepting what Ben did as sufficient penalty for Owen.

When David Butler received word of Grace Woolley's suicide, he disappeared for a few years. Some say he joined the army in the war against Mexico. But eventually he returned, was rebaptized into the church, and raised a large family with his only wife, Alice.

With plural marriage winding down, Madge left her polygamist husband and married Flat Nose George, who took her and Little George to the stone cabin in the McPhearson Mountains. However, this was not before she mailed her new husband's dried up hand to U.S. President James Garfield, asking him to accept the hand as evidence that the government was coming down too hard on the Mormons. Shortly thereafter, 26 Mormon prisoners were released from Sugarhouse Prison. Billy Parkin was not included, having been transferred to the jail in Park City. As for Flat Nose George, his name became famous a few years later, when one of the outlaws riding with Butch Cassidy picked up the alias.

Stella left her aging husband, with hard feelings on both sides, and took her baby with her to California, where she married a prosperous non-Mormon farmer and raised a large family.

Priscilla returned to Grantsville, settled in a small cottage of her own to raise her child and several more that came in later years, two after the manifesto. I never found out which church leader she was married to.

Moroni managed to stay in Salt Lake, taking care of his families while avoiding arrest. After the manifesto all charges against him were dropped. He became somewhat of a legend in his time, due to his ability to find lost items with his seerstone, though he pretty much stopped giving patriarchal blessings.

Sam and Kathryn adopted the Indian boy Abinadi and moved to Canada, establishing a large cattle and horse ranch in the foothills of the beautiful mountains northwest of Cardston, Alberta. Sam eventually fathered three children by a plural wife named Ramona Kelly, whom he first met after escaping from the Detroit prison.

Prison guard Rudolf Wolfstein was terminated by the Detroit prison when he suffered a permanent disability after falling into a 22-foot hole behind the prison mess hall.

I stayed in American Fork, and to avoid the appearance of polygamy, I built a new home for my second wife, Sarah, and Pat's widow, Beth. It was close to the old house where Caroline lived, so our lives didn't change very much. My old friend Ike continued to drop in once or twice a year, usually in the fall, in time for a hunting trip together. He came by for the last time in 1898. I never saw him after that, and don't know what happened to him. Old Indians—and he was more Indian now than black—had a way of just riding off into the mountains and disappearing.

As for Ben, he took the advice of John Taylor and moved to the Mormon colonies in Mexico, taking Lobo with him. At first Ben couldn't persuade Nellie to join him. It took her about a month to decide once and for all that Ben was the man she wanted to share her life with.

As her train pulled to a stop in Mexico, she looked

through the window to see Ben standing on the platform, a pretty young woman beside him, her arm in his. To Nellie, life was repeating itself. All too clearly, she remembered arriving in Salt Lake from England to be met at the station by David Butler and his wife, Alice. Now it was happening again. At first she felt panic, then anger. She charged off the train, determined to give Ben a piece of her mind.

Seeing her coming, Ben just grinned, then quickly explained that he had no romantic interest in the woman on his arm. Spontaneously, and perhaps thoughtlessly, he had asked the stranger to take his arm to have a little fun with Nellie.

Though she felt relieved, Nellie was still angry. She didn't appreciate what she thought was a cruel attempt at humor. Only a very sincere apology from Ben prevented her from getting back on the train and returning to Utah. It wasn't until years after their marriage that she was able to laugh at his ill-conceived practical joke.

I wish I could say that Ben and Nellie lived happily ever after, but I can't. Revolution broke out in Mexico, and Pancho Villa and his men began harassing the Mormon colonies. But that's another story.

Lee Nelson Books Available By Mail

The Storm Testament, 320 pages, $12.95

Wanted by Missouri law for his revenge on mob leader Dick Boggs in 1839, 15-year-old Dan Storm flees to the Rocky Mountains with his friend, Ike, an escaped slave. Dan settles with the Ute Indians where he courts the beautiful Red Leaf. Ike becomes chief of a band of Gosiutes in Utah's west desert. All this takes place before the arrival of the Mormon pioneers.

The Storm Testament II, 293 pages, $12.95

In 1845 a beautiful female journalist, disguised as a school teacher, sneaks into the Mormon city of Nauvoo to lure the polygamists out of hiding so the real story on Mormon polygamy can be published to the world. What Caroline Logan doesn't know is that her search for truth will lead her into love, blackmail, Indian raids, buffalo stampedes, and a deadly early winter storm on the Continental Divide in Wyoming.

The Storm Testament III, 268 pages, $12.95

Inspired by business opportunities opened up by the completion of the transcontinental railroad in 1870, Sam Storm and his friend, Lance Claw, attempt to make a quick fortune dealing in firewater and stolen horses. A bizarre chain of events involves Sam and the woman he loves in one of the most ruthless schemes of the 19th Century.

The Storm Testament IV, 278 pages, $12.95

Porter Rockwell recruits Dan Storm in a daring effort to stop U.S. troops from invading Utah in 1857, while the doomed Fancher Company is heading south to Mountain Meadows. A startling chain of events leads Dan and Ike into the middle of the most controversial and explosive episode in Utah history, the Mountain Meadow Massacre.

The Storm Testament V, 335 pages, $12.95

Gunning for U.S. marshals and establishing a sanctuary for pregnant plural wives, Ben Storm declares war on the anti-Mormon forces of the 1880s. The United States Government is determined to bring the Mormon Church to its knees, with polygamy as the central issue. Ben Storm fights back.

Rockwell, 443 pages, $14.95

The true story of the timid farm boy from New York who became the greatest gunfighter in the history of the American West. He drank his whiskey straight, signed his name with an X, and rode the fastest horses, while defending the early Mormon prophets.